"A ROMULAN SUBCOMMANDER STRIKING A STARFLEET OFFICER," HARRIMAN SAID.

"My crew put in danger, possibly injured or killed." He gestured toward the city, where the thick, dark smoke continued to rise from the sites of the two explosions. "Those are provocative actions, Admiral Vokar. At a time when your people are negotiating peace with mine—"

"We do not bargain for peace," Vokar declared calmly. "We fight to retain our manifest right to live without constraint, and to deny the encroaching imperialism of the Federation. Imperialism, of which your presence on this planet is an example."

"This is neutral territory, Admiral. We are visitors here, and we make no claims on this world or its people."

"In the beginning, you are always visitors," Vokar said. "And in the end, you always stay. But it is of no matter with respect to this planet. You are trespassers in Romulan territory, and you will leave at once."

And there it is, Harriman thought, understanding that the months and years of diplomatic ebb and flow had ceased, and that the military tide had crashed through the levees and now threatened a devastating flood. And in risking that first move, the Romulans had also taken a strategically valuable asset.

"This is neutral territory," Harriman said again. "The people here don't even know that sentient life exists beyond their world."

Vokar turned to glance up at his ship hanging above the city, the fires raging below. "They know it now."

STAR TREK®

THE LOST ERA

SERPENTS AMONG THE RUINS

2311

DAVID R. GEORGE III

Based upon STAR TREK
created by Gene Roddenberry

POCKET BOOKS

New York   London   Toronto   Sydney   Singapore   Algeron

The sale of this book without its cover is unauthorized. If you purchased this book without a cover, you should be aware that it was reported to the publisher as "unsold and destroyed." Neither the author nor the publisher has received payment for the sale of this "stripped book."

This book is a work of fiction. Names, characters, places and incidents are products of the author's imagination or are used fictitiously. Any resemblance to actual events or locales or persons living or dead is entirely coincidental.

An *Original* Publication of POCKET BOOKS

POCKET BOOKS, a division of Simon & Schuster, Inc.
1230 Avenue of the Americas, New York, NY 10020

Copyright © 2003 by Paramount Pictures. All Rights Reserved.

STAR TREK is a Registered Trademark of Paramount Pictures.

This book is published by Pocket Books, a division of Simon & Schuster, Inc., under exclusive license from Paramount Pictures.

All rights reserved, including the right to reproduce this book or portions thereof in any form whatsoever. For information address Pocket Books, 1230 Avenue of the Americas, New York, NY 10020

ISBN: 0-7434-6403-6

First Pocket Books printing September 2003

10 9 8 7 6 5 4 3 2 1

POCKET and colophon are registered trademarks of Simon & Schuster, Inc.

Cover design by John Vairo Jr.

Manufactured in the United States of America

For information regarding special discounts for bulk purchases, please contact Simon & Schuster Special Sales at 1-800-456-6798 or business@simonandschuster.com.

To Jennifer Lynn George,
who blazes through my life like a shooting star,
constantly dazzling me,
shining with her wit,
illuminating with her intellect,
and brightening with her love, kindness, and support

         . . . I see
Moments as stones in the trails of time:
Serpentine paths cast among the cinders
Of a life weighed down by the faithful climb
To ends not my own. Loss cannot hinder
The progress gained for the promise of peace,
As stepping sidelong through the remnant ash,
I focus on the goal, my mind at ease
With the menace of war soon to be passed.
  And what designs, I wonder, will I draw
  As through the ruins of lifetimes I crawl?
        —Phineas Tarbolde, "Sonnet XIII,"
           The City After the Fire

We are but dust and shadow.
    —Quintus Horatius Flaccus, "Ode VII,"
          Odes, Book IV

HISTORIAN'S NOTE

This story is set in the year 2311, eighteen years after the presumed death of Captain James T. Kirk aboard the *U.S.S. Enterprise*-B in *Star Trek Generations*, and fifty-three years before the launch of the *Enterprise*-D in "Encounter at Farpoint."

PROLOGUE: COUNTDOWN

He heard the explosion before he saw it, and as he turned and peered down into the valley to witness walls of flame surging skyward, he knew that he'd found what he'd come here seeking. His intuitions had been realized. So too had his fears.

Captain John Harriman crouched in the tall grass, but not so low that he lost sight of the alien city spread out below the surrounding hills. The orange-red fire stood out at the edge of the municipal sprawl, the most vibrant hue among the flat whites and grays and blacks of the steel-and-concrete construction. The heavy report of the blast rolled over Harriman, drawing out agonizingly as he watched seared debris rain down on the streets and buildings bordering the inferno. The rumble, though softened by distance, contrasted dramatically with the gentle midmorning sounds that had preceded it. The lilting mesh of birdsong here in the hills had vanished now, the occasional calls and movements of other animals stilled by the artificial thunder of destruction. Even the sough of the constant breeze sifting through these undulating grasslands had been lost, overwhelmed by the deep notes now saturating the air.

Harriman reached to the back of his hip, beneath the native crimson tunic he wore so that he would blend with the inhabitants of this world; the other members of the landing party wore similar clothing. He pulled out his communicator and flipped it open. "Harriman to *Enterprise*," he said, resisting the impulse to contact his first officer. The commander led the reconnaissance team currently searching the city, and Harriman wanted to know right now that the ten members of his crew composing the team had not been injured, or worse, in the explosion. But his first officer knew her job—all of his people did—and she or one of the others would contact him as circumstances allowed.

When no response came from the ship, Harriman checked the power level of the communicator. The indicator read well into the green. "Harriman to *Enterprise*," he tried again. "Come in, *Enterprise*." He heard urgency in his voice, but otherwise his tone remained even, belying the apprehension growing within him. He had long ago learned of the need in his position for composure; his crew looked to him for direction, and they followed the cues he provided.

Still no response.

Harriman eyed the dark billows of smoke rising into the sky, the thick plumes pushed aslant by the wind. Beneath sat the southern verge of the city, an area given over to industry. He recognized the ground-vehicle manufacturing plant as he watched that building and two adjoining warehouses burn. He could make out the shapes of people fleeing the blaze, although at this remove, several kilometers away, he could not identify any who might be *Enterprise* crew members. He dreaded the thought of how many casualties the Koltaari would suffer—now, and during what would surely come in the weeks and months to follow. Harriman found himself hoping, with a desperation he resented, that the conflagration below would ultimately reveal itself to be the result of an industrial accident, and not the prelude to an invasion. But he knew better.

Harriman studied his communicator, intending to execute a diagnostic on the device, but then motion to one side caught his attention. He glanced in that direction to see Lieutenant Tenger racing back toward him. The security chief's short, well-muscled legs were hidden by the flows of tall grass, his broad torso visible above, as though sailing across the sea of green stalks. The color of his flesh nearly matched that of the lea through which he moved. His speed seemed effortless, his brawny arms barely pumping as he ran.

After the recon team had earlier detected an anomalous energy reading emanating from the hills, Tenger had accompanied Harriman out of the city in search of the reading's source. The sensor spike had lasted only seconds and might well have been a scanning ghost or reflection, or even the product of a power surge in the tricorder itself. Considering the current circumstances, though, Harriman had been unwilling to risk ignoring anything even remotely suspicious.

Now the security chief settled on his haunches beside Harriman. "Captain," he said, his voice resonant despite being not much louder than a whisper. "There's some sort of interference. I can't take any readings of the city." He worked his tricorder, doubtless attempting to configure it in some manner that would allow him to scan successfully.

"I can't raise the ship either," Harriman said, holding up his communicator.

"I can't be certain," Tenger said, "but there appears to be a dampening field in operation."

"A dampening field," Harriman echoed, looking away from Tenger and back down into the valley. His gaze followed the skyline of the city, from buildings that reached up several dozen stories at its center, out to those rising just one and two stories on its outskirts. The fire had spread to another structure, he saw, and dark masses of smoke continued to coagulate above the urban wound. The roar of the explosion had faded now, replaced by the plaintive screams of sirens. The shrill wails sounded to Harriman like the keen of the city's population, in mourning for the mutilated and dead suddenly delivered into their midst by an unseen enemy. "It's them," he avowed, referring to that enemy, convinced of the conclusions he had drawn from the clues he and his crew had encountered during the past days—conclusions that had led him to bring *Enterprise* to this world.

"Yes," Tenger agreed.

Harriman knew that this land would offer its conquerors valuable resources—dilithium, pergium, cormaline, bilitrium—and the civilization here—technological, but prewarp—would provide the slave labor to mine and process those minerals and compounds. He also understood that those resources would be used against the Federation in the coming war. And there would be war, Harriman realized resignedly. If a world such as this could be taken—a world in disputed space, offering strategic value, with a planetbound population of two billion that posed no threat—then the delicate and increasingly tense political relations among the major spacefaring powers could collapse at any time.

Harriman thought of Amina, stationed on what would be the front lines, and then pushed away the emotions that followed. He turned back to his security chief. "What's your assessment?" he asked.

"It's a message," Tenger said at once. Though hardly laconic, he tended to offer his words sparingly, saying only what needed to be said. As with many of the security officers Harriman had known during his Starfleet career, Tenger tended toward a measured and serious demeanor. "They know we're here," he went on. "They've seen *Enterprise* in orbit, and they've surely scanned the planet's surface for our personnel."

Harriman regarded the lieutenant. Tenger's eyes, normally dark, distant pits, now mimicked those of the Koltaari, with large golden irises, and vertical almond shapes for pupils. His hair had also been altered, his normally short black locks now longer and lighter. Dr. Morell and her staff had similarly modified the appearance of each member of the landing party, taking the additional step of disguising their flesh; Koltaari skin color—like that of Tenger, an Orion—was pigmented a lustrous green. But all of those changes—synthetic lenses inserted into the eyes, a hairpiece set atop the head, a dye for the skin—were cosmetic, not substantive, and sensor scans would readily reveal the presence of the *Enterprise* crewmembers on the planet.

"It's not *just* a message," Harriman noted.

"No, sir," Tenger said, slowly shaking his head from side to side. "It's a challenge."

"Yes," Harriman said. "It's also a warning. And a threat." But could they beat back that threat? It remained unclear whether or not the Klingon Empire would fight beside the Federation if war erupted. Despite nearly eighteen years of peace between the two powers—*Or maybe* because *of it,* Harriman thought—the allegiance of the Klingons could only be characterized as uncertain. If forced to stand alone, the Federation would face a daunting future, where even eventual victory, if it came, would cost incomprehensible losses.

Harriman stood to his full height, and Tenger followed suit beside him. Although almost a head shorter, the burly security chief probably outweighed him by twenty kilos. "Let's go meet that threat," Harriman said with a confidence he did not completely feel, but that he felt it important to project. He placed his communicator back beneath his tunic, and Tenger stowed his tricorder in a leather satchel he carried on a shoulder strap. Harriman led the way through the tall grass to a travel-worn dirt path, and the two men began down the hill.

They had reached the paved road that would lead them into the Koltaari capital when the second explosion rocked the city.

Demora Sulu ran. Panic flowed around her like a river, the inhabitants of the city streaming past, the collective din of footfalls, screams, and sirens bounding along the building façades like water rushing along stony banks. And like the impending menace of a waterfall around a bend up ahead, the fire—the *second* fire—roared without pause somewhere in the distance.

She struggled through the tide of Koltaari, racing in the opposite direction of the fleeing throng. Shoulders, arms, legs, and feet struck her as people dashed by. She changed direction for a moment and fought her way across the living current to the side of the street. Then, using the buildings to protect her on one side, she hurried on.

No lights shined within the broad windows of the storefronts she passed, and she guessed that the second bombing had damaged or destroyed the city's power plant. She and Lieutenant Trent had left that site not an hour ago—and just last night, members of the landing party had visited the manufacturing part of the city, where she believed the first explosion had occurred. Sulu might have considered the timing fortuitous had she not immediately dismissed the notion that events had been coincidental. No, she and Trent and the others hadn't been lucky; they'd been permitted to leave those sites before the attacks. Although she hadn't been able to contact anybody using her communicator, she felt sure that the rest of the landing party had escaped injury in the blasts. As heinous as killing innocent and essentially defenseless Koltaari was, the act did not carry with it the political implications of an assault on Starfleet personnel or Federation citizens.

The dry taste of ash filled Sulu's mouth as she raced in the direction of the fire. The air grew warmer as she ran, the autumnal cool of the morning bleeding away, as though the calendar were somehow slipping ahead to the high heat of a summer afternoon. The crowd thinned as she continued forward, and she hoped that she would not arrive too late to help bring others to safety.

The ambient light wavered, shadows fluttering across the scene. She peered up past the buildings lining the street to see inky trails of smoke intermittently obscuring the Koltaari sun. Flakes of soot floated down from the sky like blackened snow. Even without being able to see the fire itself, Sulu was beset by a sense of disaster.

How could they do this? she asked herself in frustration. The Koltaari had not done anything—lacked the capability of doing anything—to warrant these attacks. Their society had matured to the point of uniting beneath a single government, but they had taken only the smallest steps out into their solar system, and they knew nothing of life beyond their own world. Their planet, though long valued by the various powers of the Alpha and Beta Quadrants for its abundant and untapped natural resources, had benefited from its position beyond established political boundaries. Its strategic location had actually protected the Koltaari, for any incursion onto their world by one power could easily be interpreted by the others as an act of aggression. For decades, that threat of interstellar conflict had kept the Koltaari safe.

Until now, Sulu thought bitterly.

She pressed on, the flood of Koltaari running past her now reduced to a trickle. She reached an intersection and turned onto the road leading directly to the power plant, expecting to see the structure in flames just a few hundred meters away. Instead, the fire only peeked out here and there from beyond a veil of dense gray smoke. But even hidden, the blaze roared, its gusty voice punctuated by hissing and cracking and the sporadic clamor of ruin: what sounded like a ceiling timber crashing down, a wall toppling, the metal of machinery moaning as the fierce heat robbed it of its strength.

A Koltaari man suddenly lurched out of the chaos, teetering as he limped forward. He coughed violently, and Sulu saw that his green flesh had discolored around his nose and mouth, the black smudges there obviously noxious trails the smoke had left. His eyes were tightly shut, his arms held out before him like those of a blind man navigating an unfamiliar environment.

Sulu sprinted forward, ducked down, and threw a shoulder beneath the man's arm. "I'll help you out of here," she said, and only after the words had left her mouth did she realize that she had yelled them. Along with the noise of the fire, the sirens had grown louder now, and she could visualize the Koltaari firefighters heading for the blaze, the chain of bright blue, ovoid hovercraft impeded by the people clogging the streets.

For a moment, Sulu feared that the man had not heard her above the tumult, but then he leaned heavily on her, allowing her to guide him. She walked him quickly away, back the way she had come. Once around the corner, she settled the man against the brick wall of a building. He slumped, his eyes still closed. She reached up and took his face between her hands, experiencing an odd instant of disconnection at the sight of her own skin colored green.

The man's eyes opened, but he didn't seem to see her. His pupils had contracted into narrow slits, and Sulu wondered if shock would prevent him from being able to get himself away from here. "You have to keep moving," she shouted. The man blinked twice, and then his gaze found her. He nodded his head in apparent understanding. "I have to go back," she told him, dropping her hands from his face. "You need to keep moving." The man nodded again, then pushed off of the wall and started away. She watched him for only a few seconds before turning and heading back toward the inferno.

Around the corner, the smoke had surged forward, the length of the street left visible shorter now. "Hello!" Sulu called, cupping her hands around her mouth. She strained to listen for any voices, then called out twice more. When she heard nothing, she started forward, reaching an arm out to the side of the nearest building, intending to use it as a guide once she entered the dark clouds. With her other hand, she stripped off the belt that cinched her traditional

Koltaari tunic at the waist, then pulled the hem of the yellow garment up to cover her nose and mouth. Drafts of heated air pushed past her exposed midriff.

She plunged into the maelstrom of smoke and ash, and at once visibility dropped to almost nothing, as though a light had been extinguished in a windowless room. She moved along the building quickly but cautiously, alert for any Koltaari she might encounter. "Hello!" she called out again, briefly taking the makeshift filter from her mouth. "Can anyone hear me?" The only reply was the ravenous cry of the fire's fury.

She kept moving, slowing her pace, but continuing to call out. Despite holding the bottom of her tunic over her face, she breathed in traces of smoke, and finally she began to cough. Soon, her throat burned as though she had inhaled a mouthful of smoldering gravel. A series of deeper coughs racked her body, and she quickly dropped to her hands and knees, bending her head low in search of breathable air. Her eyes stung and watered, and she closed them against the relentless smoke. As she brought her face within centimeters of the street, though, she found a shallow band free of the foul clouds. She gulped at the clear air, and fought to bring her hacking under control. She knew that she could go no farther.

Then an image rose unexpectedly in her mind: a woman lying on an infirmary biobed, her delicate features glistening with perspiration, her long, straight black hair in knots, her body convulsing from yet another coughing jag. Sulu thought of her mother frequently enough, but not usually from those final days on Marris III and Starbase 189. She most often remembered her mother in one of her sleek, ultramodern outfits—a woman vibrant and confident, her impossibly green eyes threatening mischief—or in one of the traditional gowns she had occasionally worn—still vital, still strong, but her eyes instead promising mystery. Right now, though, those cherished recollections could not chase away the specter of her mother in that infirmary, in that biobed, her body ravaged by Sakuro's disease, set afire from within.

Sulu opened her eyes, an attempted defense against the unpleasant picture in her mind. She saw the pavement stretching away from her beneath the roiling sea of smoke, the brick of the wall she had followed visible just a meter or so away. She inhaled deeply, then stood and retraced her steps along the building. Even as she pulled the hem of the tunic up over her nose and mouth once more, another bout of coughing rasped her throat, but she concentrated on keeping her legs in motion, and on reaching air that had not yet been poisoned by the fire.

Five steps. Ten. And still the smoke engulfed her. She began to feel lightheaded, and she feared that she might not make it out into the open air. She tried to maintain her focus on following the wall, on the rough-hewn texture of the brick as her fingers passed over it, on the—

She tripped.

She went down hard, her hands scraping along the street, her knees striking the unyielding pavement. Pain shot through her limbs, sharpening her attention. Instead of rising, though, she reached behind her, to whatever she had fallen over. Cloth and something beneath it gave way to her touch: a person.

Sulu climbed back to her feet, then stooped down and walked her hands along the body until she located its arms. She hauled the victim to their feet—they seemed slight, perhaps no taller than a meter and a half, more than a dozen centimeters shorter than Sulu—and then up onto her shoulders in a classic rescue carry. After wrapping an arm around a leg and arm, Sulu reached for the wall with her other hand. She couldn't find it, but decided to trust her bearings and started once more through the smoke.

Beads of sweat slid down Sulu's brow and into her eyes. Her Koltaari garments had soaked through and clung tightly to her body. Her breathing came in gasps now, and she wondered how many more steps she would be able to take. She stumbled once, almost overbalancing, but somehow retained her feet. She continued stubbornly forward, but worried that she might have lost her direction when she had fallen, that she now headed deeper into the smoke rather than out of it.

And then she passed back into daylight. The clouds of smoke had advanced nearly to the intersection now. She rounded the corner, then lowered her charge to the street. It was a young Koltaari woman, she saw, unconscious, perhaps twenty years of age. As with the man Sulu had helped to safety, the woman had dark patches around her mouth and nose, clearly the effects of respiring the smoke.

Sulu rested a moment, gathering her strength. Sunlight dappled the street, obviously the effect of the smoke rising haphazardly into the sky. The sirens had grown much louder now, implying that the emergency vehicles would be here soon. Still, she wanted to get farther from the fire and the encroaching smoke, and she would try to carry this young woman at least another couple of blocks.

As she set herself to lift the woman again, Sulu spotted a figure in her peripheral vision. She peered over at the intersection and saw a Koltaari man standing there. He turned quickly away, but then reversed direction and headed toward her. He was lean and fit, and stood not much taller than she did. He had a narrow face and angular features, appearing to be in his late twenties or early thirties. He carried a small satchel over one shoulder.

Only when the man had neared to within a few meters did Sulu recognize Grayson Trent, *Enterprise*'s chief computer scientist and a member of the landing party. *Thank goodness*, she thought. Trent had gone to another part of the city—his mission, beyond simple reconnaissance, had been to scan Koltaari computers for any hints that they had been infiltrated or compromised—but he had obviously come back here to the power plant to help the victims of the fire, just as she had.

Trent marched up to Sulu and raised a hand to her neck. She could not hear any hiss above the cacophony, but she recognized the pressure of a hypospray. Trent leaned in, bringing his mouth close to her ear, though he still had to speak loudly for her to hear him. "Tri-ox," he told her, identifying the medication with which he had injected her. She nodded her acknowledgment, pleased that he had somehow managed to secure a medkit, and then she pointed to the Koltaari that she had carried here. Trent reset the hypo, then ministered to the young woman.

When the lieutenant rose, Sulu leaned in close to him and asked, "Have you contacted the rest of the landing party, or the ship? Does anybody know what's happened?"

"No," he told her. "There's a dampening field in the city blocking communications and sensors." That explained Sulu's inability to raise anybody on her communicator. It also supported the captain's suspicions, since the Koltaari didn't possess the technology required to project such a field.

Beside them, the young woman stirred, the tri-ox compound evidently taking effect. She looked up with an expression of confusion and fear. Sulu squatted down beside her. "There's been an explosion and a fire," she said, yelling the words so that she could be heard; the sirens seemed extremely close now. "You have to get out of here. Can you walk?"

Sulu saw the woman say, "Yes," but the word did not carry above the sounds of the fire and the wails of the sirens. Sulu reached out and helped the woman up. Once on her feet, the young Koltaari swayed once, but then seemed to steady herself.

Just a couple of blocks down, a connected series of four

egg-shaped vehicles, bright blue, turned around a corner, hovering just above the street and heading in this direction. Several Koltaari, clad in protective gear—also blue—hung from the sides of the fire-control machines. The string of vehicles slowed as it neared, its sirens piercingly high as it passed. It turned at the intersection onto the road that led to the power plant. The sirens suddenly shut off, and Sulu guessed that the firefighters had stopped to make their stand.

"Let's get out of here," she called out, placing a hand on the young woman's back and gently urging her forward. Along with Trent, they started down the street.

As they walked, the sounds of the fire diminished behind them, and Sulu hoped that was more than a function of distance. She intentionally lagged behind the Koltaari woman so that she and Trent could speak without being overheard. "Are you all right?" she asked.

"Yes," Trent told her. "A little singed around the edges, but I'm okay." Sulu studied him for a moment and was pleased to see that he at least showed no visible signs of injury. "What about you?" he asked.

"I'm all right," she said, knowing that Dr. Morell would ignore such a statement in favor of a thorough examination. "I inhaled some smoke," she said, the throaty tone of her voice underscoring her words, "but I'll be okay." She rubbed at the side of her mouth and felt a grainy texture there. When she looked at her fingers, she saw that the tips had come away stained an ashy gray. She shook her head absently, ignoring thoughts of her own condition and turning to more important matters. "Let's try to contact the others again," she told Trent. "If we can't, if the dampening field is still in effect, then we'll head for the beam-down point," she said, citing standard procedure for circumstances such as these.

She pulled out her communicator, opened it, and used

both hands to hide it as she raised it to her mouth. "Sulu to Captain Harriman, Sulu to Captain Harriman." She waited a few seconds, eventually tried reaching other members of the landing party, and then finally the ship. No responses came.

As she replaced the communicator at the back of her hip, beneath her tunic, a gloom settled suddenly along the street. Unlike the inconstant murk thrown by the smoke, this darkness did not waver. Ahead, the young Koltaari woman turned and peered up, then took a quick step back, recoiling in obvious terror. Sulu turned her own gaze skyward. Dark clouds continued to rise from the fire, she saw, but it was not smoke that blotted out the sun. Hanging above the buildings, a massive expanse of gray-green metal filled Sulu's view. She could see dark lines and edges and other shapes on its surface, and she distinguished hatches, a shield grid, weapons turrets. Alien characters marched along one section, the identity of the language no surprise to her.

"Come on," Sulu said, already starting to move. "We've got to find Captain Harriman." Trent fell into step beside her, and the two headed down the street, rushing along beneath the shadow of the Romulan warship.

Harriman stopped in the road and stared. Lieutenant Tenger stood at his side. The two had almost reached the city when the air above it had begun to shimmer and shift, like a body of water flash-freezing in sudden and intense cold. And then the effect diminished, the previously empty sky solidifying into the form of a massive starship. Its main body, curving laterally from the tip of its bow back to its linear stern, stretched nearly as long and wide as all of *Enterprise*. A flat, thick neck reached forward to a smaller, aquiline structure, and two warp nacelles sat atop broad, winglike supports that arched outward and upward from the main section. The design evoked a distinctly avian feel, as of a hawk swooping down on its prey—an image chillingly appropriate in this case, Harriman thought. He recognized the vessel at once as a Romulan ship of the line.

"Imperial Fleet, *Ivarix* class," Tenger said, putting voice to Harriman's thoughts. "Armed with disruptors, photon torpedoes, and plasma-energy weapons," he added soberly, obviously focusing on the enormous threat to the Koltaari. The security chief did not offer speculation on the particular identity of the vessel, but Harriman's instinct told him that it was the flagship. Although it was unusual for a starship to descend so low into the atmosphere of a planet, Harriman immediately understood the reason for the maneuver: the Romulans wanted to instill awe and fear in the Koltarri.

"We need to—" he started, but a low-pitched hum interrupted him. Similar to the whine of a Federation transporter, but deeper, the drone rose from a point about ten meters ahead, an indication that the dampening field no longer operated here. Electric-blue motes danced across the width of the road, coalescing into shapes and gaining substance. Beside Harriman, Tenger moved with uncanny speed, a phaser appearing in the lieutenant's hand as if by magic. But as ten Romulan soldiers materialized, each with a disruptor pistol held at the ready, it became instantly clear which side would prevail in a skirmish.

An officer in the middle of the line stepped forward, lowering her disruptor to her side. Clad in a standard Imperial Fleet uniform—a formfitting black-and-silver mesh reminiscent of chain mail, with a colored strip running down the right third of the top—she distinguished herself from the others both by her manner and by the right arm of her uniform, also colored. The jade hue, Harriman knew, designated tactical operations, and its place on her arm, her position in command of that discipline aboard ship. The stylized starbursts at her throat specified her rank as subcommander.

The officer closed to within a couple of meters, looking only briefly at Lieutenant Tenger before turning her full attention to Harriman. She stared at his face, seeming to study his features. After a few moments, she said, "Captain Harriman," her words somewhere between a statement and a question. He surmised that the doctored shade of his skin added some difficulty in identifying him, although the Romulans likely would have expected the use by the *Enterprise* crew of such camouflage. The officer said no more, evidently awaiting a response.

Instead, Harriman slowly looked to his security chief. "Stand down, Lieutenant," he said with feigned nonchalance. Tenger did not take his gaze from the Romulans, but he lowered his weapon without comment. Harriman then peered past the subcommander to see that the members of her landing party continued to wield their disruptors. The soldiers on the flanks had moved away from the group and now surveyed the surrounding areas, presumably to protect against the unexpected.

Harriman at last looked back at the subcommander. A greenish tinge had risen in her high, sallow cheekbones, a hint that his disregard had roused her dudgeon. A small advantage, perhaps, engaging the subcommander's emotions, but Harriman's experiences through the years with the Romulan military had proven to him that *any* advantage over them was worth having. "Yes," he finally told her, "I'm Captain Harriman."

She raised her empty hand to her mouth and spoke into a communicator mounted around her wrist. "Admiral Vokar, this is Linavil," she said. "We've located him."

Vokar, Harriman thought. He'd been right, then: the vessel looming above the Koltaari capital *was* the Imperial Fleet's flagship.

Harriman heard no reply on Linavil's communicator, but within seconds, the whirr of a Romulan transporter again filled the air. This time a single figure materialized, appearing between the line of soldiers and the subcommander. The admiral wore a uniform similar to Linavil's, but with a strip and arm of royal purple, indicating Vokar's advanced position within the command structure of the Imperial Fleet. His hair had silvered more since the last time Harriman had seen him, and the lines etched into his face around his mouth had grown deeper and better defined.

The admiral spotted Harriman immediately. Linavil stepped aside, allowing him to approach directly. Vokar paced carefully over, lifting his gaze to make eye contact with Harriman. Of small stature—not even a meter and two-thirds, and thin—the admiral nevertheless projected a powerful presence. His face showed his age, but his flinty gray eyes exposed vigor and a startling intensity.

"Harriman," Vokar said, his gentle voice managing to carry with it a subtle dash of contempt. "It has been some time since last we met."

Harriman nodded and offered a humorless smile. "Not quite long enough to suit me, Aventeer," he said, attempting to convey his own disdain by employing the given name of the ever-formal admiral. Vokar seemed unmoved by the comment, but Subcommander Linavil took a quick stride forward and threw the back of her closed fist across Harriman's face. He felt his teeth dig into the inside of his cheek, and the metallic taste of blood filled his mouth. He lurched back a step in order to keep himself from going down, then righted himself. In a flash of movement, the subcommander bent and reached her empty hand into her boot, pulling out a long, narrow shape. She flicked her arm toward the ground, and the sheath flew off from the object, revealing an obsidian blade.

Beside him, Lieutenant Tenger tensed, but did not act. As

so often happened, the security chief's restraint impressed Harriman. Despite being overwhelmingly outnumbered and outgunned, many security officers would've responded in kind to an assault on their captain. In most cases, such a reaction would simply have proven foolhardy, earning the officer and the captain more physical pain. In this situation, though, such a reaction could've had far greater repercussions: what occurred here in the next few minutes might well influence the course of war. Tenger knew that, and his restraint demonstrated his commitment to serving this mission.

"A Romulan subcommander striking a Starfleet officer, threatening him with a knife," Harriman said to Vokar. "My crew put in danger, possibly injured or killed." He gestured toward the city, where the thick, dark smoke continued to rise from the sites of the two explosions. "Those are provocative actions, Admiral."

"Your crew are unharmed," Vokar said. Harriman had expected as much, believing that the Romulans would not commit to battle via direct action against the Federation, but he felt relief at the news anyway.

"Still," Harriman persisted, "at a time when your people are negotiating peace with mine—"

"We do not bargain for peace," Vokar declared calmly. "We fight to retain our manifest right to live without constraint, and to deny the encroaching imperialism of the Federation. Imperialism, of which your presence on this planet is an example."

"*Our* presence?" Harriman said, surprised by both the absurdity and the audacity of the assertion. "This is neutral territory, Admiral. We are visitors here, and we make no claims on this world or its people."

"In the beginning, you are always visitors," Vokar said. "And in the end, you always stay." The admiral rounded on his heel and paced away, then turned back to his captives before addressing them once more. The movement reeked of theatricality, although for whose benefit—the Romulan soldiers' or the Starfleet officers'—Harriman could not tell. "But it is of no matter with respect to this planet," Vokar continued. "You are not visitors, and you are not invited to stay. You are trespassers in Romulan territory, and you will leave at once."

And there it is, Harriman thought, the need for supposition and analysis gone. The Romulans had decided to act first, though they would assert otherwise, claiming their actions to be *reactions* incited by the Federation. Harriman understood that the months and years of diplomatic ebb and flow had ceased, and that the military tide had crashed through the levees and now threatened a devastating flood. And in risking that first move, the Romulans had also taken a strategically valuable asset.

"This is neutral territory," Harriman said again, making the attempt he must make, despite being convinced that nothing short of battle would prevent Vokar from accomplishing the task he had come here to perform. "The people here don't even know that sentient life exists beyond their world."

"They know it now," Vokar said, turning to glance up at his ship hanging above the city, the fires raging below. "And we have made our intentions clear to them." By *intentions,* Harriman knew, Vokar meant the ability and willingness to sow destruction and promote fear.

"The Federation and the Empire have long had a tacit understanding that this world is off-limits," Harriman went on.

"An understanding?" Vokar said. "Perhaps. But an agreement? I am sure that is not correct." His words contained the arrogance of victory already achieved. "No matter the interpretation of past exchanges, this planet now lies within the sovereign domain of the Romulan Star Empire."

"Vokar," Harriman said, taking a step toward him. Subcommander Linavil quickly moved forward, interposing herself between the two men. She brandished her knife, and Harriman raised his hands, prepared to fend off any attack. Tenger also started forward.

"Stop," Vokar said quietly, the single word more powerful for not having been shouted. The subcommander froze, then lowered the knife and backed away.

Tenger stopped, and Harriman let his hands fall back to his sides. He heard two short tones—somebody trying to contact him on his communicator—and ignored them. "Don't do this," he told the admiral. "Allow your negotiators and ours to continue their work." For many months, Federation, Romulan, and Klingon representatives had been attempting, without success, to find their ways through the ever-deepening and dangerous morass existing among the three powers. "Don't undermine the peace process," Harriman said. "Don't do *this*." He motioned toward the starship menacing the Koltaari city.

Vokar raised his chin before speaking. "It is already done, *Captain* Harriman." The minor emphasis on rank seemed intended as derision. "And I see that you still are a captain after all this time. Is Starfleet unwilling to entrust you with greater responsibilities, or are you simply afraid to assume them?"

Harriman smiled again, but this time, he actually felt like laughing. It amused him that Vokar had so completely misread his vulnerabilities, but more than that, the admiral's words might well have revealed a vulnerability of his own. "Still a captain," Harriman agreed, the smile not leaving his face. "And I see that you're an admiral . . . again."

This time, Vokar himself lifted his hand to strike, moving with remarkable speed for a man of his years. Still, Harriman saw the attack coming and had time to defend himself. Instead, he chose to do nothing. Vokar's blow landed, driving into Harriman's face. His head snapped back, and he allowed his knees to give way. He fell onto his back, the hard road unforgiving beneath him. Anticipating the next attack, he looked up, but the admiral simply peered down at him.

"Contact your ship and get out of here," Vokar hissed.

Harriman pushed himself up onto his hands. "Mr. Tenger," he said. As he climbed back onto his feet, he heard the chirp of a communicator being activated, and then the security chief called up to *Enterprise.*

"This is Linojj," came the response from the ship's second officer. Harriman detected the concern in her tone even before she continued. *"Are you and the captain all right?"*

"We are," Tenger said. "Can you locate the rest of the landing party?"

"We've already beamed them aboard," Linojj reported. *"You and the captain are the only ones left on the surface."*

"Lock on to us and prepare to transport," Tenger told her, then said, "Captain?"

Harriman tasted blood again, and he coughed to clear his throat, then turned and spat onto the road. He looked at Vokar. "Get us out of here, Lieutenant," he said.

"Energize," he heard Tenger say. A moment later, the world of the Koltaari faded from view.

Silence and the eerie scarlet glow of alert lighting suffused the bridge of *Enterprise.* Lieutenant Commander Xintal Linojj had ordered the klaxons off and the flashing of the lights stopped, but the pandemonium of the initial call to battle stations now seemed preferable to this grave atmosphere. She peered around at the crew—DeYoung and Kanchumurthi at the freestanding tactical-and-communications console, Fenn at sciences, Tolek at navigation, and Verant in Linojj's stead at the helm—and saw her own troubled feelings reflected in their faces.

Except it's worse for me, isn't it? she thought. *It's more personal.* She looked ahead from the command chair at the main viewer and felt wounded by what she saw there. The emerald-and-white Koltaari planet—so similar in appearance to Cort, the Boslic homeworld—arced across the lower left corner of the screen, a Romulan warship hanging threateningly in orbit above it. The sight recalled too well for her the fractured years of her childhood when her own people had confronted an alien invasion. It had taken almost a decade for the Boslic to completely repel the attackers, and though the final battles had been fought more than a quarter of a century ago, she found that the difficult memories of those days had lost little of their emotional force for her.

Off to her right, the starboard doors whispered open, and she glanced in that direction, grateful for the distraction. Captain Harriman and Lieutenant Tenger entered the bridge from the turbolift, the captain barely recognizable in native Koltaari garb and with his skin dyed green; several dark patches, like birthmarks, also decorated his features around his nose and mouth. The flaxen, shoulder-length hairpiece he had worn down to the planet now dangled from one hand, though, and she thought that his own short brown hair, swept back and dusted silver along the sides, at least helped his long, narrow face seem more familiar.

Linojj stood from the command chair as Harriman stepped down from the outer, raised circle of the bridge. Behind him, Tenger moved aft to the tactical position and relieved Ensign DeYoung. Unlike the captain, the security chief had not yet removed his wig, but neither the long blond tresses nor the colorful Koltaari clothing could disguise Tenger's stern countenance.

"Report," Harriman said, acknowledging Linojj with a nod and then looking to the main viewer. Standing beside the captain, she saw that his lower lip had been split open, and she realized that the dark patches she had noticed on his face were actually smears of blood.

"There are four Romulan ships in all, Captain," she said. "At least, there are four that we know of." Romulan cloaking technology generally advanced in parallel with Federation detection equipment, the two alternately outdistancing each other. The Romulans currently held the advantage, their cloaked vessels effectively invisible to Starfleet sensors. "They appeared all at once," Linojj went on, "three *D'Vorix*-class ships in orbit, and the *Ivarix*-class ship perched above the Koltaari capital." Since the captain had transported down to the city with the landing party, she assumed that he already knew about—indeed, must have seen—that fourth ship.

"You got no indications of their drives before they decloaked?" Harriman asked. The Romulans operated artificial quantum singularities to power their warp engines, and it was most often those microscopic black holes that permitted Federation technology to detect the cloaked ships.

"No, sir," she informed him.

Harriman seemed to consider this, still looking at the viewscreen. "Did they fire on the city?" he finally asked.

"It's hard to tell," she said. "Ship's sensors were impeded by a dampening field that blanketed the capital during and for several minutes after the explosions. We're not sure why."

Harriman turned toward Linojj, but he seemed not to see her, instead looking into the middle distance. "Because Admiral Vokar didn't want me to transport off the planet," he said, apparently coming to a realization. "He wanted to explain the Romulans' intentions to a captive audience."

"Vokar's here?" Linojj asked, surprised. As secretive as the Romulans could be, the name of Aventeer Vokar had been known within Starfleet for years. Now fleet admiral after a long career, Vokar had been involved in several encounters between the Empire and the Federation during his ascent to power. Starfleet Command, she knew, considered him both hostile and dangerous.

"He's here," Harriman confirmed, his eyes focusing on Linojj. "That's the flagship down there." He pointed a finger toward the image of the planet on the viewer.

She shook her head slowly from side to side, reaching up and running a thumb and forefinger along the smooth, raised ridges of her brow. A wisp of her long purple hair fell across her face, and she brushed it aside, irritated. She had hoped that the appearance of the Romulans here—and even that their attack on the city—might have been only a warning to the Federation, a cautionary signal that would not include the actual taking of this world and its people by the Empire. But Vokar's presence put the lie to such a hope; the Romulans would not have sent a fleet admiral merely to deliver a message. No, Vokar had come here to lead an occupying force.

To the captain, Linojj said, "After the dampening field went down, we scanned the city. There were no residual readings characteristic of energy weapons, so we believe that explosive charges were actually set on the surface. The Romulans may have intended them to detonate simultaneously."

Harriman seemed to consider this for a moment, and then said, "No, I don't think so." He walked slowly around the navigation station and paced toward the viewscreen, then looked back toward her. "I think they set off the first charge so that the Koltaari would commit most of their emergency-response resources to that area, and then set off the second to maximize the bedlam and horror in the city." He peered at her with a knowing and pained expression. "It's an old Romulan ploy: demoralize your enemies before they even know who's attacking."

"And then appear and show themselves to be the source of the destruction," Linojj concluded.

"Yes," the captain agreed.

She looked at the Romulan vessel on the viewscreen, her stomach churning in anger. "When the ships decloaked, we had a few tense moments," she said, continuing her report. "But the Romulans made no moves against the *Enterprise*. When the dampening field went down, the members of the landing party began calling in. You and Lieutenant Tenger were the last two on the planet. We tried to contact you, but when you didn't respond, we scanned your location and found the Romulan landing party there as well. We were about to beam you up when the lieutenant contacted the ship."

Harriman nodded, then asked, "Where is Commander Sulu?"

"In sickbay," Linojj said, "being treated for smoke inhalation. Dr. Morell says she'll be fine."

"And the rest of the landing party?"

"Unharmed," she told him. "Although the doctor's insisting on examining each of them. And she's already contacted me to demand that you and Lieutenant Tenger report to sickbay as soon as possible."

"Of course she did," Harriman said, offering a wan smile. The doctor possessed a shipwide renown for overprotecting the crew, a trait for which she was continually teased. Looking past Linojj, Harriman said, "Lieutenant Tenger, secure from general quarters."

"Aye, sir," came the crisp response from the security chief. Linojj looked around and watched him operate his console. An instant later, the red alert indicators blinked off, replaced by the standard lighting of alpha shift.

Harriman stepped forward and rested a hand along the front edge of the navigation console. "Ensign Tolek," he said, "plot a course for Starbase Iridani."

"Aye, Captain," the navigator replied, sending his long, dexterous fingers dancing across his console.

"Sir, we're leaving?" Linojj asked, dismayed, speaking out even before she'd had a chance to consider her words. But unlike the other commanding officers under whom she'd served, Captain Harriman invited questions on the bridge. His command style mixed strength and decisiveness with patience and informality; he made decisions quickly, but allowed any of the crew to ask about those decisions. When she had first come aboard, she had found Harriman's approach confused and even dangerous, but she had soon come to discover its merits. The crew appreciated their access to the captain, and felt valued by his willingness to listen to them; they trusted him because he trusted them. Linojj often wondered how much of that had been a reaction to Harriman's experiences with his father, now an admiral in Starfleet Command, a man noted as a hard and unforgiving leader; she and Demora had often speculated with each other about it.

"Course laid in, Captain," Tolek said.

"The helm answers ready, sir," Ensign Verant added.

"One moment," Harriman told Tolek and Verant. He circled back around the navigation console and eased into the command chair. "You have concerns, Xintal?" he asked.

"I don't think we should abandon the Koltaari," she said honestly.

"We're not abandoning them," Harriman said evenly. "The Koltaari don't even know that we exist."

"Begging the captain's pardon," Linojj said, "but after what the Romulans have done, aiding the Koltaari could hardly be considered a violation of the Prime Directive, if that's what you're suggesting." She looked over at the main viewscreen, training her eyes on the Romulan warship suspended above the planet. She recognized the design of the vessel—with its bulbous command section at the end of a long, narrow neck, and its wide nacelle mounts below its angular main body—as from an older class manufactured into the 2290s, but not beyond that time. All three Romulan ships in orbit hailed from that older class, and while all must have been refitted over the years, none could approach the capabilities of *Enterprise*, itself fully refitted just four years ago, right before she had joined the crew. In her head, she ran numbers and attack strategies, attempting to estimate *Enterprise*'s chances of dispatching the three older vessels before having to face the much more powerful Romulan flagship.

"No, this isn't a Prime Directive matter," Harriman allowed. "But even if we could somehow defeat all four of the Romulan vessels, what then? A direct attack on Romulan personnel would be considered an act of war."

"Isn't this attack on the Koltaari an act of war?" she said.

"Against the Koltaari, yes," Harriman said, "but not against the Federation. Aggressive, yes. Dangerous, yes. But not something that automatically instigates war."

"So we're just going to allow the Romulans to take this world, to enslave these people?" she persisted, her emotions rising. "Because that's what they'll do. They've enslaved the Remans for centuries."

"Xintal," Harriman said gently, "the Romulans have already taken the first steps to occupy this world. If we fight now, it will cost Koltaari lives."

"It's already cost that," she argued. "Hundreds of them, maybe thousands, in the two explosions."

"Yes," Harriman said, and he cast his gaze downward for a moment, clearly saddened himself at the circumstances that had unfolded here. "But the Romulans are pushing us. They either believe that war is inevitable, and that they should therefore gain as much advantage as possible, or they believe that they've already gained some advantage that will assure them victory. Either way, they're pushing us, inviting us to commit. And we're not ready."

"Captain," Linojj said, almost pleading, she realized, for people she had never even met. "To allow this to happen to the Koltaari, even to avoid war . . ."

Harriman looked at her, the stare of his blue-gray eyes intense. "We're not going to avoid war," he said. "Not by leaving the Koltaari to the Romulans, and not by confronting the Romulans right here, right now. We'll delay it by stepping back at this point—we *need* to delay it—but . . ." The captain let his voice trail off to silence, just as she had, and Linojj saw something like conflict in his expression.

No, not conflict, she thought. *Struggle.* As though he had already begun to search for the solution that would deny the inexorableness of war with the Romulans. She tried to see what he saw, that their inaction here now was necessary, that in the long run, and perhaps in the short run, even the Koltaari would be better off if the crew of *Enterprise* did not fight today. To Harriman, she simply said, "Yes, sir," signaling an end to her opposition. "I understand." She bowed her head once, a Boslic sign of respect, then turned and tapped Ensign Verant on her shoulder. The ensign quickly operated a control to freeze the helm, then stood and retreated to a secondary station at the periphery of the bridge. Linojj sat, quickly scanned the readouts to familiarize herself with the ship's current status, then reached up and reactivated the console. "Helm still answers ready, Captain," she said.

"Break orbit, Commander," Harriman told her. "Go to warp eight when it's safe to do so."

She worked the helm, the thrum of the impulse engines rising as they engaged. She looked up at the main viewscreen just once, as the arc of the Koltaari world slipped from sight. Linojj felt a tightness in her belly, a sick, sinking feeling at leaving the peaceful people to the marauding hands of the Romulans. But she also thought once more of her own homeworld, and of the hundreds of other aligned and nonaligned planets in and around the Federation, their billions of inhabitants, and she knew that Captain Harriman was right: Starfleet was not yet prepared to go to war, and if the crew of *Enterprise* had attempted to liberate the Koltaari today, the results would have been disastrous—both for the Federation and for the Koltaari.

It might still be disastrous, she thought. War had been coming for a long time, she knew, but it had never been closer than right now. Today, Vokar and the Romulans had begun the countdown.

MINUS TEN: FOXTROT

The asteroid hung in space like an afterthought, a barren, craggy rock the universe seemed to have flung together for no particular purpose. Foxtrot XIII, irregularly but unremarkably shaped, bore no conspicuous variations from any of its dozen namesakes. Less than five hundred kilometers along its greatest dimension, it appeared lifeless and alone against the glittering backdrop of stars.

No, not alone, Lieutenant Commander Rafaele Buonarroti saw as he peered at a monitor in one of *Enterprise*'s cargo holds. On the small viewscreen, a gleam of light had emerged from beyond the asteroid, a distinctive gray-white shape. *Enterprise* had been scheduled to rendezvous here with *Agamemnon*, but Buonarroti would have immediately identified the ship—or at least its class—anyway. The curved engine nacelles of the *Odysseus* vessels represented an experimental Starfleet design three decades old—a design that, while functional, had been abandoned when theorized efficiencies in warp-field generation had never materialized. Only two of the eight ships built remained in active service, and Buonarroti had heard recent talk that *Agamemnon* itself might soon be decommissioned. For now, though, the old vessel kept company with the dun, seemingly empty asteroid.

Seemingly empty, Buonarroti knew, but not *actually* empty.

Beside him, Captain Harriman reached down and pressed a touchpad on the detached console into which the monitor was set. The image shifted, bringing Foxtrot XIII and *Agamemnon* closer. The old ship measured only about two-thirds as long as *Enterprise,* Buonarroti recalled from the specs, and carried a corresponding crew complement of approximately five hundred. But despite its smaller size and the still-ultramodern appearance of its bowed nacelles, *Agamemnon* looked bulky and boxy to him, particularly when compared with the sleek, streamlined form of *Enterprise.*

"Are we ready to go once we're in range, Rafe?" the captain asked, pronouncing Buonarroti's nickname with a short *a* and long *e*: *Rah-fee.* The two men stood on the other side of the console from the expansive square stage of a cargo transporter. Buonarroti looked up from the monitor and over at Harriman before responding.

"Yes, we're all set, Captain," he said, then peered around at the cargo that *Enterprise* had hauled here from Space Station KR-3. Throughout the hold, outsized metal containers of various shapes had been stacked high. Security mechanisms, a trio of green lights glowing steadily on each, had been affixed to all of the containers. One light indicated an engaged magnetic lock, the others the active states of sensor and transporter inhibitors. If any cloaked Romulan vessels penetrated the nearby Neutral Zone to gather intelligence—and Starfleet Command believed such reconnaissance to be commonplace these days—then their crews would be able neither to scan the contents of the containers nor to transport them away; the inhibitors obstructed sensors and prevented the containers from being beamed from anywhere but directly atop a transporter pad. "I've already received the coordinates from the outpost," Buonarroti told Harriman, "and I've modified the transporter protocols not to record the details of what we beam down." He paused, then added, *"La lotta continua."*

Owing to his appreciation for his heritage, Buonarroti had an affinity for employing Italian phrases. Combined with his slightly drawn-out cadences—common to humans raised in the Alpha Centauri system—it made for a distinctive way of speaking. He remembered, back when he had first been assigned to *Enterprise,* the captain's inability to contain a smile whenever Buonarroti had spiced his dialogue with Italian, but Harriman had long ago become accustomed to such verbal idiosyncrasies. Buonarroti had served under the captain for fifteen years now, the last half as his chief engineer.

Now, not only didn't Harriman smile, but his jaw tightened. "I'm afraid that's an understatement, Rafe," he said. A saying Buonarroti used often enough that just about everybody on board understood its meaning, *La lotta continua* translated as *The struggle continues.*

The captain gazed around the hold at the cargo containers, his expression drawn, his body language hinting at his weariness. The last couple of years had been difficult for all of Starfleet, with the uncertain relations among the Federation, the Romulans, and the Klingons threatening the peace more and more each day. Seven months ago, immediately after the Romulans had taken the world of the Koltaari, *Enterprise* had been assigned to Foxtrot Sector to patrol the Federation side of the Neutral Zone and conduct defense-readiness drills at the thirteen outposts in the region. And just nine weeks ago, *Enterprise* had been ordered to team with *Agamemnon* to deliver enhanced weaponry to the outposts and to rotate outpost personnel. Buonarroti knew that Starfleet crews stationed full-time along the Neutral Zone were routinely reassigned to other posts in order to minimize fatigue and stress, a policy Starfleet Command had recently reinforced by choosing to rotate out entire crews from the outposts, at shorter intervals.

The incongruity of the operation, as far as Buonarroti was

concerned, lay in the anxiety it had produced in the crew of
Enterprise and, he was sure, in the crew of *Agamemnon*. *Enterprise* ferried weapons from Space Station KR-3 to the Foxtrot asteroids and then returned to the starbase with the
reassigned outpost crews, while *Agamemnon* delivered the
new crews and also provided special technicians to install
the new weapons. The tasks served as constant reminders of
the precarious state of interstellar relations, and the repetition
of those tasks for each outpost only helped to heighten the
feeling of dread aboard ship—probably for no one more so
than the captain, Buonarroti thought. Beyond carrying the
burdens of his crew, Harriman also must have felt pressure
from Starfleet Command; each time *Enterprise* arrived at
KR-3, he would invariably be called into hours of meetings
with the top brass. Buonarroti knew of the captain's experiences with the Romulans through the years, and the engineer
was sure that the admirals wanted to make use of whatever
the captain had learned as a result of those experiences.

"Well, it sure looks like an impressive amount of fire-
power," Buonarroti observed optimistically. Although Starfleet Command had classified the contents of the containers,
it had been an open secret that, in recent days, the Federation had been designing and manufacturing improved—
and perhaps even new—armaments. He only hoped that the
weapons experts on the Federation side of the Neutral Zone
performed their jobs better than their counterparts in the
Romulan and Klingon Empires, and that if shots eventually
did blaze through the darkness of space, the enhanced weaponry would prove decisive for the UFP.

"Yes, it does look impressive," Harriman said.

"I'd love to see what Starfleet Tactical's come up with,"
Buonarroti told the captain. He had voiced such desires before, during *Enterprise*'s runs to the other outposts. He understood that times of military necessity often resulted in
impressive leaps of technological progress, and as an engi-

neer—as with other engineers he knew, and perhaps *all* engineers *everywhere*—he enjoyed getting his hands on whatever advanced equipment he could. That had been one of the primary reasons he had joined Starfleet: on a starship, the opportunities to work on different technologies were numerous—from life-support and environmental control, to warp and impulse engines, to weapons and defensive systems, to sensors and scientific equipment. For him, *Enterprise* essentially constituted an enormous playground.

"Sorry, Rafe," Harriman said. "You know how careful Command is being these days." As always happened during periods of interstellar tensions, suspicions had been raised about the possibility of Romulan operatives having infiltrated not only the Federation, but Starfleet as well. Such occurrences, Buonarroti knew, were not without precedent. The most notorious episode of Romulan espionage had occurred just three years ago at the Antares Advanced Design Laboratories, where Starfleet worked to develop, among other things, means of penetrating the latest cloaking technology; a woman who'd been working there for several years had been unmasked as an Empire spy. And Buonarroti knew that Starfleet had conducted its own covert operations in Romulan space; at least as far back as forty years ago, another *Enterprise* had violated the Neutral Zone and two Starfleet officers—Captain James T. Kirk and Commander Spock, if Buonarroti remembered his history correctly—had purloined a cloaking device, an incident that had sparked the conflicting consequences of increasing friction between the two powers, and at the same time averting war because of the technological parity engendered by the theft.

"I understand Starfleet's concerns, Captain," Buonarroti said. But before he could say more, two short electronic tones interrupted him, followed by Commander Sulu's voice on the ship's intercom.

"*Bridge to Captain Harriman,*" she said.

Harriman touched a control on the console, opening the channel. "This is Harriman," he said. "Go ahead."

"*We've arrived at the outpost along with the* Agamemnon," Sulu said. Buonarroti glanced down at the monitor and saw that *Enterprise* now orbited Foxtrot XIII. "*Both Commander Sasine and Captain Rodriguez have signaled that they're ready to begin.*" Buonarroti looked up at the captain, but Harriman gave no indication of anything but professionalism. Still, Buonarroti assumed that the captain's heart must have begun to beat a bit faster at the mention of Sasine's name; the two had been romantically involved for eight years now. Sasine had served for a brief tour of duty aboard *Enterprise,* but she and Harriman hadn't become a couple during that time. She'd left the ship after less than a year as second officer to take on the position of exec aboard *New York,* and from there she'd moved on to commanding various starbases and outposts. After her time on *Enterprise,* she and the captain had met again at a Starfleet briefing on Romulan activity, and they'd been together ever since, although usually across many light-years.

"Acknowledged," Harriman said evenly. "Lower the shields, Demora, and inform Amina and Esteban"—Commander Sasine and Captain Rodriguez, Buonarroti knew—"that we'll commence transporting down the matériel immediately."

"*Yes, sir,*" came Sulu's brisk reply.

"Harriman out." The channel closed with a brief tone, and then the captain said, "Let's get going, Rafe. We've got a long night ahead of us."

"Sir, are you sure you don't want me to assign somebody else to this duty?" Buonarroti asked. He'd made the same suggestion during *Enterprise's* stops at each of the other Foxtrot outposts, but the captain had always insisted on taking on the task himself, and he did so again now.

Harriman bent and retrieved a meter-long device covered on one long side with grappling pads, and with a cylindrical handle at each end: an antigrav unit. Buonarroti stooped and picked up his own antigrav, then followed the captain to the nearest cargo container. The two men would use the antigravs to move each of the containers onto the transporter pad so that they could then be beamed down to the outpost. It would not be backbreaking work, but it did require an effort to maneuver the massive containers without allowing them to drift into a bulkhead. There were also a lot of containers, and it would likely take the two officers more than six hours to complete the task. Having already completed a full day shift, Buonarroti knew that he would be exhausted when they had finished in the hold. Still, he felt privileged to have been selected by the captain for the task. Because of the sensitive nature of this mission, Harriman obviously felt most comfortable doing it himself, and other than the three officers at the top of *Enterprise*'s chain of command—Captain Harriman, Commander Sulu, and Lieutenant Commander Linojj— Buonarroti carried the highest security clearance on the ship; coupling that with his transporter expertise, the captain had clearly believed him to be best suited to assist.

At first, the two men worked in relative silence, the only sounds the slightly metallic clanks of their footfalls on the decking, the low hum of the antigravs, and the treble whine of the transporter. Having been through this process twelve times previously, Buonarroti and Harriman set to the job with a clear sense of the effort needed, along with a grim seriousness that naturally accompanied preparing for war. For his part, Buonarroti simply wanted to get past this duty, not just here at Foxtrot XIII, but at all of the outposts. The entire crew of *Enterprise* no doubt felt the same, he thought, and then realized that the captain must actually have looked forward to arriving at Foxtrot XIII.

"We're making good time," Buonarroti said as he and Harriman settled an enormous cubic container, more than four meters on a side, onto the transporter pad.

"We are," Harriman said, deactivating his antigrav with a tap to its control pad. "We must be getting good at this."

"Maybe we can sign on as stevedores on a merchant ship if our Starfleet careers don't work out," Buonarroti said with a chuckle.

"Some days, Rafe," Harriman said, "that doesn't sound like such a bad idea."

Buonarroti deactivated his antigrav, pulled it from the surface of the container, and then walked with the captain back over to the console. He rechecked the settings for about the hundredth time, triggered the sequence, then slid the three activator controls up the lengths of their channels. The high-pitched quaver of the transporter filled the hold, and then the container shimmered out of its existence on *Enterprise*.

As the two men made their way to the next container, Buonarroti said, "I think I know another reason why at least one of us is moving so quickly."

"Oh?" Harriman said without looking up, instead simply reenergizing his antigrav and setting it against one surface of a dodecahedral container that reached to just above their heads.

"You've got a date tonight, don't you?" Buonarroti asked, smiling.

Now Harriman glanced up, and Buonarroti was pleased to see a grin creep onto the captain's face. "Yeah," he admitted. "I do."

"Well, say hello to the commander for me," Buonarroti said. He switched his antigrav back on and attached it to the container.

"Somehow, Rafe," Harriman told him, "I don't think your name's going to come up tonight."

Buonarroti laughed, a hearty guffaw that echoed loudly through the hold. "No," he said, "I don't suppose it will."

Harriman took hold of the handles of his antigrav, and Buonarroti did the same. "All right, one, two," the captain said, and on "three," the two men hefted the container, then slowly maneuvered it toward the transporter pad. "I've been looking forward to this time with Amina for quite a while," Harriman said as they moved.

"I believe it," Buonarroti said. Even though *Enterprise* had been in Foxtrot Sector for the last half-year or so, the crew's grueling schedule had not allowed for any down-time at any of the outposts. Harriman and Sasine had seen each other for only the shortest of times, and only on official business. The captain had stayed focused during that time, Buonarroti knew, but he also guessed that Harriman would have greatly anticipated being able to spend time again with his *innamorata*. Today, after they had finished transporting the containers down to the outpost, that time would finally arrive. As the specialists aboard *Agamemnon* took over to install the weapon systems, the *Enterprise* crew would have a day of light duties before beaming up the current Foxtrot XIII crew in favor of their replacements. "How long has it been since you've seen each other?" Buonarroti asked. "I mean, since you've spent any significant time together?"

"Eleven months," Harriman said, peering around the container at Buonarroti. "Eleven and a half, actually. We took that vacation on Pacifica."

"That's right," Buonarroti said, remembering back a year ago to when both the captain and the executive officer had taken leave, and Lieutenant Commander Linojj had taken temporary command of the ship for nearly a month. "What I recall about that trip of yours is that you came back to the *Enterprise* more exhausted than when you left it."

Harriman stepped up onto the transporter platform and moved slowly across it. "That's right," he said. "Amina and I never managed to relax, but we sure had a wonderful time." The captain's eyes shifted upward, and Buonarroti imagined him visualizing that romantic trip. "We swam and sailed, and hiked the Peragoit ruins. And almost every night, we ended up dancing at this bistro in Jennita . . . it's this little town that sits at the top of a cliff overlooking the ocean." The beautiful cobalt blue waters of Pacifica were well known throughout the Federation. "And the dance floor in the club actually projected out beyond the edge of the cliff . . . it was breathtaking. And our bungalow—" Harriman stopped, looked over at Buonarroti, and blinked, apparently embarrassed by his reverie. "Sorry," he said, and then, "One, two, three." As before, they coordinated their movements, this time lowering the container to the transporter pad.

"It's all right, Captain," Buonarroti said. "I've been to Pacifica, so I know that it's conducive to *amore*."

"It is," Harriman agreed, "but right now, I'll take that hunk of gray rock out there. It may be an asteroid with a military base buried beneath its surface, but for me, it's an oasis in the desert."

"I understand," Buonarroti said. "Don't forget to sip a little water for the rest of us."

"Don't worry, Rafe," Harriman told him. "Once we're finally done here and return to Space Station KR-3, I've put in for at least a few days of R and R for the crew."

"That's great, Captain," Buonarroti said. "I think we need it."

"I do too."

It took them just short of six hours to empty the cargo hold, a tiring exercise despite the use of the antigravs. It put an end to a long day for Buonarroti, but despite his fatigue, he felt energized for Harriman. For so long now, the captain had been Starfleet's point man in readying for battle with the Romulans, and Buonarroti could see the heavy days weighing on his captain. So as much as war might be waiting for them all in the near future, Buonarroti felt happy that, at least right now, on Foxtrot XIII, the captain's love would be waiting for him.

* * *

Harriman's footsteps echoed along the series of corridors that led from the transporter room to the section of the subterranean outpost that housed crew quarters. The walls, floor, and ceiling extended away from him in matte shades of leaden gray, interrupted every few meters by support columns and beams, along with an occasional access panel. The stark illumination provided by the overhead lighting panels did little to liven the sterile atmosphere. The cold, colorless setting seemed not only unoccupied, but uninhabitable, a man-made congener of the desolate asteroid surface somewhere above.

Of the 271 Starfleet personnel stationed here at Foxtrot XIII, Harriman knew, a third would be on duty at their stations, a third would be asleep, and the rest, while off duty, would likely be in either the mess hall, the gymnasium, or their quarters. This far from the main body of the Federation, and this close to the Neutral Zone—and to the Klingon border, for that matter—few opportunities for recreation would present themselves. The significant power demands of the small outpost for its sensor, defense, and weapon systems rendered most luxuries unsustainable. Harriman could readily understand Command's rationale for regularly reassigning the crews of such installations. Unlike their counterparts aboard starships, who could travel to any number of locations for shore leave, those who staffed distant outposts were effectively bound by their responsibilities to them—bound to fragments of frozen rock beside borders that could in a flash become the front lines in a war.

The corridor jogged to the right, past an exposed conduit that had obviously been repaired recently; a patchwork of optical fibers emerged from several openings and wound around like the web of a disoriented spider. Harriman sidled by, distinguishing another characteristic of duty at the periphery of the Federation, namely the necessity of performing makeshift maintenance. Supply ships never called often enough.

As he continued on, he thought of his own crew. Though

not posted to a base along the Neutral Zone, they had been at the vanguard of the Federation's delicate and dangerous contacts with the Romulan Empire for years now, without any real respite. Prior to spending the last seven months in the precarious Foxtrot Sector, there had been the Romulan occupation of the Koltaari, and before that, *Enterprise* had been embroiled in half a dozen other tense ship-to-ship encounters with Imperial vessels.

And then there had been the clandestine mission to Devron II. That had not involved the entire crew—only Sulu had accompanied him from *Enterprise*, together with five officers from other Starfleet postings—but that had been a year ago, and it brought home to Harriman the reality of just how long this strife with the Romulans had been plaguing the Federation. The operation on Devron II—a planet in the heart of the Neutral Zone—had been especially brutal. Harriman remembered trying to mitigate the horror of the experience for himself by believing that the efforts of his team would ultimately prevent hostilities from breaking out. Instead, good women and men had died—and worse—for nothing; all this time later, war still impended.

One of the officers who had served at Devron II had been Commander Michael Paris—known as "Iron Mike," an odd moniker for so frail-looking a man, Harriman had thought at first, although the commander's constitution and determination had soon explained the nickname. Paris had taken leave from his position as first officer of *Agamemnon*—the same ship in orbit about Foxtrot XIII right now—in order to take part in the covert assignment, and he'd comported himself admirably. He'd risked his life to save Sulu's, and it had been his courageous and quick-thinking actions that had allowed the team—or what had been left of it—to escape the Devron system. Ironically, Harriman thought, in order for his current mission regarding the Romulans to succeed, he would once again require the assistance of Iron Mike Paris.

He reached an intersection. Down the cross-corridor, to both the left and right, numerous doors led to crew quarters. He checked for the number of Amina's cabin on a directory mounted on the wall, and confirmed its location down the corridor to the right. He turned in that direction and hurried on.

What Harriman had told his chief engineer earlier, back in *Enterprise*'s cargo hold, had been no exaggeration: he'd been looking forward to this time with Amina—to *any* time with Amina—for quite a while. They hadn't been together since their week on Pacifica a year ago; although his crew believed he'd been there the entire month he'd been away from *Enterprise*, he'd actually spent the first three weeks on the Devron II mission.

Since they'd become involved, this had been the longest period during which they had spent no time together. They'd sent missives and messages to each other often, and after *Enterprise* had been posted to Foxtrot Sector, they'd actually been able to speak to each other in real time on several occasions. They had even seen each other in person once or twice, but because of *Enterprise*'s rigorous schedule along the Neutral Zone, only briefly, and only as part of their Starfleet duties.

Harriman reached the door to Amina's quarters and stopped. The sounds of his steps continued on for a second or two and then faded to silence, as though swallowed up by the corridor. He tugged at the base of his red uniform jacket, straightening it, then lifted a hand to the epaulet on his right shoulder, making sure that it was secured properly. Satisfied, he reached for the door signal. His heart raced. He felt like a schoolboy, arriving to collect his date for the prom.

A moment later, the door panel slid open with a soft rush of air. Inside sat a small room that belonged unmistakably to Amina. Harriman stepped inside, his gaze drawn to the wall directly across from him, to a mounted copy of an immigration certificate to the Martian Colonies. He'd seen the document before, and knew that it helped to tell the story of

Amina's grandmother's grandmother, the first of her fore-bears to leave Earth. Next to the certificate hung a poem, a sonnet entitled "For Now and Ever"; Harriman had written it for Amina just six months into their relationship.

The wall lay covered by those objects and others—by art-work; by small, semicircular shelves laden with numerous and varied artifacts; but mostly by framed photographs. Harriman saw Amina's parents at the party their children had thrown to celebrate the couple's fiftieth wedding anniversary. He saw her siblings—a brother and three sisters—two of whom he'd met, and two of whom he'd only ever seen in pictures. Amina's beautiful, smiling face peeked out from a few of the prints, but the images were mostly of others, of those people who meant something special to her. He saw himself, in his Starfleet Academy graduation picture—a painfully thin boy from thirty years ago that he barely re-membered anymore—and in a shot taken with Amina in Jennita, atop a cliff overlooking the sea's magical sapphirine waters.

"Captain John Jason Harriman the Second," said a silky voice to his left, "are you just going to stand there, or are you going to say hello?" The words carried the faint hint of French pronunciation—Amina hailed from the Republique de Côte d'Ivoire, in Africa—an accent Harriman had always found exotic and romantic. Despite her mellifluous tones, though, Amina somehow still managed to express her strength and confidence, two characteristics that he had al-ways found most appealing in her.

Harriman turned. Amina stood there in a gold silk dress, the plush fabric accentuating the beauty and sheen of her dark chocolate skin. Sleeveless, with a pleated skirt that reached to the middle of her calves, the dress had been one she'd worn in Jennita when they'd gone out dancing, the skirt lifting and twirling spectacularly as she spun, her move-ments lively and graceful. Her straight, jet black hair framed her lovely features, curling inward slightly as it caressed the tops of her shoulders. She was radiant.

"Amina," Harriman said, his voice catching as he spoke the name of this woman he adored—and had missed—so much. He crossed the room in two strides, sent his arms around the small of her back, and hugged her tightly to him. Her arms encircled his shoulders—she stood slightly taller than he did—and embraced him back. He loved the feel of her long, lithesome body against his; they fit well together.

Harriman pressed his lips against Amina's neck and kissed her, taking in the sweet, wispy scent of her flesh. In an instant, the months of separation fell away, the yearning undertone of their many letters to each other now a remote memory only. The rightness of their relationship, their essential need to be together despite the millstone of physical distance that often kept them removed from one another, asserted itself once more. It had always been like this, from the very beginning. They parted only because of necessity—she had her career, he had his—and whenever they rejoined, whatever emotional hardships they had endured crumbled into dust.

"Amina," he said again, and he pulled back so that he could look into her eyes. Her green irises, flecked with grains of hazel, seemed to peer back at him with as much love as he himself felt. She looked good, her skin smooth and lustrous. Lines imprinted into her face along the sides of her mouth revealed a person who laughed easily and often, but did not add to the years in her appearance. At forty-eight, Amina could have passed for a woman in her early thirties, although the dignity and self-assurance with which she carried herself conveyed her maturity.

"I missed you, John," she said, softening the first letter of his name to a *zh* sound.

"I missed you," he said. He leaned in toward her, and their lips met, gently at first, and then in a harder, more passionate kiss. Harriman felt a fire with this woman as he had felt with no other.

When they parted this time, Harriman took a few steps away, looking around the room. There wasn't much to the place. Amina stood beside a half-wall that divided her quarters in two. Behind her sat a bed and a built-in dresser in a small sleeping area, too small to have been comfortably enclosed. Past the bed, a closed door no doubt led to a bathroom. In this section, a desk—topped with a computer-and-communications interface—and two chairs filled at least a third of the floor space. Still, as spartan as the accommodations were—save for Amina's adornments—Harriman was certain that these quarters, the *commander's* quarters, were the largest on the outpost. By comparison, his cabin on *Enterprise* seemed lavish.

"This place is . . ." Harriman started, and then searched for an adjective to adequately express his thoughts. "This place is very much you," he finally settled on, referring to Amina's penchant for taking and keeping photographs.

"You mean the pictures," she said, clearly in tune with him. "All my albums are back in Aboisso with Mère and Père." Though they traveled a great deal, Amina's parents still kept a home in the African harbor city. "Starfleet didn't give us a lot of storage space out here," she said.

"That's all right," Harriman told her. "There's still plenty of room for both of us."

"Oh?" she asked, in apparent mock surprise. "Are you planning to move in?"

"Ask me again," Harriman said seriously, moving to her again and taking her upper arms in his hands, "and I'll never leave."

"Oh, certainly, Mr. Starship Captain," she teased, reaching over and brushing the tips of her fingers through the hair at the side of his head. "Mr. Warp Factor Nine, Mr. Ten Thousand Light-Years, Mr.—"

"How about Mr. Sasine?" he interrupted quietly.

"Is that a proposal?" she asked, smiling. In the eight years they'd been together, they'd each asked the other to marry countless times. The answers had always been yeses, and yet they had never progressed beyond that, had never discussed actually having a wedding. For his part, Harriman could not imagine pledging such vows and then saying farewell as Amina returned to whatever base she commanded and he returned to *Enterprise*. And yet—

"Will you marry me?" he asked.

The smile did not leave Amina's face, but her expression changed somehow, from one of simple good humor to one of love and joy. "Yes," she told him. "Of course."

And for the first time, Harriman asked the next question. "When?" He surprised himself, but as other questions threatened—Would they continue to be apart most of the time, or would one of them give up, or at least change, their career? Where would they live? Could they make it work?—as those questions and others began to flood his thoughts, he managed to stem the tide and push them away.

Amina looked into his eyes for a long time, her expression never wavering. He loved her so much, and he knew she loved him. *When will we get married?* he thought again, and waited.

At last, Amina said, "Every day."

Harriman's lips parted in a way he could not control, his smile feeling as though it filled his entire face. "I love you," he said.

"I love you."

He slipped his right hand around to the small of her back, clasped her right hand with his left, and then danced her into the sleeping area. They eased down onto the bed together, moving effortlessly in each other's arms. It felt as though they had never parted.

They did not sleep for hours.

* * *

Sasine woke first in the morning. She usually did when they were together. Lying in the dark, she glanced over to the chronometer on the shelf beside the bed, the digits on its face glowing faintly. She'd woken half an hour before the beginning of her shift, she saw, and although she'd slept only six hours, she felt more rested than she had in a long time—probably since she and John had last been together, back on Pacifica. With him beside her, she always slumbered more soundly. When they were together, the strength and certainty of their relationship provided a feeling that, no matter the circumstances in the rest of the universe, her world was whole and happy. As at no other time, she experienced a remarkable sense of peace.

In the darkness, Sasine could hear the slow, gentle susurrus of John's breathing. She felt the desire to roll over and take him in her arms. She wanted simply to hold him, to feel the warmth of his body and the love in his embrace. But he needed to rest, she knew, and she did not wish to wake him. Like her, he'd been sleeping poorly of late, and he had not needed to explain why in order for her to understand. They had both been living for months at the verge of Romulan space, and so had faced many of the same pressures and uncertainties. More and more, war seemed inevitable.

Located near both the Romulan and Klingon borders, Foxtrot XIII—as well as the other dozen outposts in the sector—sat on the first line of defense for the Federation. But functioning more as a monitoring station and depot, the outpost hardly constituted a primary military force. Sasine's crew could certainly defend themselves, and they could even launch effective short-range attacks, employing both the weaponry installed on the asteroid and the small squadron of shuttles housed below the surface. But for all of that, and even with the more powerful weaponry currently being installed, there were limitations on what you could do from a rock in space.

Sasine yawned and stretched, arching her back carefully so that she would not disturb John. Then she moved slowly across the bed, slipped her legs over the edge, and rose to her feet. Her body temperature having dropped as she slept, she felt cold, and she hugged herself against what she perceived as the morning chill. Reaching for the chronometer, she deactivated the signal that would have awakened her in just a few minutes, and then she reset it for John. Most days, the signal did awaken her, rudely interrupting her sleep. She would get up and groggily get ready for the day, seeming to really come awake only once she had left her quarters and made her way to the operations center.

Now she made her way around the bed and into the bathroom, where she quickly prepared for her shift. In the sonic shower, she thought about the challenges facing John. As captain of the Federation flagship, one of the most powerful vessels in the fleet, his assignment to Foxtrot Sector these past months had been an obvious choice by Starfleet Command. Like the outposts, *Enterprise* would be on Starfleet's first line of defense, but as an offensive force, fighting not just to identify and slow invading vessels, but to beat them back or even destroy them. The responsibilities John shouldered were significant.

After showering, Sasine opened the bathroom door, leaving the lighting panel on a low level so that she could see in the sleeping area. She retrieved her uniform and underclothing from the built-in dresser and slipped them on. In the dim light, she spied her gold dress from last night lying on the floor, and she picked it up and draped it across the half-wall. Then she retrieved her shoes and exchanged them for the uniform boots sitting in the corner.

Ready for her shift, she walked to John's side of the bed. She bent down and watched him for a few moments as he slept. In repose, he looked less like the confident and experienced starship captain he was, and more like the young man who peered out at her every day from his Starfleet Academy graduation photograph. She could see in him now the innocence of his youth, unburdened by the responsibilities that both adulthood and duty had brought on. At the same time, she could also see the man he would become—*had* become—surmounting the hardships of a strange and occasionally tragic childhood, growing into somebody she respected and appreciated—and who could always make her laugh.

Just thinking of that, Sasine smiled. She actually considered asking Lieutenant Commander Civita to take her shift for her so that she could spend more time with John. Today would be a relatively light day of duties for her, her last on Foxtrot XIII. She had been assigned to the outpost less than a year ago, and it had surprised her that Starfleet Command had chosen to rotate out the crew as quickly as it had. She supposed that the mounting strain between the Federation and the Romulan Empire had a great deal to do with the decision. She absolutely understood and appreciated the motivation of alleviating some of the pressure and tension her crew had been feeling for so long without surcease. But her crew had also accepted such pressures with equanimity; they had known what their duties would entail before accepting assignment here.

Sasine stood up and peered over at the chronometer. Alpha shift would begin in just a couple of minutes, she saw, and even though the preparations for leaving the outpost for another crew had already been made, she still had some small but important tasks to perform today. Chief among them, she wanted to address *her* crew, some of whom would not be serving under her at her next posting. She would also oversee their transport up to *Enterprise,* aboard which they would make the trip back to Space Station KR-3 before being reassigned. Once the small group of engineering specialists from *Agamemnon* had completed their work—the new weapons had been classified at such a high level that even Sasine had not been permitted to observe their installation—the outpost's new crew would begin beaming down, also from *Agamemnon*.

At the moment, she was not sure where her next assignment would take her—she'd been told of several possible postings—but what pleased her most about the transfer was the travel time aboard *Enterprise*. While John would be standing his normal watch, that would still allow them to spend the evening and night together. And whether at a lush, beautiful resort or aboard a functional and relatively sterile starship, any time that she could spend with John was time she would treasure. They believed in the same things, laughed at the same things, viewed the universe in the same ways; they belonged together. They meshed. Even last night, in a cramped cabin beneath the pockmarked surface of a dead asteroid, poised on the edge of the Neutral Zone, they had managed to smile and laugh and love.

Sasine looked down at John, then went into the bathroom and extinguished the lighting panel. In the darkness once more, she carefully padded over to the door to her quarters. She felt for the panel set into the bulkhead beside it and worked its controls. The door slid open, and light spilled in from the corridor. She took one last look across the room toward the bed. Over the half-wall, she could just make out John's sleeping figure. "I love you," she whispered, and then turned and left.

By the time she had reached the operations center, she had already begun to count the time until they would be together again.

MINUS NINE: ALGERON

Ambassador Gell Kamemor watched the Klingon bring his fist down on the conference table, the stars visible through the viewing port beyond him. "No!" he bellowed at her, then bolted to his feet with such force that his chair flew backward and toppled to the floor with a clatter. "No!" he roared again, then flung himself forward and hammered the center of the long, elliptical tabletop once more, this time with both fists. The fleshy parts of his hands pounded down atop the image of the stylized bird of prey, a planet in each talon, that symbolized the Romulan Star Empire. "Qo'noS will never permit outsiders to inspect our weapons facilities." Spittle shot from his mouth, Kamemor observed with distaste, one tiny bead hanging up in the young Klingon's dark beard.

Kamemor waited to react. She knew without looking that the eyes of all the delegates—of everybody present—had turned toward her. Thirteen people occupied the room right now: Ambassador Kage and his two aides, one of whom had been the one to rage at her; Federation Ambassador Paulo Endara and his staff of four; her own Romulan delegation of three; and two of the six waitstaff. Of those half-dozen service personnel, Kamemor had yet to ascertain who belonged to the Romulan Intelligence Service, though she had no doubt that the treaty negotiations were being closely monitored by the secretive organization.

A tense silence descended. The versicolor glow of the Algeron Effect, just a few hundred thousand kilometers from the space station, angled through the viewing port and stippled the far wall. Kamemor remained quiet, though not completely still. She tilted her head upward slightly and regarded the Klingon agitator with measured disinterest; she neither challenged him nor withdrew from his ire. Although he did not frighten her, the tall, broad-shouldered Klingon seemed dangerous—not on the basis of his imposing form, but because of the surety with which he acted and spoke. That likely indicated either the bravado of youth or the vicarious strength of powerful friends, and Kamemor suspected the latter. She knew that Chancellor Azetbur, leader of the Klingon High Council for nearly two decades now, had faced increasing opposition at home of late, and Kamemor fully expected that opposition to be represented here. As much as Azetbur had designed and driven the rebuilding of her civilization's infrastructure after the accidental destruction of their primary energy-production facility, she'd done so both by promoting peace and by accepting charity from the Federation, and neither policy had been particularly palatable to the Klingon military.

As Kamemor peered across the table, she took note of the young Klingon's immaculate raiments: a silver, metallic vest worn over a black shirt; black pants with high, matching boots; a dark, heavy cloak; and a scarlet version of the tripartite emblem of the Klingon Empire worn on the front of his left shoulder. The attire resembled a military uniform too much, she thought, to have been selected arbitrarily. No, the aide clearly functioned as a puppet of the Klingon Defense Force, and he obviously felt no reluctance about demonstrating his loyalties.

"Perhaps we should recess for an hour or two," Ambassador Endara suggested from one end of the table. The young Klingon said nothing, instead holding Kamemor's gaze. Just before she looked away, she saw hatred flash across his already angry eyes. The observation served only to frustrate her. While she did not hold with the arrogant and too-common view of her people that Romulans were innately superior to all other races, she could see how the behavior of Klingons such as this one could foment such an opinion.

Kamemor looked down the beautiful table—its rich blond top had been carved whole from the trunk of an *urukan* tree, she had been told—and over to where the Federation ambassador sat flanked by his aides. Endara, an older human with short black hair and a bronze complexion, had demonstrated as much confidence during these negotiations as the young Klingon, but confidence born of an entirely different source: the Federation ambassador possessed a lifetime of diplomatic experience. Still, as the weeks here at the Algeron station had run into months, and as the months now raced toward becoming years, Kamemor had seen her own dissatisfactions with the proceedings reflected in Endara.

"Perhaps a recess would be in order," Kamemor agreed.

"No," came another voice, and Kamemor turned back to look directly across from her, to where Ambassador Kage sat beside his volatile aide. Unlike the young upstart, the seasoned Kage dressed the part of an ambassador for his people, wearing long, heavy robes embellished respectfully with the glittering icons of dozens of worlds. "It is not even midmorning," the grizzled ambassador said, his manner and tone unusually quiet for a Klingon. "I do not think a recess will be necessary." He leaned forward in his chair, reached out, and rested a hand atop his aide's closed fist. "Will it, Ditagh?" he asked softly.

The gentle nature of the physical contact and of the appeal surprised Kamemor. Even after all this time tussling over so many issues with him, she had not yet become accustomed to the demeanor of the Klingon ambassador. Not nearly as impressive physically as his fiery aide, Kage could still command a room. But as firm and demanding as he had been during these negotiations, he nevertheless had conducted himself with tact and sensitivity. *One of Azetbur's disciples, to be sure,* Kamemor thought, not for the first time. It also seemed clear to her that Kage faced challenges not only with Romulus and the Federation, but within his own faction.

The Klingon aide did not look down at Kage, but pulled back from the table, managing to extract his hand from beneath the ambassador's without growling. Behind him, as one of the Romulan waitstaff left the room, another set down the ewer she carried and quickly righted the fallen chair. The aide grabbed it away, and the server shrank back as though she had been struck.

"Thank you, Ranek," Kage offered. The woman looked at the ambassador and nodded politely, then retrieved the ewer and hastened for the door. Kamemor felt her eyebrow rise involuntarily, and she consciously brought it back down. The server who had picked up the chair was a new addition to the waitstaff, having arrived at the station only within the last few days. Kamemor had not yet learned the woman's name, and it said something about Kage that he had.

The Klingon aide set his chair back at the table with a thump, then dropped into it. "Now then," Kage said, returning his attention to Kamemor, "I believe that you were speaking about limitations on the types of weapons allowed under a new treaty, Ambassador."

"I was," Kamemor concurred. She glanced at her two subconsuls, who sat to her left, then folded her hands in front of her and recalled the point she had earlier been advancing. "I believe that it would be in the best interests of all concerned if we can devise a means of preventing the creation of metaweapons. After all, where there are no such weapons, there are no possibilities of triggering their use. Of course, for an agreement of this type to succeed, it would require trilateral monitoring." This time, Kage's aide grunted, but he stayed in his chair, eyes cast downward, hands in his lap.

"Yes," Kage said. "I understand your viewpoint. But how, precisely, would you define a 'metaweapon'?"

Again, Kamemor felt her eyebrow climb. She had not anticipated the question. "I don't have a ready answer to that," she told Kage, "but I'm certain that we could construct a definition satisfactory to all."

"Perhaps," Kage said noncommittally. "But it is an important question, one that begs an answer *prior* to any discussion of this issue."

Irritation welled within Kamemor, and behind that, anger. With no substantial progress in these talks recently, she had thought that they could be advanced by the settling of even a single minor point. She had raised the matter of metaweapons—at the suggestion of one of her subconsuls—because she had believed it one on which all parties could easily agree.

Diplomacy is a charge for the forbearing, Kamemor reminded herself. Still, she remained angry, and so she stood up, using the movement to cover her emotions. "I'll try to respond to that, Ambassador," she told Kage, then walked along the table, past her subconsuls, and over to the viewing ports. She peered out at a line of objects shining against the darkness of space like gems against a jeweler's cloth. She raised her hand and lightly touched her fingertips to the port. A dull melancholy washed over her, drowning her choler in a tide of memories. Even all these years later, she could not escape the anguish she had felt—that all Romulans had felt—when the tragedy had occurred.

"A planet once orbited out there," she said. "A planet that—" She stopped. She had been about to describe the scope of the disaster by referring to the size of the colony's population. But not only was it not her place to reveal such information to outworlders, she also did not wish to speak of the horrific details. "A planet that no longer exists," she went on, "because of an isolytic subspace weapon." The planet—Algeron III—had not even been fired upon, but when a nearby enemy ship, fighting a losing battle against a bird-of-prey, had unleashed the weapon, a rent had formed in the fabric of subspace. The tear had been drawn to the power sources on Algeron III and had sliced through the planet with devastating result. The home to so many Romulans had been reduced to ruin so quickly that there had been no possibility of defending against it. At the same time, the force of the destruction had sealed the fissure, and had also crystallized many of the resultant planetary fragments, which now orbited the system's star and refracted its light into the colors of the spectrum. The effect was magnificent to behold, but it also marked the graves of millions.

Kamemor turned to face Kage, her hand still on the port. "This is your answer," she said. "This is what we must prevent."

"Ambassador, I am terribly sorry for your loss, for the Romulan people's loss," Kage said with apparent sincerity. "But I must point out that my people did not—"

"No, they didn't," Kamemor snapped, cutting him off. Then she paused, slowed her breathing, dropped her hand from the port. She concentrated on regaining her composure. "Nor am I suggesting that any sane Klingon, any sane individual or group, would commit such a monstrous act." Her words began to come quicker, reflecting the passion of her resolve. "But there are insane Klingons, insane humans, insane *Romulans*. If we could be assured that no such weapons would ever be used, because none were ever made, would we all not breathe easier?"

"Ambassador Kamemor," Kage said, "I do understand your view. And my colleague misspoke a few moments ago when he implied that a Romulan presence at a Klingon weapons facility would be unacceptable. Under appropriate circumstances, Chancellor Azetbur would welcome Romu-

lan representatives—and Federation representatives as well."
Next to Kage, the young aide lifted his hands up onto the
table, tensing them into fists, and Kamemor thought that he
might actually strike the ambassador; instead, he simply
looked away. "The difficulty I see," Kage continued, "is that
there are powers beyond our three. The Gorn are certainly
capable of developing metaweapons, as are the Tholians,
and even the Tzenkethi. By agreeing never to do so ourselves, we would therefore be allowing these powers to
create such weapons and attack us without fear of commen-
surate retaliation."

"Pardon me, Ambassador Kage," Endara said, "but that's
hardly the case. The might of the Klingon Defense Force
could be brought to bear. Or the might of Starfleet or the
Romulan Imperial Fleet. We could even consider a mutual
defense pact."

"But of course, metaweapons could potentially cripple the
fleets," Kage argued. "Do not misunderstand me. The Klingon
Empire opposes any employment of these weapons, and even
the construction of them. But we do not want to sign a treaty
that we might one day have to break in order to survive."

"At the risk of introducing another intractable issue into
these proceedings," Kamemor said, "I submit that this is
worth exploring."

"I agree," Endara said. "Standing Federation policy dic-
tates that we would favor the inclusion, in any treaty, of a
covenant to ban the production of these weapons."

"*PetaQ*," Kage's aid muttered. Kamemor recognized the
Klingon invective.

"Ditagh," Kage chided, almost inaudibly.

"No," the aide responded loudly. He stood back up again,
though not as quickly this time, and his chair remained up-
right. "This *petaQ*—" He pointed a thick finger toward Endara. "—hurls lies at us and I'm not supposed to speak of it?"

"Ditagh," Kage repeated, more firmly. "These are diplomatic proceedings. You will therefore conduct yourself *diplomatically*."

"Wait," Kamemor said, stepping away from the outer bulkhead and into the center of the room. "What lies?" She had seen no reason to respect the peevish Klingon aide, but none of his churlishness, his inexperience, or his status as somebody's pawn precluded his statement from being true. Kamemor had worked for months to fashion an agreement for a meaningful and prolonged peace among the three powers, but if she was being lied to, she wanted to know it.

"Federation representatives sit here spouting peace—" He waved a hand dismissively in the direction of Endara and his staff. "—while at the same time they're trying to develop a weapon to wipe out the Klingon Empire."

Endara stared at the aide with what Kamemor could only interpret as a complete lack of comprehension. "Ambassador Kage," Endara said at last, expressly addressing the statesman rather than his subordinate. "The Federation has been a friend to the Klingon Empire for years—for *decades*. What's just been suggested is not only patently false, but absurd in the extreme."

"How would you know?" the Klingon aide barked, finally turning toward Endara. "Does Starfleet keep you informed of its—"

"Ditagh," Kage interjected. He rose slowly from his chair as his aide spun in his direction. The ambassador fell well short of the young Klingon's height and build, but Kamemor still thought the older man seemed the more formidable of the two. "Sit down," Kage ordered. The aide hesitated only briefly, and then he returned to his seat, evidently realizing that, no matter who pulled his strings, he was on his own right now, in this room.

"My apologies," Kage said, looking around to include both Kamemor and Endara. "Ditagh does not speak for our people. He is my aide, and obviously . . . enthusiastic. But I am the official Klingon representative at these meetings."

Kamemor bowed her head, acknowledging Kage's declaration. "Perhaps, though, it *would* be best to recess until after the midday meal," she said.

Kage opened his mouth as if to protest, then looked down at his aide and seemed to change his mind. "A fine idea, Ambassador."

Kamemor looked to Endara for his approval. "I have no objection," he said, then rose, his staff collecting the reference materials they'd brought to the meeting and spread out on the table. At the same time, the young Klingon got up and hurried out of the room, and the second Klingon aide, silent throughout the meeting, followed. Kage took the time to excuse himself, then exited too. A few moments later, Endara and his staff also departed, leaving Kamemor in the room with her two subconsuls.

"What is the question I have in my mind right now?" she asked without preamble, walking over to face her assistants across the table.

"Why are the Klingons really against a prohibition on the production of metaweapons?" said N'Mest, a woman who'd worked with Kamemor for six years, and who could often anticipate Kamemor's reactions to diplomatic parleys. But not this time.

"No," Kamemor said. She looked to the other subconsul, Merken Vreenak, a young man who'd come to work for her less than a year ago. She'd so far found him sharp and industrious, an asset to her despite his overt chauvinism; Kamemor loved her people too, but not in such an unreasoning, aggressive manner.

Vreenak returned her gaze. "Is Ditagh correct?" he said. "Is the Federation constructing a metaweapon?"

"Yes," Kamemor said, her lips curling up slightly on one side, impressed by the subconsul's acuity. "I want both of you to find out what you can. Check intelligence reports, fleet logs, even rumors on the public comnets, anything at all." In Kamemor's experience, she did not think it likely that the Federation and Starfleet would be attempting the creation of some ultrapowerful weapon, but neither did she trust their officials and officers—not most of them, anyway.

"Ambassador," said Vreenak, "I've already heard rumors supporting Ditagh's claim."

"You've already heard?" Kamemor snapped. "And you didn't think to inform me?"

"They were rumors only, Ambassador," Vreenak proffered as justification. Kamemor dismissed it.

"Pursue those rumors," she ordered. "Locate their sources, ascertain their veracity."

"Yes, Ambassador," Vreenak said. Kamemor turned and headed for the door, which slid open at her approach. Before she left, though, she stopped and peered back over her shoulder toward the conference table. "Do not allow your distrust for non-Romulans to color your inquiry, Subconsul Vreenak," she said. Kamemor did not wait for a response before she continued out of the room.

Kage walked unhurriedly down a corridor on the habitat level, considering carefully what he would say when he reached his destination. In his youth, as a soldier, he had regarded himself a man of action, willing to charge headlong into any situation, but his mindset had shifted as he'd grown older. Rash behavior had given way to forethought, and he'd eventually quit the physical rigors of the Klingon Defense Force in favor of the mental challenges of civil engineering. But his subsequent successes in that realm had failed to sate his natural desire for battle, and so when Azetbur, newly installed as chancellor, had called upon him to join her government, Kage had accepted. He'd learned the artful combat of diplomacy under Azetbur's tutelage, and had come to relish the struggles it often provided: the subtle machinations, the blatant lies, the different colors of truth when viewed through different eyes. In his tenure as an ambassador, Kage had furthered Klingon objectives with the Lorillians, the Tholians, the Vedala, the Lissepians, the Otevrel, and dozens of other species. But the Romulans . . .

At an intersection, Kage turned left into another empty corridor, tinted green by indirect lighting. Of the few sections he'd been permitted to visit on the space station, only the habitat level stood free of security personnel. The apparent attempt at Romulan hospitality rang false to him, though, and he felt certain that his delegation—and that of the Federation—remained under constant, covert surveillance. Not that the station contained anything of value to the Klingons; had it, the xenophobic paranoia of the Romulans would likely have prevented them from hosting the negotiations here. Still, that same intense distrust for people beyond their borders would have driven the Romulans to continuously monitor their alien guests.

The station itself seemed utilitarian, a series of rings of increasing and then diminishing diameter, set one atop another to approximate a sphere. The structure put Kage in mind of something a child might cobble together out of blocks. Kage assumed that the facility had been constructed as quickly as possible after the destruction of the planet in this system, and that it functioned primarily as a platform from which the effects of the isolytic subspace weapon could be studied. Judging from Kamemor's reaction today, though, Kage supposed that the station might also serve as a memorial, as a place mourners could visit to be near the place where their loved ones had died.

Kage passed the door to his own guest quarters and stopped at the next one. He quickly reviewed what he might say and how he might say it, depending on how the conversation developed, and reminded himself of his goals: foremost, to gain information, and secondarily, to limit his liabilities in the ongoing discussions with the Romulans and the Federation. Then he jabbed at the signal control on a panel set beside the door. He heard a tone, unwavering and tedious—*Like the Romulans*, he thought—followed by a voice.

"What?" came the irritated response.

Anticipating that the quarters would not be locked, Kage pressed another control. The door glided open, revealing Ditagh standing at an open food synthesizer across the room. In his hand, he held a tall glass half-filled with a dark, red liquid. *Bloodwine*, Kage guessed, and he shuddered to think what a Romulan version of the hearty Klingon potable might taste like.

"Ambassador," Ditagh said, his employment of the title clearly not intended as a sign of respect, but as an epithet.

Kage stepped inside, the door easing closed behind him. "Ditagh, we must talk," he said.

"Talk," Ditagh said with unveiled contempt. "I am tired of talk. I've had months of it, and I've had enough." He brought the glass up to his mouth and upended it, imbibing the remaining liquid in two massive gulps.

Kage took another step forward, quickly glancing around the room. Though smaller, Ditagh's quarters mirrored his own. A rectangular front room, conspicuously devoid of decoration, contained only a sitting area—a quartet of chairs surrounding a low circular table—a food synthesizer, and a comm system. An open doorway in the far wall led to a simple bedroom. *Good*, Kage thought. *No surprises.*

"If you've had enough, then I can have you reassigned," he said, an offer he knew Ditagh would not accept. Several months ago, the volatile aide had replaced one of Kage's most trusted lieutenants, Roneg. The appointment had been officially handed down by Azetbur, but Kage understood now that other members of the High Council had maneuvered Ditagh into the position. The circumstances of Roneg's departure from the negotiating team—his father had been killed in an industrial accident, requiring that

Roneg return to Qo'noS to lead their House—had at first seemed unambiguous. But Kage's vigilance in protecting the needs of the Empire had driven him to have the accident quietly investigated, and the results, while inconclusive, had at least seemed suspicious. Roneg's father had been killed in an area of the shipyards nobody could recall him ever having visited, at a time when he normally would have been off. All of which had led Kage to believe that Ditagh had been installed in the delegation for a purpose counter to Kage's own—and counter to Azetbur's. And as time had passed, Ditagh's tongue had loosened, speaking up during negotiations—as he had today—in ways seemingly designed to slow, or even derail, the peace process.

"I do not need to be reassigned," Ditagh said. "I will endure my lot for the good of the Empire."

"Then you will conduct yourself in accordance with my direction," Kage said, dropping his voice low for emphasis, "rather than that of your . . . sponsor." Kage had chosen the last word carefully, intending it as a disparagement of Ditagh's manhood.

Ditagh laughed, a guttural, confident sound that Kage hoped also contained the taint of fear. "I am *your* aide, no one else's," Ditagh claimed, then slammed his empty glass down on the shelf of the food synthesizer. He pushed the tips of his thick fingers against the device's control panel, and a door dropped into place in front of the shelf. Kage saw menus and submenus flash up onto the panel, and Ditagh navigated through them until he stopped at a particular entry—Klingon bloodwine, Kage assumed, though he could not read the words from where he stood. Ditagh selected the beverage, and the buzz of the device filled the small room. A moment later, the door of the food synthesizer slid upward, revealing a full glass of what appeared to be bloodwine on the shelf. As Ditagh grabbed it up, Kage crossed the rest of the short distance between them.

"If you are my aide, then listen to me," he said, staring up into Ditagh's face. "I will brook no more interruptions in the negotiating sessions, no more disruptions." Kage paused, seeking the words that would enrage his aide. "You will speak only when I so deem."

Ditagh's face went through a rapid succession of transformations, from anger, to acceptance, to confidence, and finally to amusement, a smirk emerging from beneath his beard. "As you wish," he said, lifting the bloodwine to his lips.

Kage moved without hesitation, swinging his open hand up and batting the glass from Ditagh's grasp. Kage did not look away, but he heard the glass strike the wall, then fall to the floor and shatter. "I'm not toying with you, Ditagh," he said. "Do not test me."

Ditagh turned his head toward where the glass had broken, then glared back down at Kage. "Test *you*, old man?" he said. "What possible glory could I find in doing battle with a broken-down peace-lover?" Ditagh moved even closer to Kage, standing over him and obviously trying to intimidate him with his sheer size.

Kage did not flinch. "Isn't that why you're here?" he asked. "To fight me? To prevent me from completing my mission?"

"I am here as your aide," Ditagh maintained, evidently unwilling to take Kage's bait.

"And to act on behalf of the High Council," Kage ventured. "Or at least some of those on the Council." He had not intended to be so straightforward with his accusations, but Ditagh was perhaps not as foolish as he seemed. Even though Kage had wanted to learn the identity of the power behind Ditagh surreptitiously, he would settle right now simply for knowing.

"I am *your* aide," Ditagh repeated.

Kage returned Ditagh's cold stare, at the same time searching for the tactic that would tell him what he wanted—what he needed—to know. Finally, he smiled up into Ditagh's face, then turned and headed for the door. "It is a weak man who works in the dark for another," he said as he went.

"It is *you* who are weak," Ditagh called after him, and Kage stopped just as the door swept open before him. "And you make the Empire weak as well."

Now Kage turned back around and stepped away from the door, which he heard close again behind him. "I am attempting to strengthen the Empire," he said. "There is no dishonor in not fighting. There is only dishonor in not fighting well."

"You avoid fighting," Ditagh told him. "You seek peace at any cost. You are willing to give up anything for it, including the will of your own people."

"Klingons do not want war with the Romulans and the Federation unless we can win such a war," Kage said. "And right now, we can't. We still need to strengthen our infrastructure and fully resupply our military."

"What Klingons want," Ditagh pronounced, "is their birthright. We are warriors." He paused, then added derisively, "At least, most of us are."

"Say what you want to say," Kage told him.

Ditagh apparently needed no further invitation. "You are a lackey for peace," he accused. "Qo'noS should withdraw from these talks and let the Romulans and the Federation destroy each other for us."

"Is that what you really want?" Kage asked. "To sit back and allow our adversaries to decimate themselves, then for us to march in and defeat the battle-weary? Would you also kick a three-legged *targ*?"

"A three-legged *targ* does not possess a weapon capable of laying waste to much of the Klingon Empire," Ditagh argued.

"Nor does the Federation," Kage said, and at last, he thought he saw a direct path to the information he needed. "The general is wrong or misguided," he said, then hurried on, trying to avoid drawing attention to the statement. "Such stupidity and shortsightedness were what weakened the Empire twenty years ago. You were only a child, Ditagh, but surely you remember the destruction of Praxis." The Klingon moon had housed the Empire's primary energy facility, which had been taxed beyond its capacity in order to prepare for war with the Federation. A massive explosion had resulted, blowing half of the moon out into space and raining destructive fallout on Qo'noS. "The accident left us crippled and unable to provide enough energy for everyday life, let alone to take us into battle. If we move too quickly toward war again, we will once more be left weakened."

"The Klingon people grow tired of accepting Federation handouts," Ditagh said, "and of begging for peace with the hypocritical Federation and the disloyal Romulans."

"But Ditagh," Kage implored, "there is no honor in fighting a battle you cannot win."

"There is no honor in believing your own people are unable to win battles," Ditagh countered.

"We *can* win battles," Kage avowed. "But we don't need starships and disruptor banks to do so. The Romulans and the Federation are on the brink of war between themselves, but neither dare attack without an alliance with us. As far from full strength as the Klingon Defense Force is right now, our ships would be the difference in any war, whichever side we choose to fight with. So we can wield our political might, reestablish our power that way, and at the same time, prevent the devastation war would bring upon us, even in victory."

"Political power," Ditagh said, an expression of disgust on his face. "You are an old man, filled with the cowardice of a little girl . . . or a big girl. Azetbur is a plague on the Klingon people."

"*Chancellor* Azetbur is the leader of the High Council," Kage said seriously, "and deserving of your respect." He paused, then decided to try again: "The general would lead no better." It was a gamble; although numerous generals sat on the Klingon High Council, the name Kage was looking for might not have belonged to one of them.

But Ditagh finally bit. "General Gorak is a great man," he said indignantly. "He would return honor to the Council, to all of Qo'noS. And he would end this pathetic peace conference."

Kage charged the few steps back across the room, wanting both to deflect attention from the information just divulged, and to deal with Ditagh's outburst in today's session. As he reached Ditagh, Kage threw his hands out and straight-armed the larger man. Caught off guard, the younger Klingon did not have time to brace himself, and he sailed backward into the wall. Kage lunged after him, thrusting a forearm up into his neck and applying pressure. Ditagh gasped for air, his eyes wide with surprise. "You will speak no more of ending this peace conference," Kage hissed through gritted teeth. "If you interfere anymore with what I'm trying to accomplish here, with what Chancellor Azetbur wants me to accomplish, I'll snap your neck." To underscore his words, Kage pushed his arm forward. Ditagh's face darkened, his eyes bulged.

Finally, Kage pulled back. Ditagh doubled over, dropping to his knees as he choked and coughed. Kage watched him for a moment, then leaned in next to his ear and said, "Do not underestimate this old man." Then he straightened and headed for the door.

As Kage passed back into the corridor, he heard Ditagh sputter, "Azetbur is a pretender. She will fall." Kage did not stop or look back. He already had what he'd come here to get: the name of the power behind Ditagh. General Gorak was the traitor on the Klingon High Council.

MINUS EIGHT: UNIVERSE

Sasine stood before John at an open airlock on Space Station KR-3, the two of them in their Starfleet uniforms. An *Enterprise* corridor stretched away beyond the airlock, the great vessel waiting to take him away once more. She supposed she could have resented the ship because of that—perhaps *should* have resented it—but why waste such emotional effort on something so foolish? She loved John, and she would miss him terribly once he had gone, but captaining a starship contributed to who he was as a person, and was therefore something that she loved about him. She never once entertained the notion of wanting him to give that up. She would support whatever choices he made for his life, as long as they fulfilled him and did not deny the man he was.

"I'll miss you," John told her.

"And I'll miss you," she replied. As she gazed into his blue-gray eyes, she thought she saw a mix of emotions there. She knew that he did not want to say goodbye—neither of them ever did—but they both carried greater burdens than that. In the days since they had arrived here at KR-3, they'd been able to continue their time together, but they'd also been required to prepare for their next assignments. John would be leaving on *Enterprise* in just a few minutes on a classified mission, and tomorrow she would be leaving for her new posting, Helaspont Station, near the Tzenkethi border.

"I love you, Amina," he said.

"I love you." She glanced in each direction down the corridor on KR-3, and then past John into *Enterprise*. Seeing nobody, she leaned forward and kissed him, softly, romantically.

When she pulled back, he said something that neither of them ever said: "Be careful."

Sasine had always assumed that the risks inherent in their positions prevented them not only from saying such things, but even from thinking too much about them. She knew that if she focused for any length of time on the danger John faced as a matter of course—and even more so in the current political climate—she would be unable to function at her best. She simply had to accept the nature of his duties and trust in his abilities, just as he did with her. Admonitions to "be careful" or "stay safe" were unnecessary, and even potentially dangerous; as experienced Starfleet officers, neither would act recklessly, but if, at the wrong moment, thoughts of their commitment to each other intruded into their minds, it could undermine their decisions and thus pose a threat to themselves and others.

And so John's comment surprised her. Rather than reproving him for it, though, she simply said, "I'll be careful. I always am." Then, playfully swatting him on the shoulder, she said, "You know that."

"I know," he said. "I do. I just . . ." He shrugged. "I just love you, and I don't trust the Tzenkethi."

"You're a wise man, John Jason Harriman," she said. "I mean, I don't know about the Tzenkethi, but as far as women are concerned, you have exceptional taste."

John smiled, and she was happy to see that. In the past few days with him, she'd seen it a great deal. And John rarely smiled in a small way; when happy or amused, his mouth widened broadly, his joy apparent. She had always loved that about him: he enjoyed being happy. It seemed an odd thing to consider, but Sasine had known many people who could not exist within a moment, could not live for the simple but important pleasures life could offer. But John loved life as he loved her: fully. That did not mean that he didn't suffer difficulties or doubts—life always provided such obstacles— but John never appeared to take for granted the things that brought him happiness.

"Yes, I do have great taste in women," he joked, "but I have to wonder about your taste in men."

"I do too," Sasine said with a smile. "I mean, a *mere* starship captain? You'd think I'd rate a commander in chief."

John playfully wrinkled his nose. "Admiral Sinclair-Alexander isn't really your type, though, is she?"

Sasine shook her head. "No. A little too severe for me," she said. "Which means I suppose I'm stuck with you." She leaned forward and whispered into his ear, "So will you marry me?" Then she stepped back and looked at him, allowing him to answer.

"Yes, of course," he said.

"When?" she asked, just as he had when she'd first seen him back on Foxtrot XIII.

"Every day," he said.

Sasine smiled, perfectly content with the vitality of their commitment to each other. "I'll contact you once I'm settled in at Helaspont," she said.

John nodded, and then turned and boarded *Enterprise*. She watched him go, and when he turned a corner and disappeared from sight, she headed for the nearest turbolift. She would go to an observation lounge with a view of *Enterprise* and watch as the ship departed the station. It would allow her to feel connected to John for just a little bit longer. And even after the time they'd just had together, she wanted to continue to experience that connection, even if for just a few more seconds.

* * *

As Harriman watched the image of Space Station KR-3 start to recede on the bridge's main viewscreen, he decided that he detested farewells. He pictured Amina back on KR-3, where they had just parted, and imagined her standing at a viewing port, gazing out at *Enterprise* as it fled into the eternal night of space. The thought saddened him. He supposed that he should have become inured to such experiences by now—after all, his relationship with Amina had strung together a long series of goodbyes over eight years—but he found each new parting more difficult to bear than the last.

"Viewer ahead," Harriman said from the command chair, fully aware of both the irony and the denial inherent in the order. For reasons personal and professional, though, he actually *would* look ahead to the future. But he also knew that there would be no renouncing his emotions; he might be able to bury the sadness of his separation from Amina, but it would never leave him.

"Viewer ahead," Lieutenant Tenger echoed from his side of the tactical-and-communications console. The main screen blinked and the scene on it changed, the three-armed, honeycombed form of KR-3 disappearing in favor of an empty starscape.

"Ensign Tolek, plot a course for the Bonneville Flats," Harriman ordered.

"That course has already been plotted, Captain," the navigator responded. He tapped the controls on his console with the long, slender fingers common to many Vulcans, then turned and glanced over his left shoulder at Harriman. "And now it's been laid in," he said, and smiled.

Harriman felt momentarily startled, still not quite accustomed to Tolek's demeanor. Harriman had served with several Vulcans during his Starfleet career, but until Ensign Tolek had come aboard *Enterprise*, none who'd ever smiled—or laughed, or frowned, or fraternized with the crew, or engaged in any number of other behaviors considered anathema to Vulcans. To *most* Vulcans, anyway; there were also the *V'tosh ka'tur*—Vulcans without logic—but Harriman knew that Tolek did not count himself among their number.

"The helm answers ready," Lieutenant Commander Linojj reported.

"Take us to warp nine, then," Harriman said.

"Warp nine, aye," Linojj replied, her hands skipping nimbly across her station.

Around Harriman, *Enterprise* came alive, an awakening more felt than heard as the warp drive engaged. After eighteen years commanding this vessel, Harriman could tell the condition of the engines simply by feel. And as the stars began their relative movement on the main viewscreen, he knew *Enterprise* was not just healthy, but *vigorous*.

"Time to arrival at the Bonneville Flats," Tolek said, "forty-seven hours, fifty-three minutes."

"Thank you," Harriman acknowledged. Tolek had been assigned to *Enterprise* less than two years ago, and promoted to alpha-shift navigator just within the last six months. Despite his unusual manner, at least in terms of typical Vulcan customs, Tolek claimed to live as most Vulcans did: according to the tenets of Surak, a philosopher who, two millennia ago, espoused the employment of logic and the suppression of emotion.

When Tolek had chosen to enter Starfleet, though, and therefore to live among humans and members of other emotive species, he had concluded—by way of logic, Harriman assumed—that he and his crewmates would be best served if he could develop a means of smoothly integrating with them. With that goal in mind, he had set out to become a student of social interaction, eventually putting into practice what he learned. According to Tolek, no happiness resided behind his smiles, no humor behind his laughs, no sorrow behind his frowns; he only emulated such expressions in the appropriate contexts in order to better interrelate with his crewmates.

Except that, no matter what Tolek claimed, there seemed to be more than mere imitation behind his conduct. If there hadn't been, then no matter how much he attempted to fit in with his crewmates, he would have been perceived as dishonest. Harriman believed that Tolek acted as he did in order to satisfy, at the very least, an intense curiosity about other species and other individuals. And so his behavior did not simply reflect his abilities to mimic others, but his genuine interest in their lives, their beliefs, and their activities.

By all accounts Harriman had heard, Tolek had succeeded well, even holding a measure of popularity among the crew. He had even been known, on occasion, to entertain them. Not long ago, Harriman had been passing by the crew mess and had heard Tolek telling a rapt group: "A Vulcan, a human, and a Klingon are stranded on an uninhabited planet." Harriman hadn't had time to stop, but he'd intended to ask Tolek later to share the rest of the joke.

The memory of that incident suddenly made Harriman feel alone. He peered around the bridge at his crew—at Demora Sulu and Xintal Linojj, at Tenger and Ramesh Kanchumurthi, at Borona Fenn, at Rafe Buonarotti up from engineering—but doing so failed to alter his sense of isolation. Harriman considered these people closer to him than family, but he felt disconnected from them right now.

Uncomfortable, he stood from the command chair. "Commander Sulu," he said, unable at that moment to use her given name, "you have the bridge. I'll be in my quarters."

Sulu looked up from where she stood beside Ensign Fenn at the sciences console on the port side of the bridge. "Sir?" she asked, obviously surprised, but Harriman headed for the turbolift without offering an explanation. "Yes, sir," he heard her say behind him, acknowledging and accepting the order.

He entered the turbolift and waited for the doors to close. Once they had, he stated his destination, then leaned heavily against the wall. *What's wrong with me?* he thought as the lift descended. This feeling of seclusion that had washed over him, this melancholy . . . he didn't understand where these emotions had originated.

Maybe it was *saying goodbye to Amina again,* he speculated. Maybe he just hadn't wanted to leave her again. The times they'd spent with each other during the last several days—first on Foxtrot XIII, then on *Enterprise,* and finally on KR-3—had been absolutely wonderful. Unlike their trips together, when they met in some interesting place to enjoy one activity or another—sailing the garnet seas on the Canopus Planet, donning artificial wings to soar through the low gravity of Izar's Shroud, spelunking the bottomless ice caves on Catulla—they'd remained almost exclusively in their quarters this time. With Amina commanding Foxtrot XIII—and soon Helaspont Station—and Harriman commanding *Enterprise,* propriety would not have permitted them to do otherwise.

The lift slowed its descent, came briefly to a halt, then started to glide laterally. Harriman shifted his weight and straightened from where he had been leaning against the wall. Thinking of the last few days with Amina, he smiled. They'd talked and laughed, they'd danced, they'd watched some of the old films that they both loved so much: Greer Garson in *Mrs. Miniver* and *Random Harvest,* Frank Capra's amazing *It's a Wonderful Life,* the magical and powerful *An Ancient Season.* And more than all of that, they had simply reveled in sharing each other's company. Parting today had been torturous, unquestionably more difficult for him than it had ever been.

But isn't that the way it always is? Harriman asked himself. Isn't the most recent farewell always the most difficult? That made sense; time blunted memory, assuaged emotion. That would be the case this time too, he was certain: as time passed without Amina by his side, the ache of their goodbye would fade.

Except that he was no longer sure that he wanted time to pass without Amina by his side. But then, that was one of the prices he paid to be a starship captain.

The turbolift eased to a stop and the doors opened. Harriman exited into the corridor and started for his quarters. On his way, he passed several of the crew, and he nodded automatically in their direction as he passed them, a long-standing habit of a life lived almost entirely aboard starships. Harriman had been born on *U.S.S. Sea of Tranquility*, and then had moved to numerous other vessels as his father—John "Blackjack" Harriman, now an admiral—had advanced through Starfleet. As a result of Blackjack's life aboard starships—and therefore of his own such life—the first time that Harriman had spent more than a couple of weeks planetside had been when he had traveled to Earth to attend Starfleet Academy. His three years there—he'd been approved to take an accelerated course of study, in addition to receiving credits for duties he'd performed aboard his father's ships—had been the only time in his life when he hadn't called a Starfleet vessel home.

He reached his quarters and strode inside. He stopped for a moment, considering what to do. He eyed the arc of his desk sitting in the near left corner of the cabin, but realized that he didn't feel up to concentrating on any work right now. The door to his bedroom stood open in the wall beyond the desk, but neither did Harriman feel like sleeping. Instead, he crossed the room to the outer bulkhead and stared out at the stars slipping by as *Enterprise* warped through space. His quarters sat on the starboard side of the ship, so the stars raced from left to right across his view.

After a few minutes, his thoughts wandered back to Amina, and his emotions back to being apart from her. Frustrated, Harriman dropped onto his back on the sofa, thinking that perhaps he could rest for a while and refocus his thoughts. He attempted to blank his mind, closing his eyes to shut out the rest of the universe, but before long, he found himself staring at the ceiling.

That's something that never changes, he joked to himself: starship overheads. They all had that same off-white color, that same beam-to-beam construction, that same pattern of lighting panels. *And I should know,* Harriman thought; for the vast majority of his life, such a ceiling had been his sky.

He recalled those first weeks he had spent on Earth after he had joined the Academy. He'd felt helpless, and even fearful, being outdoors and under a wide, open sky so often, a condition he'd self-diagnosed as mild agoraphobia. He had never revealed that experience to anybody but Amina—and certainly *not* to his father. At the time, he had chosen to suffer through the unhealthy emotions, convinced that he could help himself past the problem. He'd read psychological texts regarding the condition, and had researched the techniques people utilized to overcome it. Within just a couple of months, he had gotten better, and by the end of his term at the Academy, he'd actually come to appreciate and take pleasure from outdoor activities.

Once he had graduated, though, Harriman's Starfleet career had taken him back aboard ship. He had never really wanted another way of life. Truthfully, he had never even considered it.

Of course not, he thought. *The admiral saw to that.*

He swung his legs down to the floor and sat up on the sofa. *Is that it?* he wondered. Was Blackjack's presence on the upcoming mission what had led to his own pensiveness and sense of disconnection? Other than in an official capacity, the admiral hadn't spoken to him in seventeen years, since an incident in which Harriman had transported Blackjack from the bridge of *Enterprise* and into the brig. At the time, Harriman had been under orders from Starfleet Command to track down *Excelsior* and escort it back to base. He had instead

helped *Excelsior*'s captain—Hikaru Sulu, Demora's father—
rescue her from Askalon V; Demora, *Enterprise*'s navigator
back then, had previously been believed dead.

After the incident, Harriman had gone to his father and
convinced him not to empanel a court-martial for the actions of either starship's captain. But relations between father and son had cooled after that, and a few silent months
later, it had become clear that their relationship had
foundered. They had spoken during the years since, but only
in their official capacities within Starfleet, including some
important meetings within the last year or so. Two days from
now, though, their respective roles in the *Universe* project
would require more interaction between them than they'd
had since . . . well, since all those years ago.

*And maybe that's affecting me more than I've been willing
to admit,* Harriman thought. *Maybe—*

No. He had long ago come to terms with his estrangement from his father. For despite all of the time they had
spent together on the various starships to which his father
had been assigned, they had never really shared a father-son
bond. Even as a boy, Harriman had been treated more like a
subordinate than like a child; Blackjack seemed to have
been grooming him for service in Starfleet even then.

He pushed up from the sofa, but he didn't move from
there, his feet remaining planted and his thoughts remaining
in the past. By the time Harriman had graduated the Academy, his father had attained the rank of rear admiral, a position that had allowed him some influence in forwarding his
son's fledgling career. Doors of opportunity had opened
early and often for Harriman, more so than his performance—as good as it had been—had merited. More so than
anybody's performance would have merited. He had initially
felt divergent emotions about this: on the one hand, he had
appreciated the chance to rise rapidly through the Starfleet
ranks, but on the other, his pride and personal ethic had

made him want to earn his promotions solely on the basis of his accomplishments and abilities. He had also resented that his father had not apparently believed him capable of such a career on his own.

Except that his father had thought him neither capable nor incapable, Harriman had eventually realized; the admiral's actions had been motivated not by his opinions of his son, but by his opinions of *himself*. Blackjack had worn his son's career as he would have a medal, as something that reflected upon him. It had taken Harriman a long time, but on that day seventeen years ago when the admiral had essentially taken command of *Enterprise* from him and had prepared to fire on the undefended *Excelsior*, he—Harriman— had finally faced the depth of his father's self-involvement. He wished it were otherwise, wished that his father were different from the man he was, but in actuality, Harriman did not really like or respect him, and so also did not miss him.

But if this feeling of segregation from the crew was not about his father, as awkward as it might be to work with him in the next few days, and if it was not about Amina, much as he loved and missed her, then what was it about?

He paced across the room to his desk. He reached over it and turned the desktop computer interface around so that he could see it, then toggled it on. The image of *Enterprise* appeared on the display. "Computer," he said, "show me *U.S.S. Universe*, NX Twenty-nine Ninety-nine. External views, bow and starboard."

"Please state identity and authorization code," the computer responded in its mature, female voice.

"Identity: Harriman, Captain John J.," he said. "Authorization: beta thirty-one meteor green."

"Voiceprint and security code confirmed," the computer said. *"Displaying requested data."*

On the computer screen, the *Enterprise* vanished, replaced an instant later by split-screen images of *Universe*; a view from in front of the vessel sat on top, and a view from the side on the bottom. With a particularly wide beam and shallow depth, the starship looked as though it had been compacted top to bottom, and spread port and starboard. The primary hull, a narrow ellipse with its major axis running fore and aft, had no rise to it at its center. The secondary hull, another level, narrow ellipse, but smaller, connected to the primary hull directly, the forward section of the former lying directly below the aft section of the latter. A pair of thin struts, angling backward, connected each of the two warp nacelles to the secondary hull. The nacelles themselves were flat and wide, flaring out broadly from their midpoints aft. The two-hull, two-nacelle alignment suggested a resemblance to other Starfleet vessels, but departed dramatically from those other designs in execution.

This *is what's troubling me,* Harriman thought. He circled around his desk and sat down in the chair behind it, pulling the computer interface around as he did so. *This is what's dividing me from my crew.* Not the work to be done with Blackjack, not the goodbye with Amina. This.

He stared at *Universe,* a ship he had taken a key role in planning, from its unconventional appearance to its unorthodox employment of cloaking technology. The threatening uncertainty with the Romulans and the Klingons—and particularly with the Romulans ever since they had occupied the Koltaari world—had led him to this perilous course. And although his crew understood that they would be assisting in the final flight trials of the strange ship, Harriman knew that they did not comprehend the full importance of those trials. Billions of lives in the Alpha and Beta Quadrants depended on the success of this mission.

Harriman reached forward and jabbed at a control on the computer interface, blanking the screen. *Not Blackjack, not Amina,* he thought again. His own knowledge of the importance of the *Universe* trials was what separated him from his crew.

That, and the fact that he knew that they would only have one opportunity to get this right.

Ensign Borona Fenn sat at her sciences station on the bridge of *Enterprise*, studying two readouts. With her left eye, she scanned a geographical abstract from the library database, and with her right, the sensor readings provided by a series of class-one probes. Her eyes functioned independently of each other, and the structure of the Frunalian brain allowed her to process both sets of information simultaneously.

The title *Bonneville Salt Flats* headed the geographical précis, which also included historical notes about the area. Existing in a region of Sol III's North American continent called the Great Basin, she read, the twelve-thousand-hectare desert formed during the final desiccative phases of an ancient inland lake. The old lakebed continued to be remade annually, though, when a shallow volume of snowmelt evaporated slowly from the salt surface, as winds leveled it into an immense, extremely flat plane. Because of the unusual evenness of the surface, humans had utilized the area four centuries ago to set land speed records; incredibly, wheeled ground vehicles had traveled faster than a thousand kilometers per hour there.

That explained the nickname that had been given to this region of space, Fenn realized. Starfleet traditionally field-tested new starship and engine designs here, with experimental vessels often surpassing velocity benchmarks. Of course, while it seemed reasonable that the word *salt* had been omitted from the area's moniker, it made little sense to her that the word *flats* had been retained; the space-time continuum could hardly be described as two-dimensional.

Humans, she thought, smiling, amused yet again by their proclivity for imprecision. Her roommate at Starfleet Academy, a human himself, had insisted that the proper term for such mental inexactitude was *poetic license,* but Fenn believed that distinction to be merely semantic, not substan-

tive. Still, despite the recurrent assaults on her natural
Frunalian instinct for meticulousness, she remained content with her decision to take her scientific studies into
Starfleet. In the seven years since she had graduated the
Academy, Fenn had relished her part in conducting scientific exploration—although there had been little of that recently. Her duties aboard *Enterprise* had required her to
function in a wide array of disciplines—including such di-
verse fields as geology, chemistry, cosmology, and physics—
and she had found the experience intellectually and
emotionally fulfilling.

On the second display Fenn studied, probes seeded along
the Bonneville Flats supplied sensor readings of the surrounding space and of the three other Starfleet vessels there.
The small support ships *Canaveral* and *Ad Astra* had joined
Enterprise to assist, observe, and record *Universe*'s flight testing. Fenn knew that such field trials typically involved the
abetment of more ships and more personnel—*Canaveral*
and *Ad Astra* each carried crews of only a few dozen—but
she surmised that, given the current diplomatic turmoil,
Starfleet Command had not wanted to draw attention to
Universe. The radical design of the ship not only promised
increased efficiencies in warp-field geometries, but also afforded a test bed for a new propulsion system, a development neither the Romulans nor the Klingons would likely
appreciate.

Enterprise's crew had been given few details about *Universe*, other than the fact of its installation of so-called hyperwarp engines. Fenn assumed that Starfleet intended the new
drive as a replacement of the failed transwarp program,
which had been initiated a few decades past. If successful,
the crew had been told, hyperwarp would revolutionize
spaceflight and launch a new era of exploration—goals Fenn
found both laudable and exhilarating. Nor was she alone in
her views. Since *Enterprise* had departed KR-3 two days ago,

the topic of what the achievement of hyperwarp drive would mean had occupied the crew, and the sense of anticipation and excitement aboard had been palpable. Right now, only moments before *Universe* would make its first test run, the atmosphere on the bridge felt electric.

"Captain, we are being hailed by the *Ad Astra*," Fenn heard Lieutenant Kanchumurthi say at his side of the tactical-and-communications console.

"Put Saren-Sah through," Captain Harriman said.

"It's not Captain Saren-Sah, sir," Kanchumurthi said. "It's Admiral Harriman."

Fenn turned from her station and gazed over to where the captain sat in the command chair. Since *Enterprise* had arrived at the Bonneville Flats, contact with *Ad Astra* had included Saren-Sah and his officers, but not the admiral, and Fenn wondered how Captain Harriman would react. Although she knew from her long service with him that he did not have a good relationship with his father, she saw now that he did not appear flustered or anxious, but simply professional.

"Then put the admiral through," he said. "On screen."

"Yes, sir," Kanchumurthi said, and worked his console.

Fenn glanced over at the main viewer with her left eye, leaving her right trained on the captain. On the viewscreen, an empty field of stars was replaced by the image of Admiral Harriman. Broader than his son, with a rugged appearance and a head of hair that had silvered completely, the admiral looked very much like a man in charge. Fenn could see the resemblance between father and son, but even before the admiral said anything, she also noted that the two men carried themselves differently. In her time aboard *Enterprise*, Fenn had always appreciated how accessible and even-tempered Captain Harriman had been, and how his easy confidence had in turn inspired the crew's confidence in him. By contrast, the admiral's mien made him appear angry and unapproachable, and though he was likely a man very sure of himself, Fenn doubted that his conviction would motivate her to want to follow him into battle.

"*Captain Harriman*," the admiral rumbled, his voice rough and loud, giving the impression that yelling came naturally to him. "*What's the status of your ship and crew?*" From the admiral's lips, the standard question sounded somehow like an accusation.

"*Enterprise* is in position, Admiral," the captain reported. "All the probes have been deployed along *Universe's* flight path, and my crew have completed all of their pre-test duties." While *Canaveral* and *Ad Astra* would monitor *Universe's* field trials from either end of the Bonneville Flats, Fenn knew, *Enterprise* would hold a position midway along the test route, its crew observing and recording both through direct sensor contact and via the sensor packages on the probes.

"*Reconfirm the operation of the probes*," the admiral ordered, unnecessarily, Fenn thought. But she immediately spun back to her station, anticipating the captain's command.

"Ensign Fenn," he said, obviously not feeling the need to repeat the admiral's demand.

"Checking, sir," she responded. As she scrutinized her readouts, she sent the four fingers on each of her hands racing across her controls, testing the strength of the communication signals traveling to and from the probes. The semitransparent, chitinous membrane that encased her fingers—as well as the rest of her body—tapped rapidly on the console. As quickly as she could, she verified the active status of each of the probes, as well as the stability of *Enterprise's* comlinks with them. When she had completed the task, she turned back toward the captain. "Reconfirmed, sir," she said. "The probes are fully operational and the contacts with them are strong and steady."

"Thank you, Ensign," the captain said, nodding in her direction before looking back at the main viewscreen. "Admiral?"

"*All right*," the elder Harriman said. "*Let's open the continuous comlink between all four ships.* Canaveral, *this is Admiral Harriman aboard the—*"

To Fenn's left, the port-side doors opened, drawing her attention away from the admiral. She looked over and saw Commander Sulu step onto the bridge from the turbolift. The ship's first officer stopped for a moment and looked over at the captain, then turned and walked over to the sciences station. "Borona," Sulu said, leaning in beside Fenn, "anything to report on the navigational deflector?" Sporadically over the past eighteen months, Fenn's sensor scans had detected a random dispersion of the force beam that *Enterprise* projected ahead while in flight, in order to push matter from its path. The cause of the intermittent problem had so far been elusive. Although it was not a threat to the ship, triggering only an infinitesimal and nearly undetectable power drain, Commander Sulu had asked Fenn to be alert for more occurrences of the dispersion.

"Not since just after we left KR-3," Fenn said. Shortly after *Enterprise* had departed the starbase, the problem had recurred, but it had lasted only a few seconds before resolving itself. "I've been working all shift with the probes we sent out to monitor *Universe*, though," she added, "so I haven't inspected the logs today. Let me check them now."

"Thanks, Borona," Sulu said with a smile.

Fenn worked her console to locate and then access the sensor logs. As she pressed one control surface, pain suddenly shot through her hand and up her arm, as though a knife had been thrust into her palm and then dragged through her flesh up to her shoulder. She suppressed the urge to cry out, but could not prevent a quick expulsion of breath. Sulu must have heard her, because she asked, "Are you all right, Borona? Are you—"

The first officer stopped abruptly, and when Fenn looked

down at her own hand, she saw why. A five-centimeter section of her exomembrane had fallen off of one of her fingers and now lay atop her console like a dead insect. Where the exomembrane had fallen away, her gray-green flesh had been completely exposed.

"I'm all right," Fenn said, although she doubted that she sounded very convincing. The sharp pain had already subsided to a dull ache, but the shock of seeing her bare skin remained. *It's too soon*, she thought. She was too young to be starting the Shift—

—except that wasn't true. Fenn was young for the process to be commencing, but not *too* young. A small percentage of Frunalians did undergo the Shift this early in their lives, and she certainly could not dispute the evidence of a piece of her exomembrane falling from her body.

"Do you need to see Dr. Morell?" Sulu asked, the concern in her voice plain. Fenn knew that the first officer had been informed about the metamorphosis Frunalians underwent during their lives, and Fenn had even spoken with her about it on two occasions. Sulu must therefore have understood the significance of what had just happened.

"I'm all right," Fenn repeated, though still without much conviction. She felt anxious and even scared, despite the amount of education she had received throughout her life about this event and how she could and should deal with it. One of the things she knew, though, was that the first shedding of a section of exomembrane preceded the main stage of the Shift by three to six months. For now, at least, she could continue to function in her duty.

Sulu leaned in very close to Fenn. "Borona," she said gently, "you don't sound or look 'all right.' "

Fenn wanted to protest, wanted to stay at her post, a means of attempting to deny what had just happened, she supposed. Instead, she said, "I do think I need to go to sickbay."

"Go ahead," Sulu said at once. "I'll let Dr. Morell know you're on your way. We'll cover for you here." She reached a hand up and grasped Fenn's forearm reassuringly. "It's going to be okay, Borona."

Fenn forced a smile onto her face, then stood and headed for the turbolift. Her thoughts and emotions whirled. She would have to take a leave of absence from *Enterprise*. She would also have to find the strength to endure the pain of the Shift, a menacing prospect that, until now, had always been safely hidden away in the remote future. *How am I going to get through this?* she asked herself as she entered the lift. How would she be able to cope with the complete loss of her exomembrane, or with any of the other numerous changes both her body and mind would experience? Her skin would toughen, she would lose the raised ridges on the backs of her shoulders—the vestigial remnants of wings, some Frunalian biologists believed—her quartet of mammary glands would mature, as would her internal sexual organs, and she would develop a new sensory appendage, which would stretch from her brow, across the top of her head, and down her spine, like a fleshy mane. And she could not even begin to know how she would be able to deal with the major hormonal and chemical changes that would occur.

"Sickbay," Fenn said in the turbolift, and now she could hear the uncertainty in her voice. Uncertainty, and fear. And as the lift doors slid closed, one question glowed in her thoughts like a supernova in a dark nebula: when her Shift was complete, would she still be herself, or someone else?

Sulu thumbed the comm channel closed after letting Dr. Morell know about Ensign Fenn's situation. Sulu liked Fenn a great deal, and appreciated the consistently high quality of her work, as well as the enthusiasm with which she carried out her duties. She hoped that the young woman would be all right. Years ago, when Ensign Fenn had been assigned to *Enterprise*—the only Frunalian aboard, then and now—Captain Harriman had been told about the hemimetabolous phase that she would one day go through, and he in turn had enlightened his senior staff about the process. Sulu therefore knew something of what Fenn would be facing—and she'd also spoken with Fenn herself about it—but she certainly could not comprehend what it would be like to live through such an experience. *Childhood and puberty were hard enough,* she thought wryly.

Sulu sat down at the sciences station and took a quick inventory of the readouts. She familiarized herself with the data being transmitted to *Enterprise* by the probes, noted *Universe's* unique sensor profile, along with the life signs of its skeleton crew of fifty-one, then turned and looked toward the captain. He was already peering in her direction, evidently having noticed Ensign Fenn's departure from the bridge. The captain raised his eyebrows, asking a question without having to speak it: *Is everything all right?* Sulu nodded her head.

"*All right,*" she heard a voice say—a deep, harsh voice she immediately recognized as belonging to Admiral Harriman. "*Confirm four-way comlink and ship readiness.* Universe?"

"Universe *confirms comlink,*" said a voice Sulu did not know, but that must have been that of Adrienne Kuwano, whom they'd been told would captain *Universe* during the flight trials. "*We are at full readiness and await final confirmations.*"

"*Acknowledged,*" Admiral Harriman barked. "Canaveral?"

"Canaveral *confirms comlink and ship's readiness,*" said Captain Jack Breshar, an old space dog Sulu had known for many years, and who had once been a colleague of her father.

"Enterprise?" the admiral asked.

Captain Harriman responded in the affirmative, then asked Sulu to establish a visual of *Universe* from the probe nearest to it. She turned and operated the controls of Fenn's console, then looked up at the main viewer to see the unusual form of the experimental starship sitting motionless in space. Finally, the admiral called out the name of the ship on which he was himself stationed; the repetition of his words made him sound to Sulu like an automaton. The captain of *Ad Astra*, Saren-Sah, gave the appropriate confirmations.

"*All right*," Admiral Harriman said. "*It's your show*, Universe."

Sulu felt her stomach jump with excitement. Once these test flights had successfully been completed, dramatic and thrilling changes would be in store for interstellar exploration. And although she had not spoken to Captain Harriman about it, she understood that a significant improvement in warp-engine performance, even short of hyperwarp drive, could easily have a positive impact on the precipitous state of affairs with the Romulans and Klingons.

"Universe *acknowledges*," said Captain Kuwano. "*All our boards show green. Engineering, helm, and navigation preparations are complete. We are beginning sixty-second sequencing to hyperwarp . . . now.*"

As *Universe* warped out of sight on the main viewer, Sulu turned back to the sciences console and checked the readouts. "The first probe has begun telemetering data," she reported. "The *Enterprise* has the *Universe* on long-range sensors."

"*Warp one,*" Sulu heard a woman say, and she assumed it was *Universe*'s helm officer, Lieutenant Seaver. Sulu had taken a glance at *Universe*'s personnel roster earlier today.

"*All three hyperwarp computers are engaged,*" came another voice, a man's, probably that of *Universe*'s chief engineer, Lieutenant Commander Chernin. "*Primary and secondary hyperwarp computers are in synchronous operation.*"

"*Fifty seconds to hyperwarp,*" Captain Kuwano said.

Sulu felt her heart race, gripped by the moment. *Fifty seconds away from a revolution,* she thought. She did not know the specifications of hyperwarp, but her imagination sent her soaring across the Milky Way.

"*Warp two,*" said Seaver.

"*Articulated dilithium matrices are focused and aligned,*" Chernin said.

"*Forty seconds.*" Captain Kuwano.

Sulu saw another set of readings begin to register on her panel. "The second probe now has the *Universe* in range," she said.

"*Warp four.*" Seaver.

"*We have matter entering the flux chamber. Warm-starting antimatter flow.*" Chernin.

"*Thirty seconds.*" Kuwano.

In these breathless moments, Sulu thought of her father. She recalled how, when she'd been attending Starfleet Academy, he would send her recorded messages telling her stories he had wanted to share with her: the first sustained powered flight by the Wright Brothers at Kill Devil Hill, Neil Armstrong and Buzz Aldrin setting down on Earth's moon, Verna Mitrios surviving the first landing on Mars, Zefram Cochrane traveling at warp in *Phoenix.*

"*Warp six.*"

"*We register influx of antimatter.*"

"*Twenty seconds.*"

As Sulu announced *Universe* now in range of the third probe, she gave thought to how these next few moments would be recorded in history. It energized her to be a participant in such a momentous event.

"*Warp eight.*"

"*Hyperwarp generators are online.*"

"*Fifteen seconds.*"

At the sciences station, an energy waveform suddenly surged across one of the displays. Sulu did not recognize its shape or structure, and she quickly worked her controls to isolate its source and identify it.

"*Warp nine.*"

"*Beginning hyperwarp reaction.*"

"Ten seconds."

As Sulu scanned space for the origin of the energy wave, she also queried the library computer about it. An answer appeared at once on a readout, and Sulu felt as though she'd been punched in the stomach. The only source known to generate such a waveform was a Romulan cloaking device.

"Warp nine-point-three," *Universe*'s helm officer, Seaver, said.

"Confirming hyperwarp initiation," the engineer, Chernin, said.

"Five seconds." Captain Kuwano.

Sulu opened her mouth to shout a warning to *Universe*'s crew, to alert them to the presence of a Romulan vessel in nearby space, maybe even to end the test run right now. If the Romulans had sabotaged the field trials—

But in that instant, sensors ascertained the location of the waveform's source: *Universe* itself. Somewhere aboard the experimental Starfleet vessel functioned Romulan cloaking technology, or the Federation equivalent. This clearly had been the reason for Starfleet's security measures with respect to these trials.

"Warp nine-point-five."

"We're on track."

"Three seconds . . . two . . . one."

On the readouts of the probe data, the numbers began to change not just quantitatively, but qualitatively. The readings no longer described a starship traveling at warp velocities. Sulu held her breath.

"We are at hyperwarp, factor one," Seaver said, and Sulu could tell that the woman had spoken with a wide smile on her face. Sulu exhaled in relief, and then couldn't resist squeezing her hand into a fist and jabbing the air in celebration. Applause went up on the bridge of *Enterprise*, and she was sure, on the bridges of the other ships as well.

"Congratulations, Universe,*"* Admiral Harriman said.

Across the bridge from Sulu, at a starboard engineering console, Rafe Buonarroti said, "Those engines must be *le bellezze.*" He saw her looking over at him, and he smiled. She smiled back.

"Our joys as wingèd dreams do fly," Sulu thought, unsure of the source of the quote, but feeling that it applied here. Her father had passed his sense of romance down to her.

"Maintaining hyperwarp one," Seaver said.

A moment later, Sulu thought she heard someone gasp. Then: *"Look at the stars."* It was Captain Kuwano, speaking almost in a whisper.

"Capt—" somebody began to shout, and then a thunderous sound swept across the bridge of *Enterprise.* In an instant, the sound was gone, and behind it followed only silence.

Sulu looked at the readouts. All of the numbers had dropped to zero. She felt the blood drain from her face and her skin grow cold.

"Universe, *this is Harriman,*" the admiral roared. *"Come in, Universe."*

And still, there was only silence.

"We have no comlink with the *Universe,*" Kanchumurthi said.

"I'm reading a malfunction," another disembodied voice said.

"Captain," Tenger said, "there's been an explosion."

Sulu felt as though her heart had stopped in her chest.

"What have we got?" Captain Harriman wanted to know, standing from his chair. "Tenger? Demora?"

Sulu checked the readouts from the probes twice, and then *Enterprise*'s own sensor readings twice, before answering. Finally, she had no choice but to say the unthinkable. "Captain . . . the *Universe* is gone."

Harriman stood staring at the empty starscape on the viewscreen. For the first time on the bridge of *Enterprise,* he did not know how to act, what to say. What his crew must be feeling right now . . .

"Captain," Tenger said, his tone urgent. "The explosion sent out a shock wave, concentrated in one direction. *Ad Astra* was in its path."

"Shields up," Harriman said, no longer at a loss for words, even as he remembered that there had been another time when he had not known how to act or what to say on *Enterprise*'s bridge: during the ship's maiden voyage. "*Ad Astra,* this is *Enterprise.* Come in."

No response.

"The comlink has been knocked out," Lieutenant Kanchumurthi explained. "Now we've lost contact with all the ships."

"Tenger," Harriman asked, "can we make it through the shock wave?"

"We're not in the path of the main wave," Tenger said. "With shields up, we should have no problem."

"Xintal, best speed to *Ad Astra,*" Harriman said. "Tolek, coordinates from Lieutenant Tenger."

Linojj and Tolek both responded verbally even as they began working their consoles.

"Ramesh," Harriman said to Kanchumurthi, "try to raise *Canaveral.* See if they can assist."

"Yes, sir," Kanchumurthi said.

And as *Enterprise* leaped to warp, Harriman thought the same two things that he had during his vessel's disastrous first flight eighteen years ago: that he hoped he could rescue the crew of a ship in trouble, and that this hadn't been supposed to happen.

Blackjack Harriman stood on the bridge of the support vessel *Ad Astra* and waited to hear the words.

"*We are at hyperwarp, factor one.*"

Around Blackjack, the other four people on *Ad Astra*'s bridge—the ship's captain, the helm and navigation officers, and a sensor technician—all clapped. Over the comlink, Blackjack heard applause from the crews of the other ships as well. He tried to imagine his son's reaction, then quickly put the thought out of his mind.

"Congratulations, *Universe*," Blackjack said, playing his role as the ranking officer in the operation. He looked around the bridge—with barely enough room for its five occupants, the small area would more aptly be called a control room—and saw the *Ad Astra* officers all exchanging celebratory glances.

Somebody said something unintelligible over the comlink, and then Blackjack heard, "*Maintaining hyperwarp one.*"

And then somebody gasped, and on the heels of that: "*Look at the stars.*"

"*Capt—*" came a shout, clipped off by a deafening noise, followed by a horrible quiet. Blackjack moved past Captain Saren-Sah in the command chair and leaned over the sensor technician. On the scan readouts, he saw that all of the entries had changed to zeroes.

"*Universe*, this is Harriman," he bellowed. "Come in, *Universe*."

No response.

"*We have no comlink with the* Universe," somebody said.

"I'm reading a malfunction," said *Ad Astra*'s sensor technician.

"*Captain, there's been—*" The comlink ended as abruptly as though it had been sliced in two by an axe.

Suddenly, the deck canted sharply to one side, and Blackjack was thrown from his feet. He brought his hands up, but too late; his chest collided with the arm of Saren-Sah's command chair. He felt his breath leave him as he tumbled onto the deck. His shoulder struck hard, and even with the din now filling the bridge, he heard the sickening snap of his bones.

He heard yelling, but could not make out any words. But then the noise diminished enough that he could hear Saren-

Sah issuing orders to the crew: to raise shields, to bring the ship about, to map the shock wave and chart a course into and through it. Blackjack reached up and grabbed for the arm of Saren-Sah's chair, pulling himself to his feet. His injured arm hung limply at his side. He took a few seconds to catch his breath, and tried to steady his gaze in the badly shaking ship. In the dim red flash of alert lighting, he saw Saren-Sah leaning in over the helm as the other officers all struggled back toward their stations, obviously having been tossed from their chairs.

This wasn't supposed to happen, Blackjack thought, and he headed for the navigation console. He was almost there when the room spun again, inertial dampers failing under the stresses of conflicting forces. He sailed backward, leaving his feet. He saw a chair fly past his face, missing him by only centimeters. He waited for the impact he knew would come from behind, and attempted to brace himself for it. In that moment, the alert lighting failed, plunging the bridge into darkness, the only faint illumination coming from the various control stations. Blackjack had just enough time before he hit the bulkhead to wonder whether the consoles would also lose power.

And then everything went black.

Fleet Admiral Aventeer Vokar stared at the main viewscreen and carefully studied the tactical display superimposed there. The powerful shock wave expanded in a three-dimensional arc from its point of origin, hurtling through space with destructive force. His flagship seemed to sit well beyond what would likely be its range, but—

"Shield status," he said without looking away from the screen.

"Shields functioning at twenty-five percent," Subcommander Linavil answered at once.

Now Vokar turned in his chair—raised above the deck at

the aft end of the oval bridge—and peered over at the sub-commander. She sat at the main tactical console, the re-flected light of her readouts glimmering on the torso of her uniform. As with all the stations here, Linavil's faced toward the center of the bridge, allowing her ready sightlines for-ward, to the main viewscreen, and aft, to the command chair. "Increase to full," Vokar ordered. His ship would prob-ably be safe this far from the detonation, but he had not risen to his position at the top of the Romulan Imperial Fleet by taking unnecessary risks.

"Sir," Linavil said. She hesitated only a second before adding, "Yes, sir." She operated her console, but Vokar un-derstood her almost imperceptible delay for what it was: dis-agreement, bordering on insubordination. The ship's cloak required an enormous amount of power to operate, and stan-dard procedure—even during incursions into enemy space, such as this one—mandated minimizing the utilization of other systems, including defensive shields. Linavil knew that, of course, and her hesitation revealed that she believed there to be insufficient cause to alter that strategy. "Shields now functioning at one hundred percent," she said.

"Yes," Vokar said, giving a moment's thought to whether or not it would pay to reprimand the subcommander. She had long been a loyal follower—sometimes almost *too* loyal, her militant support of both his command and his other objec-tives threatening to draw unwanted attention. Still, she pos-sessed other tangible assets, including an uncle in the Senate, and the ear of a centurion in the praetor's cabinet. At the same time, she had lately taken issue with Vokar, mostly in subtle ways, and he had begun to wonder whether her own personal objectives had come to supersede her support of his.

Vokar stood, descended to the deck, and paced into the center of the bridge, returning his attention to the tactical display on the viewscreen. "Analysis, Sublieutenant Akeev." Vokar already had his suspicions—more than that, his judgments—about what he was witnessing, but he wanted to hear an unbiased scientific view as well.

"The detonation is massive, Admiral," Akeev replied from his station near the main viewer. He detailed the output of the explosion, a staggering figure. "Its profile reads almost like the blast caused by the catastrophic failure of a Starfleet warp core, but it is far more powerful."

Vokar looked over at the science officer. Wearing the gray ensign of military technical disciplines down the right third of his uniform top, Akeev had long since lost the youthful appearance he'd had when Vokar had handpicked him from the Beryk Institute a decade ago. The scientist had graduated at the top of his class, and combined with the military proficiencies he'd shown as a boy in the Youth Guard, he'd been a commodity too potentially valuable for Vokar to overlook.

"*Could* the explosion have been a warp-core failure?" Vokar asked. They had detected three Starfleet vessels in the area, and a fourth object that had resembled a ship, though he believed that it had likely been something else.

"I don't think so," Akeev said. "Besides being too powerful, the explosion was also too focused to have been a random blast."

"Then what do you think it is?" Vokar asked. The answer seemed perfectly clear to him. Starfleet had spent a great deal of time recently conducting battle simulations at their outposts along the Neutral Zone, as well as upgrading the weapon systems in those installations, both activities obvious preparations for combat. When Imperial Fleet Command had received word of those operations, Vokar had taken his ship into Federation space to observe. Now similar information had brought Vokar and his ship here, and there seemed little doubt that the Federation was continuing its provisioning for a war it professed not to want. The hypocrisy sickened him, but the Federation would be made to pay for its dishonesty.

"I think it's a weapon, Admiral," Akeev said. "I think the fourth object out there was a weapons platform Starfleet was testing."

"Not just a weapon," Vokar said, looking back up at the viewscreen. The arc of destructive force had lost much of its power, he saw, but not before passing through a considerable volume of space.

"No, not *just* a weapon," Akeev agreed. "A *meta*weapon."

Vokar looked over again at the scientist. "A piece of information the praetor would surely like to have, wouldn't you say, Akeev?" He smiled thinly, disgusted by the duplicitous Federation even as he foresaw its downfall. "Something even the Klingons would enjoy knowing."

"Yes, Admiral."

Vokar rounded on his heel and strode back to his command chair. "Tactical, return shields to one-quarter," he said. "Navigation, plot a course for the Arandra Entry. Helm, maximum warp. I want to get a message to Romulus as soon as possible." Vokar's officers acknowledged his orders as they set about executing them. "Clear the screen," he added. "Viewer ahead."

On the main viewscreen, the tactical display winked off, a starscape appearing in its place. Vokar felt the thrum of the ship's engines as they engaged, and a moment later, the stars on the viewscreen started to fall away to port. The Romulan flagship *Tomed* changed course and headed for home.

MINUS SEVEN: AFTERMATH

The medical scanner whirred as Morell passed it over her patient, the gentle sound just one of many in this section of Space Station KR-3's infirmary. The soft, too-slow pulse that echoed the beating of her patient's heart emanated from the diagnostic panel above the biobed, and a respirator hissed its sad but vital operation. *The funeral dirge of modern medical equipment*, Morell thought, not without bitterness. She usually appreciated such sounds, thinking of them not as a dirge, but as the accompaniment of the journey back to health of those she treated. But in a case such as this, when her best efforts—when *any* physician's best efforts—would likely be insufficient, nothing could adequately fill the silence left by a missing voice.

Morell reviewed the scanner readings on a medical tricorder. She saw nothing unexpected on the display, and worse, she saw nothing encouraging. Setting the instruments down on a nearby cart, she took one more look at the diagnostic panel, as though it might show her something different than the scanner just had. Though she'd been a doctor for forty years, this aspect of her work had never gotten any easier. But then, as the first CMO under whom she'd served had told her, it *shouldn't* get easier; being unable to save the sick or injured should always be hard.

As Morell reached up and dimmed the display above the biobed, she heard the door to the intensive-care section sigh open. She turned and headed in that direction, suspecting that she knew who had just come in, and thinking that it would be best if she could move him out of here as quickly as possible. If she had to, she would quote the technicality that, at this late hour, visitors were not even supposed to be here.

Morell exited her patient's room—sectioned off, but lacking a fourth wall, the "room" was really more of a bay—and approached the visitor. A nurse at the other end of the intensive-care section had also started in this direction, striding past the other, thankfully empty, bays, but Morell waved him away. "Captain," she said when she reached the wide door, which had closed behind him. She saw immediately that he had not been getting much rest; his eyes appeared glassy, with dark patches hanging in the flesh beneath them. He also still wore his uniform, though his shift had ended hours ago. "Let me prescribe something for you to help you sleep," she said. She placed her hand on his upper arm and urged him back toward the door.

"Thanks, Uta," Captain Harriman said, but he didn't allow her to lead him away. He slipped his arm from her grasp and glanced toward the bay from which she had just emerged. "How is he?" he asked.

Morell briefly considered suggesting that they talk elsewhere, even thought about ordering the captain out of the infirmary, or at least out of intensive care. But she did none of those things, understanding that nothing would ease this burden for either one of them. "He's not good," she said. "The surgery went as well as it could, but there was so much damage to his brain . . ." She let the sentence trail off, something she did not typically do, and she realized just how tired she also felt. Because of the extent of the head trauma Admiral Harriman had sustained, coupled with the number of injured crew from *Ad Astra* that she and her staff had needed to treat, Morell had chosen to place the admiral in stasis for most of the time it had taken *Enterprise* to return to KR-3. They'd arrived back at the space station earlier today, and the CMO here had agreed to allow Morell to continue to treat the elder Harriman. She had spent several hours in the operating theater here, opening up three sections of the admiral's skull in order for her to remove the subdural hematomata that had been caused by the blunt force to his head. The surgery had been successful, but . . . "It'll take some time before we know the permanent effects of the cerebral swelling."

"Has he regained consciousness?" the captain asked.

"No," Morell said. "And I'm afraid I can't tell you when he will, or even *if* he will."

The captain nodded slowly, as though trying to decide what to do with this information. Finally, he said, "But there's a chance he might wake up."

Morell offered a tight, closed-mouth smile, hoping it masked how badly she felt for the captain. "There's always a chance," she said. She reached up and put her hand on his upper arm again, this time in a comforting gesture. "But it's not a good chance, Captain," she told him, because she saw little benefit in hiding the truth. "You should make peace with that."

Again, he nodded slowly, then patted her hand where it rested on his arm; his fingers, she noticed, were cold. "All right," he said, then looked past her again, in the direction of the admiral's biobed. "Can I see him?" he asked.

Morell paused, never knowing how to answer that question. For some people, having a last opportunity to see a badly injured loved one helped provide closure; for others, it stripped away the ability to remember the loved one in the fullness of health. "You can go see him, Captain," Morell

said at last. "But you might not want to. He doesn't . . ." The
words came hard. *Ad Astra* had been battered by the shock
wave from the explosion, and so had its crew, although the
admiral had been the only one whose injuries might prove
fatal. "He doesn't look very much like himself."

The captain continued to stare past her for a few moments, and then said, "Okay." He pulled his gaze away from
the direction of where his father lay dying and looked back
at Morell. "Thank you, Uta," he said. He patted her hand
once more, then turned and stepped away. The wide door
between intensive care and the main section of the infirmary slid quietly open, and the captain walked through it
and toward the infirmary exit.

"Captain," Morell said, stepping forward to prevent the
door from closing. When he stopped and peered back at her,
she found that she had nothing to say, despite wanting very
much to find some way to help the captain. "Good night,"
she finally said.

"Good night, Doctor." Morell watched him leave, and
only after the door had closed behind him did she remember that she had wanted to give him something to help him
sleep. She took a step, intending to go after him, but then
she stopped. The captain was a secure enough man, she
knew, that he if needed help, he would ask for it.

Morell thought about returning to her quarters aboard
Enterprise and trying to sleep herself, but she felt too unsettled for that right now. She considered the café down on the
Plaza, but quickly discounted that possibility as well, not
wanting either to socialize or to sit alone in a public place.
Finally, without even really making a conscious decision,
she headed back into intensive care, back over to where the
admiral lay comatose. She retrieved a chair from the corner
of the bay and pulled it up beside the biobed. She didn't talk
to the admiral, or take his hand, but just sat quietly beside
him. She stayed with him for a long time, unable to help

him any more than she already had, but unwilling to let her patient go.

The sound penetrated into Sulu's dream, but only after it had come again did it rouse her from sleep. In an instant, she bounded out of bed, unsure if a red alert had woken her, but taking no chances and responding as though it had. As she stood tensed in the middle of her bedroom, waiting to hear information from the bridge or the next blare of the alert klaxon, the memory of what had happened to *Universe* and its crew rose hauntingly in her mind. The last two days had been filled with moments like this, the horror of the tragedy inescapable. She also knew that there would be many more such moments in the weeks and months ahead, and that she would always bear emotional scars from the terrible disaster.

The door signal buzzed, apparently for the third time, and Sulu tried to concentrate on the present. "Computer, what time is it?" she asked in the pitch-dark room. Before she had retired for the night, she had shuttered the viewing ports above her bed, just as she did every night, because she had difficulty falling asleep in even the faint illumination provided by the stars.

"The time is zero-one-thirty-five hours," the computer replied.

"One-thirty-five?" Sulu repeated, surprised that somebody would be calling on her now. No wonder she felt so tired. She shook her head, trying to clear away her grogginess. "Just a minute," she called out into the main room of her quarters. "Computer, lights up half."

As the lighting panels came on, Sulu moved to a circular armchair in the corner, where she had draped her robe before going to bed. She pulled the red, floor-length garment on over her body, tied its sash about her waist, and headed out of her bedroom.

At the entry to her quarters, she touched a control pad set

into the bulkhead, and the doors glided open. Captain Harriman stood in the corridor. "Captain," she said, but in the next second, she saw the torment in his face, the fatigue in his carriage. "John," she said, concerned not just about her commanding officer, but about her friend. "Come inside." She reached a hand to his elbow and guided him into her quarters.

"I'm sorry to wake you," Harriman said as the doors closed behind him. "I just needed to talk."

"Of course," Sulu said, walking with him over to the sofa that sat against the outer bulkhead. Here too, she had shuttered the viewing ports for *Enterprise*'s simulated night. Harriman sat down, and Sulu took a seat in an easy chair across a low table from him. It occurred to her to ask him if something had happened to upset him, but of course something had: *Universe* had exploded in a soundless flash in the middle of deep space, ending the lives of fifty-one members of Starfleet, and threatening the life of Harriman's father.

He leaned forward, his forearms resting atop his knees, and looked over at her. "I don't know where to begin, Demora," he said. He looked not just tired, but exhausted. She suspected that he'd barely slept since the accident.

"You don't have to know where to begin," she told him. "The last couple of days have been painful for all of us. I know you feel that, and that you also carry the crew's wounds in addition to your own. That's an awful lot to bear."

Harriman sat up and leaned against the back of the sofa. "I do feel terrible about the crew, about the loss they must feel," he said. "But it's also more than that."

"Your father," Sulu said, her tone sympathetic. Even though she knew that Harriman had not had much of a relationship with Blackjack for many years, she also understood that the threat of losing a parent changed things.

"My father, yeah," Harriman allowed. "But I'm not even

sure that's it. I've been feeling like this, feeling . . . disconnected . . . for a while."

Sulu had actually noticed a difference in Harriman during the past few months: he hadn't been as quick to laugh or to socialize, and he'd been sterner and more formal with the crew than she'd previously known him to be. The alteration in his behavior had not been drastic, though, and nothing she hadn't ascribed to some of the same pressures and concerns she'd been feeling herself. For too long, the crew of *Enterprise* had been involved less with the exploration of space and more with interstellar politics. Word had spread from Qo'noS that many Klingons had begun to clamor for Chancellor Azetbur to jettison the "embarrassment" of accepting Federation aid, while the Romulans continued to make noises and take actions that promised a coming conflict. All of which had taken a toll on her, and she'd assumed, on the captain as well. And ever since the Romulans had forcibly occupied the world of the Koltaari, Harriman had been involved in numerous high-level Starfleet meetings about how to address the mounting threat, a process that she guessed had worn him down further.

"I think it must be easier now than ever to feel disconnected," Sulu said. "The galaxy doesn't seem to be a very friendly place these days, does it?"

Harriman raised his eyebrows, the left side of his mouth curling into a humorless half-smile. "No," he agreed, "it sure doesn't."

"Well, why don't we do something about that?" she said, slapping her hands down on the tops of her knees. She knew that Harriman wanted to talk, but she thought that a change of tone might help him. "How about something to drink?" she asked, not waiting for an answer before getting up and crossing the room toward the food synthesizer.

"Sure," Harriman said behind her. "Why not?"

Rather than selecting something from the ship's menu, Sulu touched a control away from the food synthesizer. A different door slid open in the bulkhead, revealing a large compartment, about a meter square and half as deep. Inside stood a frame containing several dozen bottles of wine lying on their sides, their corks facing outward. An oenophile, Sulu had requested the special modification to her quarters a decade ago, when she had been promoted to be the ship's executive officer. Wine appreciation had been among her father's many leisure pursuits, one she had taken to during the course of her travels in Starfleet. "How about some port?" she asked, looking back over her shoulder.

Harriman shrugged. "Fine," he said, but this time he smiled with some apparent good humor. He knew of her passion for wines, and he had always professed an appreciation for people with passions; a "philophile," he liked to call himself.

Sulu peered into the compartment and found a Late Bottled Vintage port, 2289, from Argelius II. She reached into the climate-controlled environment—twelve degrees, with high humidity—and pulled out the bottle. She closed the compartment, then retrieved a stylish metal rack from a nearby shelf. After placing the port in the center of the rack, where it sat between a pair of hanging, stemmed glasses, she carried it over and set it down on the low table in front of the sofa.

"I think you'll like this," Sulu said, recalling which wines Harriman had enjoyed in the past. She used her thumbnail to break the seal at the top of the bottle. "It's dense, with a rich, full-fruit nose. Full-bodied, but it's got finesse and a great style." She circled her hand around the cap of the cork stopper and pulled, twisting it back and forth until it came free.

"At this point," Harriman said, "I'd settle for anything short of a phaser blast to the chest." He paused, then added, "Then again . . ." Sulu was pleased to hear him joke.

"Trust me," she said, pouring the fortified wine. "This will knock you off your feet better than a phaser blast." The port came out of the bottle opaque, so deeply purple that it almost appeared black. When she finished pouring, she set the bottle down and handed a glass across the table to him. "What shall we drink to?" she asked, sitting back down and lifting her own glass.

"To peace," Harriman suggested, leaning forward, a telling remark as to his state of mind, Sulu thought.

"To peace," she said, but then another toast came to mind. She quickly tried to assess whether or not she should offer it. After a moment, she did: "To Admiral Blackjack Harriman."

The captain looked at her for a few seconds without saying anything, his expression frozen, and she worried that she had upset him or hurt him by saying the wrong thing. But then he reached forward and touched his glass to hers. "To Blackjack," he said. He raised his glass toward his mouth, but then hesitated, apparently waiting for Sulu to drink first. She did, sipping the grape nectar. It tasted as good as she'd expected, and even better than when she'd first sampled it on Argelius a few years back. She only wished the occasion could have been celebratory, rather than mournful.

"I'm very sorry about your father, John," she said.

Harriman nodded his head. "I'm sorry too," he said, "even though I'm not entirely sure why. I mean, I don't want him to die, of course, but it's also not as though he and I were close. Except for admiral-to-captain discussions, we haven't even talked in years." He seemed to consider his statement for a moment, and then said, "Maybe we've never even *really* talked."

"It doesn't matter," Sulu said. "He's your father. He's a part of you—*literally* a part of you—and a part of your life. Whether you're close or not, you're connected to each other."

"By genetics?" Harriman asked. "By blood?" He set his glass of port down on the table. "Is that enough?"

"It's certainly enough for some things," Sulu said, hoping that she could offer her friend some words to bring him to an acceptance of his feelings. He had just toasted to galactic peace, but she thought that what he might benefit most from right now would be peace of mind. "It's enough to make you feel sad that his life's been put in jeopardy."

"I feel like a hypocrite," Harriman said. He stood up, moved out from behind the table, and paced across the room. "I've had no personal relationship with the man for years, and I think he's arrogant and self-involved. He's strict and unyielding, and he sees the universe in black and white and nothing in between." Harriman stopped and turned to face Sulu from near the food synthesizer. "The universe just isn't like that," he said.

"No, it's not," Sulu concurred. "It's a lot more interesting than that." Sulu had met and worked with the admiral on several occasions throughout her career, including being debriefed by him after the mission to Devron II, so she knew firsthand his shortcomings. More important, from her long friendship with Harriman, she understood the impact that Blackjack's behavior as a father had landed on his son.

"I've never figured out why he feels the need to be so strident," Harriman said.

"It's his way or the spaceway," Sulu said, invoking the old boomer saying. "That's for sure."

"He'd simply call it confidence," Harriman said, walking back over to the sitting area. "Something he never thought I had much of."

"Oh, I don't know about that," Sulu said. "From what Commander Dane told me, you showed the admiral quite a bit of confidence at Askalon Five." She easily recalled the story she had been told almost twenty years ago by *Enterprise*'s executive officer at the time, about how the captain had transported the admiral from the bridge and into the brig.

"I doubt Blackjack thought of it as confidence," Harriman countered. "Something more like insubordination."

"Either way," Sulu said, "you impressed him."

"Yeah, I guess so," Harriman admitted. He was quiet for a

moment, and his gaze drifted from Sulu. "This wasn't supposed to happen," he finally said.

For a second, Sulu didn't know to what he was referring,
but then concluded that he must mean the accidental destruction of *Universe*. "No," she said, unable to keep a note
of sadness from entering her voice.

"I think one thing that's bothering me is that I don't like
my father," Harriman said, looking back down at Sulu. "But
I want to."

Sulu sipped at her port, remembering similar feelings
she'd had about her own father. "When my mother died and I
had to go live with my father," she said, "a man I'd never even
met before that, I hated him. Right from the beginning, without even getting to know him. But when I got to know him,
you know what? I still didn't like him. But I also didn't *want*
to like or love him, because he represented things to me: his
own absence from the first six years of my life, the loss of my
mother, change. But even though I didn't want to, when I let
go of those things, I eventually did come to like him and love
him." She paused, wanting to emphasize what she would say
next. "Maybe you can do the same with your father."

"Maybe," Harriman said slowly. He turned and walked
back across the room again. For as long as she'd known him,
Harriman had been peripatetic; even in staff meetings, he
had a tendency to wander from his chair and walk about the
conference room while speaking. "But there's really nothing
to let go of. I haven't liked my father for a long time, but I
have forgiven him."

"For what, exactly?" Sulu asked. She sipped again at her
port.

Harriman reached the end of the room and headed back
toward the sitting area. "For whatever he did that made him
fail to be a father to me. For most of my life, he's simply be-
haved like my commanding officer. But I don't harbor that
anymore. I used to, and I suppose I still could, but why

would I? What good would it do me, or him, or anybody else? Mom's gone, Lynn's gone, my grandparents are gone; the only ones left are him and me."

"And Amina," Sulu said.

Instantly, Harriman's bearing changed. He seemed to draw himself up, the troubles affecting him falling away. "Yes, there's Amina," he said softly. He navigated around the table and sat back down on the sofa. "And there's you and Xintal and Rafe and the others. I didn't mean that there aren't people who I love, or that there aren't people who love me. I meant family."

"You have two families, John," Sulu told him. "The one you were born into, and the one you choose every day of your life."

"Yes," he said. "And my chosen family is very important to me. But I feel . . . adrift, I guess . . . that I don't have the other. I know I haven't had it for a long time, but I've still always had the potential for it. But if my father dies . . ."

"I think it's natural to feel those things," Sulu said. "I also think it's all right to dislike your father. What would be worse would be to pretend to like him, or even to actually like him despite his bad behavior. Then you'd truly be a hypocrite."

"I feel sorry for my father," Harriman said, looking down. "He was estranged from his own father when *he* died, and for his own life to end with him estranged from his son . . . it's just sad."

"It is," Sulu said. "But you can't change your father; only he can do that."

"I guess I need to accept that," Harriman said. "Accept all of it." He sat quietly for a few minutes, and Sulu let the silence stretch out, wanting to allow him to deal with whatever he was thinking and feeling. At last, he looked up and said, "I'm also worried about my chosen family, Demora, and about the extended family of the *Enterprise* crew."

"We've been through a lot recently," Sulu said.

"I want you to make sure they're all right," Harriman told her. "Work with the medical staff to get them through this difficult time. Morell and Benzon and some of the nurses have some psychiatric training."

"I will," Sulu said. "I was going to ask you if we should make counselors available to the crew."

"Let's encourage activities too," Harriman said. "It's been hard for a while. I know we've had little downtime, and we're not likely to get much more right now. I've noticed a decline in social activities throughout the ship, so I'd like to do what we can to change that. I want the crew to have some enjoyment in their days, and to lean on each other when they need to." He raised his arms and wiped his hands down his face, sighing heavily. "I hate that they're going through this."

"It's not just them, John," Sulu said, realizing that Harriman had not bothered to include himself as being affected by recent events.

He looked at her in shock, as though it had never occurred to him that the *Universe* tragedy had impacted him the same as it had the crew. But then he seemed to recover from his surprise. "I know," he said. "I'll speak to Uta too. So should you."

"Yes, sir," Sulu said, recognizing the command as something more than friendly advice.

Harriman stood up from the sofa. "I should let you get back to sleep," he said. "Thanks for listening. Sorry for stopping by so late."

Demora got up from her chair. "At least I got to try some of this port," she said. She lifted her glass, drank the small amount left in it, then set it down.

Harriman walked out around the table and headed for the door. Just before he got there, though, he stopped and turned back. He didn't say anything right away, and he looked to Sulu as though he was trying to make a decision about something. Finally, he said, "I keep thinking about Iron Mike Paris."

"He saved my life," Sulu said, her reaction almost automatic. The memory of the events on Devron II remained as fresh for her as though they had happened yesterday.

Harriman nodded, and Sulu expected him to say more about Iron Mike, but instead, all he said was "Good night, Demora."

"Good night," she replied. As he left, she looked after him, sensing that he had just attempted to tell her something. She thought about it, but then, unable to conclude anything, shook off the feeling. She watched the doors slide closed, then sat heavily back down in the chair. On the table, she saw, Harriman's glass of port sat untouched. She thought about drinking it herself, but instead, she got up and went back to bed.

It was a long time before Demora fell back to sleep, though, and when she did, she dreamed of Captain Harriman, Iron Mike Paris, and those horrible days on Devron II.

Azetbur, leader of the High Council, chancellor of the Klingon Empire, seethed. Even after she had calmed the uproar in her office, it required all of her willpower not to dive across the length of the table and wrap her hands around the throat of the Romulan envoy. Instead, she calmly rose, conscious not to allow her hands to roll into fists, though tempted by the release the feel of her sharp fingernails against her palm would have given her. "Thank you, Consul Vinok," she said. "Please express my appreciation to the praetor for providing the Klingon Empire with this information." She imagined the green blood of the envoy spurting through her fingers as she squeezed his ignoble life from him.

"Chancellor," Vinok said, standing himself and bowing his head in her direction. "Thank you for seeing me on such short notice."

Azetbur nodded, but thought, *As if I could have done otherwise.* The praetor had sent word of the Starfleet treachery to the senior members of the Klingon High Council, and not simply to Azetbur herself—not technically a violation of the diplomatic protocols between the two governments, but a move clearly designed to undermine Klingon relations with the Federation. Had the Romulan intelligence been delivered to her exclusively, she would have quietly sought to confirm or deny it, with the hope of being able to preserve the relationship between Qo'noS and Earth. But now . . .

Consul Vinok withdrew from Azetbur's office, his footsteps echoing on the stone floor, the tall, ornamented doors swinging open at his approach. Beyond the threshold, four members of Klingon Internal Security stood guard. Two of those, Azetbur knew, would escort the Romulan from the fortress of the Great Hall.

"Chancellor," Brigadier Kuron blustered. "We must—"

"Silence," Azetbur said firmly, waiting for the doors to shut behind Vinok. She could see the ire on Kuron's long, angular face—ire for the Federation and for her, she was sure—but he quieted, just as he had done when she'd quashed his vociferous reactions during the Romulan's presentation. The doors, climbing halfway up the stone walls to the vaulted ceilings and arcing to a peak, swung closed with a loud thump, resounding in the great room. "Your opinion is of value to us, Kuron," Azetbur said with tact, a weapon her father had taught her to use in her youth. "But it is not of value to the Romulans, nor is it their place to hear it." She sat back down at the head of the table, her right hand automatically coming up to take hold of the walking stick leaning against her chair. In front of her, to her left, a number of isolinear data spikes sat heaped on the tabletop.

"The Romulans already know what I have to say," Kuron protested. "What *all* of us should have to say." He raised a leather-gloved fist, triangular silver teeth marching up the fingers, and pointed around the table at the three other High Council members present, though he refrained from gesturing toward Azetbur. "I say that the Federation is our enemy and seeks to crush us."

Azetbur waited, her hand tightening about the top of the walking stick, hoping that she would not have to be the first one to defend the Empire's relationship with the Federation. In the wake of her father's death eighteen years ago, she had stepped forward and assumed the mantle of Klingon leadership. She had signed the Khitomer Accords, enacting the peace with the Federation for which her father had so desperately worked, and she had strived since then to maintain that peace. But because of her years of service to that cause, her voice now carried less weight than it once had; her positions were so well known and so well established that the actual content of what she said now was often overlooked.

"Do you really think that the Federation is our enemy?" Councillor Kest asked across the table from Kuron. The only one of the senior Council members not in the Klingon Defense Force—he worked for Imperial Intelligence—he still cut an imposing figure. Bald, with a thin mustache falling past the sides of his mouth to his chin, he appeared almost sinister. "Do you really think the Federation has given us food and energy and other aid for all these years, helped us rebuild our infrastructure and keep our military intact, so that they could then face a reinvigorated opponent in battle?"

"Klingons would," Kuron declared. "Klingons would seek the glory of battle against a worthy adversary."

"Klingons, yes," Kest allowed. "But humans? Vulcans? *Betazoids?*" Azetbur saw that she had been right to convene the four senior Council members for this meeting, rather than the entire Council, more than two dozen strong. While Kest no longer openly allied himself with Azetbur—few did these days, amid the public grumbling about the ignominy of continuing to accept Federation charity—he at least provided a thoughtful, stabilizing voice, a voice that could easily have been lost in a larger gathering.

"The Federation does not seek honorable battle," Kuron persisted. "They seek to wipe us out with a single weapon."

"If that were true," Azetbur said, "then they had that weapon in their grasp years ago. After Praxis was destroyed, all the Federation had to use to defeat us was apathy. If they'd ignored us, if they hadn't responded to our sudden and significant needs, then we would not now be able to feed our people, much less be able to go into battle."

"We are not now able to go into battle," General Kaarg said. "Not full-scale battle against a fully committed adversary. Yes, the Federation provides us aid, but not enough for us to make ourselves as strong as possible." The general, one of the highest-ranking officers in the Klingon Defense Force, had sat through the Romulan envoy's presentation saying very little, as had his peer in the military, General Gorak. Both commanded large segments of the KDF, but the similarities between the two men ended there, Azetbur knew.

"General," Brigadier Kuron said, "do you doubt the might of the Empire?"

"I do not doubt the Empire, Kuron," Kaarg said. "But as Kahless the Unforgettable told us, 'Destroying an empire to win a war is no victory.' " Kaarg, beefy and physically sluggish, had earned a name for himself as a battlefield tactician, defeating enemies not on the basis of force, but through careful planning and clever strategy. Two years ago, he had managed to forestall a Tholian incursion into space claimed by the Empire, utilizing a squadron of vessels dwarfed by his foe's. Azetbur had heard some classify him derogatorily as a backroom planner, a thinker who lacked the ability to genuinely lead. Yet he had still stormed up the ranks of the Klingon military to his present position, and to an upper seat on the High Council.

"In whatever battles we fight," General Gorak offered, "we will be victorious, or we will die honorable deaths. That is the Klingon way." A stark contrast to Kaarg, Gorak was lean and muscular, and had developed a reputation as a warrior's warrior, leading his men on the front ranks. Within the last year, he had crushed a major uprising on Ganalda IV, charging the battlements himself and slaying the rebel leader with a *d'k tahg* through the heart. From every report Azetbur had received, Gorak's men worshipped him, and would follow him all the way to *Sto-Vo-Kor*. "But we need a reason to go to battle," Gorak finished. He said nothing about how one of his men, Ditagh, worked even now to provide him with that reason by undermining the trilateral peace negotiations.

"There is the fact of Federation treachery," Kuron fumed.

"It is a fact in name only," Azetbur insisted, but she understood at once that the veracity of the Romulan assertion was irrelevant. The praetor would not have sent an envoy with sensor logs demonstrating the Starfleet testing of a metaweapon if those logs could have been easily dismissed. In one way or another, she would have to address the Romulan allegation, as well as its implications.

"Do you doubt what we just saw, Chancellor?" Kuron said, leaping to his feet and pointing at the clutch of data spikes. Azetbur and the councillors, along with the Romulan envoy, had viewed the contents of some of the spikes on a large monitor set into the wall to the left of the table, opposite the great chair that sat raised on a dais to the right. "Do you doubt—"

Azetbur swung the walking stick—the long, tapered incisor of some long-extinct saber-toothed beast—in a wide arc and brought it down on the tabletop, filling the chamber of her office with a loud report. The data spikes jumped. "Do not question me, Kuron," Azetbur said. "I doubt everybody and everything. That is my duty as chancellor." She paused, fixing the brigadier's gaze with her own. "Now sit down," she commanded him.

Kuron remained standing, though, and Azetbur thought that the challenge to her leadership from within the upper

High Council had finally come. She tightened her hand around the walking stick—it had belonged to her father—and brought her free hand up to the *d'k tahg* she wore at her waist. She prepared to vault to her feet and fight—for her chancellorship, and for her life. She had fought traitors to assume and keep her position, had survived early attempts from almost all quarters to see her relinquish it, and had daily battled her own prejudices and her own instinct for violence in order to do what was best for her people. She would not step down quietly.

But then General Kaarg stood from his chair, rising slowly. When he reached his full height, he turned his gaze upon Kuron, his eyes peering intensely from the soft, slack flesh of his face. "The chancellor told you to sit," Kaarg told the brigadier calmly, though there was no mistaking the menace in his voice. Azetbur saw Kuron flex the fingers of both hands, the material of his gloves making scraping sounds as he did so. She thought for a moment that he might actually engage Kaarg, but then he returned to his seat, fixing his eyes downward.

It would not be the last time that the soft-brained partisan would confront her, Azetbur was sure, but that assessment concerned her very little; the brigadier's blatant and headstrong opposition called too much attention to itself to be truly dangerous. What gave her pause had been the reactions of Kest and Gorak to Kuron's brief challenge: neither of them had moved to defend the Chancellor of the Klingon Empire. She might have expected that of Gorak, considering his furtive machinations to sabotage the peace process, but that also told Azetbur something she needed to know about Kest. Public dissent for the Empire's current relationship with the Federation must have been stronger than she thought for him to fail to come to her defense. Now more than ever, she would have to proceed with caution and vigilance. At least General Kaarg had revealed his loyalties to her.

As Azetbur pulled the walking stick from the table, returning it to its place at her side, Kest asked, "Federation treachery or no, what action will you take now, Chancellor?"

"I will have the Romulan information analyzed," she said, dropping her hand onto the collection of data spikes. "If necessary, I will demand an explanation from the Federation."

"An explanation," Kuron repeated disgustedly, but he did not look up and he said nothing more.

"Will an explanation be enough?" Kest asked.

"We will see," Azetbur said, but she already knew that an explanation would *not* be enough. Fury boiled within her, and she imagined wielding her walking stick like a bludgeon, pounding the treacherous life out of whoever had put her in this position. Either the Romulans had manufactured the tale of a new Starfleet metaweapon, or the Federation had lied to her about their condemnation and repudiation of the creation of such weapons. Whichever the case, Azetbur would now be forced to react. And she would do so, but she pledged to herself that the action she would take would be of her own choosing, and not dictated by the political maneuverings of either the Romulans or the Federation. "I will do whatever I must to protect the Empire," she concluded.

"Even if it means opposing the Federation?" Gorak asked.

Azetbur knew that she would seek to preserve the peace, because that served all sides, but she also knew that her only true loyalty was to her people. If she had to, she would fight against the Romulans or beside them, she would fight against the worlds of the Federation or beside them, as long as, in the end, the Klingon Empire remained standing. And it would matter not at all to Azetbur if that meant standing amid the dead bodies of Romulans, or the dead bodies of humans and Vulcans and Betazoids. All that mattered was Qo'noS.

"Yes," she said, "even if it means opposing the Federation." All eyes turned toward her then, even those of Kuron, all no doubt attempting to take the measure of her words. Azetbur did not wait for them to reach their judgments. Instead, she stood and addressed them. "I will convene a gathering of the full Council in a few days," she told them. "We will discuss these matters and my decisions about them then." She lifted her walking stick, turned, and walked away from the table, effectively dismissing the councillors.

Azetbur strode over to the wall opposite the door, in which a dozen tall, peaked windows stood open. As the sounds of chairs scraping along the floor and of retreating footsteps reached her from behind, she peered out from the top floor of the Great Hall at the First City, the capital of Qo'noS. In the distance, she spied the ritual flames of the Temples of Rogax and Molgar, both reaching upward like fiery fingers clutching at the sky. The spires of imperial structures dotted the urban landscape, proud and mighty symbols of a proud and mighty race. And down below the window, marking the entrance to the Great Hall, stood the great bronze statue of Kahless and Morath, depicted in their epic twelve-day battle over honor.

Azetbur gazed out of the window in silence for long moments, until she heard the door to her office open and somebody enter. She turned to see her efficient aide, Rinla, approaching.

"Chancellor," Rinla said. "Do you require anything?"

"Yes," Azetbur said, because she had already begun to formulate a means of dealing with the Romulans and the Federation. "Contact the Romulan space station Algeron," she said. "I want to talk to Ambassador Kage."

MINUS SIX: SMOKE

Los Tirasol Mentir swam with abandon. He flexed his muscles with all of his strength, sending massive sinusoidal motion coursing through the length of his body—down from his head, through his torso, and into his tail structure and caudal fin. The walls and floor of the artificial watercourse dashed past to either side and below, a ceiling of air above. He could feel the cooling touch of the lubrication he secreted, allowing a laminar flow of water past his scales.

Inside, though, he felt only heat. His grief manifested as anger, the terrible end of *Universe* and its crew seeming like a betrayal by life itself. Nor had the tragedy finished its taking; Blackjack Harriman, a man Mentir had called a friend for half a century, lay comatose in the station's infirmary, waiting helplessly for the black tides of death to envelop him and carry him away.

Mentir thrust his tail left, right, and on, channeling his rage into movement. He sliced through the water with ease, his short but limblike pectoral fins swept back along his sides and, together with his smaller dorsal and pelvic fins, keeping his body stable as he swam. Once, twice, half a dozen times around the two-hundred-meter elliptical canal, racing like a silvery torpedo, Mentir sought to exhaust himself. He spent the energy he could, attempting to starve his emotions of their force.

Finally, another half-dozen circuits at speed, and fatigue set in. His fury abated, but in its wake came a mournful emptiness. Mentir stilled his tail, and he slowed and dropped, until he floated just a few centimeters above the floor of the waterway. He closed his eyes and tried to blank his mind, but unwanted images assaulted him: he pictured the silent explosion that had torn apart *Universe* and its crew, envisioned the expanding shock wave that had pummeled *Ad Astra*, saw his friend smashing headfirst into a bulkhead.

Seeking to distract himself, Mentir tried to imagine being back home in the depths of Alonis. But the water here, maintained as it was for all the inhabitants of Space Station KR-3, could not compare to his native seas. Here, the color, the density, the motion, the solids content, all varied too much from his home waters to allow him even a moment's fantasy. And although he had designed his quarters and office here on the station to more closely mimic the familiar environment of Alonis, he still often found himself longing for the oceans of his birth.

A pair of short midrange tones pulsed through the canal, followed by a spurt of muffled clicks and squeals. Mentir opened his eyes, immediately recognizing the communications signal, as well as the sound of somebody attempting to contact him, though he could not at this distance distinguish the "words." He switched his tail once, moving slowly forward and upward, until he rose to the midpoint of the channel. Then he surged into motion. A third of the way around, he arrived at an underwater communications console, one of three installed on the station. Another had been set up in his quarters, and another in his office.

Mentir swam in close to the console and focused. His people had no opposable digits, but they possessed a short-range psychokinetic ability, which they utilized to manipulate water into effectively solid tools. With his mind, Mentir pushed a concentration of water against an activation pad, then opened his short, flat snout and issued a quick series of snaps and chirps. The universal translator in the communications console, he knew, would broadcast his sounds as "This is Admiral Mentir. Go ahead."

"*Admiral, this is Dr. Van Riper in the infirmary,*" came the response, interpreted into the language of the Alonis. "*I thought you'd want to know: Admiral Harriman has regained consciousness.*"

At once, Mentir felt a rush of energy course through his body. After being operated on a day and a half ago, Blackjack had remained in a coma, with the prognosis for his recovery indeterminate at best. The news that his chief medical officer had just delivered came as a welcome surprise.

A string of questions flooded Mentir's mind—*Is Blackjack lucid? Has he recovered any of his strength? Does this mean he'll be able to recuperate completely?*—but he would ask those once he arrived at the infirmary; right now, he wanted only to see his friend. "Thank you, Doctor," he clicked and twittered. "I'll be right there. Mentir out." He closed the channel with a burst of thought.

Just past the communications console, a small spur led from the main oval of the watercourse. Mentir swam into it, to where he had left his environmental suit when he'd entered the channel. He slipped his head inside the helmet, then settled his body atop the open, formfitting suit, which he maneuvered closed around him using his psychokinesis. He heard the cottony *sniks* of the electromagnetic locks as they fastened, followed by the whisper of the environmental controls as they automatically activated. The suit held a layer of water against Mentir's scales, and adjusted the characteristics of the water so that it more closely matched that of Alonis. The unit also included an aquatic rebreathing device.

Once secure in his portable artificial environment, Mentir swam forward to the antigrav chair in which he traveled when not in water. He settled back into the seat and directed it upward, operating it with slight but specific body movements. The chair slowly lifted out of the channel, water spilling back down with a splatter. As he rose, he saw few people in the natatorium—the elliptical waterway surrounded a long, wide swimming pool—and those present swam quietly and alone. Since the news that a starship had been lost had reached KR-3, the mood among Mentir's crew had been understandably somber.

Mentir floated into a locker room adjoining the swim center, and then to a smaller room within. There, several fans dried both his environmental suit and his antigrav chair. Then he exited into a corridor and headed for the nearest turbolift. The infirmary was actually housed on this level, but in a different one of the station's three arms. Only five decks through, Space Station KR-3 looked from above like a letter Y, the wide arms of the station meeting at obtuse angles.

Mentir entered the lift and identified his destination, a device in his helmet transmitting the sound of his sub-aqua voice out into the air. The antigrav chair swayed slightly as the turbolift began its horizontal journey, and Mentir felt momentarily unsettled. He realized that he had anxiety about visiting the infirmary. He had not seen Blackjack since his old friend had been brought back to KR-3 after the accident; Mentir had instead heeded the counsel of *Enterprise*'s chief medical officer, who had suggested that staying away might be the better course.

Blackjack, Mentir thought. They'd met fifty-seven years ago, when the Starfleet vessel *Allegiance* had arrived at Alonis on a diplomatic mission. Mentir had just been embarking on what would turn out to be a fleeting political career, and Ensign Harriman had been one of *Allegiance*'s officers selected to accompany the Federation delegation. They'd met during the conference and had quickly become friends; Mentir had particularly appreciated Blackjack's straightforward manner and punctilious nature, characteristics that had only grown stronger through the years.

The turbolift slowed, crossing the threshold into the station's hub. Mentir felt the lift sweep into a broad arc, then pick up speed again as it passed out of the hub and into another of the station's arms. The infirmary, he knew, was not much farther.

After the summit on Alonis all those years ago, Mentir had stayed in contact with Blackjack, and the two had grown close. Back in those days, they'd often joked that they knew far more about each other's culture than did the diplomats. And years later, when Mentir had decided to apply to Starfleet Academy, Blackjack—a starship captain at that point—had helped him become only the second Alonis accepted. These days, several more of Mentir's people served in Starfleet, and a dialogue had begun on his homeworld about whether or not to submit a request for membership in the Federation. Although Mentir knew that numerous issues would have to be resolved before Alonis would be invited to join, he hoped that it would happen within the next two or three decades. And Blackjack had supported that position, becoming an outspoken proponent for the Alonis over the past several years. There were few people in Mentir's life whom he respected and appreciated as much as his old friend.

The turbolift slowed again, this time coming to a stop. The doors parted, revealing one of the entrances to the infirmary directly ahead. Mentir eased from the lift, crossed the corridor, and entered. He moved through the main section of the infirmary, past a series of empty biobeds, and over to the wide door leading to the intensive-care section. The door opened as he reached it, and he floated inside.

As the door closed behind him, he spotted KR-3's chief

medical officer standing at a console to the right, studying a readout. "Doctor," Mentir said, and the lanky physician turned at the sound of his voice.

"Admiral," Van Riper said.

"How is he?" Mentir asked. Then, feeling the need to say his friend's name, he asked, "How is Admiral Harriman?"

"We don't know," Van Riper said, walking over from the console. "But he doesn't appear to be appreciably better, even though he's no longer unconscious."

"So you haven't upgraded your prognosis?" Mentir asked, surprised. He had expected better news than this.

"We haven't," Van Riper said. "There's just no way to tell how fast or how well Admiral Harriman's brain will heal."

"But surely waking from his coma must be a positive sign," Mentir said, seeking some measure of hope.

"Yes," Van Riper said cautiously, stretching the word out, "but that's not in itself cause to believe that the admiral can overcome his injuries."

"I see," Mentir said, though he wasn't necessarily sure that he did. "Is he lucid?"

"He seems to be," Van Riper said, "but he's also extremely tired, and Dr. Morell has reported that he's shown some signs of distress." Even though Blackjack was being treated on Space Station KR-3, Mentir knew that he still remained in the primary care of the *Enterprise*'s CMO, who had first treated him.

"Distress?" Mentir asked, but then he heard the door open behind him. He turned his antigrav chair to see Blackjack's son enter.

"Admiral," Captain Harriman said, his expression stoic. He did not look as though he'd been sleeping particularly well, though.

"Captain," Mentir returned. He knew that there must be some physical resemblance between father and son, but he had never been able to see it. Nor had he ever seen much similarity in their personalities. But then, few people could match up against Blackjack; he cut such a commanding figure, tall and muscular, with a strong, self-assured presence. Captain Harriman was his own man, of course, and a fine commander, but he was not his father. "I assume that Dr. Van Riper contacted you about your father."

"Actually, I did," came another voice.

Mentir looked around to see Dr. Morell approaching from one of the intensive-care bays. "Doctor," he greeted her.

"Admiral," Morell said, and then, looking with some apparent concern to the younger Harriman, "Captain."

"May we see him?" Captain Harriman asked.

Morell hesitated, peering at Mentir and Dr. Van Riper in quick succession before looking back at Harriman. "May I see you privately for a moment, Captain?" she asked. Mentir thought that she seemed very uncomfortable.

"It's all right, Doctor," Harriman said, and Mentir got the impression that the captain knew what Morell had to tell him. Mentir thought that he knew as well. "Go ahead."

"I mentioned to Admiral Harriman that you and Admiral Mentir would be coming to see him," Morell said, still clearly ill at ease. "He got . . . um . . . agitated."

"He doesn't want visitors?" Dr. Van Riper asked, but Mentir knew that was not the case.

"He doesn't want *me*," Captain Harriman said.

"No, sir," Morell agreed. "And I'm afraid, under the circumstances, it wouldn't be a good idea for you to go in. The admiral's in no shape to be upset."

"I understand," the captain said, and Mentir could see that he did, although Mentir himself did not—at least not entirely. He knew that a rift had long ago developed between father and son, but he had never known why that had happened, or why the two had never resolved whatever issues lay between them. Mentir had inquired a few times many years ago, but Blackjack had always deflected the conversation elsewhere, never once bringing up the subject himself.

Captain Harriman started to leave, but Mentir stopped him. "Would you like me to tell your father something for you?" he asked.

"Tell him—" the captain began, but then he seemed to catch himself. "No. No thank you, Admiral." He turned and exited.

A stony silence drifted into the room, which Mentir finally broke. "I'd like to see him then," he said.

"Of course," Morell said. "This way." She gestured toward one end of the long room. "I'll have to ask you to stay only a short time, Admiral. Just a couple of minutes at most. Admiral Harriman is obviously very weak and very tired."

"I understand, Doctor." Mentir followed Morell to the bay in which Blackjack lay. She walked up to the side of the biobed and leaned down near her patient's face, blocking him from view.

"Admiral Mentir is here to see you," she said quietly. She backed away, allowing Mentir to maneuver his antigrav chair in beside the biobed. He peered over at his friend and felt horrified by what he saw. Bandages swathed the entire top of Blackjack's head, and covered most of one side of his face. But even where his head and face were not visible beneath the gauze, the impression was that of flesh that had been compromised, bone that had been fractured. His complexion barely contrasted with his bandages, so pallid did it appear. His lips had thinned into an ashen line. A respirator encircled his chest and evidently breathed for him. Blackjack looked bloodless, his body seeming too frail to hold life within it.

Mentir leaned in toward his longtime friend. "Blackjack," he said gently, "it's Tirasol." Blackjack's one visible eyelid fluttered, but did not open all the way. His eye appeared hazy and unfocused, as though attempting to see through a fog. He looked not just exhausted, but hurt.

In pain, Mentir thought. Both physically and emotionally.

He waited a few moments, and when Blackjack said nothing, and seemed to see nothing, Mentir thought that he should probably leave. But as he prepared to move away, Blackjack's gaze found him. "Tirasol," he said in a voice barely strong enough to be called a whisper, the syllables almost lost in the murmur of the respirator. "I wanted . . . to tell you . . . it worked."

" 'It worked'?" Mentir repeated, unsure what Blackjack meant. Was he coherent, or had his medical condition rendered his words meaningless?

"The . . ." Blackjack sputtered. "The Romulans . . ."

Mentir waited for Blackjack to continue, but he said no more. "What about the Romulans?" he finally asked. "Blackjack, what about the Romulans?" But Blackjack's eyelid flickered closed. Had he been hallucinating, or disoriented, or had he actually been trying to tell Mentir something? "Blackjack," Mentir said. "Blackjack."

"Admiral," Dr. Morell said, moving back in beside Mentir. "I think that's enough."

"Can you revive him, Doctor?" Mentir asked. "Can you bring him more awake?"

"I don't know," Morell said. "But certainly not without putting him at risk."

"All right," Mentir said. He looked at his friend, and felt as though he didn't really recognize him. "If he gets stronger, if he can talk," he said, "I want to know immediately."

"Yes, sir."

Mentir backed his antigrav chair away from the biobed, taking one last look at Blackjack. Then he turned and headed out of the bay, wondering if his friend would ever be the same again.

The Klingon recording device sailed through the air in a high arc, nearly striking the ceiling before it descended to the conference table with a crash. The device skittered across the flaxen surface, until it came to rest not far from where the Federation ambassador, Endara, sat. He looked at it, Kage thought, as though it might leap at his throat at any moment.

"What is your explanation for this?" Kage asked angrily from across the room, from where he had tossed the recorder. The storm he forced into his voice belied the calmness within him. The data on the recorder had been transmitted directly to him by Chancellor Azetbur yesterday, and she in turn had received it from the Romulan government. Kage assumed that Ambassador Kamemor had by now been provided the information as well. Both yesterday and today had been scheduled as open days in the Algeron talks, when no negotiating sessions would take place, but after Kage had learned of the Romulan sensor logs and consulted with the chancellor about them, he had requested this special session. He suspected that if he had not done so, Kamemor would have.

At the end of the conference table, among the other four members of his staff, Ambassador Endara seemed to compose himself. He looked up from where the recorder had landed and over at Kage. "Am I to infer that you want me to examine the information on this device, Ambassador?" Endara asked, his tone steady and not acerbic, even if his words were. He made no move to pick up the recorder.

Kage walked slowly—and he hoped, menacingly—toward the Federation ambassador. He glanced at Kamemor and her two aides, sitting facing him from the center of the table. Their attentions, he noted with satisfaction, were firmly on him, as were those of his own two aides, who sat on the nearer side. Kage took his time approaching Endara, wanting to maximize the tension in the room. For the same reason, he had been uncharacteristically but intentionally late to the session this morning.

When he reached the table, Kage bent over it and rested

his palms flat on its surface. He leaned in over the corner toward the Federation delegation, his eyes focused on Endara's. "No," he said.

"No?" Endara asked, clearly confused. "You throw this device in my direction—" He gestured toward the recorder. "—demand some sort of explanation, and you don't want me to look at it?" Endara actually peered toward the Romulans, evidently seeking their support. Kage did not look away from the Federation ambassador, though, so he did not know how Kamemor and her aides reacted, but they said nothing.

Kage waited until Endara looked back up at him, and then said, "No, I don't want you to examine the data on the recorder. What I want is for you to explain why the Federation has developed and tested a metaweapon—a *first-strike* weapon—and why you lied about it."

"What?" Endara said, incredulous. "Ambassador Kage, with all due respect, those claims are absurd."

"'Respect'?" Kage roared, forcing himself to anger. He knew where he needed to take this meeting for the good of the Klingon Empire, and on the journey he took to arrive there, he would have to be convincing. "You sit here all these months and tell us lies. What do you know of respect?" Kage reached across the table and snatched up the recorder, then slammed it down in front of Endara. "Here are the sensor readings of the Starfleet test," he said, his voice still loud. He glared across the device at the Federation ambassador.

Slowly and carefully, Endara rose from his chair and faced Kage across the corner of the table. "I'll thank you not to threaten me, Ambassador," he said.

Kage smiled coldly, then turned and walked dramatically across the room, his performance worthy, he thought, of the best Klingon opera. He turned back toward the table. "But it is all right for your people to threaten mine. Worse, to plot for their demise." Kage saw that Ditagh and his other aide, Gorreg, seemed to be enjoying the confrontation, and that even one of the Romulans, Vreenak, appeared pleased by the developments.

"Ambassador," Endara said, "whatever information you think you have—"

"Look at it," Kage yelled, pointing at the recorder.

For a moment, the Federation ambassador did not move, and Kage considered what other tack he might have to take in order to accomplish his aims. But then Endara reached forward and picked up the recorder. He studied the device for a few seconds, then touched a button and watched the readout. When he finally looked up again, he wore an expression of shock and disbelief.

"Where did you get these readings?" Endara wanted to know.

"From our Romulan friends," Kage said, emphasizing the last word. Of course, before this, the Romulan and Klingon governments had shared nothing but antipathy and distrust for decades, since a series of technological trade agreements. But Kage needed to put the Federation ambassador—and the Federation itself—on the defensive.

Endara sat down heavily, dropping his hands—one holding the recorder—onto the table. "These sensor readings appear to have been made in Federation space," he said, still visibly stunned.

"A violation minor compared to the Federation's treachery," Vreenak hissed. Ambassador Kamemor said nothing, but continued to observe the proceedings.

Endara peered over at the Romulan delegation. He breathed in heavily and seemed to try to regroup, then addressed Kage once more. "If these readings are accurate," he said, "they present no breach of established treaty. Just the other day, Ambassador, you balked at the possibility of Qo'noS agreeing not to build metaweapons."

"I took issue with signing a treaty that would, in extreme cases, enfeeble my people," Kage said. "But I also clearly indicated our opposition to the use and even the construction of such weapons." He attempted to goad Endara into making the accusation he must make, and that would ultimately serve the goals of the Empire. "I mentioned wanting the opportunity to develop them only if threatened by another power, such as the Gorn or the Tholians. But you promised to sign a treaty banning metaweapons, and the Federation president has also pledged to Chancellor Azetbur, on several occasions, that your people did not and would not make such armaments."

"We were all told that," Vreenak spoke up again, addressing Endara, "and yet there is the proof of your deceit." He pointed at the recorder. Again, Kamemor said nothing, but simply sat by and watched.

"You presume that these readings are accurate," Endara said to Vreenak, a note of defiance entering his tone. "I am not convinced that they are." He looked over at Kage. "You have personally dealt with the Romulans for decades, Ambassador," he said. "Do you always take them at their word?"

"The Federation lies," Vreenak charged, rising to his feet, "and you dare to hurl aspersions at us?" He pushed his chair back. "Ambassador Kamemor, we should end these talks right now. If we cannot trust the Federation to bargain in good faith—"

"Sit down, Vreenak," Kamemor said without looking up at him. "Ambassador Endara, I do not wish to believe this information either," she said, and Kage knew that he had not misjudged her; her commitment to peace was as strong as his own. "Nor do I want to end these talks. But I'm afraid that on behalf of my government, I must demand a satisfactory explanation. If these readings indicate what they appear to indicate—"

"Gell," Endara said, using Kamemor's first name almost as a plea, "I truly mean no disrespect to you or your people, but readings can be manufactured."

"Our scientists have reviewed the sensor logs," Kamemor said, "and they've ascertained them to be authentic."

"I see," Endara said, and then he turned back toward Kage. The Federation representative looked as though he'd just been slapped. "And you, Ambassador? Are you as convinced?"

And that was the final question Kage had needed to be asked. He now had what he required to reestablish the might of the Empire. "No," he said. "I am not." For Kage, the reality of what the Romulan sensor logs purported to show was irrelevant. He walked back across the room to the table so that he could face all of his adversaries at close range. "But something did happen. As a human once wrote, 'There can no great smoke arise, but there must be some fire.' Either the sensor readings are genuine, or they are not. If they are, then it demonstrates two things to me: that the Federation has lied and is girding for war, and that the Romulans violated the Neutral Zone, itself an act of war. And if the readings are not genuine, then the Romulans are attempting to instigate hostilities. Whichever the case, the Klingon Empire will not stand idly by and allow our region of space to be destabilized."

"What does that mean, exactly?" Kamemor asked.

"It means that the Klingons will fight for peace," Kage avowed. At last, Chancellor Azetbur would be able to appease both those in the Empire who desired peace, and those who desired the restoration of Klingon might; in this case, that might would come in the form of political power. "If either the Federation or the Romulan Empire take one more provocative action," he further declared, "Qo'noS will immediately side *against* the aggressor."

"The United Federation of Planets seeks only to avoid war," Endara maintained.

"As does the Romulan Star Empire," Kamemor asserted.

"That is good," Kage said. "Then there will be nothing but peace." Except that Kage knew that would not be the case. Either the Romulans or the Federation—or both—

were moving steadily against the other, and he believed that nothing would stop them from the eventual inception of battle.

There would be war. But he and Chancellor Azetbur had just made certain that, in the end, it would be the Klingons who decided everybody's fate.

When the transport *Andoria* had arrived at Space Station KR-3, Lieutenant Elias Vaughn had made sure to be in an observation lounge on the ship. Although he seldom these days reflected on the wanderlust of his youth, he still took enjoyment from looking at the great vessels of exploration. And few of those ships, if any, possessed a more storied past than those that had borne the name *Enterprise*.

Vaughn had stood at a viewing port as *Andoria* had approached the space station. They'd passed *Enterprise* to port, where the illustrious starship sat docked at the end of one of KR-3's three honeycombed arms. Vaughn had followed the beautiful contours of the Excelsior-class ship from aft to bow with his gaze: the long, narrow warp nacelles; the unusually configured secondary hull, with its shallow aft half expanding to the bulging "belly" of its forward section; and the relatively small, almost flat circle of its primary hull.

Now Vaughn stood in another observation lounge, this one aboard *Enterprise* itself. From the viewing port here, on the starboard flank of the ship, he could see only stars. Behind him, he heard the footsteps of his commanding officer as she paced about the room.

As an academic exercise, Vaughn attempted to identify some of the stars he saw as he peered out into space. From this unfamiliar vantage—he had never before traveled to this region of the Federation—he encountered some initial trouble. But after a few minutes of concentration, his decade of deskbound analysis with Starfleet special operations—his apprenticeship, as he thought of it—allowed him to begin naming the brilliant specks in his view.

Belak, Algorab, Achernar, Unroth, Devoras . . .

Vaughn shifted as he studied the sky, not entirely comfortable in the charcoal gray suit he wore. For years with special ops, while he'd studied and interpreted intelligence reports and learned a vast array of disparate skills, he had looked forward to the days when he would finally throw off the shackles of his office and take his turn in the field. Vaughn had known back then that he would meet continual challenges once he left his desk behind, that he would face difficult, sometimes impossible obstacles, that he would likely have to endure great hardship in the performance of his duties, but he'd never anticipated how much he would despise the clothing. He felt comfortable in his crimson Starfleet uniform, the single gold bar on his right shoulder and his left sleeve, but during his five years in the field, he'd discovered that when he'd been required to outfit himself differently for his various missions, he frequently had trouble finding something comfortable to wear.

. . . Chaltok, Gasko, D'Deridex, Tranome Sar, Nequencia . . .

He had only covered a handful of the "major" stars when the doors leading into the observation lounge hissed open. Vaughn turned from the viewing port to see John Harriman, the *Enterprise* captain, stride into the room. Vaughn was familiar with Captain Harriman—and just about every other Starfleet officer, as well as numerous enlisted personnel—from his work with special ops; when a mission had to be undertaken, it paid to know whose abilities best fit the requirements of the task. Vaughn did not yet make final decisions regarding personnel assignments, but he had helped cull the names of candidates for several missions now. In this case, though, as far as he knew, he had himself been selected by his commanding officer for whatever lay ahead.

As Captain Harriman entered the room, Commander

Gravenor approached him, her hand extended. She wore a stylish, tailored dress of navy blue. "Captain, I'm Drysi Gravenor," she said, avoiding the use of her Starfleet title, no doubt because this mission called for her—and for Vaughn—to assume roles other than as Starfleet officers. Still, Harriman surely knew their identities and actual positions in special ops.

The captain and the commander shook hands, hers swallowed up in his grasp. Commander Gravenor was petite, barely a meter and a half tall, and probably not even forty-five kilos. She had dark, straight hair that hung down to the middle of her back, a sharp intellect, and a fiery determination. She had served with special ops, Vaughn knew, for almost twice as long as he had, and he considered her a mentor to him.

"Ms. Gravenor," the captain said. "John Harriman."

The commander turned toward Vaughn, who started around the conference table over to where she stood with Harriman. "This is my colleague, Elias Vaughn," she said. Her voice held the hint of a lyrical accent, a relic of her upbringing in Wales. Vaughn shook hands with the captain.

The introductions made, they all sat down, Harriman at the head of the table, Vaughn and Gravenor to either side of him. "I've been told that you both have gray-level security clearance," the captain said. "Is that correct?"

"It is," Gravenor said. "Mr. Vaughn has silver clearance, I have slate."

"Good," Harriman said. "Then you know about the Starfleet vessel lost five days ago in the Bonneville Flats."

Commander Gravenor peered across the table at Vaughn and nodded her head. "Only that it was an accident," she said. "The C in C informed us before we boarded *Andoria* that this assignment would involve the lost ship, and that Mr. Vaughn and I—" She waved a finger over the table to include the two of them. "—would be operating as special Federation envoys." Starfleet's commander in chief, Admiral Margaret Sinclair-Alexander, had personally assigned Gravenor to this mission, Vaughn knew. "But we have heard rumors about the lost ship," the commander finished.

"Yes," Harriman said, "I've been told that word is spreading throughout Starfleet, and even into the civilian population." He lifted his elbows onto the table and folded his hands together in front of him. "Admiral Sinclair-Alexander has now reported to the Federation Council, and the Council will soon release the following details about the incident. That an experimental starship, *U.S.S. Universe*, was conducting classified tests of an advanced propulsion system dubbed 'hyperwarp.' That a Romulan vessel conducting covert surveillance detected the tests, and that the Romulan government has misinterpreted the long-range sensor scans taken by that vessel. That the praetor believes Starfleet to be developing a metaweapon that will provide us with a first-strike capability. And finally, that because of this, the Klingon Empire is on the verge of joining the Romulans in a military alliance against the Federation."

Vaughn managed to keep his mouth from dropping open, but only with a conscious effort. Beyond the obvious tragedy of what had happened to the crew of *Universe*, he saw now that the Federation faced an even greater loss. Starfleet could not stand against a combined Romulan-Klingon force. He also understood why Captain Harriman had been selected to lead whatever action special ops would now take. Considered an expert on the Romulan space fleet in general, and on some of its highest-ranking officers in particular, the captain had a great deal of experience with the Romulans.

"How far out from armed conflict are we?" Commander Gravenor asked.

"Not far," Harriman said. "The Romulans have begun mobilizing their fleet, shifting massive amounts of matériel toward their borders with Federation space. The Klingons have also begun redeploying their vessels, and Starfleet has had little choice but to match them."

"No, that probably doesn't leave us much time," the commander said. "What's our role going to be in this?"

"We are going to begin by generating a strategic political response to the Romulans," Harriman said. "The Federation president has already requested permission from the Romulan praetor for *Enterprise* to travel to the site of the peace negotiations, so that we can meet with their highest-ranking ambassador. The Romulans mistakenly believe that the Federation has been developing a metaweapon so that we could launch a first strike against them. We're going to prove to them that they're wrong, that what they took to be a metaweapon was simply a new form of starship propulsion."

Vaughn doubted whether even the best-planned political action would make a difference in this situation, but something even more troublesome occurred to him. "Captain," he said, "wouldn't the creation of an advanced propulsion system also provide Starfleet with a first-strike capability?"

Harriman looked at Vaughn. After a silent moment, he said, "It would."

"So then convincing the Romulans that Starfleet was developing a new warp drive rather than a new weapon won't change anything," Vaughn concluded.

"No," the captain agreed.

"Then what are we going to do?" Vaughn asked.

And Captain Harriman told them.

"You're going to what?" Sulu asked, her voice rising with disbelief. She dropped her hands heavily onto her desk as she peered across her quarters at Captain Harriman.

"I'm going to deliver the hyperwarp drive specifications to the Romulans and the Klingons," he repeated. His words made no more sense to her now than when he'd said them the first time.

"Captain," Sulu said, standing up, "if either the Romulans or the Klingons are able to perfect hyperwarp drive before we do, then they'll have what they've accused us of trying to develop: a first-strike potential." She moved out from behind her desk and started across the cabin. "And unlike the Federation," she said, "both the Romulans and the Klingons would be willing to commit a first strike."

"That's true," Harriman said haltingly. "But I don't believe that's what's going to happen."

Sulu crossed the final distance to the captain and faced him from just a meter or so away. She waited a moment for him to offer up some justification for his last statement, but he said nothing more. Into the silence, Sulu said, bristling, "Begging the captain's pardon, but . . ." She hesitated, wanting neither to overstep her bounds nor to address her commanding officer—and her friend—with such stridency.

"It's all right, Demora," Harriman said. "Go ahead. You can tell me what you're thinking."

"All right," she said. "I think this is insane. We've been at the flash point of war for months, desperately trying to prepare ourselves for a long, hard battle, and now we're going to provide our enemies with technical specs that could ultimately help them defeat us? It makes no sense."

Harriman breathed in slowly, then out slowly, as though evaluating his response before offering it. "I know what you're saying," he told her. "But if we don't do this, then war will come fast—a war we can't win."

Sulu held her arms out to either side in a gesture of frustration. "So we're going to delay that by improving the offensive capabilities of the Romulans and Klingons even more?" She felt uncomfortable with her loud, incredulous tone, but she'd been unable to express her feelings otherwise. She dropped her hands back to her sides with a slap.

"I know that's what it sounds like," Harriman said. "But it is the opinion of Starfleet's propulsion-design engineers that the Romulans and Klingons won't be able to make hyperwarp work."

"Those are the same engineers who just cost fifty-one members of Starfleet their lives," Sulu blurted, regretting her words even before she'd finished speaking. Upset with the situation, and with herself for her volatile reactions, she turned and walked back across her cabin. She knew that nobody had intended for the crew of *Universe* to die, but still—"Captain," she said, turning back around to face Harriman from the other side of her quarters, "why did Starfleet Command decide to develop and test hyperwarp *now*? With the political situation the way it's been these past couple of years, it seems like such a risky idea."

Again, Harriman inhaled and exhaled slowly before answering. Then he said, "It was my recommendation to proceed at this time."

"Your—?" Sulu said, thunderstruck. The idea seemed so preposterous that her first thought was that the captain had never even had the time to be a part of such decision-making. But then she recalled all of the meetings he'd been asked to attend on Space Station KR-3 during the past few months.

She looked away from Harriman, trying to determine what to say, what to feel. Finally, all she could do was look back at him and ask, "Why, John?"

Harriman returned her gaze, but said nothing.

"You didn't . . . Starfleet wasn't *trying* to develop a first-strike potential, was it?" she asked, her voice dropping low. The notion of Starfleet designing a technology for the purpose of launching an unprovoked attack against anybody seemed completely antithetical to everything for which the Federation stood.

Harriman continued to look at her, opening his mouth once, then again, without saying anything. He appeared to be struggling to find a response—which probably answered her question, Sulu thought. But then Harriman said, "Honestly,

Demora, no. The goal of hyperwarp drive was never, for one second, to allow us the capability of striking the Romulans or Klingons first. Never."

Sulu peered at the captain—at her friend—and knew that he had just told her the truth. She felt relieved and foolish. "I . . . I'm sorry," she said. "I didn't mean to—"

"It's all right," Harriman said, moving across the room over to where she stood by her desk. "I know that these are difficult times for all of us."

Sulu gazed up at Harriman, and felt guilty not only for having questioned his motives, but also for forgetting how much he'd been through lately. His father, still critically injured, and still refusing to see him . . . "I'm sorry," she said again. "I know you're making the best choices that you possibly can."

"I'm trying," he said. "Believe me."

"I do," she said, but something else bothered her. She moved back around her desk and sat down there. "Do you know the nature of the technological leap that's supposed to make hyperwarp possible?" she asked.

"Demora," Harriman said, taking a seat across the desk from her, "I can't talk about it."

"That's all right," Sulu said. "Because I can. I was monitoring the *Universe* during its test run. When their crew began the hyperwarp reaction, the *Enterprise*'s sensors detected a distinctive waveform. At first, I thought it must be emanating from another ship in the area, but I pinpointed the source as the *Universe* itself. There was no question."

"I see," Harriman said noncommittally.

"John, if the use of cloaking technology is at the heart of hyperwarp drive, and if we give the Romulans and Klingons the drive specifications, then isn't it possible—isn't it *likely*—that with their decades of experience in cloaking technology, they'll be able to perfect hyperwarp before we do?" The possibility, clearly real, did more than concern her; it frightened her.

Harriman looked silently at her for a long time. Sulu

waited, and as she did, she noticed something. Where over the past few days she had sensed great sadness in Harriman—for the crew of *Universe*, for the grief the *Enterprise* crew felt, and for his injured father—she now saw something . . . less than that. Something less, coupled with a resolve that she did not entirely understand. When Harriman at last spoke, he said only, "I don't think the Romulans or the Klingons will develop hyperwarp before we do." He gave no reason for his opinion, something not like him. As the *Enterprise* bridge crew could so well attest, the captain often answered their questions even in the middle of a crisis. His silence now seemed unusual, and she suddenly got the feeling that there was something that he was not telling her. But Sulu had been Harriman's executive officer for ten years now, and she'd served with him for eight years prior to that, and in all of that time, he'd never given her a reason to mistrust him.

"Okay," she said, although in truth, she hadn't been this scared in a long time—maybe not since she had been a child, since her mother had been stricken ill.

"Okay." Harriman stood up and started for the door. Before he got there, Sulu called after him.

"John," she said. When he turned back toward her, she said, "I know that the admiral . . . your father . . . I know he said he won't see you, but . . . maybe you should visit him anyway." Sulu did not know how she would have handled her mother's death had she not been able to spend time with her in those last days—and to say goodbye to her.

"Yeah," Harriman said, nodding slowly. "I've been thinking about that myself. I've decided that I will go see—"

"*Bridge to Captain Harriman*," the voice of Lieutenant Commander Linojj interrupted him.

Harriman walked back to over to Sulu's desk and touched a control there. "This is the captain," he said. "Go ahead, Commander."

"*Captain*," Linojj said, "*you're receiving a priority message from Starfleet Command.*"

Harriman glanced at Sulu before responding. "I'm in Commander Sulu's quarters," he said. "Pipe it down here."

"*Aye, sir.*"

"Harriman out." He thumbed the channel closed as Sulu reached up and spun the computer interface monitor around so that it faced him. He operated the controls, and after just a few seconds, she saw the light of the display reflected on his face. "Admiral Sinclair-Alexander," he said. If Starfleet's commander in chief was contacting Harriman directly, Sulu thought, then it must have to do with the Romulan-Klingon situation.

"*Captain*," Sulu heard Sinclair-Alexander say. "*The Federation president just received word from Romulus.*" Her manner was nothing but professional. "*Enterprise has been granted permission to deliver the two Federation envoys to Space Station Algeron, where you and they will meet with Romulan Ambassador Gell Kamemor.*"

"We'll leave KR-3 immediately, Admiral," Harriman said. "At maximum warp."

"*When you reach the Neutral Zone*," Sinclair-Alexander continued, "*you will rendezvous with a Romulan vessel, which will escort you while you're in Romulan space.*" Sulu knew what the admiral would say next, even before she said it. "*It will be their flagship*, Tomed."

"Acknowledged," Harriman said. Sulu saw no reaction on his face to the news that *Enterprise* would be in such close proximity to Admiral Vokar's ship.

"*Good luck, John*," Sinclair-Alexander said. Harriman nodded once. "*Sinclair-Alexander out.*" The light from the display reflecting on Harriman's face vanished as the communication ended. The captain worked the controls again, and then said, "Harriman to bridge."

"*Bridge*," came the immediate response. "*Linojj here.*"

"Commander, contact Admiral Mentir and inform him that *Enterprise* will be departing KR-3 immediately," he said. "Then set course for Romulan space station Algeron, maximum warp."

"*Sir?*" Linojj said, obviously surprised by the orders.

"Do it, Xintal," Harriman said. "I'm on my way to the bridge now. I'll explain when I get there."

"*Aye, sir.*"

"Harriman out." He closed the channel with a touch to a control, then stood up and looked at Sulu. "Don't worry," he told her, and while his manner seemed serious, he also sounded extremely confident. And as Sulu had done for a long time now, she chose to trust that strength and surety.

As Harriman headed for the door, Sulu's mind drifted to *Tomed* and to its commanding officer, Admiral Vokar. She knew that Captain Harriman had endured several tense encounters with the admiral through the years, most recently on the world of the Koltaari. She also knew that the admiral had a personal animus for the captain, stemming back to their first meeting, many years ago.

Before he reached the door, Harriman stopped and looked back over his shoulder at Sulu. He looked as though he would say something, but then he continued out of her quarters, on his way to the bridge—and to the Romulan Neutral Zone, she knew, and another encounter with an old enemy.

MINUS FIVE: HISTORY

Lieutenant John Harriman feverishly worked the helm, hurling the wounded Starfleet vessel into further evasive maneuvers. He threw his leg against the side of the astrogation console, trying to keep himself in his chair as the inertial dampers adjusted late to the ship's rapid change in attitude. The incessant whine of the impulse engines filled the *Hunley* bridge as the demands on them increased. Smoke stung Harriman's eyes, and he smelled the acrid scent of melting fiber optics and scorched metal, even as the desperate gasp of a fire-suppression canister sputtered somewhere behind him.

"Fire at will!" Captain Linneus yelled, his commanding voice cutting through the uproar.

"Unloading port torpedo bay," Lieutenant Grinager called from the tactical station, her tone steady despite the chaos of the situation. Harriman looked to the main viewscreen, its aspect locked on the enemy vessel and following it across the sky. A sweep of bright red projectiles streaked away from *Hunley*, and he realized that the ship must be in trouble for the captain and security chief to be attacking like this, spending their munitions in such a scatter-shot manner. They clearly hoped for a chance hit that might just allow *Hunley* to limp away to safety, even if that would mean abandoning S.S. *Dakota*, the freighter they'd come here to assist.

On the viewer, the Romulan ship swooped and dived, its crew obviously seeking to evade the photon torpedoes sent after them. The *Ventarix*-class battle cruiser—squat and long-necked, composed primarily of straight lines and edges, but with a bulbous projection at the fore end of the thin neck—belonged to a new squadron of vessels upgrading the Klingon-designed D7 heavies that the Romulans had been using for the last decade or so. Harriman looked down at his console as he brought *Hunley* around, then glanced back up to see one of the photon torpedoes land on its target. He felt momentarily elated, but the reprieve was transitory: a bright flash of blue pinpoints concentrated along the area of impact told him that the Romulan ship's shields had protected against the full force of the detonation.

Narrowly eluding the remaining torpedoes, the Romulan vessel arced into a wide turn and rounded back toward *Hunley*. "Evasive!" the captain cried, but Harriman had never stopped piloting the ship. He alternately watched the viewscreen and his readouts as he hove *Hunley* about, searching for an escape. Energy signatures marched across the helm display and told him that the Romulan vessel had fired its weapons again.

Hunley rolled to starboard at one-eighth the speed of light, too slow to avoid the disruptor salvo. Two of the bolts—two out of a spread of a dozen, Harriman saw on his panel—two of the bolts were going to find their marks. Trailing the intermittent blue fiber of its laser-assisted propulsion as though it had dripped from the Romulan ship's weapons bank, the first bolt struck the top of the saucer section forward of the bridge. *Hunley* shuddered violently, and Harriman had to fight to stay in his chair.

"Deflector grid is down," Grinager yelled, her voice competing with the increasing drone of the impulse engines. "Firing all phase—" she started, and then the second disruptor bolt pounded into *Hunley.* A massive explosion rocked the bridge, followed closely by the sounds of tearing metal and wind—

Wind?

In the next instant, Harriman flew upward. His knees struck the bottom of the helm station, reducing his momentum for just a second, and he grabbed instinctively for the nearest surface. His hand found purchase on the astrogation console, his fingers squeezing the thin metal hood surrounding it, but the rest of his body continued up, as did seemingly everything else on the bridge. The chair in which he'd been sitting glanced off his back as it rushed by him. Harriman seemed to dangle upside down, and when he looked up past his feet, he saw the chair tumbling end over end out into space, the stars a terrifying backdrop— the disruptor bolt had sheared off the roof of *Hunley*'s bridge.

Air rushed past Harriman, trying to carry him out into the void. The sounds of the swift currents filled his ears, and he could hear nothing else. He felt his hand cramping as he clung desperately to the astrogator hood.

And then Harriman witnessed the unthinkable: Captain Linneus soared through *Hunley*'s gaping wound and out into space. For what must have been only a fraction of a second, but which felt longer, Harriman saw Linneus's face: his eyes wide, his mouth open in a silent scream, his profound terror unmistakable. And then the captain was gone, his figure disappearing quickly as it receded into the darkness.

Harriman's fingers slipped along the surface of the astrogator hood, and he clenched his hand tightly, as though attempting to punch a new handhold in the metal. He tried to reach his other arm down and grab on to something else, but he felt his fingers slide again along the hood, until finally his closed fist held nothing. Harriman sailed upward. His heart leaped in his chest, and he opened his mouth to scream. He shot toward the stars, and toward the cold, hard vacuum that separated them.

Harriman struck something. The unexpected impact came along his right side, and then he plummeted back to the decking. He landed in the open space between the command chair and the helm and navigation consoles, bringing his arms up in time to protect his head. He crashed down on his left side, his shoulder giving way with a loud snap. The breath was forced from his lungs as pain flowed through his body like an electric current. He gasped, trying to inhale.

There was no air.

The wind had stopped, he realized, the atmosphere of *Hunley*'s bridge now entirely gone, blown out into space. Gulping wildly as he suffocated, Harriman rolled off of his injured left side and onto his back. The stars stared down at him through the hull breach, and then they began to wink out one after another as something moved in front of them. He recognized the form of the Romulan vessel as it passed, and he could even read the rounded, runelike block characters on its hull: *Daami*. As he lay dying, he unaccountably recalled the Romulan-language courses he'd taken during his time at the Academy.

In just a few seconds, the Romulan vessel had gone from view, leaving only the unfeeling starscape above him. His vision began to fray at the edges. His lungs ached.

Finally, darkness took him.

Admiral Aventeer Vokar, master of the Romulan vessel *Daami*, stood at the front of his ship's bridge, staring at the primary viewscreen there. On it, he saw the wounded form of the Starfleet vessel drifting undirected in space. The two warp nacelles on either side of its circular hull had gone dark, and its bridge had been demolished.

Vokar smiled to himself. *Hunley*'s crew had come here into Romulan territory in response to the other vessel's distress signal, and yet they hadn't even been able to help themselves. He had seen to that. *Daami*'s crew had detected *Dakota*'s call for assistance—originating in Romulan space—and had moved immediately to intercept the supposedly civilian freighter. *Daami* had arrived on the scene after *Hunley* had, but not too late to take action.

"Bring us about," Vokar said, turning to face his bridge crew. "Let's finish what we came here to do in the first place." The crew's acknowledgments crackled in the dim lighting, no doubt motivated by Vokar's recent promotion in rank. But he had no intention of stopping or even slowing his progress through the hierarchy of the Imperial Fleet, and today he would demonstrate that to all by bringing the Empire another victory.

He turned back to the viewscreen and watched as the crippled *Hunley* slipped away to starboard, *Daami* rounding onto its new heading. Both the *Hunley* and *Dakota* captains had claimed to know nothing of the recently modified Romulan borders, of the expanse of interstellar territory the praetor had claimed for the Empire. And Vokar supposed that had been the truth—the freighter had needed assistance after it had struck a perimeter mine—although the incursion might also have been an attempt at espionage by the deceitful Federation. Whichever the case, they would pay, either for their ignorance or for their treachery.

On the screen, the image of *Dakota* slid into view. Vokar regarded the old, seemingly decrepit freighter with contempt. The damage it had sustained when it had struck the mine showed at the bow of its single warp nacelle, a jagged, blackened patch reaching a quarter of the way back along the engine structure. If the crew of the hoary vessel had been conducting an intelligence mission, *Daami*'s sensors had told Vokar, then they had been doing so with antiquated equipment. Unlike *Hunley*, the aged hulk provided Vokar no opportunity for spoils.

"Ready disruptors," Vokar said, calling back over his shoulder. Again, the crew responded sharply. He peered back at the viewscreen, at the defenseless Federation vessel in *Daami*'s path, and smiled to himself once more. He would vanquish the interlopers, and then he would collect *Hunley* and return to Romulus, where he would personally deliver his prize to the praetor.

Consciousness returned to Harriman surreptitiously, surrounding him in its folds like warm water gradually and unexpectedly rising around him. He became aware by degrees, not knowing whether he had been out for a minute or an hour or a day. He only knew that he was not . . . was not—

Not dead.

Harriman opened his eyes. Above him, he saw the starscape still staring threateningly down on the *Hunley* bridge. But a blue haze flickered where the roof of the bridge had once been, and he realized that an emergency forcefield had automatically activated in order to close the breach. Likewise, environmental-crisis protocols must have pushed an atmosphere back into the resealed space.

He moved his arms back so that he could prop himself up on his elbows, but his left shoulder wailed in pain. He felt tenderly along the silver uniform sleeve covering his injured arm, grateful not to find any bones projecting from beneath his flesh. Everything seemed to be intact, at least, though he had clearly suffered internal damage.

Rolling onto his right side, Harriman pushed himself up and stood. Eerily quiet, the bridge sounded and looked wrong. Virtually everything that had not been somehow secured to the ship had vanished: chairs, handheld equipment, the smoke . . . and people. He tried to recall how many of the crew had been on the bridge when the Romulan ship had engaged them. Eight? Ten? There had been the captain and the first officer, the security chief, Anner'-namin at navigation, Harriman himself at the helm . . . somebody at the sciences station . . . and one or two people had been working to quell whatever fires had broken out . . .

However many of the crew had been on the bridge, now only two others besides himself remained: Lieutenant Grinager, lying near the tactical station, and a member of the crew he didn't recognize, her body in a heap near the portside turbolift. Harriman bounded up the two steps to the outer, raised portion of the bridge. As he approached the unfamiliar crewperson, he saw that she lay with her neck twisted at an unnatural angle—at an *impossible* angle for a human. Still, he knelt beside her and reached two fingers out to the side of her neck, feeling for a pulse. He found none.

As he rose to go check on Lieutenant Grinager, movement on the viewscreen—amazingly still intact and functioning—caught his attention. The viewer, continuing to track *Daami*, showed the Romulan vessel approaching *Dakota*. Harriman knew that the freighter carried no weapons of any kind, and that beyond navigational deflectors, it flew essentially undefended. The ship's crew of thirty-nine men and women had met danger here because they'd had the simple misfortune of traveling the same flight path they'd plied dozens of times previously, without knowing that the Romulans had decided without warning to claim the surrounding space for their own. Nor had the crew of *Dakota* been permitted to correct their unwitting trespass, their vessel striking a Romulan mine and losing warp capability in the process. *Hunley* had responded to their distress call, but *Daami* had arrived on the scene before long, declaring the two Federation vessels to be in violation of their sovereign territory. Captain Linneus had not disputed the unforeseen assertion, instead asking only for the opportunity to repair *Dakota* and escort it back to Federation space. The Romulans had replied with the full force of their disruptors on *Hunley*.

The ensuing battle had been relatively one-sided, the light cruiser *Hunley* outgunned and outperformed by the larger, faster, newer *Daami*. The Starfleet vessel had also been hampered by the need to protect *Dakota*, Harriman knew; fortunately, Captain Linneus had been wise enough to transport the freighter's crew off of their ship, although lowering *Hunley*'s shields had cost the ship some disruptor-inflicted damage. Only the command and combat skills of the captain had prolonged the confrontation for as long as it had lasted. *Hunley* had even managed to inflict its own share of damage on the Romulan ship.

Harriman watched as the blue pulse of disruptor bolts flashed across the screen. *Dakota* took hits amidships first, in the middle of its long cylindrical cargo container. Then *Daami*'s assault widened, blasting at the small control structure at the bow of the ship, and at the lone warp nacelle. Harriman saw the control center break off from the ship, followed by the warp engine. The great bulk of the cargo container split in two, and then an explosion flared, encompassing all of *Dakota*. When the light dimmed, only *Daami* and a field of wreckage remained.

Harriman tore his gaze from the viewscreen and moved toward the supine figure of Lieutenant Grinager. As he approached her, he saw blood seeping from her nose, but he also saw her chest rising and falling: she was alive. He bent down beside her and tried gently to wake her, but she did not stir. He got up and went over to the tactical station, where he touched a control to open a communications channel. "Lieutenant Harriman to sickbay," he said, his voice sounding strange to him on the still bridge. He waited for a response, and when none came, he tried again. "Harriman to sickbay." Then: "Harriman to engineering," and "Harriman to environmental control." Nothing.

He looked over at the viewscreen, and saw *Daami* turn and start back toward *Hunley*.

His mind raced as he bent to scoop up Grinager in his arms. Pain exploded in his left shoulder, but he gritted his teeth and did his best to ignore it. He felt sweat cold on his face as he carried the lieutenant to the port turbolift. He wanted to get medical aid for her, but more important, he wanted to get to the rest of the crew and help them find a means of repelling the Romulans. At the Academy, he had studied the mysterious and secretive empire in depth, furthering a curiosity first provoked by his father's stories of the Earth-Romulan war; Blackjack had heard the stories himself from his own father, who had lived through the conflict as a boy.

Stepping carefully past the body of the dead woman, Harriman stopped short at the turbolift doors, which did not open as he neared them. The lifts would have shut down automatically, Harriman realized, once the bridge had been compromised. Without hesitation, he turned and kicked at the knockout panel beside the turbolift. The small emergency door swung open on its hinges, revealing an access tube beyond it. He knew he could not carry Lieutenant Grinager in the cramped shaft, so he squatted and laid her back down on the decking, the pain in his shoulder easing dramatically once it had been freed of its burden. As soon as he could—*if* he could—he would send help back to her.

Before Harriman entered the access tube, he took one last look at the viewscreen. *Daami* drew nearer. The Romulan crew would not destroy *Hunley*, Harriman knew; they would want the Starfleet vessel for their own. Doubtless having jammed Captain Linneus's messages to Starfleet, the Romulans would count on *Hunley*—and *Dakota*—being presumed lost, with no apparent causes.

But Harriman also knew another fact about the Romulans, something he had heard numerous times, not just aboard *Hunley* and back at the Academy, but throughout his entire life. Even back in his childhood, Blackjack had uttered the phrase to him.

Romulans don't take captives.

Vokar sat in his command chair, raised above the level of the bridge around him. On the viewscreen, the Federation vessel slowly rotated, more or less along a line running from port side forward to starboard aft. The ship looked dead, a dark, worthless carcass, easily defeated by the might of the Empire, and now a mute witness to the superiority of the Romulan people.

Except that *Hunley* would not be worthless. Collected and taken home to Romulus, the Starfleet vessel would provide insight not only into Federation technology, but also into the culture of their military. The Empire had waged a war against Earth more than a century ago, but contemporary contacts with the Federation had been few; reliable information about the UFP was therefore considered a valuable commodity. Vokar had even heard rumors recently that there had been deliberation at the highest levels of the Imperial Fleet about capturing Starfleet personnel, should the opportunity arise, for the purpose of prolonged interrogation. But no such orders had come down to Vokar, and he would carry out his duty as current fleet policy dictated.

"Still no response, Admiral," announced the communications officer, who had been attempting for several minutes to open a channel to *Hunley*. "I can't be sure that they're receiving us because of the radiation." When *Daami* had returned to the Starfleet vessel, sensors had revealed low-level radiation distributed throughout much of the ship, likely a result of the disruptor strikes. Just as the radiation inhibited sensor scans, it might also be interfering with communications.

"Voldat," Vokar said, calling to his first officer. The elder, graying centurion, slightly thick through the middle, appeared immediately to Vokar's right, almost as though he had transported there.

"Yes, Admiral," Voldat said crisply.

"How many are still left alive aboard that ship?" Vokar asked, preparing the endgame with *Hunley*.

"Indeterminate overall," Voldat said. "Our scans cannot penetrate the radiation, which has spread through ninety percent of the ship. But prior to our last assault, sensors detected two hundred thirty-one life signs."

"And how many would you estimate now?" Vokar asked.

Voldat peered at the viewscreen, clearly to assess the damage that *Daami* had inflicted on the Starfleet vessel. Numerous dark patches marred the silvery-white surface of the ship's main body, a circular structure twelve decks deep, and the bridge had been opened to space. "I would approximate twenty-five to seventy-five dead."

"Leaving at least one hundred fifty," Vokar said. "Section the cargo holds to confine ten to an area, then transport them over. Identify the highest-ranking officers so that I can question them before we put them to death."

"Admiral," Voldat said, "because of the radiation, we cannot establish a transporter lock anywhere but along a relatively small section at the stern, and we read only seven life signs in that area."

Vokar took in this information reluctantly; he did not appreciate disruptions to procedure. "Transport the seven aboard when the holds are prepared," he told Voldat. "Form boarding parties and beam over to the uncontaminated section of the ship, and herd its crew into that area so that they can be transported to *Daami*."

"Yes, Admiral," Voldat said, and he started to move away.

"Voldat," Vokar said, and the centurion stopped. "Take no chances over there. I want to interrogate their officers, but not at the expense of Romulan lives. If any of them offer the slightest resistance, kill them at once."

"Yes, Admiral," Voldat said, and he continued on his way.

Vokar looked at the viewscreen again, at the beaten Starfleet vessel displayed there, and he wondered how much of an effect this would have on his career. He had attained the rank of admiral far faster than most in the Romulan military, but that fact did not satisfy him by itself. Vokar had ambitions beyond a simple admiralty. He would lead the Imperial Fleet one day, conceiving and executing victories befitting his people—victories that, today, too many in the upper strata were content to wait for, eschewing preemptive action in favor of reactive policies.

Vokar would change that mindset. He had already done so aboard his ship, and he had set about influencing Imperial Fleet Command as well. Beyond that . . . well, he did have ties in the Senate, and he had no trouble at all envisioning himself one day among their number, leading his people from the highest levels of power.

From *the* highest level of power.

In the future, the Federation, the Klingons, the Tholians, and all the others would bow before the might and natural superiority of the Romulans. And the Empire would be led by Praetor Aventeer Vokar.

Harriman moved through *Hunley*'s engine room, waiting anxiously for word from Lieutenant Bexx. He paced back and forth behind the chief engineer, trying not to disturb her as she worked at an environmental-control console, but—"Anything?" he asked, stopping beside her. From an intellectual standpoint, he understood the requirements of command, and the need to allow people to do their jobs, but however much time they had, he knew that it must be running out quickly.

"Just a moment," Bexx said, not taking her gaze from her work. The engine room stood mute around them. Most of the engineering staff had already left to join the rest of the crew in the ship's cargo holds, and the few who remained observed quietly.

Harriman felt no apprehensions about having to lead a starship crew for the first time in his career, beyond the horror of being seventh in the chain of command and the only one of those seven still alive and conscious. The captain, first officer, science officer, and navigator had all been lost when the bridge had been hit and the hull breached; the second officer had not been heard from since the last disruptor strikes, and might have been among those killed when the penultimate bolt had struck the ship and brought down the deflectors; and the security chief, Lieutenant Grinager, still lay unconscious on the bridge, though Harriman had reported her injuries to sickbay personnel, who would send somebody there to treat her.

"All right," Bexx said, looking up from her console. "I've overridden the radiation protocols and retracted the emergency bulkheads, except in the stern sections." She reached up and wiped a bead of perspiration from her forehead, from beside the bifurcated ridge that ran across her bald skull and down the center of her face. Harriman only now noticed the sheen on Bexx's light blue flesh, an indication of the anxiety she must be feeling.

"Good work," Harriman said, then put his hand on Bexx's forearm, squeezing it softly. "It'll be okay," he told her. "This will work." He felt far less sure than he hoped he sounded, but he'd learned from observing his father over the years that confidence, like fear, could be infectious.

Bexx nodded, though she seemed unconvinced. "I wouldn't recommend keeping the emergency bulkheads open too long," she said. "The Romulan sensors won't be able to find us, but they won't have to if the radiation kills us."

"Dr. Latasa has informed me that we have sufficient hyronalin aboard to treat the entire crew," Harriman said, side-stepping the obvious detail that the medication would be useless to a ship of corpses. "So, are we all set?" he asked.

"Aye," Bexx said, walking over to another engineering station and consulting it. "Passive sensors are functioning in the stern sections, and also in the hangar deck and in all the docking ports, in case the Romulans decide to board that way."

"And communications?" Harriman asked.

"All channels are still open below deck two," Bexx said.

"Good," Harriman said. He turned to face the other four engineers standing at consoles around the room. "All right," he said, "you all know your jobs." As heads nodded in acknowledgment, Harriman started for the doors. Before he left, though, he stopped and told the engineers, "Good luck." Then he hurried on, headed for a cargo hold, and a desperate attempt to save the *Hunley* crew.

Centurion Rentikin Voldat stepped onto the transporter platform and took a moment to scrutinize the first boarding party. The eleven men all appeared alert and serious, each with a disruptor pistol held in his hand, and with a breathing mask strapped across his nose and mouth; intelligence reports indicated that at least some Starfleet vessels incorporated anesthetic gas as part of their intruder-control systems.

Satisfied, Voldat lowered his own mask across his face, then drew the disruptor that hung at his hip. He looked to the transporter operator and nodded. As the operator worked his controls, the blue particles of dematerialization formed in Voldat's vision, dissolving his view of the transporter room as they multiplied.

And then, in what seemed to be no time at all, and with no perceived lack of consciousness, Voldat saw his eyesight begin to clear. In place of the transporter room aboard *Daami*, he now saw a dark, unfamiliar corridor. "Sensors," he said, and at once, he heard the buzz of a portable scanner in use.

"I read no life signs in this section of the deck, Centurion," reported Lieutenant Arnek. Earlier, scans performed aboard *Daami* had detected seven of the *Hunley* crew here, but they must have abandoned the area, clearly realizing that, at least for a short time, the radiation in the other portions of their ship would mask their location. It did not matter, of course. There would be no escape for these Starfleet officers.

"What about the other decks in this section?" Voldat asked.

The scanner continued to hum. "Negative, sir," said Arnek. "I read no life signs in any of the stern sections, on any of the—" As soon as Arnek stopped speaking, Voldat knew something had gone wrong. "Sir, the radiation on the ship has cleared. I'm reading human life signs all over—"

And then the pinpoints of light that marked the dematerialization process filled Voldat's vision once more. Except that this time, the pinpoints were not blue, but white.

Lieutenant Bexx stared unrelentingly at the console before her, determined to act as swiftly as possible when—*if*—the time came. She felt the runaway beat of her heart pounding in her chest, a consequence of her fear and anticipation for what lay ahead. If Lieutenant Harriman had been—

The readings she had been waiting for raced across the display on her panel: twelve transporter signals, deck seven, aft. "Now," she yelled, even as her hands sped across her console, working the *Hunley*'s environmental controls. She heard the other engineers operating their own consoles behind her. All over the ship, she knew, emergency bulkheads began sliding into place, containing the radiation caused by the disruptor strikes. She had to wait only a second before the red indicator lights on her panel all turned green. Then she sent the predetermined signal to each of *Hunley*'s cargo holds.

For probably the tenth time, Harriman checked the setting on his phaser, then adjusted the tricorder he carried on a strap over his shoulder. Fifteen of his crewmates stood in a semicircle beside him, and another, Ensign Gabe Márquez, stood studying a console a few meters in front of him. They all waited for the signal that they hoped would come from Lieutenant Bexx or one of her engineering crew.

They did not have to wait long.

Ensign Márquez said nothing as Harriman saw him suddenly move into action. The ensign rapidly and silently worked the controls of the cargo transporter.

A moment later, Harriman dematerialized.

"Admiral," the tactical officer said, "the radiation on the Starfleet vessel just dissipated."

Vokar sat forward in his command chair, concern unfurling within him like a flag before the wind. "All at once?" he asked.

"No, not all of it," the officer said. "There continues to be radiation around where our disruptor bolts landed. But the rest of it—"

"Shields up," he yelled, understanding the deception that had taken place. "Lock weapons on the Starfleet ship. Destroy it."

"Admiral," the weapons officer said, "our boarding parties are over there."

"Do it," Vokar yelled.

But then the whine of a transporter filled the *Daami* bridge.

As soon as he saw Romulan personnel, Harriman felt a powerful urge to squeeze the trigger of his phaser. His desire for retribution almost overwhelmed him, the image of Captain Linneus being thrown into space a haunting memory that he knew would never leave him. But vengeance would not serve the captain, Harriman understood, or any of the others who had lost their lives aboard *Hunley*. What Captain Linneus would have wanted, more than anything else, would have been the safety of the rest of his crew.

At the far end of the bridge, a Romulan officer dashed toward a door. "Stop," Harriman called, and he leveled a phaser shot past the man, careful to aim away from any consoles; he could not risk damaging the bridge controls he would likely need. The beam streaked into the bulkhead beside the door and erupted in a shower of sparks. The Romulan stopped.

Harriman's crewmates quickly fanned out. Four took up positions beside the bridge exits—two monitoring each door—and the others covered each of the seven Romulans present, moving them away from their stations. One Romulan did not sit at a console, but in a large, raised chair at the aft end of the bridge. As he stepped down onto the decking at the point of a phaser, Harriman strode over to stand before him. "Are you the captain of this ship?" he asked, even as he noticed the uniform insignia denoting the rank of admiral.

"I am," the Romulan said in a voice unambiguously defiant. "I am Vokar." Much shorter and thinner than Harriman, the Romulan nevertheless cast a strong aura of authority. His gray eyes held on Harriman's face, the intensity of the admiral's stare conveying the fury he clearly felt.

Ire rose within Harriman, his craving for vengeance surging again. The notion that this Romulan who stood before him felt angry for having been prevented from exterminating the rest of the *Hunley* crew, this Romulan who had already overseen the unprovoked and unnecessary deaths of Captain Linneus and the others—the very idea enraged Harriman. In a flash of bitterness, he pictured himself raising his phaser to Vokar's head and applying pressure to the trigger.

Harriman looked away, almost unable to contain the emotions roiling within him. Trying to focus on his duties, he lifted his tricorder and, his phaser still in his other hand, carefully worked the controls. The display blinked to life, and told Harriman that *Daami*'s shields were up, as he'd suspected they would be. He had considered attempting to beam *Daami*'s entire crew from their ship once the Romulans had lowered shields to transport their boarding parties— and as soon as the radiation had subsequently cleared aboard *Hunley*—but there wouldn't have been enough time to transport all four hundred before they had managed to raise shields again.

Harriman looked back up at Vokar. "Where are the shield controls?" he asked.

Vokar glared at Harriman. "There is an old Romulan saying that tells that if all around you lies in ruins, either fault yourself, or seek the serpent. Are you the serpent?"

Harriman said nothing. Instead, he turned and walked over to the freestanding console that sat between Vokar's command chair and the forward viewscreen. As he did, he peered up at the viewer, and saw the image of *Hunley* drifting through space, battered and seemingly beaten. But Lieutenant Bexx had assured him that her engineering team would need only an hour or two to restore warp power, and so the ship would soon be on its way back to the Federation.

From the markings on its controls, Harriman identified the first console he examined as hosting a combination of helm and navigation functions. He quickly moved to the freestanding consoles rimming the bridge, studying the Romulan symbols on them. The fourth panel he came to appeared to contain tactical controls, and Harriman soon found characters spelling out SHIELD FUNCTION. He reached forward and touched the deactivation switch, then checked his tricorder again. Finally, he raised his wrist and spoke into the communicator he wore there. "Harriman to Bexx," he said.

"This is Bexx," the engineer responded.

"Lieutenant, we've lowered the shields on the Romulan ship," he said. "You can begin transport." The Romulans would be beamed, sans any weapons they carried, into *Hun-*

ley's cargo holds, where they would be restrained by the ship's heavily armed crew. They would be held there until *Hunley* reached a Federation starbase.

"*Understood*," Bexx said, relief evident in her voice.

"Wait," Vokar said, the word delivered as though the admiral were still in command.

Curious, Harriman said into his communicator, "Lieutenant, transport the bridge crew last."

"*Aye, aye*," Bexx said.

Harriman walked back over to Admiral Vokar, waiting for him to continue. But Vokar only glared at him, his hatred readily apparent. Again, Harriman felt the rush of his own powerful emotions, and found himself not just wanting to shoot the admiral, but to throw him to the deck and beat him.

Vokar stared at Harriman without saying anything for long seconds, and Harriman quickly tired of whatever game the admiral was playing. He had started to move away when Vokar finally spoke again.

"Kill me," he said simply.

Harriman thought he understood. Although little information had come out of the Romulan Empire in the decade and a half since contact had been reestablished with them—the Romulans had essentially isolated themselves in the century after the Earth-Romulan war—Starfleet Command had drawn some conclusions about the Imperial Fleet. When faced with the possible capture of their vessels, Romulan commanders had, on at least three occasions, chosen instead to destroy their own ships. And while Vokar did not have the capability of taking such action now, he clearly did not want to have to face the consequences of losing his vessel to Starfleet.

With the condition of *Hunley*, though, and the apparent claim to this space by the Romulans, Harriman would not risk towing *Daami* back to the Federation. Nor would he even spend the time here that it would require to download

Daami's files, as much as it might have benefited Starfleet to have such information. Instead, he would order *Hunley*'s phasers trained on the Romulan vessel once it had been emptied of its crew.

He said none of this to Vokar, though, discovering that he had nothing at all that he wanted to say to this thug. He turned away, intentionally showing the admiral his back.

"Kill me!" Vokar roared, his tone one of command.

Harriman turned back to face the admiral. Then he raised his phaser, pointed it at Vokar's chest, and fired.

Vokar awoke slowly. He felt disoriented, unsure of where he was, or even of what he'd been doing before falling asleep. A vague recollection of being aboard *Daami* rose in his mind, but he could not—

It all came rushing back.

Vokar opened his eyes, wanting to know where he was. He lay on his back, and light glared on a clear pane several centimeters above his face. To either side, and down past his feet and above his head, the walls of a container surrounded him. Vokar recognized Federation markings, and although he'd never seen the UFP version of the device in which he now lay, it bore enough of a resemblance to its Romulan counterpart that he knew what it was: a stasis chamber. An emergency medical device, the unit was most often utilized to keep an injured individual in a state of suspended animation until they could receive medical treatment. It apparently also functioned effectively as a prison cell.

The Starfleet officer—Harriman—had shot him, but obviously hadn't killed him. Worse, Harriman had made him a prisoner of the Federation. Rage coursed through his body, and he felt his hands clench into fists. At the earliest opportunity, he would find a Federation throat and choke it until—

The clear panel above him began to move, retracting into one side of the stasis chamber. *Now*, Vokar thought, re-

alizing that his opportunity had come sooner than he could
have hoped. A shadow fell across him, and he tensed, waiting to see the face of the Federation citizen he would kill.

"Get up," a man's voice said in a cold tone.

Vokar reached up to the sides of the chamber and slowly
pulled himself up to a sitting position. He turned, ready to
leap at the first person he saw. Somebody moved into his
line of vision, but as Vokar set to act, he saw something that
stopped him: a Romulan Imperial Fleet uniform. Slowly, he
tilted his head up to look at the narrow face and hard features of the man who wore it, a man he knew well.

"Get up," Admiral Hiren said again, and he stepped forward and threw the back of his hand across Vokar's face.

Vokar's head snapped to the side, and he felt the flesh of
his cheek open beneath what must have been a ring on one of
Hiren's fingers. The pain fueled his anger, not for the Romulan admiral who had just struck him, but for the Starfleet officer who had put him in this situation. He looked back up at
the unforgiving expression on Hiren's face, and saw two security guards standing behind the admiral.

Vokar knew that he still lived only because of his connections in the Romulan Senate. He must have been returned
to the Empire, perhaps exchanged for one of the Federation
spies recently unmasked, who'd been kept alive specifically
to be used for such a purpose. And the Federation had probably believed that the Imperial Fleet would punish Vokar far
more than they ever would.

And they would have been right.

"Get up," Hiren said again, and he reached forward and
grabbed Vokar by the front of his uniform. Hiren pulled him
from the stasis unit and threw him across the room. "Get
up," the admiral repeated. "Get up, Sublieutenant."

The last word chilled Vokar, telling him his future: he
would be made to remain in the Imperial Fleet, reduced in
rank and carrying the burden and shame of his failure with

him. His ties in the Senate had spared his life, but that
would not necessarily be preferable to the fate to which he
had now been consigned.

"Get up, Sublieutenant," the admiral said again, striding
across the room toward Vokar. Hiren did not stop saying it
for hours.

MINUS FOUR: CLOAK

Sulu entered the *Enterprise* bridge a few minutes before the change of shift. For days, she'd been intending to speak with Ensign Fenn about what had happened to her—about the section of chitin that had fallen from Borona's finger. Sulu knew that such a loss of exomembrane by a Frunalian often signaled the preliminary stages of what they called the Shift. And while she couldn't understand what it would be like to face such a metamorphosis, she had seen the expression of fear Fenn had worn when confronted with the prospect. Sulu had been concerned about the young woman, and she'd wanted to make sure that Fenn would be all right.

After the *Universe* tragedy, though, Sulu's attentions had been diverted in other directions. In addition to dealing with her own grief, she'd been trying to assist the crew with theirs. She'd also been worried about the captain, who not only had the weight of the entire crew's troubles on his shoulders, but who carried sizable trouble of his own: though he was no longer comatose, Admiral Harriman's condition had improved no further.

As Sulu walked around the raised perimeter of the bridge, passing behind Lieutenant Tenger and Lieutenant Kanchumurthi at the tactical-and-communications console, she saw the captain glance over his shoulder at her from the command chair. He nodded a greeting to her, and she returned the gesture. As Sulu circled past the port-side turbolift, Ensign Fenn looked up with both eyes from the sciences station. "Hi, Borona," Sulu said.

"Commander," Fenn replied. "I was about to contact you. I detected another occurrence of the dispersion in the navigational deflector."

"Were you able to track it down?" Sulu asked. She noticed a bandage wrapped around Fenn's wounded digit.

"No," the ensign said. "The effect lasted less than a second. But I've set up some monitoring programs, and they had enough time to eliminate some systems as the cause of the problem: the warp drive and impulse engines, sensors, and environmental control."

"Well, that's a start," Sulu said with a wry smile. "Maybe in another year and a half, we'll actually figure out what the source of the dispersion is, rather than what it isn't." Realizing that her statement could be construed as criticism, which she had not intended, Sulu added, "Good work, Borona."

"Thank you, Commander."

Sulu paused, allowing a moment for her to alter the course of the discussion. "Did you see Dr. Morell about what happened?" she asked, pointing offhandedly toward the bandage around Fenn's finger.

"Yes, I did," Borona said, but then she said nothing more.

"I don't mean to pry if you don't want to discuss it," Sulu said. "I just wanted to make sure that you were all right."

"No, no," Fenn said, somewhat hastily. "I mean, yes, I'm all right." She peered down at her hand, splaying her fingers as she did so. "I'm beginning the Shift." Fenn looked back up. "I thought Dr. Morell would have told you."

"She's probably informed the captain," Sulu guessed. "Are you in any pain?"

"The doctor prescribed some Frunalian medication for

me," Fenn said. "I think she's been prepared for this to happen."

"Dr. Morell is nothing if not attentive to the needs of the crew," Sulu agreed. "How long will it be?"

"The doctor estimates I won't begin the main phase of the Shift for another eighteen to twenty weeks," Fenn said. She looked down, apparently embarrassed. "I'll need to take a leave of absence before then," she said. "In about fourteen weeks."

Sulu knew that Frunalians never allowed themselves to undergo their metamorphosis off of their planet. "It's all right, Borona," she said, attempting to reassure her. "Your position as science officer will be here when you return."

"Yes, Commander," Fenn said, nodding. Although she did not appear to disbelieve what Sulu had said, she still seemed troubled by what lay ahead for her.

"Captain, we are being hailed," Kanchumurthi said. Sulu peered over and saw him operating his communications console. "It's the *Tomed*."

Sulu looked back around at Fenn. "Borona, I'm on alpha watch tomorrow," she said quickly. "Let's have dinner." Fenn nodded, and Sulu gave her shoulder a pat.

"How long until we reach the Neutral Zone?" Captain Harriman asked. Sulu stepped down into the lower, central portion of the bridge and walked over to stand beside him.

"Twenty-seven minutes," Linojj answered from the helm.

Harriman looked at Sulu. "Sooner than Vokar wants to see us, I'm sure," he said. "Put him through, Ramesh."

"Yes, sir," Kanchumurthi said. Then, after a moment, he added, "Captain, it's not Admiral Vokar."

Sulu felt her brow furrow in confusion. Had something happened to remove Vokar from command of the Romulan flagship? Had he perhaps been injured, or even killed?

"Put the message through," Harriman said.

"Yes, sir," Kanchumurthi replied, and the starscape on the main viewscreen disappeared, the image of a lean Romulan woman appearing in its place, the dark, green-tinged setting of the bridge on which she stood visible behind her. She wore the insignia of a subcommander, the color of tactical operations, and the guise of command. Her cheekbones sat high on her narrow face, her flesh extremely pale and yellowish, even for a Romulan.

"Captain Harriman," she said.

"Of *U.S.S. Enterprise*, yes," the captain said. "And you are?"

As Sulu watched, color rose in the woman's cheeks, an olive tone that clearly marked her ire. "I am Subcommander Linavil," she said evenly. "First officer of *Tomed* under Admiral Vokar." Sulu remembered Harriman's report of his experiences on the planet of the Koltaari, and that this woman had struck him and knocked him to the ground, then threatened him with a knife.

"Subcommander," the captain said, and Sulu noted an almost imperceptible curl along one side of his lips. "It's a pleasure to meet you."

For a tense beat, Linavil said nothing. *What can she say?* Sulu wondered. Any attempt to remind Harriman that the two had met previously would simply have underscored how she had apparently made no impression on him. If Vokar had intended his absence during this communication as an insult to Harriman, the captain had clearly returned it to the admiral's executive officer.

Finally, Linavil said, "Once *Enterprise* reaches the Neutral Zone, you will reduce velocity to warp factor five and lower your shields."

"We are not traveling with our shields raised," Harriman responded. "We expected there to be no need for us to defend ourselves. Our mission here is one of peace."

Linavil's lips parted and she expelled a short burst of air, the Romulan equivalent, Sulu supposed, of derisive laughter. "Whatever your mission," the subcommander said, "you will reduce your velocity and continue with your shields down. *Tomed* will escort you to Space Station Algeron. You are not permitted any communications while within Romulan territory."

"Even with your ship?" Harriman asked, and Sulu thought she could see the mischief behind his eyes.

Again, Linavil paused, her features tensing, her rage seeming barely contained. "At the first transgression of these requirements, *Tomed* will fire on *Enterprise*." The subcommander turned her head sharply to one side, clearly looking to somebody offscreen, and an instant later, her image vanished, the stars ahead of *Enterprise* appearing once more.

Sulu looked at Harriman, who returned her gaze. "I don't think she likes you very much," she said.

"Funny," the captain said. "I just don't seem to be able to make friends among the Romulan military."

"No, sir," Sulu said. Directly ahead of her, the doors to the starboard turbolift opened, and Lieutenant Trent and Ensign DeYoung stepped onto the bridge, the computer scientist and the tactical officer now obviously arriving for beta shift. Others would also be appearing shortly, she knew.

"Do as Linavil . . . ah, requested," Harriman said. "When we reach the Neutral Zone, keep the shields down, reduce speed to warp five, and maintain radio silence." He stood up from the command chair. "And let me know immediately if anything seems suspicious to you, Demora."

"Yes, sir," she said. As Harriman made his way to the turbolift, Sulu took her place in the command chair. She still did not feel comfortable about Starfleet providing the Romulans and Klingons with the hyperwarp-drive specifications, and she certainly did not trust either power. But she did trust John Harriman, and as *Enterprise* headed for hostile territory, she tried to focus on that fact. For eighteen years, the captain had commanded Starfleet's flagship through uncounted dangers, and always, he had successfully protected the ship, the crew, and the Federation itself. Right now, she simply had to trust that he would so one more time.

"Here are the research notes, the design specs, and the sensor logs of all the testing," Harriman said. He stepped up to the conference table and set down one of the three personal-access display devices he carried. On its screen, numbers, letters, and symbols marched in formulas along the bottom, below an animated line diagram that described warp fields being generated around an accelerating starship frame.

Harriman stepped back and glanced around the room. All eyes, he saw, had found the padd. At first, nobody said anything, reinforcing Harriman's conviction that Ambassadors Kamemor and Kage wanted to believe what they had just been told by the Federation envoys, and that both wanted to do what they could to avoid war.

"And you wish us to trust you?" Admiral Vokar asked, his voice thick with skepticism. He stood behind the table, near where the Romulan ambassador and her staff sat. In addition to the Federation, Romulan, and Klingon diplomatic parties to whom the special UFP envoys were making their presentation here on Algeron, Harriman had joined the summit to represent Starfleet; Vokar had subsequently demanded permission to take part in the meeting as well. One of the Klingon ambassador's aides, a large, imposing figure named Ditagh, had also made noise about wanting a Klingon Defense Force representative present, but Kage had quickly shut him down.

"No, Admiral, we actually do not expect you to trust us," said the lead Federation envoy—in reality, Commander Gravenor. Lieutenant Vaughn stood behind her, to her right. Both wore raiments befitting their alleged professions, Gravenor in a dark blue jacket and skirt over a white blouse, and Vaughn in a dark gray suit, also with a white shirt. "That is the purpose of our visit here," Gravenor continued. "That is why Starfleet has agreed to furnish both the Romulan Star

Empire and the Klingon Empire with all data relating to our hyperwarp project. It is our hope that your scientists will confirm what we've told you, and for you to see that what the crew of the *Tomed* witnessed was not the trial of a new weapon, but the tragic loss of a starship and crew testing the experimental drive."

"And what happens when we confirm something different than that?" Ditagh snapped. Ambassador Kage looked at his aide, but did not stop him from going on. "What happens when we confirm that Starfleet *was* conducting tests of a metaweapon?"

Kage peered over at Gravenor. "That is a legitimate question," he said.

"For you, yes, it is," Gravenor allowed. "But not for us. Because we know that Starfleet has created no such weapons, we expect that your scientists will be able to provide the necessary verification. There is nothing else that they can verify."

"So you claim," Ambassador Kamemor said carefully. "It is clear that the Federation understands the repercussions of their developing and testing a metaweapon; I trust you further understand the repercussions of then attempting to lie about it." Harriman watched her as she spoke, trying to measure the woman he saw now with the one he had met fifteen years ago at another diplomatic summit. Back then, he and Kamemor had established a rapport, one that had grown during four succeeding encounters. Harriman had even provided her with some guidance for her son regarding the young man's then-fledgling military career, guidance which had served the son well, Harriman had later found out. Now, though, Kamemor seemed to studiously avoid his gaze. Even when he had first entered the room and been introduced by Federation Ambassador Endara, her attention had passed quickly over him, as though even the slightest acknowledgment of their prior relationship could foul these talks—which, Harriman supposed, might well be true. "If the Romulan Empire is unable to authenticate the Federation's claims," Kamemor went on, "the consequences will be severe."

"Begging the ambassador's pardon," Vaughn said, "but since we are telling you the truth, the only consequence should be peace."

Kamemor nodded. "Let us hope so," she said.

Beside Kamemor, Vokar moved, striding behind the Romulan delegation and down the length of the table to its end, where he scooped up the padd Harriman had set down. "I will duplicate these data so that I can scrutinize them myself," he said, his tone clearly signaling a challenge to Harriman and the Federation envoys. Ripples of color wavered across Vokar's features, and Harriman glanced out the viewing port. In the distance, the remnants of the planet that had once orbited here refracted the light of this system's star. Although he could not see from this vantage where *Enterprise* sat docked at the large central ring of Algeron, Harriman spied the underside of *Tomed* as the ship orbited the space station. "The scientists and engineers on Romulus can check these readings," Vokar continued, "but I know what my crew observed, and I will have them examine the Federation assertions firsthand."

"Please," Gravenor said, "by all means, Admiral."

"The Klingon Empire demands its own set of data," Ditagh said.

"Of course," Harriman said. He moved forward again and placed the other two padds on the table. "I brought complete copies for each of the delegations."

"You may take a set of data, Ambassador Kage," Gravenor said. "Please feel free to match what we have provided you with what we have provided the Romulans. We wish there to be no misunderstandings."

Kage nodded in Gravenor's direction. "Thank you," he said to her, his voice unusually mellow for a Klingon, Harriman thought. He had never met Kage before, but he knew that the Federation Council held the ambassador in high regard. Evaluated to be one of Chancellor Azetbur's most trusted and loyal adherents, Kage was therefore believed to be a strong proponent of peace.

"I will repair to my vessel now," Vokar said, holding up the Federation padd, "so that my crew can begin to analyze these data."

"Pardon me, Admiral," spoke up one of Kamemor's aides, an intense young subconsul named Merken Vreenak. "With your permission, sir, and with yours, Ambassador—" Vreenak looked to Kamemor. "—I would like to examine the readings myself." When Kamemor said nothing, he added, "So that I may provide a direct report to you and this delegation." He smiled thinly, an expression Harriman imagined people wore when sliding a dagger smoothly and slowly into somebody's back.

"That will be acceptable," Kamemor said at last. "That is, if Admiral Vokar has no objections."

"Not at all," Vokar said, and Harriman felt suddenly certain that the admiral and the subconsul had worked together previously. Vreenak stood from his chair and emerged from behind the table, following Vokar as he passed Harriman and headed for the door. Before leaving, the admiral turned and addressed the assemblage. "I hope to have some preliminary findings within the day," he said. Then, looking directly at Harriman, he added, "Perhaps within hours." His message—that he expected to uncover evidence of Federation duplicity—was unmistakable.

"Excellent," Harriman said, unfazed. "We look forward to your conclusions." Vokar rounded on his heel and left, Vreenak trailing after him.

Good, Harriman thought as the meeting began to break up around him. Vokar's predictable insistence on having his crew study the hyperwarp documents at once would likely keep *Tomed* and *Enterprise* docked at Algeron for several more hours. And that would be enough time for Harriman to do what he had actually come here to do.

Sulu paced her quarters anxiously. The sounds of her footsteps, muffled by the carpeting, reached her ears too easily, underscoring the stillness of *Enterprise*. Tethered to an alien space station, inside the territory of a hostile power, the ship seemed vulnerable. Should political tensions finally give way to warfare, the crew of *Enterprise* would be immediately endangered, cut off as they currently were from the rest of the Federation.

"Damn," she muttered. She felt powerless, unable to take any meaningful actions as events unfolded around her. Captain Harriman remained on Algeron with the special UFP envoys, presumably handing over hyperwarp technology to the two powers who posed the greatest threat to the Federation. *Enterprise* sat undefended and silent, its shields lowered, its communications blacked out. And Sulu shuttled back and forth across her quarters, arms folded across her chest, searching for something that she could do to help.

"Damn," she said again. She considered going to the bridge and relieving Xintal, but she knew that there would be no point; standing another watch would not put her mind at ease, nor would it do for the crew to see her in such an apprehensive state. But she felt that she needed to do something.

Sulu walked to the outer bulkhead and peered out through the viewing ports there. Above, the tiered, circular form of the Romulan space station rose away from *Enterprise*, the lights from the station's own ports evidence of the inhabitants and visitors aboard. Beyond Algeron, the unblinking stars rested in the firmament, voiceless observers to all that transpired within the galaxy.

Without consciously choosing to do so, Sulu picked out the two stars that roughly defined the ends of the Bonneville Flats. Like a recurring nightmare, the moments of *Universe's* hyperwarp tests came back to her: the excitement she had felt, the numbers that had streamed across the sciences station readouts, the voices of the *Universe* crew. The sound of the explosion.

And then the silence. The terrible, cruel silence.

She knew that the specter of the *Universe* tragedy would haunt her for the rest of her life. She would learn to live with it, of course, and there would eventually come days that passed free of the horrible memories, but it would never leave her completely. *We have no comlink with the* Universe, Lieutenant Kanchumurthi had said from his communications station, and Sulu had known at that moment that tragedy had struck. There had been the sound of what could only have been an explosion, there had been the painful silence after it, there had been the zeroes on her readouts, but when Ramesh had reported the loss of communications with *Universe,* the certainty of what had happened had come to Sulu.

Each morning since the events out on the Bonneville Flats, she had awoken with thoughts of *Universe* in her mind. She had found some salve in working with the *Enterprise* crew to ease their pain, but only so much. Words and thoughts and actions could bring understanding and acceptance, and perhaps even closure, but the loss could never be lessened. Fifty-one people—fifty-one *heroes*—had given their lives in pursuit of a dream, a dream of exploration that would have been shared by all. Now, only the memories of those lives remained.

Sulu turned from the viewing port and walked over to the inner corner of her quarters, to her desk. She sat down and activated the computer interface there. It chirped to life, the image of *Enterprise* appearing on the display. "Computer," Sulu said, "list the crew roster of the U.S.S. *Universe.*" After the Romulans had revealed their knowledge of the testing out on the Bonneville Flats, and after Starfleet had opted to respond by fully disclosing what had taken place, all records of the incident had been declassified.

On the monitor, a list of Starfleet personnel appeared, blue letters on a white background. Sulu began to read through them, noting that Captain Kuwano had not actually held the rank of captain, but commander; an engineer by trade, according to the document, she had been designated acting captain for the *Universe* trials. Sulu recognized the names of the helm officer—Lieutenant Seaver, whose given name had been Doris—and the chief engineer—Lieutenant Commander Chernin, whose given name had been Alexei.

A knot formed behind Sulu's eyes, and she reached up and rubbed her forehead. *What am I doing?* she asked herself. She understood the grieving process, recalling the emotional storms she had weathered during other times of loss throughout her life. But was that what she was doing now? Was she working through her shock and sadness, or obsessing over them, staying mired in her sorrow?

Maybe the captain was right, she thought. *Maybe I should talk to Dr. Morell.*

Sulu dropped her hand into her lap and looked again at the *Universe* roster on her desktop display. She had no desire to diminish the memories of these women and men by fixating mindlessly on their loss. She wanted instead to honor them, to find the words or gestures that would exemplify her grief, and in so doing, venerate the lives of the *Universe* crew.

And that's what she would do, she decided.

Sulu stood from her desk and retrieved a small, round candle from her bedroom. She returned to the front cabin with it, and set it down before the desktop computer interface. After lighting the candle, she sat and folded her hands together. The yellow flame flickered once, then settled down to burn steadily. Sulu focused on it for several moments, before raising her eyes once more to the *Universe* crew roster.

"Commander Adrienne Kuwano," she said, her voice firm and clear. She peered again at the candle flame, bowing her head as she memorialized her fallen compatriot.

Finally, after a silent minute or so, she looked back up at the screen, at the next name on the list. "Lieutenant Commander Alexei Chernin," she recited, and bowed her head once more.

It took more than an hour for Sulu to read through the entire list of names.

A recognizable and steady tone signaled the arrival of the visitor at Kamemor's quarters. "Enter," she said from her place on the sofa, and the door slid open to reveal Captain Harriman standing beyond it. Behind him, a muscular security guard towered over him, evidence of station protocols that required guests to be accompanied when outside their habitat and conference sections.

"Ambassador Kamemor," Harriman said, bowing his head and closing his eyes in what she took to be a sign of respect. After the meeting with Harriman and the Federation envoys—and the vulgar Vokar—the three had been assigned separate quarters, despite the uncertainty of how long the trio would be staying on Algeron. From his cabin, Harriman had contacted Kamemor and asked for an audience with her. It had demanded some consideration for her to accede to his request; concerned that even the smallest misconception could pose a problem for the treaty negotiations, she did not wish to risk the impression of impropriety. But she realized that far greater problems than that now plagued the peace talks, and in the decade and a half that she had known the Starfleet captain, she had always found him an honorable and trustworthy man.

"Captain Harriman," she said, standing. "Please come in." The captain strode inside, and the security guard followed, stopping in the doorway. "Thank you, that will be all, Lieutenant," Kamemor said, dismissing him. He withdrew back into the corridor, the door closing behind him.

"*Jolan tru*, Ambassador," Harriman said, offering the traditional Romulan greeting. His pronunciation, impressively, lacked even the slightest hint of a human accent.

"Good evening, Captain," Kamemor returned, trusting in her own language skills to reciprocate Harriman's show of deference. "Please, have a seat," she said, opening her hand in the direction of a chair across from where she had been sitting.

"Thank you for seeing me," Harriman said as he moved farther into the room. He circled around the chair and sat down.

"It is my honor," she said. "May I offer you something to drink? Some ale perhaps?" She recalled the last time she had seen Harriman, at another treaty negotiation more than five years ago, on a moon in Tholian space. The two, celebrating the signing of a trade accord, had shared more than a liberal amount of the famed Romulan intoxicant.

Harriman looked up and smiled, clearly understanding her reference. "I think I'll pass on the ale today," he said. "But a glass of *carallun* would be refreshing."

"Of course," Kamemor said, struck again by the captain's knowledge of Romulan culture. As far as she knew, *carallun*—a lightly flavored citrus beverage made from fruit native to Romulus—was generally unknown outside of the Empire. She walked from the sitting area to the other side of the room, to the food synthesizer set into the bulkhead there. As she operated the control panel, walking through several menus and submenus, she asked, "How is Ms. Sasine?" Kamemor had once met Harriman's romantic partner, and Ms. Sasine had been the topic of conversation on more than one occasion.

"Good, very good, although I miss her," Harriman said. "And how about Ravent?" he added, asking about Kamemor's own mate.

"Excellent, thank you," Kamemor said. "Although I miss her as well." Arriving at the submenu item for *carallun*, she selected it, specifying her request for two glasses of the beverage. "So, Captain, is this a social visit, or an official one?"

"I'm afraid it's neither," Harriman said.

"Neither?" Kamemor questioned. "Then this is an unofficial visit, and not one intended for social purposes."

"Yes," Harriman agreed. "That's right." The hum of the food synthesizer filled the room, and its small door slid upward to reveal a pair of tall, narrow glasses on the shelf within. Kamemor picked them up and crossed back to the sitting area. As she handed one of the pale yellow drinks to Harriman, she saw him peering around her quarters. She followed his gaze as it passed over the artwork adorning her walls, a collection of realist works, mostly oil paintings, but also including a pair of busts she had acquired over the years. She saw the captain's attention settle on a still life portraying an IDIC pendant sitting atop a stack of books on an antique desk. "That painting is by a woman named Raban Gedroe," she told him. "It is entitled *Still Life, with Philosophy*."

"It is impressive," Harriman said. "But I'm a little surprised to see a Vulcan symbol depicted in a piece of Romulan art." He obviously referred to the medallion in the painting, an ancient Vulcan icon embracing the concept of "infinite diversity in infinite combinations."

"Tolerance and acceptance are ideals hardly exclusive to the Vulcans," Kamemor said.

"And yet not practiced widely enough," Harriman said as Kamemor sat back down on the sofa. "It's good to see you again, Ambassador. You're looking well."

"I am well, thank you," Kamemor said, sipping at her drink. "Although I am also frustrated at the often torpid pace of the peace negotiations."

"I understand," Harriman said.

"And you?" Kamemor asked. "Are you well? You appear . . . fatigued." The captain's features seemed drawn, his eyes red.

"I am fatigued," Harriman admitted. "The situation with the hyperwarp drive . . . that's why I'm here."

"But not in an official capacity," Kamemor said, attempting to understand the purpose of Harriman's visit.

"No," the captain said. "I wanted to tell you . . . I wanted to *assure* you . . . that the new drive was never intended to provide the Federation with a first-strike capability."

"I see," Kamemor said, not disguising her tone, which clearly reflected the uncertainty she felt about Harriman's claim.

"I can tell you that I've been involved in the project from the outset," he continued. "It's been in development for years, the next logical step after the failure of Starfleet's transwarp program."

Kamemor leaned to her left and set her glass down on a small table at the end of the sofa. "All these years since the transwarp program, Captain," she said. "Two, two and a half decades? And a starship equipped with the next generation of propulsion systems appears now, at the height of tensions between the Empire and the Federation?"

"An unfortunate coincidence," Harriman maintained. "But after all, Starfleet's primary purpose is exploration, and we are always moving to advance our abilities to carry out such endeavors."

"You'll forgive me, Captain," Kamemor said, "if I point out the heavy armaments carried by so many of Starfleet's vessels."

"I said exploration was Starfleet's *primary* purpose," Harriman said, "not its only one. I don't deny the defensive imperative of Starfleet. But I am telling you that hyperwarp was not developed as a weapon or a defense, but strictly as a tool of discovery."

"I am trying to decide, John," Kamemor said, "whether you are attempting to convince me of this, or whether you are attempting to convince yourself."

"Ambassador," Harriman said, his tone beseeching.

"Captain," Kamemor said. "I know that you're not naïve.

And I don't need to dispute your personal intentions for hyperwarp drive—or even the intentions of Starfleet itself. But are there not admirals within Starfleet Command who would employ any technology, any means, to defeat my people? Are there not those admirals who likely viewed the development of hyperwarp drive as an opportunity to end this cold war we've been waging, and not by declaring peace?" Kamemor paused, hoping to allow her words to penetrate past Harriman's stated opinion. "If I recall the content of my intelligence briefings, is not your father an admiral with a reputation as a so-called hawk?"

"I cannot deny the existence of such admirals," Harriman said, "although they are well in the minority. But neither can you deny the presence in the Romulan Imperial Fleet of such individuals."

"Of course not," Kamemor said. "And in the Senate as well."

"But I am not my father," Harriman said, "and you are not a warmongering diplomat."

"No," Kamemor said, "but if the hyperwarp data you have provided do not corroborate Starfleet's claims, there will be no stopping the Romulan hawks."

"Gell," Harriman said, employing her given name for the first time. He leaned forward and set his drink down on the low table between them. "There will be no stopping them anyway."

"What do you mean?" Kamemor wanted to know.

"I mean that I have information to give you," Harriman said. "For one thing, believe me when I tell you that the data provided today will verify the Federation claims: hyperwarp drive is not a weapon, nor can it reasonably be utilized as one. And as far as first-strike capabilities are concerned, the Romulans and Klingons now have as much data about the new drive as Starfleet; there will be no unbalancing of power."

"I am gratified to hear that," Kamemor said.

"But none of that will matter," Harriman went on. "Not to one man."

"One man?" Kamemor asked, although she already suspected the identity Harriman would reveal.

"Aventeer Vokar," the captain said, confirming Kamemor's suspicions.

"But if the data you provided prove the Federation claims," Kamemor said, "then the admiral will be able to do nothing."

"Nothing sane," Harriman said. "But he has a plan, Gell. And when data fail to provide him with the excuse he needs to attack the Federation, he will do so anyway."

"What?" Kamemor asked, her voice rising in surprise. She stood up, unable to remain seated. Slowly, Harriman stood as well, facing her across the sitting area.

"Vokar is going to commit an act of terrorism," he said. "He is going to attack a facility across the Neutral Zone in order to lure the Federation into a war. He knows that if we are attacked without provocation, we will be unable to refrain from launching an immediate counterstrike."

"But that is madness," Kamemor said, appalled at the picture Harriman had painted for her. "If the Federation is attacked, the Klingons will side with them in any subsequent conflict, and such a combined force would be able to overcome the Empire."

"You believe that," Harriman said, "and I believe it. But does Vokar? Or does his zealous nationalism blind him to reality? Does he trust so much in the natural ascendancy of the Romulans that he believes their defeat impossible under any circumstances?"

Kamemor looked away from Harriman, her mind working over what she had just been told. She knew the admiral, both by reputation and through her own dealings with him, and she recognized Harriman's characterization of Vokar as accurate. She had recently seen the beginnings of such attitudes in one of her own subconsuls, Vreenak, and she had vowed to herself to counsel the young diplomat in other directions.

Kamemor sat back down on the sofa, then looked back up at Captain Harriman. "Why are you telling me this?" she asked him.

Harriman returned to his seat as well, his eyes never leaving hers. "Because I need your help," he said.

"To do what?" she said, although the answer seemed clear.

"To stop Vokar," Harriman said. "To prevent a war that, no matter who ultimately wins, will see unprecedented numbers of casualties on all sides."

Kamemor thought again of Vreenak, and of her other subconsul, N'Mest, but she knew that she would never be able to tell anybody of this meeting with Harriman. "How can I trust you?" Kamemor asked, searching his face for an answer she knew she would not find there.

"That's a question only you can answer," Harriman said. "Despite living on opposite sides of the Neutral Zone, we've known each other for a long time now. I've never lied to you, and I'm not lying now. Like you, all I want is peace."

Kamemor nodded her head, not in agreement, but in simple, absent movement. She found herself believing the Starfleet captain, both because of her long relationship with him, and because of the narrow-minded, xenophobic, almost fanatical mindset she had always known Vokar to manifest. And in those terms, the decision came easily to her.

"What do you want me to do?" she asked.

MINUS THREE: SHADOWS

A bead of perspiration trickled from Harriman's hairline down to his brow. The air in the Jefferies tube felt still and close, like a windless day in a humid clime. The times he'd spent on Pacifica with Amina rose in his mind, but he immediately dismissed those thoughts; this was no vacation. He wiped at his forehead with the back of his hand, smearing the sweat across his already-slick skin.

Lying on his left side, Harriman lifted a handheld device up before his face. He examined the simple readout—one indicator for status, another for range—and verified the accurate operation of the fist-sized apparatus. After reattaching it to the belt of his uniform jacket, he reached for another piece of equipment he had carried here. He picked up the heavy rectangle of metal from the decking and studied its curved surface, about half a dozen times the size of his open hand. A control module and a small display jutted out from its other side. A normal component of impulse-drive systems, the deuterium-flow regulator controlled the introduction of hydrogen isotope fuel into the fusion reactors.

This particular regulator, Harriman knew, was defective. Though not visible to the unaided eye, a microscopic fracture zigzagged across its face. Additionally, a dropped parity bit in its firmware would prevent self-detection of the flaw. When engaged, the regulator would fail to correctly control the stream of deuterium entering the impulse reactor. Temperatures would rise rapidly in the core, releasing radiation and threatening an explosion. Unchecked, the runaway fuel flow would result in disaster.

Harriman adjusted the position of his body, pushing up onto his knees. He turned and reached forward with both hands, into the exposed equipment beyond the open engineering panel. Magnetic and mechanical locking mechanisms snapped closed around the regulator as he set it delicately into place. He withdrew his hands from the open panel and grabbed his tricorder, also hanging from his belt. A quick check showed the impulse system in apparently perfect working order.

He returned the tricorder to his belt, then closed up the panel and retrieved the flow regulator he'd earlier removed. Before completing his tasks here, he once more confirmed the functioning of the other small device. The sensor veil remained in place, he saw, rendering him no more substantial to scans than a shadow. His presence here, and his modification of the impulse drive, would go completely undetected.

As would a single phaser blast.

The decking of the Jefferies tube clanged as Harriman put the replaced flow regulator down. He crawled backward away from it, then slipped a type-one phaser from beneath the back of his uniform jacket. He leveled the weapon at the piece of equipment and fired. The regulator vanished in a burst of high-pitched sound and red light. The burned scent of ozone filled the air.

Harriman holstered his phaser, then utilized his tricorder to exit the Jefferies tube back into the corridor without being seen. He quickly returned to his quarters, where he divested himself of his tricorder, phaser, and sensor veil. Then he headed for the *Enterprise* bridge.

"How long?" Sulu asked, peering down past Linojj's shoulder at the helm readouts. Her clipped words reflected the disquiet she'd felt ever since *Enterprise* had crossed the Neutral Zone on its way to Algeron. Not long ago, though, Captain Harriman had returned to the ship and informed her that they'd be leaving the Romulan station in two hours. Vokar's crew had evidently examined the hyperwarp specs and testing logs the captain had provided, and they'd been unable to find any discrepancies between those data and Starfleet's claims about the new drive system. Admiral Vokar had therefore scheduled the departure of *Tomed*, which would first escort *Enterprise* back to Federation space, and then travel to Romulus, where the hyperwarp data would be studied more thoroughly. "How long before we leave?" she said, clarifying her question.

"Twenty-seven minutes," Linojj answered, consulting the chronometer on her console.

Sulu absently shook her head. "Not soon enough for me," she said quietly, more to herself than to any of the crew. She knew that some of the apprehension she felt right now would ease once *Enterprise* had exited Romulan territory.

"Not soon enough for me either," Linojj agreed, looking up from the helm and staring forward, toward the front of the bridge. Sulu followed her gaze. On the main viewscreen, the layered circles of the Algeron station rose off to port, an unfamiliar outpost in unfriendly space.

Sulu crossed behind Linojj and walked over to the navigation console. She leaned in past Ensign Tolek and examined the course he'd computed for the journey back to the Federation, a simple reversal of the path along which *Tomed* had initially led them. "Ensign," Sulu said, raising her hand to the display, "I want you to calculate a series of contingency courses for us. Beginning with the space station, from every point a half-light-year along this route—" She traced the tip of her finger along the blue line that represented their presumed course. "—I want you to prepare alternate courses back to the Federation."

Tolek peered up at Sulu, one of his eyebrows rising on his forehead in obvious curiosity. "Do you anticipate difficulties, Commander?" he asked.

"Anticipate them?" Sulu said. She took a moment before answering, considering the question as she moved back to the command chair and sat down. "No," she said at last, and that was true: she didn't expect *Enterprise* to find itself in the middle of a firefight while on this side of the Neutral Zone. But she also did not trust the Romulan Imperial Fleet in general, or Admiral Vokar in particular. "While we're still in hostile territory, though," she continued, "there's nothing wrong with taking additional precautions."

"Aye, aye, Commander," Tolek said. As the ensign complied with her order, his controls garnishing the bridge with beeps and chirps, Sulu heard the starboard doors open. She looked over to see Captain Harriman enter the bridge from the turbolift.

"Captain," she said. She started up out of the command chair, but Harriman gestured to her as he approached, his hand patting down toward the deck. "We're ready for departure," Sulu said, sitting back down. "We expect word from the *Tomed* in less than half an hour."

"Good," Harriman said, nodding. "I want *Enterprise* back in Federation space as soon as possible." Although his sentiment echoed the one she'd voiced herself just a few minutes ago, his inflection and the way he'd phrased the statement seemed to carry an additional—and surprising—meaning.

"Sir?" Sulu said, asking the question with only the single word.

"I'll be staying behind on Algeron," Harriman said. "With the Federation envoys."

"For how long?" Sulu asked at once, stunned to learn of this just minutes before the ship would be leaving the Romulan station.

"I don't know," Harriman told her. "But in my absence, you will captain *Enterprise*, and Xintal will serve as your first officer."

"Sir," Sulu began, but then she stopped, unsure of what she should say. She certainly held no concerns about her own ability to command—she'd been Harriman's exec for a decade, and she fully expected to have her own ship one day—but the abruptness, the unexpectedness with which this had happened left her puzzled. She understood that the captain had more direct experience with the Romulans than just about anybody else in Starfleet—not to mention his vast experience with the Klingons—but he was a better explorer and a better soldier than he was a diplomat. It made no sense to her for Starfleet Command, in these dangerous times, to remove an officer of Captain Harriman's caliber from the command of the flagship.

"I've already transferred all command codes to you," Harriman said. "Inform the crew of my temporary reassignment. Once you take the ship back into Federation territory, proceed to Echo Sector. *Enterprise*'s orders are to patrol along the Neutral Zone in that region. You'll find Starfleet's latest communications in my command log."

"Yes, sir," Sulu said, though she still felt uneasy by what had just occurred. But she could see that the captain had said all he was going to say right now, and so she added, "Good luck."

"Thank you," Harriman said. Before he left, though, he looked as though he might say something more to her, and Sulu hoped that he might offer an explanation for why Starfleet wanted him to remain on Algeron. He leaned in close to her, and she sat forward in the command chair, until their faces were only centimeters apart. "You know," he said in a voice barely above a whisper, "I still keep thinking about Iron Mike Paris."

Sulu felt her eyes narrow as she stared at the captain. Harriman had mentioned Mike Paris to her only one other time since the debriefings after the mission to Devron II, and that had been just a few days ago, on the night when he'd come to her quarters to talk about his father. And as with that first time, Sulu felt as though the captain's words held some deeper meaning that she could not immediately decipher. Before she could respond to him, though, Harriman rounded on his heel and headed back toward the starboard turbolift. In only seconds, he was gone.

Sulu sat back in the command chair, uncomfortable with what had just happened. In front of her, at the helm, Linojj turned and looked back over her shoulder. "Twenty-one minutes now until departure," she said, and then added with a wry grin, "Captain."

Sulu smiled thinly, an acknowledgment that contained no good feelings in it. The true captain of *Enterprise* had just left the bridge, she knew, and he'd soon be leaving the ship as well. Sulu glanced back over at the turbolift doors, at where she had last seen Harriman, and suddenly, she wondered whether she would ever see him again.

Lieutenant Vaughn sat stiffly in a chair in Commander Gravenor's quarters. Taking advantage of the quiet and the stillness in these last few moments, he forged through a series of mental disciplines he'd picked up during the last few years. As he'd moved from behind his desk at Starfleet special operations and out into the field, he had discovered himself challenged in ways he'd never anticipated. On some missions, he had been tested physically, an eventuality for which he *had* prepared; the intense fitness regimens required of all field operatives had so far seen him through the most difficult of circumstances. And he had trained himself mentally as well, sharpening his powers of deduction and observation, of memory and strategic thinking, and those skills too had stood him in good stead.

But there had also been other, unexpected trials, trials surprising for their simplicity: things such as boredom, and discomfort, and frustration. Vaughn had once shadowed a Benzite engineer for three months, a man suspected of trafficking in purloined Starfleet technology, but who'd ended up being nothing more than an honest and extremely dull person. Another operation had required Vaughn to wear prosthetic appliances—most notably on his face—for weeks in order to infiltrate a Tellarite mining facility. Still others of his missions, while justified and perfectly executed, had failed to yield the desired results.

Through the course of his field service, Vaughn had learned numerous and varied mental exercises that allowed him both to prepare for and to endure such psychological adversities. He had been taught some techniques by other special ops officers—primarily by Commander Gravenor— while he had discovered some on his own. Right now, he employed them all in an attempt to ready himself for the coming mission.

They weren't working.

Vaughn rubbed at his eyes, concerned by what he felt, and by his inability at the moment to deal appropriately with it. While boredom, discomfort, and frustration likely would not threaten Vaughn in the hours and days ahead, another feeling had already taken hold of him: fear. The emotion had not developed from a concern for his own safety or survival, he knew—he had become adept at facing personal danger with relative composure—but out of his concerns for others. If something went wrong on this mission—and there were so many ways in which something could—then people—*lots* of people—would die. And that risk haunted him.

A single-toned chime sounded in the quiet room. Vaughn stood from the chair, intending to answer the door, but Commander Gravenor immediately emerged from the bedroom and said, "Come in." As she crossed to the door, it opened, and Captain Harriman entered the room. He waited until the door had slid closed behind him before speaking.

"*Enterprise* and *Tomed* will be leaving the station in a few minutes," he told the commander. "Are we prepared?"

"We are," Commander Gravenor said. She glanced over at Vaughn, as though seeking to confirm his readiness. He nodded once in response. "I've got our things laid out in there," she said, looking back at the captain and pointing toward the bedroom.

"Good," Harriman said. He reached beneath the bottom of his uniform jacket and withdrew a small handheld device. Vaughn recognized the piece of classified equipment at once as a sensor veil. He and Commander Gravenor wore them as well. "Let's go."

The commander turned and strode back toward the bedroom, the captain close behind her. Vaughn followed, and as he crossed the room, he felt his heart rate begin to climb. *Stop it*, he told himself, knowing that he would have to find some way to banish—or at least rein in—this sense of dread. *You have a mission*, he thought, a mantra that he had adopted on a recent, exceptionally grueling assignment. *You have a mission*, he thought again, trying to focus his mind.

In the other room, Captain Harriman and Commander Gravenor gathered up the few items they would be taking with them. Vaughn quickly did the same. Then, with a bloody war in the Alpha and Beta Quadrants hanging in the balance, they waited.

Linojj tapped at the thruster controls, maneuvering *Enterprise* away from the Romulan space station. *Tomed*'s first officer, Subcommander Linavil, had confirmed the return route back to the Federation, and now Linojj started the ship along that path. She watched the readings on the helm display carefully, paying close attention to *Enterprise*'s position relative to the station. "We've departed Algeron," she said when the numbers indicated that the ship had pulled away sufficiently. "We are free and clear to navigate."

Free and clear? Linojj thought, acknowledging to herself the folly of what she had said. *We can't be that free with an* Ivarix-*class warship chaperoning us through space.*

"Take us to full impulse," Sulu ordered. She sat behind Linojj, in the command chair. "Let's get out of this system."

"Engaging impulse power," Linojj said. She walked her fingers across the helm panel, coaxing the slower-than-light drive to action. Around her, the ship stirred like a living thing, as though rising up onto its haunches and preparing to spring forward. The low growl of the impulse drive grew, and an almost imperceptible vibration coursed through the ship's structure like the tensing of muscles. In a short time, Linojj knew, *Enterprise* would leave the Algeron system behind, and then the ship could leap to warp. "One-quarter impulse," Linojj said, reading the velocity from her display. She saw the momentary fluctuation in the ship's acceleration the instant before Lieutenant Commander Buonarroti reported it.

"I just read a slight instability in the deuterium stream to the port impulse reactor," he said from the starboard engineering station. By the time he'd finished speaking, the flux had vanished.

"Is it a problem?" Sulu asked. Linojj kept her eyes on the helm readouts, monitoring the velocity curve to see if the fluctuation would recur.

"I'm not sure," Buonarroti said. "It may have been an isolated—" Again, Linojj saw the situation on her display right before the chief engineer announced it. This time, though, the ship's acceleration did not steady. "There it is again," Buonarroti said. "And now the stream isn't stabilizing."

"What's causing it?" Sulu wanted to know.

"I don't know," Buonarroti said. "I'm trying to pinpoint the problem now."

"We're at one-half impulse," Linojj said. She heard the sound of the ship change, an inconstant whine now joining the hum of the impulse engines. The velocity indicator continued erratically upward.

"Fluctuations are increasing," Buonarroti said. "Both in number and in size."

Linojj saw movement in her peripheral vision, and she looked in that direction to see Sulu striding toward the engineering station. "Are we in any danger?" the commander asked.

"Not yet," Buonarroti said. "But the temperature is beginning to climb in the core."

"Do we need to shut down the impulse engines?" Sulu asked.

"Possibly," Buonarroti said, "but . . . let me try to adjust the deuterium flow, try to control the instability." Linojj watched as the chief engineer expertly worked his panel.

"Captain," Tenger said from the tactical station. "The radiation level in the port reactor is also increasing."

Sulu did not hesitate. "Shut them down, Xintal."

"Acknowledged," Linojj said. Her hands fluttered across her panel, working to bring the impulse drive offline.

"Rafe," Sulu said, "can you tell—"

"Captain," Linojj interrupted, startled to find herself fighting a losing battle with the helm controls. "I can't shut down the port reactor." She scanned her readouts for the ship's current velocity. "We're at three-quarters impulse and still accelerating."

"Rafe?" Sulu asked, her voice firm, her manner serious but composed.

"The core is pulling in more fuel than it should, keeping the reaction hot," Buonarroti said. "Let me shut down the deuterium stream."

"Radiation is beginning to increase significantly," Tenger said. "The temperature in the core is spiking."

"Eighty percent of full impulse," Linojj said.

"It's not working," Buonarroti said, turning from the engineering station to face Sulu. "The deuterium-flow regulator reads fully functional, but it's not controlling the influx of fuel into the reactor. I need to go down there."

"Go," Sulu said immediately.

Buonarroti jogged around the chair in front of the engineering station and raced for the starboard turbolift. "Gray," he said, calling across to the port side of the bridge, where Lieutenant Trent sat at the library-computer console. "You're with me." The ship's chief computer scientist took only a second to secure his station, then hurried around the perimeter of the bridge, past the main viewscreen, and joined Buonarroti in the turbolift. The doors glided closed after them.

Sulu stepped back down to the center section of the bridge and paced over to stand beside Linojj. "What do you think?" Sulu asked quietly. "Did they do this?" She did not have to identify whom she meant by *they*; Linojj had already wondered herself if the ship had been sabotaged.

"I don't know," Linojj said, looking up at Sulu. "But why would they? If the *Enterprise* is destroyed in Romulan space, even in an accident, nobody's going to believe that the Romulans weren't involved. And wouldn't that drive the Klingons to side with the Federation if hostilities break out?" As she thought through the argument she was making, Linojj found that it made sense to her. That, in turn, brought relief, to know that the first shot of the war had likely *not* just been fired.

Sulu nodded, although if in agreement or in simple acknowledgment, Linojj could not tell. "Ramesh," Sulu said, turning to face him at the tactical-and-communications station at the aft section of the bridge, "get me the *Tomed*."

Ambassador Gell Kamemor waited in her cabin on Algeron, peering out into space through the viewing port in her sleeping quarters. A sliver of her pallid face reflected on the oval pane, a sheer contrast to the onyx night beyond. Kamemor studied the arc of her waxen flesh, one ear sweeping upward to a graceful point, one eye staring relentlessly back at her. She did not appear nearly as weary as she felt.

Behind her, a clock kept time, its staccato ticking permeating the surrounding silence. Kamemor still had not completely decided on what actions she would take—or fail to take—in the next few minutes. She had pledged her cooperation to Captain Harriman, a man she had known—and trusted, at least to some extent—for some time, but what he had asked of her held danger not only for her, but for her people as well. If the captain had deceived her about Vokar, about the admiral's intentions to instigate war no matter the circumstances, then aiding Harriman at this point might itself abet the start of hostilities. Kamemor had labored a very long time for peace, had struggled against prevailing sentiment that held war to be inevitable, and yet what she did or did not do in the next several moments might decide everything.

The *tick, tick, tick* of the clock seemed to echo the beating of her heart. Her thoughts drifted with the sound. The ebony expanse of space outside the viewing port faded, as did her ashen likeness, replaced in her mind by the faces of Ravent, her mate, and Sorilk, her son. Kamemor had visited Ravent only three times during the past year, on foreshortened trips back to their homeworld of Glintara. She had seen Sorilk just once, when the starship on which he served had stopped briefly at Algeron. And yet Ravent and Sorilk inspired most of the passion Kamemor devoted to crafting a lasting peace with the Klingons and the Federation. She knew that even a war in which the Empire eventually triumphed would put her loved ones at risk, and she could not countenance such a threat.

And is not almost everyone somebody's loved one? Kamemor thought. Did the Empire not mourn the loss of even a single Romulan soldier? Would it be any different for Klingon or Federation citizens? The Klingons did not look upon the prospect of death in the same way that Romulans did—Klingons might be less reluctant to die under certain circumstances—but they still did not seek the ends of their lives.

A belief Kamemor embraced held that the measure of all sentient existence rose to infinite heights. A necessary corollary of that conviction gauged a Klingon life or a Federation life—Vulcan, human, Andorian, or whatever—as no more or less valuable than a Romulan life. The citizens of the Empire wanted none of their people to be killed in battle, but what they should have wanted was for no people, of any race, to be killed in battle. That meant seeking and sustaining peace, and Kamemor had dedicated her career to establishing equitable accords to do just that.

Tick. Tick. Tick.

Now, though, she had to decide, had to *figure out*, who had told her the truth—if anybody even had. Klingon and Federation ambassadors and aides, her own aides, the Romulan Senate, the Klingon High Council, the Federation Council . . . alleged truths had come to her from many sources. Kamemor understood that in the world of diplomacy, a single word, a particular shade of meaning, could be employed to twist the truth in order to achieve some end. Words and ideas often became arguments to persuade, to threaten, to dissemble, all simply to bring about some course of action.

Did Harriman tell me the truth? she wondered. *Did my aides?* Did she herself fully grasp the nuances of all that had transpired these past few years, of all that had been said?

Right now, it came down to this: did she really know John Harriman, and could she—*should* she—trust him? Should she be so wary of Admiral Vokar, a man whose sometimes-ruthless service record could not hide the heroic deeds he had achieved for the greater good and glory of the Empire?

A tone beeped in the room, and then repeated, vying for her attention with the ticking of the clock. Kamemor peered away from the viewing port and across the room, at the portable sensing device that sat on the shelf built into the bulkhead above her bed. Harriman had configured the scanner for her, and the signal told her that in nearby space, the crew of *Enterprise* faced disaster, and the crew of *Tomed* would shortly react to that crisis. The time had come for Kamemor to choose which course of action she would take.

She peered once more out the viewing port. She could not see *Enterprise* or *Tomed* from here, nor could she see the beautiful, glistening colors of the Algeron Effect. But she did not need to see the sparkling remnants of Algeron III to be reminded of what had occurred in this system. Kamemor thought of the horrible weapon that had been wielded here, thought of the terrible destruction and death wreaked upon her people by a merciless enemy, and she knew that she could not let that happen to anybody else, Romulan or otherwise. There were lines that should never be crossed—not in everyday life, not in peacetime, not in wartime. Kamemor might not be able to prevent Vokar from perpetrating the heinous act of terror Harriman had accused him of planning, but she could try.

She stopped on her way out of her bedroom to deactivate the signal calling from the portable scanner, then tucked the scanner inside the folds of the long scarlet robe she wore. She then walked to the door to her quarters and stopped as it opened before her. She realized that this would probably be a defining moment of her life. With luck, no Romulan would ever know about it.

Kamemor strode through the door and down the corridor. She did not look back.

"Something is happening aboard *Enterprise*," Sublieutenant Akeev said from the sciences station near the main viewscreen. Subcommander Renka Linavil peered down at the officer from the raised command chair at the rear of *Tomed*'s bridge. The sublieutenant's tone had contained a recognizable note of agitation, but his words had conveyed a woeful lack of useful data. But Linavil immediately suspected treachery, perpetrated not against the Starfleet crew, but by them. She trusted the Federation not at all.

"*Something* is happening?" Linavil questioned, not even attempting to moderate the irritation she felt. Akeev had served under Admiral Vokar for years, and therefore should have known better than to offer up less than complete information. Had the admiral been on the bridge right now, rather than off-shift in his quarters, either the sublieutenant would have acted capably, or he would have found himself relieved of duty.

"Readings indicate abnormally high levels of radiation," Akeev explained. He checked the console, and then added, "It's coming from the impulse drive."

"Full sensor sweep," Linavil ordered. "Are they raising shields? Charging weapons?" She doubted the *Enterprise* crew would be adopting an offensive—or even a defensive— posture in these circumstances, and Akeev should already have been monitoring the Starfleet vessel anyway. But her request for a complete sweep attended two purposes: first, to confirm *Enterprise*'s status, and second, to emphasize to the science officer the consequences of performing his duties less than rigorously.

"I've been monitoring continuously, Subcommander," Akeev said, clearly abashed. "*Enterprise*'s shields remain down, and its weapons offline." He consulted the sciences console before resuming. "The source of the radiation is the port impulse drive. The temperature in the reactor is also increasing."

Linavil stood from the command chair and descended to the deck of the bridge. "What is happening?" she demanded. She saw the eyes of other bridge personnel turn toward her, but she continued to focus on Akeev.

"It's difficult to know for sure," the sublieutenant said, studying the readouts, "but it reads like a malfunction."

"Are they in danger?" Linavil wanted to know. She peered at the main viewscreen, at the image of *Enterprise* as it soared through space ahead of *Tomed*.

"If the temperature and radiation maintain their rises, yes," Akeev said. "The reactor will go supercritical and explode." The sublieutenant looked up, and Linavil saw what appeared to be satisfaction in his expression. If nothing else, it demonstrated why the officer, as bright a scientist as he was, had not attained a rank beyond the one he currently held.

"Can we prevent that from happening?" Linavil asked.

"Can we—?" Akeev started, evidently confused. "Subcommander?"

"It was a simple question, Sublieutenant," Linavil said, marching across the bridge to the sciences station. "Can we prevent *Enterprise* from being destroyed?" She found Akeev's shortsightedness disturbing, but it seemed obvious to her that the destruction of a Starfleet vessel in Romulan space—however it happened—would be viewed by both the Federation and the Klingons as an act of hostility. And even if the Romulan Star Empire did not need the Klingon Empire fighting by its side, it did not need the Klingons fighting alongside the Federation either. But she did not feel the need to explain this to Akeev. Instead, she said, "The *Enterprise* crew must have detected the danger, and they clearly cannot shut their impulse drives down, otherwise they already would have done so. So is there something we can do to assist?"

"I . . . I don't know," Akeev stammered. "I'm not, uh, familiar with—"

"Shields down," Linavil said, cutting off the sublieutenant both with her words and by turning her back to him as she looked toward the tactical station. "Be prepared to transport their crew into the cargo holds."

"Yes, Subcommander," responded the tactical officer.

Linavil turned toward the communications station. "Contact *Enterprise*," she said.

"Subcommander," the comm officer said, looking up from her console, "*Enterprise* is hailing us."

"Put them through," Linavil said, and she peered toward the main viewscreen, prepared to face the enemy—and if necessary, help them.

Kamemor arrived at her destination, hastily consulted the scanner she had carried here, then quickly slipped inside. As the door slid shut behind her, the lighting in the room increased automatically from a low, standby level to station normal. She inspected the small room at once, her gaze darting from a lone, freestanding console on one side to an alcove on the other. As the scanner had told her, the room was empty.

Again keenly aware of her heart beating, Kamemor raced over to the console. *I'm a diplomat*, she thought, *not an intelligence agent, not a saboteur*. And yet here she stood, in an area of the Algeron station that, before now, she had only ever passed through.

She set down the scanner atop the console and studied the array of controls there. Captain Harriman had carefully described the layout to her, and she saw now that his instruction had been accurate. Kamemor did not question how a Starfleet officer had known such information, vaguely assuming the ephemeral nature of technological secrets.

She studied the panel closely, and at first she rushed too

much, the complexity of the console nearly overwhelming her. Kamemor thought that she would not be able to do this, and in that moment of doubt, she dreaded the consequences of her failure more than the consequences of being labeled a traitor. She hadn't fully realized it, but on her way here, and entering this room, and even standing here peering down at this console, she had not been completely committed to this course of action.

Now she was. For the good of the Empire, she had to do this.

Kamemor concentrated on the console. She did as Harriman had suggested, and isolated only those controls that she would need. She found the targeting sensors first, and then the activation sequencer. One by one, she located all the necessary controls. When she had finished, she raised her arms and positioned her hands above the panel, then reviewed the progression of actions the captain had detailed for her. Finally, knowing that her window of opportunity was rapidly closing, and wanting to finish here and flee this room, Kamemor acted.

Her fingers moved carefully across the console. She hesitated briefly before operating each control, revisiting and reconfirming her memory of what Harriman had told her to do. If she did not do this correctly, then none of her actions and none of her decisions would have any meaning.

Everything she did seemed to work. Readings and confirmation indicators appeared on the readout as she'd been told they would, until she came to the final step. Once more, she paused, not from any reservations about completing this undertaking, but because once she had, there would be no way to reverse it. And if she had done something wrong along the way, then she might just as easily kill Captain Harriman as help his cause.

Kamemor operated the last control.

A surge of emotional energy coursed through her body, and a thought—*What have I done?*—bloomed in her mind.

But she knew that she would not learn the answer to that question right away.

Using the same care that she had already shown, and continuing to follow Harriman's directions, she sent her fingers back across the console, hiding the evidence of her handiwork. When she had finished, she retrieved the scanner and verified that the corridor outside the room was clear. Then, returning the scanner to its hiding place amid the material of her robe, Kamemor exited the transporter room, walking into a future that she had just tried to cast, but not knowing yet what that future would actually hold.

Rafaele Buonarroti crawled along the Jefferies tube, the metal grating hard against his knees even through the material of the environmental suit he wore. A loud, deep drone filled the area, joined by a higher-pitched, tremulous whine. The sounds conducted through the air, through the decking, through the environmental suit, causing a sensation like insects crawling all over his body. Normal engineering procedures restricted access to this section of the ship when the impulse engines were engaged, but the situation right now had deviated far from normal.

Buonarroti tilted his head—an awkward movement with his helmet on—and peered past his feet to where Lieutenant Trent clambered along after him. They'd left their comm channels open, and Buonarroti heard Trent's breathing beginning to become a bit labored. "Are you all right, Gray?" he asked, having to raise his voice to be heard above the ambient sounds of the drive.

"Yeah," Trent said around mouthfuls of air. "I'm okay. It's just a little hot in here."

"Don't worry about the heat," Buonarroti quipped. "Long before we burn up, the radiation will kill us." Trent actually laughed at that, despite the truth contained in the joke. While the environmental suits would have safeguarded them from the standard temperature and radiation levels of the impulse engines for a matter of hours, now they would provide only minutes of protection. Lieutenant Commander Linojj had been able to shut down the starboard engine, but the port reactor remained online, deuterium fuel apparently flowing uncontrolled into its core. And that meant that somebody had to come here to attempt a repair of the problem.

Buonarroti looked ahead again, pulling himself along in the enclosed space. He glanced at the data on the readout strip sliding down the left side of his faceplate, and saw that he and Trent had only thirteen minutes left before the radiation levels here would begin affecting their bodies. The sections surrounding the port impulse engine, he knew, were already being evacuated.

A minute later, Buonarroti arrived at the engineering panel that allowed access to the deuterium-flow regulator for the port reactor. He stopped and climbed onto his knees, then reached forward to remove the panel, his movements slowed by the environmental suit. The panel came away from the bulkhead easily, the magnetic locks giving way under the force of his pull. He set it to one side and peered in at the regulator. A readout on it indicated the runaway nature of the hydrogen-isotope stream pouring through its electromagnetic control field.

Buonarroti believed that the symptoms of the problem pointed to a disruption of that control field. That likely meant either a physical defect or a programmatic problem in the regulator; because the diagnostic code in the firmware had failed to identify any physical defects, he therefore suspected the latter, which was why he had brought Trent down here with him. It had also occurred to Buonarroti that *Enterprise*, sitting docked at a Romulan space station, might have been sabotaged, but at the moment that possibility mattered little to him; he only cared about diagnosing and then repairing the problem.

He pulled a tricorder from where it hung on his environmental suit, along with two fiber-optic leads. He quickly attached the thin glass wires to the tricorder, then reached in and connected the other ends to the regulator. He worked the controls on both devices, scrutinizing their displays. He had expected the root cause of the problem to reveal itself immediately, but instead, he detected nothing wrong.

On his faceplate, he saw that he and Trent had only ten minutes of safety left. If they had not fixed the problem in that time, he knew that they would continue to search for a solution, but their probability of surviving the situation unharmed, if at all, would rapidly decrease to zero.

"Gray," Buonarroti said, and he handed the tricorder to Trent. The computer scientist took it, holding it in both of his gloved hands, his strained breathing loud over the comm system. He studied the readout for just a few seconds.

"There's nothing wrong here," he said. "The operating system is functioning perfectly."

"But how can there be no problem to report," Buonarroti asked, "when there clearly is a problem?"

Trent nodded. "Let me check the verification routines." He operated the controls of the tricorder, then looked up and pointed into the bulkhead at the regulator. "I need to get in there," he said.

Buonarroti quickly scrambled farther down the Jefferies tube, clearing the way for Trent in front of the engineering panel. Trent moved forward as well, then reached inside. Buonarroti watched as the lieutenant pressed the control pad on the regulator, causing text—lines of code, Buonarroti assumed—to march across its display.

A minute passed. Then another. Buonarroti felt perspiration rolling down his body inside the environmental suit, a result not of the heat, he thought, so much as of the time growing short. He imagined the heavy atoms of hydrogen screaming past the regulator, unconstrained as they fed the fusion reactions in the impulse engine. Like having too many logs on a fire, the increase in the number of atomic reactions in the core would eventually generate more energy than could be contained in the reactor.

Seven minutes left.

"I've got it," Trent said at last. "The diagnostics aren't checking out. The checksum routines seem to be off." He worked the controls on the regulator's panel for a moment more, then began operating the tricorder

"Can you fix it?" Buonarroti asked.

"I'm trying," Trent said. "I'm recoding the safety routines, reestablishing the parity bits."

Six minutes left. Then five.

"Uploading," Trent said, peering into the bulkhead. Buonarroti followed his gaze, and saw a warning message scroll across the regulator display. Around them, the resonant hum of the port impulse engine, along with the sickly whine permeating it, began to fade. He looked up at Trent. "Error detection is now functioning," the computer scientist said. "There's a flaw in the regulator surface. Automatic shutdown is in progress."

Buonarroti leaned in beside Trent and touched a control on the tricorder. Sensor readings of the reactor core appeared on the display. The radiation and temperature levels had stopped their precipitous climbs, and as he watched, they even began to recede.

"Let's get out of here," Buonarroti said, pointing past Trent back down the Jefferies tube.

"Bridge to Buonarroti." Sulu's voice came over the comm system as the two men began to crawl back the way they had come. "You've done it."

"Yes, Captain," Buonarroti confirmed. "Trent did."

"Good work," Sulu said.

"We're on our way back to the bridge," Buonarroti said.

"I look forward to your report," Sulu said. "Out."

As the two made their way through the Jefferies tube toward the corridor, Buonarroti checked the readout on his faceplate. Seconds continued to tick off from their margin of safety. 3:57. 3:56. 3:55.

"We had more than four minutes left," Buonarroti told Trent. "That wasn't even dramatic."

"Sorry," Trent said. "Next time."

"Yeah, next time," Buonarroti agreed. "I can hardly wait."

Sulu noticed the eyes first. The gray irises mimicked the color of ash, and appeared as cold as the remnants of a fire long extinguished. The glare of the Romulan admiral felt penetrating, even on the viewscreen.

"We have replaced the defective part," Sulu said, standing at the center of the bridge, directly behind Linojj and Tolek at the helm and navigation stations. The admiral regarded her impassively. So thin that he could almost be called gaunt, he had straight, silvering hair and deep lines drawn around his mouth.

"And you are satisfied that there will be no additional . . . mishaps?" Vokar said. The hesitation in his words clearly marked his skepticism that what had occurred aboard *Enterprise* had been accidental. But if he implied that Starfleet would have sacrificed a ship and crew in Romulan space in order to gain the allegiance of the Klingons in a war, then Vokar did not know the Federation as well as he obviously thought he did.

"Yes, Admiral," Sulu said. "We are satisfied." Buonarroti and Trent had concluded that the microfracture in the deuterium-flow regulator had probably been the result of a flaw introduced during the manufacturing process. After a certain amount of stress from usage, the flaw had given way, allowing the microscopic fissure to form. They had also theorized that the error in the firmware had been caused by the subsequent irregularity in the device's electromagnetic field. And since Sulu saw no advantage to the Romulans destroying *Enterprise* within their territory—the Klingons would never have believed that such an event had been an accident—she accepted the judgments of Buonarroti and Trent.

"We've also inspected our starboard impulse assembly," Sulu continued, "as well as our warp drive." The ship's engineering and computer-science crews had taken nearly an entire day to thoroughly examine and test all of the engines, and they had encountered no further difficulties. "We're ready to resume our journey back to the Federation."

"Excellent," Vokar said, though his expression remained stoic, and his voice as icy as his gaze. "Then you'll start at once?" He delivered the statement less like a question than an order.

"Commander," Sulu said, still looking at the image of Vokar on the main viewscreen, but speaking instead to Linojj. "Full impulse power. Get us out of here."

Vokar did not move—not a brow, not an eyelid, not a muscle—giving the impression that he might not even have heard Sulu. But then the viewscreen blinked, and a vista of stars replaced the view of the Romulan admiral.

"They ended the communication on their end," Lieutenant Kanchumurthi said.

"Acknowledged," Sulu said. She reached up and placed her hand atop Linojj's shoulder. "I meant it, Xintal," she said. "Get us out of here."

"Aye, Captain," Linojj said. "With pleasure." As she worked the helm, the bass thunder of the impulse drive rose around them. This time, it stayed steady.

Sulu sat down in the command chair, pleased and relieved to finally be under way again. A few moments later, Linojj reported that the ship had attained full impulse velocity, and shortly after that, she noted that *Enterprise* had left the boundaries of the Algeron system. "Take us to warp five," Sulu said, and Linojj executed the order.

With *Tomed* following, *Enterprise* and its crew raced for home.

Harriman stood at the base of a well that served as the junction for several equipment conduits. He continually checked his sensor veil to ensure that he, Gravenor, and Vaughn could not be detected by scans. He also consulted his tricorder regularly, performing passive inspections of the surrounding areas; just because the trio couldn't be scanned didn't mean that some Romulan might not stumble upon them by chance.

On the other side of the junction well, Commander Gravenor squatted beside an open panel, her hands buried deep inside the exposed equipment. Several fiber-optic bundles wound from out of the bulkhead and connected to a Romulan scanner sitting beside her on the deck. Beside Gravenor, Lieutenant Vaughn knelt before another open panel.

The commander looked ridiculous to Harriman. The Romulan uniform she wore—with a dark blue sash that indicated her position in engineering—seemed too bulky for her, particularly in light of her diminutive size. Her yellowed complexion and pointed ears seemed more like parts of a costume than natural components of her body. And worst of all, the wig of straight black hair she wore appeared completely out of place on her.

Peering down at Vaughn, who also wore Imperial Fleet garments, Harriman thought that he looked as silly—or maybe even sillier—than Gravenor. The lieutenant's rugged face and piercing blue eyes did not seem suited to either a Romulan complexion or the straight black hair that went along with it. Vaughn's appearance struck Harriman as so comical that he actually had to stifle a laugh, bringing his hand up to cover his mouth. He found it remarkable that he could be so amused in circumstances such as these.

Maybe that was it, though; maybe—no, *definitely*—he'd had enough of these circumstances. Harriman wanted to end all of this—with the Romulans, with the Klingons—as soon as possible. Which was why he had gone to Starfleet's commander in chief with this plan in the first place.

"Excuse me, sir?" Vaughn said, peering up over his shoulder at Harriman. "Did you say something?"

"No," he said. "Just clearing my throat." Harriman himself wore a Starfleet uniform, the insignia on his shoulder and sleeve indicating a rank of lieutenant commander. If they did encounter a Romulan officer, Gravenor and Vaughn would masquerade as Romulans who had captured a Starfleet spy. It might not work for more than a few seconds, but any time at all might allow them to extricate themselves from such a situation. Beneath the hem of his uniform jacket, Harriman carried a phaser; Gravenor and Vaughn each carried a Romulan disruptor pistol.

"Captain," Gravenor said. She examined the readout of the scanner that she had connected to the ship's circuitry. "We're turning." Harriman waited as the commander studied the display. "They've set a course for Romulus," she said. "Warp eight."

Harriman nodded. "All right," he said, glancing over at Vaughn to include him. "Let's get to work."

The three Starfleet officers moved in unison, each knowing their responsibilities as they set to take control of *Tomed*.

MINUS TWO: SINGULARITY

As Sulu entered her quarters, the lights automatically coming on to a nighttime level, she wondered about Captain Harriman back on Algeron. He would have been pleased to know that *Enterprise* had made it safely out of Romulan space, and that it now headed for its patrol assignment in Echo Sector. Certainly she felt pleased about it.

She unsnapped the fasteners of her uniform jacket, anxious to undress and roll into bed. Of late, each day ended in exhaustion for her, and each night she looked forward to whatever sleep she could manage. Bad dreams sometimes accompanied her slumber, but more often than not, she would sleep as though she had lost consciousness, not stirring at all until morning. She would invariably awake less tired than when she had gone to bed, but feeling as though she still needed more rest.

"Computer," she said, "lights down half." As the overhead lighting panels dimmed, Sulu pulled open her jacket and shrugged out of it. On her way through the sleeping area to the bathroom, she tossed it onto the nearest chair, then grabbed at the tall, ribbed collar of her white undershirt, slipping a finger inside and tugging it loose about her neck.

Inside the bathroom, Sulu bent over the basin. "Warm,"

she said, cupping her hands beneath the faucet. Water streamed out, and she splashed it onto her face. As she toweled herself dry, she thought again of the captain. She had been mildly surprised that he hadn't contacted the ship when they'd had the trouble with the impulse flow regulator. Of course, he would have had no way of knowing what had happened without being informed of it. Sulu had considered doing so herself, but had concluded that there would have been little point; he had left her in charge of *Enterprise*, and his duties right now obviously lay elsewhere—at least as far as Starfleet Command thought. She couldn't allow herself to worry about the captain not being on the ship right now.

She studied her visage for a moment in the mirror above the basin. To her surprise, she noticed three or four gray hairs in among her shoulder-length black locks. *Only forty, and already going gray*, she thought, chuckling to herself. "So much for not worrying," she said.

Except it's not really worrying, is it? She just wished that she knew why Starfleet Command had ordered the captain to stay behind on Algeron. They'd clearly had some purpose in mind, and she simply wanted to understand it. Perhaps she should've asked Captain Harriman about it before he'd left the ship, but he hadn't seemed approachable at the time. As far as she knew, he seldom kept information from her, his professed belief being that his crew could best serve *Enterprise* when they knew what he knew.

"But that's not always possible, is it?" Sulu asked her reflection in the mirror. Certain information had to remain known only at the highest levels of Starfleet. She recognized the need for classified data; for good reason, nobody aboard *Enterprise*, and only a very few in Starfleet Command, knew of her mission alongside Captain Harriman to Devron II, much less what had happened there.

Unforgettable images rumbled through Sulu's mind. The

turbulent descent through the rich, roiling atmosphere of the planet. The enormous, towering volcano hurling molten rock and ash high into the atmosphere. The gargantuan and seemingly impenetrable rain forest. The electric-blue disruptor blasts hammering into one of the warp shuttles. The crash landing. Devron II had been an experience of extremes.

Sulu dropped the towel beside the basin and returned to the living area of her quarters. Thoughts of the secret mission—considered successful at the same time that it had been disastrous—recalled those who had carried it out: Captain Harriman and herself from *Enterprise*, Iron Mike Paris from *Agamemnon*, T'Prel from *New York*, Zultu Bini and Claudine Robinson from special operations, and Creyn, from nowhere Sulu had ever been able to determine.

I still keep thinking about Iron Mike Paris, the captain had told her before departing the ship. That had been the second time he had mentioned Iron Mike recently—and those had been the *only* times he had mentioned him since the Devron mission. She wondered again whether Harriman had been trying to tell her something.

Sulu walked over behind her desk and sat down. She punched at the activation button for the desktop computer interface, which chirped in response. "Computer," she said, "show me the Starfleet personnel file for Commander Michael Thomas Paris."

"Working," the computer replied in its slightly stiff female voice. A moment later, the interface display sparked to life. The left third of the screen filled with a portrait of the officer, the right two-thirds with data about him.

Sulu looked at Iron Mike's face, and she felt a twinge of something; even a year afterward, the memories of the events on Devron II carried with them an emotional weight. Paris appeared quite youthful in the picture, just as he had at the start of the mission, though she knew that they'd both been born in the same year. A small and seemingly fragile human, with soft features and light hair, Paris looked as though it would have been impossible for him to have genuinely earned the nickname of "Iron Mike." By the time the mission had ended, though, Sulu had understood the source of the moniker: Paris had acted with unrelentingly strong mental discipline, facing dangers with bravery and selflessness.

The Starfleet personnel summary recounted information about Iron Mike, some of which Sulu had learned prior to the Devron operation. Born 17 May 2271 on Altair IV, in Hume Township. Wife, Victoria Santos. Son, Cole, born only days before Paris had left *Agamemnon* for Devron II. Graduated Starfleet Academy with honors in 2292. Served as a mathematician aboard *Colombia* before requesting and being granted a transfer to the command track. Rose rapidly up through the ranks, serving on *Excelsior* and *Mjolnir* before being assigned to *Agamemnon*. As second officer and then executive officer of *Agamemnon*, decorated seven times by Starfleet, a fact that impressed but did not surprise Sulu.

She read through the list of Paris's awards, which included such high honors as the Silver Palm with Cluster; the Grankite Order of Tactics, Class of Excellence; and the Archer Ribbon for Conspicuous Bravery. She had expected to see a decoration at the end of the list—something like the Karagite Order of Heroism—given for Iron Mike's role in the Devron mission, but of course, nothing could have been awarded for an operation that, as far as most people knew, had never taken place.

Sulu pored through the detail of Paris's Starfleet record, through to his leave of absence from *Agamemnon*—a leave that, like hers from *Enterprise*, had been scheduled to last only weeks. No explanation had been given for his time away from *Agamemnon* beyond *Personal request*. Information about—and even the very existence of—the mission to Devron II would doubtless remain classified for years to come, Sulu thought.

And then she came to the next entry in Iron Mike's personnel record, and her jaw dropped in shock. She looked at it a second time, thinking that she must have initially misread it. The stardate identified a time several months after the Devron II mission, and listed Paris's return to *Agamemnon* as the ship's executive officer.

But that had never happened, Sulu knew.

"Computer," she said, "what is the current status of Commander Michael Thomas Paris?"

"Commander Michael Thomas Paris is the first officer aboard *U.S.S. Agamemnon*," the computer answered.

Sulu stood up quickly, a rush of energy pushing her to her feet. She felt confused and . . . and *betrayed*. Something was wrong here, and she needed to know what it was.

She reached down and jabbed at a button, deactivating the computer interface. Then she moved out from behind her desk and paced across the room, her mind attempting to concoct scenarios that might be able to explain what she had just learned. She crossed her arms as she strode up to a viewing port, but though she peered through it, she did not see the stars. Instead, she saw the surface of Devron II: the lava flows, the great waterfall, the wreckage of the warp shuttle, the subterranean compound they'd found in the middle of the jungle.

And she saw Iron Mike Paris, in the moments after he had selflessly risked his life for hers. She saw his tattered flesh through the tears in his uniform, his body badly broken. She saw herself rushing to him, trying to save him, her hands becoming soaked in his blood. And she saw his last, quick intake of breath, and his eyes as the light faded from them.

A year ago, on Devron II, Sulu had watched Iron Mike Paris die.

Azetbur ran at speed across the courtyard, her legs devouring the distance to her adversary. As she neared him, she raised her staff above her head, setting up to wage her attack. She saw him brace himself as she approached, bending his knees in obvious preparation to spring away, his eyes measuring her advance.

With the gap between them closing, Azetbur opened her mouth wide and screamed, her voice loud and wild, a battle cry she hoped distracted from the rapid change she made to her handhold on the staff. Almost on top of her adversary, she brought the weapon down fast, in a move she intended to appear as a direct assault. Her adversary committed himself at that moment, leaping away to her right. But Azetbur thrust the far end of the staff into the grass-covered ground, planting it. Holding tight to the staff, she adjusted her weight and threw her body into an arc around it. She swung her feet out and caught her adversary on his right side, one of her heels landing on his biceps, the other on his chest. The impact sent him flying from his feet.

Azetbur landed and overbalanced, losing her grip on the staff as she tumbled to the ground. The aromatic scent of freshly cut grass filled her nostrils as she rolled atop it. She quickly jumped back to her feet and retrieved her weapon, grasping it in both hands and preparing immediately to wield it.

"Well done, Chancellor," her adversary said, breathing heavily. Azetbur waited as he lifted himself up onto his hands and then rose to his feet. She still held the staff up, ready to swing it, her muscles tensed, her blood coursing hotly through her veins, the taste of combat raw in her mouth as she gasped for air. Only when it became clear that her adversary would not continue the exercise did she relax her arms and let the far end of the staff drop to the ground.

"Thank you, Revik," Azetbur said. Her daily training session had already lasted nearly two hours, almost twice as long as usual. Though a diplomat, as her father had been, she never forgot her heritage; a proud Klingon, she fought most often with weapons such as words and tact, but she also kept herself proficient in the use of her fists and the traditional weapons of individual combat. Further, she regularly practiced her skills with energy weapons.

Revik, a large but agile man, walked over to Azetbur. His white, lightweight body armor, shining brightly in the morning sun, contrasted vividly with his dark coloring. He slipped off his protective gloves as he made his way over to her, then removed his headgear, revealing a mass of long black hair pulled back into a knot. "Excellent anticipation and adaptation," he commended. "I thought I'd waited until you'd fully committed, but obviously not."

"I've told you before," Azetbur said, "it's my job to figure out what people are going to do next, and plan for it." She dropped the staff onto the grass, then pulled off her own gloves and helmet, tucking the former inside the latter. She smoothed the tangles of her hair, soaked through with sweat.

"So have we finished for today?" Revik asked.

Azetbur considered continuing—the workout had been a good one, and though tired, she still felt strong—but then she spied movement past Revik, at the far corner of the courtyard. "Yes, we're done," she said.

"What shall we work on tomorrow?" Revik asked.

"Hand-to-hand combat," she said without hesitation. "No weapons."

Revik nodded, apparently not surprised. Azetbur had most often been practicing weaponless combat in their recent sessions. She supposed the reason might be her need to somehow deal with her political dissatisfactions. The resistance to her decision to sustain acceptance of Federation aid, even during the current diplomatic circumstances, frustrated her a great deal. Of late, she had come to suspect that private interests drove her opposition—both among the citizenry and on the High Council—far more than the now-common plaint of the wounding of Klingon pride.

"With your permission, Chancellor," Revik said, motioning behind her, toward where the preparation room opened from the Great Hall into the courtyard. Azetbur nodded, and Revik bowed his head, then walked past her.

Across the way, where she had seen him enter just a few moments ago, a man stood unmoving. Even if he had not asked for this meeting, she would have recognized him. He wore the heavy, metallic uniform of the Klingon Defense Force, and his large, fleshy shape was unmistakable. She lifted her hand and pointed to a stone bench along one wall of the courtyard, gesturing for General Kaarg to meet her there. He began marching in that direction.

Azetbur tossed her gloves and helmet onto the ground beside the staff, then strode toward the bench. Already she felt the muscles of her legs beginning to tighten; her workout today had been particularly strenuous. As she walked, she began unfastening the black armor surrounding her upper body. By the time she had reached the bench, she carried four separate pieces: the front of the torso, the back, and both arms.

"General Kaarg," she said when he reached her. She held the pieces of body armor out to her side and let them fall to the ground. "I was surprised to hear from you this morning. I would have expected you to be aboard a starship patrolling the boundaries of the Empire." In response to the Romulan claims of a Starfleet first-strike weapon, and to the Federation's subsequent denial, Azetbur had ordered the Klingon Defense Force to deploy significant resources along the Empire's borders with both powers. She knew that both the Romulans and the Federation had done the same. Such a military buildup risked the peace, but in light of Azetbur's decision to side against whichever government committed the next act of aggression, the Klingon military needed to be ready for battle.

"I have great confidence in my wing," Kaarg said, "and I

am in frequent contact with my officers. But considering the current political situation, I concluded that my presence here, on the Council, would be most important." He paused, and then added, "At least prior to the start of any hostilities. But I'll be returning to our borders with the Romulans and the Federation before long."

"Of course," Azetbur said. "The Empire appreciates your loyalties." Since the general had stood up to defend her against Brigadier Kuron in the meeting following the Romulan envoy's visit, Azetbur had noticed other, subtler indications that Kaarg's allegiance was to her. And after learning from Ambassador Kage about the perfidious General Gorak and his young lapdog, Ditagh, she valued, now more than ever, whatever solid support she could find.

"My duty is to Qo'noS," Kaarg agreed. "And because of that, there is an urgent matter I must discuss with you."

"An urgent matter?" Azetbur asked, wondering what information the general would want to bring directly to her, and not to all of the High Council. "Please," she said, motioning toward the bench, "sit."

Kaarg did so, settling his considerable bulk onto the stone surface. "Chancellor, I have learned that you may soon be challenged," he said soberly.

"I'm continually being challenged," Azetbur said lightly, intentionally suggesting that she had not taken his meaning, and thereby hoping to force him to disclose in detail whatever information he had—an old diplomatic technique. She did not look at him. Instead, she casually propped her foot up on the edge of the bench and began loosening the straps that bound the armor about her leg.

"Chancellor, I did not make myself clear," Kaarg said. "I meant to say that an attempt is going to be made to remove you from power."

"To remove me from power," Azetbur repeated. She pulled the armor from her leg and lobbed it atop the other pieces on the ground. It landed on the breastplate with a *crack*, then slid off onto the grass. "And what about removing me from *life?*" she asked, still not looking at the general. She set her leg down and lifted the other one, reaching for the straps securing the armor around it.

"Yes," Kaarg said.

Finally, she looked up at him. To her surprise, Azetbur felt anger rush through her. Although she had long dealt with opposition to her leadership, and even though Kage had recently confirmed the disloyal intentions of General Gorak, actually hearing that an attempt would be made to assassinate her enraged her. "And what is your point in telling me this, General?" she demanded.

"My point," Kaarg said, his expression hardening, "is to protect the chancellor of the Klingon Empire." He stood up, though he made no move toward her, and no move to leave. "To protect *you*," he finished.

"How does my knowing what you've just told me offer me protection?" she asked, suddenly realizing that the plot of which Kaarg spoke might be separate from that of Gorak's. "Am I never to leave my residence?" she asked. "Or my office? Am I to stay away from gatherings of the High Council? Such actions would see me removed from power just as quickly as a *mek'leth* in the back." She took her leg down from the bench and leaned in close to Kaarg. "Klingons," she said, "do not cower."

"I had thought that by telling you of the threat," the general said, "I could cause you to be more vigilant."

"Do you believe that I am not now vigilant?" Azetbur bristled. "Do you think that there are not a dozen disruptors aimed at you at this very moment?"

To his credit, the general did not look away, did not seek out the armed guards peering out from the grand structure of the Great Hall surrounding the courtyard. "My apologies, Chancellor," he said with unconcealed annoyance. "I can see that my assistance is not required." He turned, apparently to go. He did not ask for her leave.

Azetbur watched Kaarg's back, her fury compounded by his snub of her authority. She appreciated the practice of loyal opposition, and the need for open debate on policy, but she'd had enough of the ignominious backroom maneuvering against her. In the wake of her father's assassination, eighteen years ago, she had brought peace to her people, and from there she had fostered the rebuilding and renewal of the Empire. The destruction of Praxis had hobbled the Klingon infrastructure, and it had been her vision and leadership that had made it possible to deal with, and then move past, the catastrophe. How could it be, then, that mere talk—about the shame in accepting Federation aid—now empowered her enemies and cowed her supporters? *How dare General Kaarg—*

What? Azetbur asked herself. How dare he warn her of a threat against her? He had come here to help her, and she had allowed her anger and frustration with the current political situation—on Qo'noS, but also with Romulus and Earth—to blind her to his support.

"General Kaarg," she said, and she took several steps after him. She realized that she still wore body armor on one of her legs, but she ignored it. Right now, she needed to know what the general knew—beyond the existence of vague threats—but perhaps more important, she needed an ally on the High Council.

Kaarg stopped and spun to face her. She stopped as well, facing him across a short space. "Yes, Chancellor?" he asked, the annoyance in his voice now seemingly tempered. With a few strides, she closed the distance between them.

"Do you have specific information?" Azetbur asked.

The general appeared immediately uncomfortable. "I have been told certain things," he said, "but I cannot vouch for the authenticity or seriousness of those things."

"And yet you come to me with a warning," she said.

"Obviously, I believe in the veracity of the information," Kaarg said.

"What information?" Azetbur asked. "Specifically."

"I do not wish to impugn another member of the High Council," he said. "I have no evidence, beyond the word of certain of my acquaintances who themselves have heard things."

"From whom?" Azetbur wanted to know. She stepped forward until she stood so close to Kaarg that she could feel his breath on her skin. "Tell me the source of the threat to me, and I will determine whether or not it is true."

Kaarg looked at her for only a second before answering. "General Gorak is planning to kill you, Chancellor."

"Gorak," Azetbur echoed. She turned and paced slowly away from the general in an attempt to hide her great satisfaction with what he had just told her. There was one plot only, and it had now been confirmed. She turned back around to face Kaarg. "And you know this how?" she asked, seeking additional confirmation.

"A young officer on Gorak's staff blurted out the information in a transmission to the Romulan starbase Algeron."

"A transmission to whom?" she asked, suddenly concerned that Kaarg would try to implicate Kage, one of her most trusted confidants.

"To one of the ambassadorial aides," the general said. "Ditagh is his name."

Azetbur nodded, again pleased to hear corroboration of something she had already been told, namely that Ditagh operated under the thumb of Gorak. "When will this attempt on my life take place?"

"I know no particulars," Kaarg said, "but I believe it will be soon. And I do not think that he will challenge you in open Council."

"No," Azetbur concurred. "As loudly opposed as some on

the High Council are to my handling of relations with the Federation, I doubt many would allow such a challenge."

"And so Gorak will no doubt try to isolate you," Kaarg suggested.

"I am seldom in a position of risk," Azetbur noted.

Kaarg nodded, but the expression on his face displayed uncertainty. "Considering Gorak's position," he said, "do you trust the loyalty of *all* your guards?" The day-to-day protection of the chancellor fell under the jurisdiction of Klingon Internal Security, a branch of the Defense Force, over which General Gorak held considerable sway.

"You will surround me with your men," Azetbur told Kaarg.

"I can do that," he said. "We can safely control the access to you."

"And in the meantime," Azetbur said, "you can find Gorak's weaknesses."

"I can do that as well," Kaarg said.

They stood in silence for a short time, until at last, Azetbur said, "Thank you, General."

Kaarg bowed his head, then started back the way he had come, toward the entrance in the corner of the courtyard. Azetbur watched him go. For the first time in a long time, she felt fortified in her position as chancellor, and thought that maybe she could continue to take the Empire in the right direction as they headed into the future.

Admiral Mentir wanted to swim, wanted to hie down to Space Station KR-3's natatorium and sprint round and round the long, narrow oval of the watercourse. He felt the need to move, to expend energy in order to divert his thoughts from his responsibilities. But as he glided on his antigrav chair into his office, he knew that he could not do as he wished, precisely *because* of those responsibilities.

In the last day, Mentir's immediate priorities had been changed significantly. Starfleet Commander in Chief

Sinclair-Alexander had contacted him on a secure channel yesterday and directed him to stand in for Admiral Harriman. Mentir's old friend, it turned out, had begun a mission prior to the injuries he'd sustained as a result of the destruction of *Universe*. Because Blackjack's medical condition had not improved since then—had actually begun to deteriorate now—the C in C had needed an officer to complete his assignment.

And then Sinclair-Alexander had detailed that assignment for Mentir. He'd listened in silence, staggered both by the actions that had already been taken and by those that remained to be accomplished. His emotions had lurched from anger to fear to hope, and back again.

Now, hours later, none of those feelings had diminished.

Mentir floated across the anteroom toward a door on one side of the far bulkhead. His office consisted of three sections: this outer chamber, in which he could host air-breathing visitors; an inner, aquatic chamber approximating the environment of Alonis; and a lock between the two, allowing access and egress to the water-filled room. A desk and chairs sat in the outer office, along with several tall, leafy plants of various colors. Shelves decorated the walls, holding a collection of meticulously detailed starship models—Federation and otherwise—which Mentir had crafted himself using his psychokinetic abilities. Among the shelves hung several framed holographic prints of undersea landscapes. But the most dramatic feature of the room was a large transparent section of the far bulkhead, which allowed a view of Mentir's marine workspace, with its rocky floor, exotic undersea flora, and deep-purple water.

Just as he reached the door of the lock, he heard the warble of a communications channel opening. *"Operations to Admiral Mentir,"* came the voice of Commander Murray Sperber, the station's executive officer. The universal translator in Mentir's environmental suit modified Sperber's words into the distinctive clicks and cheeps of the Alonis language.

Mentir crossed the room to his desk, where he leaned forward and activated the comm system with a touch of his pectoral fin. "This is Mentir," he said, the sounds of his own voice interpreted as they emerged from the speaker in his ES. "Go ahead."

"Admiral, we're receiving an encoded transmission from the Enterprise," Sperber said. *"The first officer, Commander Sulu, is asking to speak with you."*

Demora, Mentir thought, and his mind naturally went to *Enterprise* and Captain Harriman, and from there to the mission. "Put her through down here," he said.

"Yes, sir."

"Mentir out." He circled around his desk—past a replica of a Nivochan asteroid runner sitting on one corner—so that he could view the monitor there. He waited only a second before Sulu's image appeared on the screen. "Commander," he said, rather formally, he realized, considering that they had been friends for two decades. Back at the Academy, she had attended a xenoculture course he'd taught, and they'd shared enough mutual interests that they had stayed in touch over the years. He had seen her during *Enterprise's* recent visits to KR-3, but only very briefly. Attempting to put aside the serious nature of his new duties and take a friendlier approach, he said, "Welcome back to the Federation."

Sulu nodded once, curtly, seeming to acknowledge and dismiss Mentir's salutation at the same time. *"Admiral,"* she said, also sounding official. *"I need to speak with you."*

Mentir felt suddenly confined in his environmental suit, the thin layer of water surrounding his body an inadequate substitute for an ocean. He feared at once that something had gone wrong. Sulu knew nothing of the mission—few did—but if Captain Harriman had been compromised . . .

"I am alone," Mentir assured Sulu. "And my exec mentioned that you were communicating on an encoded channel." Mentir also noted that Sulu appeared to be addressing him from a cabin—presumably her own—rather than from the *Enterprise* bridge.

"*Admiral, I've discovered a discrepancy in Starfleet's personnel records,*" she said. Mentir took in this information and immediately felt himself calm down, his concerns subsiding. Whatever personnel matter Sulu wanted to discuss with him, it clearly would not be an issue that involved the mission or Captain Harriman's role in it.

"I'm listening," Mentir said.

"*By chance, I found a Starfleet officer currently assigned to a starship,*" Sulu explained. "*But a year ago, I watched that same officer die.*"

"I don't understand," Mentir said.

"*One year ago, on a classified mission, I witnessed the death of a Starfleet officer,*" Sulu said. "*There was no doubt of it, no possibility that he hadn't really died, or that he'd later been revived. His body was—*" Sulu hesitated, then took a breath. "*He was dead. I'm certain of it.*"

"And you claim that he is now assigned to a Starfleet vessel?" Mentir asked, seeking confirmation that he understood Sulu.

"*Yes,*" she verified. "*Several months after the mission, Starfleet apparently reassigned him to a ship.*"

Mentir considered this for a moment. "The simplest explanation would be a mistake in the personnel records," he ventured. "This would be a strange example of poor record-keeping, but I'm sure that errors do occur."

"*I don't think this is an error, Admiral,*" Sulu said. "*It's not the only instance I found. On that same classified mission, another Starfleet officer died, and a few months later, she was also supposedly reassigned to a starship."* She paused, and then said, *"She was transferred from special operations to the* Universe."

"Universe?" Mentir said, and he suddenly realized what had happened—something Admiral Sinclair-Alexander had not mentioned to him, but that must have been the case. Eventually, if she kept digging for information, Sulu would figure it out too. Mentir glanced away for a moment, his gaze falling on the Nivochan asteroid runner, but he looked back when Sulu continued.

"Yes, the Universe," she said. *"I think these may be spies. I think—"* She hesitated, and for a moment, looked away from the screen, as though something had unexpectedly occurred to her. Then she peered back at the monitor and continued. *"For the Romulans, maybe,"* she suggested, *"or even for the Klingons."*

"But that would mean that somebody within Starfleet Command would have to be involved," Mentir said. "To falsify the reassignments . . ."

"That's why I came to you, Tirasol," Sulu said, the intent of her statement—that she could trust her friend—clear. *"Think about this: there are no records of the deaths of these officers, since they died on a classified mission; they have extensive Starfleet records; and so nobody would question their posting to a starship."*

"You may be right," Mentir said, knowing of nothing else that he could say. "What is the location of *Enterprise?*" he asked, although he was already fully aware of the ship's movements.

"We're en route to the Echo Sector," she said, *"to patrol the Neutral Zone."*

"I'm issuing you new orders, Commander," Mentir said. *"Enterprise* is to report at once to Space Station KR-3, and you are to report directly to me." He needed to recruit a starship and its commander anyway.

"*Sir?*" Sulu said.

"Demora," Mentir said, leaning closer to the screen and lowering the volume of the snaps and chirps that formed his voice, "we'll discuss what you've found when you arrive."

Sulu looked silently at him for a moment, as though trying to judge his intentions. Finally, she said, "*Yes, Admiral. Thank you.*"

"Mentir out," he said, and he saw Sulu reach forward, obviously ending the communication from her end. The screen went blank. Mentir reached forward himself and deactivated the comm system.

He sat for a while without moving, his thoughts racing. He suspected that Sulu would continue to scour Starfleet's personnel records in search of additional anomalies, and that she would eventually piece all of the information together and confirm the truth. Fortunately, he trusted few officers as much as he trusted Sulu, and so it would be no more of a risk to recruit her for the mission than it would be to recruit any other officer. *Enterprise* had not initially been considered for the assignment because of its recent trip to Algeron, but the Romulan Imperial Fleet and the Romulan Intelligence Service would know that Starfleet's flagship had been patrolling the Neutral Zone during the past few months, and so this could work.

Satisfied with his decision, Mentir made his way around his desk and headed for the lock, and for the comforting waters of his inner office. Considering the circumstances, he felt sure that Sulu would do as he asked, but he did not look forward to telling her what they had done, and what they would yet do. He could only hope that she would understand.

And forgive.

"The general is preparing to act."

Ditagh stood in front of the monitor in his quarters and smiled broadly at the welcome news. His time aboard Algeron had grown frustratingly long, and his tolerance for Kage's continued obeisance toward the Empire's historical enemies had waned almost completely. Once the general seized power, though, Ditagh knew that Qo'noS would immediately remove itself from these pathetic efforts to pacify the Romulans and the Federation. After that, he would finally be able to bolt this sterile space station and return home.

"Do you know the timetable?" Ditagh asked his compatriot, a member of the general's staff.

"Not precisely, but it's going to happen soon."

"Good," Ditagh said. "The might of the Klingon Empire will be—" The flat tone of the door chime sounded in the small room. He looked away from the monitor and over to the door, which he had taken to locking after Kage had burst in here not long ago. The ambassador no doubt stood on the other side of the door right now; no one else on the station would have cause to call on him. "I must go," Ditagh said, peering back at the monitor. He did not need the old man questioning him about his communications back to Qo'noS.

"I understand." And he clearly did, because he closed the channel, blanking the screen. Ditagh touched a control and deactivated the comm system on his end, then turned and walked to the front of his quarters. He reached up and operated a panel set into the bulkhead, and the door slid open. As he'd expected, Kage stood in the corridor.

"Ditagh," the old man said, "I would speak with you." He employed the same voice as he did in the negotiating sessions, the calm, even tones of diplomacy—the tones of weakness. It embarrassed and angered Ditagh that such a man represented the Empire.

Turning his back to Kage, Ditagh strode into the center of the room. "What do you want?" he said, showing no respect at all to the ambassador. Although he allowed Kage to maintain his appearance of authority in front of the Romulan and Federation representatives, it pleased him that the charade had ended outside of those meetings. In private, Ditagh no longer hid his disdain for the peace-loving old man. Now he rounded to face him.

"I want to know your mind," Kage said, stepping inside. The door eased shut after him. "I want to know what you think of the data presented by the Starfleet captain."

Ditagh stared at the ambassador for a second, just long enough to ascertain the seriousness of the request. When he saw that Kage actually expected an answer, he laughed, a deep, hearty guffaw filled with derision. "You want *my* opinion?" he said. "Are you now mediating harmony within the Empire?"

"Why not?" Kage asked. "We are both Klingons. Should we not battle together against our enemies, rather than fighting each other?"

Ditagh peered at the ambassador, but now found it impossible to determine the sincerity with which he had asked his questions. "The problem," he told Kage, "is that you do not know who the enemies of the Empire are, and you do not do battle against them."

"I know who *you* think our enemies are," Kage said. "I know who your sponsor thinks our enemies are." Ditagh listened to the obvious attempt to insult him and did not react; Kage's words meant nothing to him. "But is there no room in your worldview for new facts?"

"And what 'facts' are those?" Ditagh asked. He moved to the food synthesizer, intending to order a flagon of bloodwine, but then he decided against it. The Romulan approximation of the Klingon drink provided yet another impetus to flee Algeron. "Facts such as manufactured data files? Doctored sensor readings? Useless blueprints? Are those your 'new facts'?"

"Have you actually looked at the data?" Kage asked, stepping farther into the room. "Are those your genuine conclusions, or are they merely assumptions?"

Ditagh studied the ambassador, attempting to take the

measure of his questioning. Did he really want to know Ditagh's view, or did he seek something else, perhaps some item of information that he thought might help Azetbur's cause? Kage had previously acted on both motivations, although it seemed unlikely that he would wish to seriously discuss matters with Ditagh after their confrontation.

"I've examined the Federation data," Ditagh disclosed. He walked over to a chair and dropped heavily into it, his large frame filling the piece of furniture. Kage followed him over, though he did not sit down.

"You've examined the data, and concluded the readings to be counterfeit?" he asked. "What about the designs for the new drive?"

"I'm not an engineer or a scientist," Ditagh said, beginning to tire of this interrogation.

"What does that mean?" Kage asked.

"It means that I'm not qualified to make a determination about the authenticity of the Federation data," Ditagh said.

Kage leaned forward, resting his hands on the back of a chair. "But you just characterized the data as manufactured, the drive plans as useless."

"The veracity of the data is irrelevant," Ditagh said, dismissing the integrity of sensor logs and engine designs with a wave of his hand. "What matters is the intention of the Federation. They are our enemy, and so it is clear that they strive to defeat us. If the readings are genuine, then the Federation must be distracting us from some other important truth. If the drive plans are accurate, then they most certainly will fail in operation, or lead the Empire to develop starship engines inferior to whatever Starfleet is now devising."

"But your interpretations are self-fulfilling," Kage said. He circled the chair he had been leaning on and took a seat directly across from Ditagh. "You do not trust the Federation, and so you ascribe dishonorable motives to them. You then use those perceived motives as fortification for your belief that the Federation is our enemy. But since the destruction of Praxis almost twenty years ago, they have demonstrably been our allies."

"And why is it that you think they've been our allies?" Ditagh asked. "Because they've provided us food and energy?"

"Yes, of course," Kage said. "They've helped to prevent the disintegration of the Empire."

"Have they saved us, or have they found a means of controlling us?" Ditagh leaned forward, warming to the subject despite his contempt for the ambassador. "The Federation has done only so much for Qo'noS. They've stopped short of giving us what we've needed to grow as strong as we'd been before the disaster on Praxis. They've kept us from becoming a threat to them, restraining our progress by enthralling some of our people—as they've done with Azetbur. And with you."

Kage gazed at him, his eyes narrowing. "Do you not even grant the possibility that the Federation is our ally?"

"Do you not even grant the possibility that it is our enemy?" Ditagh returned. "You accuse me of finding ends based upon my assumptions, but do you not support your vision of the Federation as a Klingon ally with favorable interpretations of their actions?"

Kage lifted his chin, then glanced away for a moment. At last, to Ditagh's surprise, he said, "Perhaps." But then he asked, "Have you ever been to a Federation world?" When Ditagh did not bother to answer, he said, "I thought not."

"If you're here to try to convince me of the truth of your position, there is no point," Ditagh said. He sat back in his chair. "I would die protecting Klingons from the imperialism of the duplicitous Federation."

"Yes," Kage said slowly. "I'm sure that you would." A glimmer in the ambassador's eyes hinted that he either hoped or believed that such a fate would befall Ditagh. "It astonishes me how different our views can be, based upon the same information." He paused, and then added, "But then, I have actually been to the Federation, and worked with its people."

"Then why don't you go back to some Federation world, old man?" Ditagh stood up. "Maybe you can spend the last days of your life being administered powders and liquids for the sick. You can prolong your fearful little life in safety, absent the fires and glories of battle. Like a human, or a Deltan."

Kage peered up at him and nodded. He stood up and faced Ditagh for a few seconds—a pitiable attempt to show strength, Ditagh figured—and then headed for the door. As it opened before him, he looked back into the room. "You call me an old man," he said, "and I am. But you are out of date, and so are all of those like you. And because you are all out of power—real power—the Empire has survived, and will continue to survive." Then he continued out into the corridor.

Ditagh watched him go. "How wrong you are, old man," he said to himself. Before long, he knew, Kage and Azetbur and their ilk would be forcibly rendered obsolete. The Empire had survived under their reign, but only once they had been removed would it flourish.

He crossed the room, making his way back over to the food synthesizer. He operated the control panel, steering through its menus and submenus until he reached the selection for *Klingon bloodwine*, and then found the specification *Warm*. Ditagh would toast to the future of the Klingon Empire, which would not include Kage or Azetbur or any of their minions.

Sulu sat down across the desk from Admiral Mentir. They'd exchanged cursory pleasantries when she'd entered his office, and now she waited for him to begin their meeting. Under normal circumstances, she would have been delighted to see him again, would have wanted to have a personal conversation, but the current situation hardly qualified as normal.

On the corner of the desk, Sulu noticed, sat a model of a small sublight craft she recognized as a Nivochan asteroid runner. She'd never flown one herself, but she remembered her father telling her that he once had. She wished that she could have spoken with him about everything that had happened recently, but—

"Commander," the admiral began, confirming the formal tone of their meeting. A faint, tinny quality underlay the sound of his translated voice. "Have you spoken with anybody besides me about your concerns?" He clearly referred to her discovery of Starfleet records indicating that officers she knew to be dead had apparently been assigned to starship duty.

"No," Sulu answered. "I haven't because . . ." She stopped and looked away from the admiral, uncomfortable with what she needed to reveal to him. After their last conversation, she worried that he might view her latest concern as paranoid.

"Commander?" Mentir said. Sulu peered back over at him, the silvery scales of his face visible through the helmet of his environmental suit.

"I haven't said anything to any of the *Enterprise* crew, not even to the senior staff," she said, "because I think there's a spy on board."

"*What?*" Mentir exclaimed, obviously surprised at the revelation. "You've found records of a deceased officer assigned to your vessel?"

"No," Sulu said. "But when I uncovered those discrepancies in the personnel files, it reminded me of an intermittent problem we've been experiencing aboard the ship for months. It's a seemingly random dispersion of the navigational deflector, lasting just a second or two each time. It's occurred less than a dozen times, and so we haven't been able to pinpoint the cause. Since it hasn't impacted ship operations, though, resolving it hasn't been a priority."

"And you believe that a spy aboard *Enterprise* has sabotaged the ship?" the admiral asked.

"No," Sulu said. "But I recalled the problem during our last conversation, and so I went back and checked the logs."

She lifted a padd from her lap and activated it with a touch. "The first dispersions occurred just before and just after a confrontation the *Enterprise* had with a Romulan warship eighteen months ago. It happened again, twice, during the ship's visit to the Koltaari homeworld, when the Romulans began their occupation of the planet, and then several times during our patrols of the Neutral Zone in the Foxtrot Sector." Sulu pressed a control and scrolled down the list. "The dispersion appeared once more just before the *Universe* test—" She felt a knot tighten in her stomach at the mention of the ill-fated ship. "—and a final time just after our deuterium-flow regulator failed when we were departing from Algeron."

"Obviously there's a pattern there," Mentir said, although the surprise he'd shown a moment ago seemed to have faded now.

"There's a Romulan spy aboard the *Enterprise*," Sulu concluded, "sending them information in a communications beam hidden in the output of the navigational deflector."

"Yes," the admiral said simply.

Sulu felt relieved at Mentir's immediate acceptance of her judgment, and she said so. "I'm glad you agree, Admiral."

"I'm not telling you that I agree," Mentir told her. "I'm telling you that, yes, there is a Romulan spy aboard your vessel."

"Admiral, I don't understand," Sulu said. "You know?" Her heart began to race and she felt herself flush as she realized that she had been right, that somebody in Starfleet Command *had* helped seed spies throughout the fleet. She had obviously been wrong to trust Mentir, and she wondered if she would be able to make it out of his office alive. In her mind's eye, she imagined him lifting a phaser from beneath his desk and—

Sulu sought to restrain her frenzied thoughts. She'd known Los Tirasol Mentir for twenty years—known and trusted him. She would not have contacted him about all of this if she hadn't.

Unless he's been replaced too, Sulu thought wildly. *Like the dead officers—*

"I know," Mentir said. "I didn't until just recently, but I do now. Captain Harriman discovered the spy almost immediately after they'd been assigned to the ship. It was his idea to leave the spy in place, so that we could know what information was being passed to the Romulans, what information they were seeking."

Sulu nodded slowly. It was a sensible plan, and she understood at once why the captain had not shared the information with her. The fewer people aware of the spy's existence, the better the chance that the spy would remain unaware that they'd been found out, and the more likely that they'd continue to operate aboard *Enterprise*. Now, though, with Captain Harriman no longer on the ship . . .

"Who is it?" she asked. She expected the admiral to refuse to tell her, but he did not.

"*Enterprise*'s chief computer scientist," he said. "Lieutenant Grayson Trent."

"*Trent*," Sulu said, and she immediately remembered when she'd encountered him near the second fire in the Koltaari capital. When she had first seen him, after she'd come out of the smoke, he'd initially turned away from her, and she realized now that he hadn't wanted her to see him there. It had been too late, though; he'd seen that she'd already spotted him, and so he'd had to come over to her.

And he had a medkit with him, she recalled now. He'd given her a dose of tri-ox compound, but why would a computer scientist be carrying a medkit with him? *Because he thought he might need it for himself,* she surmised. *I also was pleased that he'd made it back to the power plant,* Sulu recalled. Trent had been assigned to a different area of the city at the time, but she had simply ascribed his presence back at the fire to his desire to help the Koltaari. But Linojj had concluded that the explosive charges had been set manually, and Sulu saw now that Trent had been the one to set the bomb in the power plant, and probably the first bomb as well. Fury rose within her.

"How much longer is Starfleet Command intending to leave him aboard?" Sulu wanted to know.

"Not another day," Mentir said. "His usefulness to us is at an end." The admiral reached forward to his desk and activated a comm channel. "Mentir to Sperber," he said.

"Sperber here, Admiral," came the immediate reply.

"We're all set here," Mentir said. "Carry out your orders."

"Yes, sir."

"Mentir out." The admiral looked over at Sulu as he closed the comm channel. "My executive officer," he said. "He'll contact Lieutenant Commander Linojj and explain the situation. Trent will be transported directly into a holding cell here on the station."

"Yes, sir," Sulu said, pleased that situation had been taken care of that quickly, at least from her perspective. "And what about the other spies?" she asked, and then something else occurred to her. "Do they have anything to do with why Captain Harriman remained behind at Algeron?"

"There are no other spies," Mentir said.

"What?" Sulu said. "But the discrepancies in the personnel records . . ."

"There are no other spies," Mentir repeated. "And Captain Harriman is not aboard Algeron."

"What?" Sulu said again. "Then where is he?"

"I can explain all of this to you, Demora, and I will," the admiral said. "But first, I need to tell you that *Enterprise* must depart from KR-3 in—" He glanced at the monitor atop his desk. "—three hours and fifty-seven minutes. You'll be returning to Foxtrot Sector, to outpost thirteen."

"Yes, sir," Sulu said. "To patrol the Neutral Zone?"

"In a matter of speaking," Mentir said. "*Enterprise* needs to be there for the start of the war."

Vaughn crawled through the dark, cramped access channel, pulling himself along with his fingers, pushing himself along with his toes. The small beacon he carried in his mouth revealed his surroundings in stark tones, throwing inconstant shadows as he moved past equipment protruding from the bulkheads. The heat, the closeness of the air, enveloped him completely, like cloth strips wrapping a mummy. His elbows and knees, knocking repeatedly against the metal decking and sides of the conduit, felt raw, even through the material of his Romulan uniform. The crew of *Tomed* clearly used this tube infrequently, if at all; Vaughn suspected that they utilized robotic maintenance devices for such areas of the ship, devices small enough to maneuver through the confined spaces. If true, then it left him less vulnerable to detection, although the narrow passage also caused the completion of his tasks to be both more uncomfortable and more difficult.

At a T-shaped intersection, Vaughn took the beacon from between his teeth and shined its beam down the tube stretching away to his left. He eyed the nearest access panels, trying to pick out the Romulan characters identifying the ship's systems they covered. He saw a word that translated as *Environment*, and knew that life-support functions could be found there, though he did not bother to read the words in smaller characters that would have specified exactly which functions.

On the other side of the tube, Vaughn spied what he needed: *Communications*, and a specific relay that supported it. He stuck the beacon back between his teeth and struggled around the corner. After hauling himself into the intersecting conduit, he paused, setting the beacon down and resting his forehead on the back of one hand. He'd been down here in the bowels of *Tomed* for a long time, working to locate and sabotage the ship's external communications system. That effort had entailed finding and reconfiguring not just one subsystem or relay, but many, including independent backups, so that when the system was brought down, the Romulan crew would not be able to repair it.

Now, finally, Vaughn had come to the last site. He positioned the beacon on the deck so that it illuminated the area in which he needed to work. The access panel came free with a metallic click, and he set it to one side. Inside the bulkhead, fiber-optic clusters twined around various pieces of equipment. Vaughn studied the layout until he positively distinguished the coupling he required. Once he finished modifying it, all the critical points of the ship's external comm system would be tied together into a single control circuit, and by way of that control, *Tomed* could be rendered mute and deaf.

Vaughn retrieved a Romulan scanner from his belt, where it hung beside a sensor veil. He checked the chronometer on the display, verifying that he would have enough time to complete his tasks, then grabbed a small pack of handheld engineering tools. After performing a thorough scan of the coupling, he reached into the bulkhead and set to work.

As Vaughn toiled over the comm system, he felt the slight pulse of its operation beneath his touch. He had executed this same series of modifications several times already, and he used the tools quickly and expertly on the equipment. In just a few minutes, he, Commander Gravenor, and Captain Harriman would be one step closer to completing their mission. Success would justify the significant personal risk, Vaughn knew, but failure . . . failure would leave the blood of many on his hands.

In recent days, as this scenario had begun to unfold, he had begun to wonder if he had chosen the right career for himself. He recalled his boyhood dreams of exploration, but circumstances and his own natural abilities had conspired to send his life in another direction—in *this* direction. He had enjoyed his years of deskwork and training for Starfleet special operations, his sense of accomplishment particularly high when his efforts had contributed to the success of a field mission.

Still, he had looked forward to his own promotion to field duties with great anticipation, and he'd found his half-decade of service in that capacity more than satisfying, despite the vagaries of special ops work. Proportionate to his talents, Vaughn's responsibilities had increased quickly and significantly, and as a consequence, so too had the stakes for which he worked. In the last two years or so, he had come to face his own peril almost as a matter of routine. But while he did not wish to die, the possibility of his own death did not scare him; the possibility of the deaths of others, though, specifically as a result of his actions, did.

As Vaughn withdrew one hand from the communications equipment in order to exchange one tool for another, he asked himself whether or not he believed in what he was doing. It did not require a great deal of introspection for him to conclude that he did; he would not have stayed in special ops otherwise. Evil existed in the universe in many forms, and he found not only necessity, but virtue, in fighting it.

The difficulties he experienced now, he realized, lay not only in the cost of failure, but in the price of success, both paid for by wounds heaped upon the innocent, and by death. The destruction of *Universe* had sent waves of anguish heaving through Starfleet, and though not destroyed, *Ad Astra* had endured damage that would probably end up being measured in a life. Vaughn did not like being a party to that. He had never believed that virtuous ends justified anything but virtuous means.

He removed one hand from within the bulkhead and dragged the sleeve of his uniform across his face, wiping away the patina of perspiration that had formed there. The

old simile *Hot as Vulcan* should have had a companion
phrase, he thought: *Hot as Romulus.* Vaughn would have removed his tunic had there been more room to maneuver
within the narrow equipment tunnel.

The modifications took nearly an hour to complete.
When he had finished, he replaced the access panel, then
packed the engineering tools back inside their case. After
gathering up his equipment—tool case, scanner, and beacon—he activated the circuit now controlling the critical
points of *Tomed*'s external comm system. For now, the ship's
Romulan crew had been cut off from the rest of the universe. So too had Vaughn, Gravenor, and Harriman.

Vaughn retreated backward down the conduit, past the
intersection, and finally headed back the way he had come.
It took him twenty minutes to reach a junction. He burst
from the access tunnel as though throwing off fetters. His
body spilled onto the deck of the junction well, and he lay
there on his back for a second, shining the beacon upward
and peering at the various tunnels—some narrower, some
wider—that connected into this area. Then he pushed himself up to a sitting position and leaned against the bulkhead, resting for a few moments and gathering his strength.
Time remained before his scheduled rendezvous with Commander Gravenor and Captain Harriman. As with him, he
knew that both officers had been charged with tasks to
accomplish once they had stolen aboard *Tomed*: the commander, to secure the helm, and the captain, to access internal sensors and—

"*Alert,*" a stilted male voice announced loudly in Romulan, accompanied by the short blasts of an alarm tone. "*Singularity containment malfunction. Containment will fail in
twenty-nine minutes.*" The words rang in the enclosed space.

Vaughn quickly rose to his feet. An artificial quantum singularity—a microscopic, synthetically created black hole—
powered the warp drive of Romulan starships, he knew. A

complex containment field about the extremely efficient power source prevented the black hole from devouring the vessel, but once the singularity had been enabled, it could not be deactivated. If its containment failed, the ship would be doomed.

"*Alert*," the voice repeated, obviously part of an automated warning system. "*Singularity containment malfunction. Containment will fail in twenty-eight minutes and forty-five seconds.*"

Vaughn shined his beacon around the junction well and picked out the right access tunnel, fortunately wider than the one from which he had just emerged. He jumped over to it and dove inside, racing to meet Commander Gravenor and Captain Harriman before *Tomed* collapsed into nonexistence.

Sulu marched through the arc of a corridor on Space Station KR-3, her feet pounding rapidly along the deck, her thoughts and emotions whirling. The briefing she'd just received from Admiral Mentir had delivered to her unexpected and even shocking information. Her perspectives on recent events—the treaty negotiations with the Klingons and Romulans, the loss of *Universe*, Captain Harriman staying behind on Algeron, her unearthing of incongruities in Starfleet personnel files—had all shifted dramatically during the meeting. Likewise, her feelings had slipped their moorings, drifting not only from the surest of her convictions, but also to unanticipated extremes. She understood what had been done—and what would be attempted—even as some of those actions had injured, and would injure, her and others. She felt conflicted and aimless, despite that she would do what had been asked of her.

A corridor intersected with the curve of KR-3's central hub, and Sulu turned right into it. She had left Admiral Mentir's office headed for *Enterprise*, forty-five minutes short of its departure for Foxtrot XIII, but partway to the air-

lock she had changed direction. Right now she did not
know if she would ever see John Harriman again, but
whether she did or not, there was something she felt she
needed to do for him.

Sulu slowed when she reached the infirmary, padding
quietly through the main room and into the intensive-care
section. A thin, long-limbed man sat working at a console off
to the right, and he turned when she entered. "I'm Dr. Van
Riper," he said, rising and walking over to her. In his hand,
he held a long, silver device, tapered at one end—some sort
of medical instrument, Sulu assumed, but one she did not
recognize. "May I help you?"

"Yes, thank you. I'm Commander Demora Sulu, executive officer of the *Enterprise*," she said. "I wanted to check on
the condition of Admiral Harriman."

Van Riper's expression changed little, but it was as
though a gloom had settled across his face. "The admiral is
not doing well," he said. "Our expectations for his recovery
have diminished."

Those expectations, Sulu knew, had never been particularly high in the first place. "Is he awake?" she asked. "May I
see him?"

"He drifts in and out of consciousness," the doctor said. "I
can take you to him, but I'll have to ask you to stay no more
than five minutes."

"Thank you, Doctor," Sulu said.

Van Riper reached back to a console and set the silver device down, then moved past Sulu and led the way to an alcove at the far end of the section. They stopped at the
threshold, and Sulu looked in to see the admiral's indistinct
shape beneath a sheet, the low arch of a respirator circling
his chest; she could not see his face. "Five minutes," the
doctor whispered gently, and then left.

Sulu moved slowly into the alcove, making her way to the
head of the biobed. As she passed the respirator—the sighs

of its operation haunting in the quiet room—the upper section of the admiral's body came into view. Sulu's hand automatically came up to her mouth, as though stifling the gasp that she consciously held back.

Gone was the Blackjack Harriman of her memory. The sturdy, broad-shouldered admiral had been replaced with a fragile skeleton of a man. His robust features had slackened and paled, the medical coverings wrapping his head and one side of his face seeming to have more substance than did his sickly flesh. His one visible eye was closed.

Sulu peered down at the admiral with a mixture of horror and pity. She had come here for her friend, not with any specific agenda in mind, but simply because she believed that she should. As she stood here, though, she felt grateful that she'd found the admiral sleeping.

Still, she didn't want to leave right away. She glanced around and saw a chair against the wall, and she picked it up and set it by the head of the admiral's bed. She sat down to spend the five minutes here that the doctor had granted her.

The rise and fall of the respirator's sounds filled the small area, an elegy meted out in mechanical breaths. For the first time in a while, Sulu thought of her mother, thought of sitting by her sickbed, keeping a vigil night after night. The hours had seemed interminable at the same time that they'd raced unflaggingly toward her mother's death.

Next to the admiral's respirator, Sulu saw several of his fingers not covered by the sheet. She considered taking his hand, just as she had so often taken her mother's during those final days. She wanted to do it, thinking that it might somehow serve her friend, but she couldn't. Not only did she feel no connection with this man, but she had built a strong resentment of him over the years, knowing how he had willfully failed his son. On so many occasions—

A sound like sandpaper rasping against wood interrupted her thoughts. She looked over to see that the admiral had awoken—or perhaps he had been awake, but had only now opened his eyes. Sulu met his gaze, but he couldn't seem to focus on her. His eyes—rather, the one eye not covered—appeared glassy and vacant. As she watched, his thin, grayish lips parted, and another scratchy mutter issued from them.

"Admiral Harriman," she said quietly.

His lips moved again, and this time, they emitted a weak voice. He seemed to speak a single, unintelligible word, something that sounded to Sulu like *Fron.*

"It's Commander Sulu," she said. "From the *Enterprise.*"

Blackjack's mouth slowly formed the last word she'd said, though he only gave voice to the third syllable: *"Prise."*

Inane questions such as *How are you?* and *Can I get you anything?* crossed Sulu's mind, and she discarded them at once. "I'm here—" she started, but couldn't complete the statement because she really didn't know why she'd come here.

"Enterprise," Blackjack said again, most of the word audible this time. "Sulu." His eye seemed at last to find her.

"Yes," Sulu confirmed. "That's me."

"Your father," Blackjack said, "violated regs."

Sulu couldn't stop from smiling. She understood the incident to which the admiral was referring—the incident that had resulted in the estrangement of Blackjack and his son—but her amusement came from what she knew she would say.

"Yes, my father violated Starfleet regulations," she agreed. "Many times."

"A cancer," Blackjack said.

Sulu felt the smile fade from her face. In an instant, she thought of countless ways to respond to the admiral, from citing the details of her father's long and illustrious Starfleet career, to simply saying how much she loved him. Instead, she decided to give the dying man before her another chance to find peace. "I'm here," she said, "for your son."

Blackjack said nothing for a moment, and Sulu thought that he might not have heard her, but then: "Johnny."

"Yes," she said. "John Harriman Junior." She paused, and then said, "He's worried about you. He wants you to get better." She waited for the admiral to respond, but when he didn't, she added, "He loves you."

Blackjack remained quiet. As Sulu watched him, though, a spark of life seemed to enter his eye, and she realized that a tear had formed there. Joy filled her heart at this moment that she could bring to her friend—*if* the captain returned from his mission.

"Johnny," the admiral said again. "Weak. Undisciplined. Un*grateful.*"

Sulu's mouth dropped open in surprise. Immediately, though, shock gave way to anger. She had come here for her friend, but she had also tried to ease the senior Harriman's suffering, to bring him some closure with his son. She thought she'd reached the admiral, but . . .

Sulu stood up. Once more, a myriad of things to say to Admiral Harriman occurred to her, and again, she said none of them. "Goodbye, Admiral." She turned and left the alcove, stopping briefly to thank Dr. Van Riper before exiting the infirmary.

As she strode through the corridor, headed for the hatch that would take her to *Enterprise*—and beyond it, to Foxtrot XIII—she thought of John and his long estrangement from his father, thought about the complex and unreconciled feelings her friend had been dealing with lately. She didn't know why the admiral was the way he was, but she understood that there must be a reason. A terrible sense of sadness swept over her— not for John, but for his father, a joyless, pitiable man who, even as he lay dying, could not find a place in his life for love.

Time grew short.

Admiral Aventeer Vokar sat in his raised chair at the rear

of *Tomed*'s bridge, staring ahead at the becalmed starscape on the main viewscreen. At the first indication of containment failure, he'd directed the ship dropped from warp and brought to station-keeping. With the engines shut down and the great thrum of their operation now absent, *Tomed* lay in space like a voiceless, wounded animal.

Below Vokar, the bridge crew searched for answers. He had ordered the grating automated alerts silenced, leaving only the sounds of the officers working their consoles. The yellow glare of the emergency lighting threw the scene into bleak contrasts, imparting to it a cold, two-dimensional aspect. Vokar observed, quiet and utterly still, waiting for the information that would dictate his next actions.

Inside, he raged.

He did not suspect Federation subversion; he was *certain* of it. The sudden deterioration of the singularity containment field would have been indication enough, but the simultaneous breakdown of the ship's external communications provided virtually unassailable proof. The two systems—containment and communications—shared no common circuitry, flouting the realistic possibility that they would go down independently and at the same time, along with their backups. He did not know how the sabotage had been perpetrated, but he knew beyond doubt the identities of the perpetrators.

"Admiral," Subcommander Linavil said, her voice just loud enough, just untamed enough, to betray her dread. Vokar looked down and to his left, to where she stood beside an engineer feverishly operating his console. "They can't stop it," she declared. "They think they *might* be able to slow the loss of containment, but it *will* fail completely."

"For how long can the engineers delay it?" Vokar asked.

"They're not sure," Linavil said. She took several steps away from the console and toward Vokar. "Minutes, maybe hours. But they may not have even enough time to determine if they *can* delay it."

Vokar nodded, carefully keeping his fury in check. He glanced at the chronometer set into a small display in the arm of his chair. If nothing could be done, then twenty-five minutes remained before the quantum singularity that powered *Tomed* would be free of its cage, an insatiable force that would demolish the ship.

No crewmember was more than seven minutes away from an evacuation pod, Vokar knew. That left a margin of safety, but a small one. After the crew had escaped, there would still have to be time enough for the ship, via preprogramming, to be sent out of the area and then stopped somewhere; the singularity could not be permitted to slip its bonds while at warp velocity, for the resultant devastation would easily reach back far enough to obliterate the crew.

Vokar looked back up at the viewscreen, barely able to stifle the scream forming behind his lips. Reluctantly, he gave the order. "Abandon ship."

Linavil acted immediately. "Navigator," she said as she strode purposefully across the center of the bridge, her body movements now reflecting decisiveness and strength, Vokar noted, and not concern or fear. "Plot a course away from here, and away from any space lanes. Helm, preprogram the ship to travel the new course at warp eight, beginning six minutes prior to projected containment failure, and ending one minute prior."

The officers acknowledged the orders and set to operating their consoles. "Intraship," Linavil said, continuing across the bridge until she reached the communications station. As the officer there worked her controls, Vokar made another decision.

"Subcommander," he said.

"Sir?" Linavil said, turning to peer up at him.

"Myself, you, Akeev, and Elvia and her top two engineers," he said, "we go last." He would provide Elvia, *Tomed*'s lead engineer, and Akeev, the ship's lead science officer, as much time as possible to find any kind of a solution. If the containment failure could be delayed until they reached the nearest repair base, then another containment field could be erected about the singularity.

"Yes, sir," Linavil said, and she looked over to where Lieutenant Akeev manned his sciences station. Vokar saw him acknowledge with a nod the unspoken question: *Did you hear the admiral's order?* As Akeev returned his attention to his panel, Linavil reached across the communications console and touched a control. "Bridge to Lieutenant Elvia," she said.

Several seconds passed. *"This is Elvia,"* a female voice finally said, sounding beleaguered.

"This is Linavil. We're about to abandon *Tomed.* You and your top two engineers will remain aboard and continue to work on slowing the containment collapse until ten minutes before it will fail." Vokar knew, as Linavil must also, that several evacuation pods were within a minute of main engineering. "Report any progress immediately."

"Acknowledged," Elvia said. *"I'll keep T'Sil and Valin with me."*

"Out," Linavil said, and then she told the comm officer once more, "Intraship." When the channel had been opened, she made the announcement to the crew. "This is Subcommander Linavil. By order of Admiral Vokar, all hands abandon ship. I repeat: All hands abandon ship. This is not an exercise."

Vokar watched as the crew—but for Linavil and Akeev—quickly secured their stations and began an exodus for the evacuation pods. Vokar waited until the last of the departing officers—helm and navigation—had left, and then he stood from his command chair and descended to the deck. In just moments, the bridge had been deserted.

"Normal lighting," he said. He did not see who, but either Linavil or Akeev complied with the order. The illusory quality lent to the bridge by the yellow emergency lights vanished, as though reality had somehow been injected back into the scene.

Vokar walked forward, past the flight-control consoles, and glared at the main viewscreen. He concentrated on controlling his wrath. *How did they do it?* he asked himself in frustration. He had been right not to trust the Federation, of course: not about the test of metaweapons that they denied; not about the so-called hyperwarp drive; and not even to travel to and from Algeron within Romulan space. No, he hadn't trusted them—had *never* trusted them—but neither had he believed that the security of the flagship could be compromised like this.

On the almost-empty bridge, the tap of Akeev's fingertips on his panel, and the occasional tones emitted by the sciences station, failed to fill the void left by the absent crew. Vokar waited to hear something from Akeev, or from the engineers working directly on the containment field, but he knew that he wouldn't. Before long, they would all have to flee the ship too.

Minutes passed.

Why? he asked himself. Why would the Federation want to destroy just one Romulan vessel? Yes, *Tomed* was the flagship, but the risk that they must have taken to attempt this within Romulan space seemed too great. *Unless* Tomed *wasn't the only vessel attacked. Perhaps the Federation has commenced a war, perhaps—*

Movement streaked across the viewscreen. Vokar saw the cylindrical evacuation pods—half a dozen, a dozen, more— as they rushed away from *Tomed*, taking the crew to safety. "Time," he said.

"Fifteen minutes until containment failure," Linavil answered from somewhere behind him.

"How did they do it?" Vokar asked as he watched more evacuation pods racing out into space. He heard the metallic toll of footfalls, which ended as Linavil stepped up next to him.

"I don't know, Admiral," she said, clearly understanding who he had meant by *they*.

"How?" he asked again. He turned toward the first officer. "We never docked at Algeron. We stayed in orbit about it specifically to maintain ship's security."

"I know, sir," she said. "The shields have been raised from the moment *Enterprise* crossed the Neutral Zone into our territory until the moment it crossed back. They couldn't have—"

The instant Linavil stopped speaking, Vokar knew that she had figured it out. "What?" he demanded.

"When *Enterprise* suffered the problem with its sublight engine," Linavil said, "we prepared to transport their crew aboard. I lowered the shields, for just a few moments, until the crisis had passed."

Vokar resisted the urge to strike her where she stood. He saw Linavil's fear of him in her eyes. "Decoyed," he said. He peered past Linavil. "Akeev."

"Sir?" the science officer said.

"How long would it take to do this in this way?" he asked. "To sabotage the containment field and its backups, external communications and its backups?"

"I'm not sure, Admiral," Akeev said. "I'd have to—"

"Minutes?" Vokar spoke over him. "Hours? Days?"

"Hours at least," Akeev said. "Probably days."

Vokar looked back at Linavil. "They're still aboard," he asserted. "Which means that they're not attempting to destroy the ship; they're attempting to seize it."

Linavil's eyes went wide. "Lieutenant, full internal scans," she said. "Find the intruders."

"Working," Akeev said as his hands flew across his console. "The sensors show only six life signs," he reported a moment later. "All Romulan." But he continued operating his controls. "Broadening search for secondary indications," he said.

Vokar waited. "Time," he said to Linavil.

She walked over to the nearest console and glanced at its display. "Twelve minutes," she said.

"Sir," Akeev said, looking up from his station to face Vokar. "Sensors are picking up a statistically significant heat fluctuation that could be caused by intruders."

"Where?" Vokar wanted to know.

"Lower engineering deck, port side," Akeev said, then checked his console again. "In a maintenance connector."

"They're somehow cloaked," Vokar said, sure that they had found the Federation saboteurs. "But they're here."

Linavil's features shifted, her emotions moving from a fear of reprisal for the blunder that had allowed intruders onto *Tomed*, to a desire for retribution.

"Get the weapons," Vokar said.

MINUS ONE: SERPENTS

Commander Drysi Gravenor scratched at her ear, trying to eliminate an itch where the pointed Romulan tip had been attached to her flesh. She glanced up from her scanner and across the equipment junction at Lieutenant Vaughn. He leaned with his back against the bulkhead, his posture revealing his fatigue. A sheen of perspiration coated his features, even as two beads slid down the side of his face, leaving quicksilver trails behind. He looked as uncomfortable as she felt.

The time aboard *Tomed* had been hard on all of them, Gravenor knew. The heat, the closeness in the equipment junctions and conduits, napping in abbreviated shifts, subsisting on condensed emergency rations—all had taken their toll. In addition, the complexity and arduousness of their tasks had pushed each of them, while the importance and pressure of successfully completing their mission had never left their minds. And right now, they'd reached one of the most critical stages of the operation.

Gravenor checked the display on her Romulan scanner. Fiber-optic lines swept from the back of the device and into a cluster of exposed circuits within the bulkhead. She'd secured a connection to the ship's helm, and while she hadn't yet taken control of it, she monitored its function. *Tomed*'s helm officer had programmed it to engage six minutes before complete containment failure, taking the ship away from the evacuated crew and leaving them behind in safety. Once that had happened, Captain Harriman would slow the degradation of the containment field—it could not be stopped—and Gravenor would head the ship toward Federation space.

The chronometer on the tricorder told Gravenor that in just four minutes, *Tomed* would go to warp. By that time, the entire crew would have vacated the ship, allowing her and Vaughn and Harriman to finish their mission. With full control of the ship, they could—

The display on her scanner jumped. She'd been observing *Tomed*'s helm readouts, monitoring the programmed flight settings and the status of the warp drive. Now the set of Romulan characters marching across the display told her something different than they had only seconds ago. She quickly read through the new text, and saw in an instant that everything had changed.

Gravenor raised her arm and activated the Romulan communicator encircling her wrist. As she did so, she saw Vaughn straighten and push away from the bulkhead, his attention firmly on her. "We've got a problem," she told him, and as though confirming that fact, she risked contacting Harriman. Until now, they'd refrained from using their communicators, which could have betrayed their presence aboard *Tomed*. "Aerel to Ventin," she said, employing the names of two of the Romulan crew that they'd chosen for themselves should the need arise.

"*Ventin*," Harriman responded at once.

"The ship is no longer programmed to go to warp," she said. "Flight control has been transferred from the computer back to the helm station on the bridge."

Silence followed, only a second or two in duration, Gravenor was sure, but the time seemed to elongate for her. She awaited Harriman's orders, anxious to take action.

"*Check internal sensors*," Harriman said at last. "*How many are left aboard?*"

Gravenor worked her scanner. She had established a link to the ship's internal sensors as a contingency measure, and she accessed that connection now. She executed a high-level scan, casting a shipwide net for Romulan life signs. "Six of the crew are still aboard," she reported to Harriman. "Three on the bridge, three in engineering—*wait*. Some of them are now on the move."

"*Take control of the helm*," Harriman ordered. "*Get us away from here*."

"Aye," Gravenor said simply.

"*I'll do my job*," Harriman said, obviously meaning that he'd do as planned, reducing the rate of decay of the containment field. "*I'll rejoin you shortly. Out*."

Gravenor deactivated the communicator, then dropped her hand back to her scanner. She brought up the helm readouts on the display, studied them for a moment, and then went to work. In only a short time, she had taken over operation of *Tomed*'s flight-control systems. Utilizing the course the Romulan navigator had earlier plotted and programmed into the computer, Gravenor engaged the ship's warp drive.

The deep hum of the faster-than-light engines rose in the equipment junction. The throbbing character of the sound differed from that of *Enterprise*'s steady drone. Here, the pulse seemed like the beating of *Tomed*'s singular heart.

As Gravenor worked, Vaughn stepped up beside her and peered at the scanner display. She waited enough time for the ship to be beyond the reach of the limited sensors in the escape pods, then adjusted *Tomed*'s course and increased its velocity to warp nine. "We're on our way," she said to Vaughn. She accessed the ship's internal sensors again, wanting to check on the location of the Romulans. She saw that the three of them in main engineering had left that location and now headed in this direction. It would not take long for them to reach—

The display went blank.

Gravenor coolly worked the controls of the scanner, even as she understood what had happened. She checked both the device itself and its connection to the ship's circuitry, confirming her suspicion: her access to the sensors had been severed. "They found us," she said to Vaughn. She activated the communicator wrapped around her wrist and raised it once more toward her mouth. "Aerel to Ventin," she said. "They found us."

"*Get out of there*," Harriman ordered. "*You know your jobs. Out.*"

As with any special operation, alternative courses of action had been established wherever possible. Being discovered at this point, with *Tomed* almost entirely abandoned by its crew and now streaking away toward Federation space, Gravenor's duty would be to prevent the Romulans from taking control of the warp drive. If she and Vaughn and Harriman were to succeed in their mission, they could not allow the ship to be stopped, slowed, or diverted.

Gravenor reached forward, grabbed the bundles of fiberoptics, and ripped them free of their connections to the Romulan circuitry. After disengaging the lines from her scanner, she stuffed them into the bulkhead. Beside her, Vaughn had already reached down and retrieved the access plate, which he replaced as soon as she had moved away. When he turned to face her, she said, "Proceed as planned, Lieutenant."

"Yes, Commander," he said. The muscles of his face had tensed visibly, and he looked serious and concerned. But young as he was, Vaughn didn't give in to panic—and wouldn't, Gravenor felt certain. If she had believed otherwise, she would not have selected him for this assignment.

"Go," she said. Vaughn drew his disruptor, then turned and climbed into a conduit. Gravenor attached her scanner to its holder at her waist, then reached for her own weapon. As Vaughn's legs and feet disappeared from view, she whirled and scrambled into a different conduit, headed for *Tomed*'s main engineering section.

As he watched Linavil stride to the weapons cache, Vokar stepped up to the nearest console—the navigation station—and opened a comm channel. "Vokar to engineering," he said.

"*This is Elvia,*" replied the ship's lead engineer, rushing through the words, her voice loud. She sounded harried, and perhaps also annoyed. "*Admiral, we have only a few—*"

"Cease your work, Lieutenant," Vokar interrupted. "There are intruders aboard. Arm yourselves and proceed to the lower engineering deck, port side, maintenance connector—" He looked over at Akeev for the location.

"Connector forty-seven," the science officer said. Vokar repeated the information to Elvia.

"*Admiral,*" she said, "*we haven't been able to slow the containment loss. My engineers and I were just about to head for the evacuation pods.*"

"I'm aware of that," Vokar said, fighting back anger at having his orders questioned. Linavil started back across the bridge, he saw, three disruptors in her hands. "The source of the containment problem has been located, and another crew is making repairs. I need you and your engineers to arm yourselves and find the intruders. You're closest to them."

Elvia did not respond immediately, and Vokar thought that she might not respond at all. Obviously fearing the collapse of the containment field and the unleashing of the quantum singularity, Elvia might simply flee the ship, choosing to suffer the consequences of her cowardice later. But then she said, "*How many intruders are there?*"

Again, Vokar looked to Akeev. "Probably not more than two or three," the science officer speculated, just as Linavil walked up to him and handed him one of the disruptors.

"Three," Vokar told Elvia. "And they are impervious to direct sensor scans."

"Yes, sir," she said. "We're on our way."

"Vokar out," he said, jabbing at the control on the navigation console to close the channel. Linavil stopped beside him and held out a disruptor. He took the proffered weapon and affixed it to his uniform at his hip, and Linavil did the same with her own. "Subcommander," he said, "cancel the program that would automatically take the ship out of the area."

"Yes, sir," she said. She moved quickly to the helm.

"Sir," Akeev said from the sciences station, "there's another crew working on the containment field?" As with Elvia, he sounded distressed.

"The intruders," Vokar explained. "The Federation saboteurs."

"I don't understand," Akeev said. "I know what the sensors indicated, but even if the intruders are still aboard, how can you be sure that they can fix the problem?"

"They *are* still aboard," Linavil offered as she worked the helm controls, "because they want this ship."

"Yes," Vokar agreed. "They executed the damage to *Tomed*, and now they'll repair it. They can't very well have the ship if it's destroyed."

Akeev nodded slowly, but seemed unconvinced. "How do you know they don't *want* to destroy the ship?" he asked.

"Because they're still aboard," Vokar said, "and the Federation doesn't launch suicide missions." He thought of the Romulan commanders who over the decades had sacrificed their lives and those of their crews rather than allow their vessels and themselves to fall into the possession of an enemy. Vokar knew firsthand that Starfleet personnel did not always lack for courage or the ability to plan strategically, but willingly giving up their lives for the greater good was an action beyond their capabilities.

"I've canceled the helm program, sir," Linavil announced. "*Tomed*'s not going anywhere."

"So the intruders sabotaged the ship to force the crew to evacuate?" Akeev asked. "And their plan was to fix it and escape when the ship automatically left the area?"

"Yes," Vokar said, "but they didn't intend for there to be any Romulans left aboard to . . ." Vokar's voice trailed off as something else occurred to him. ". . . to thwart them," he finished flatly as he began to work through his realization: the plan of the Federation operatives demanded secrecy. Even if they successfully captured *Tomed*, it would do them no good if the Romulan Empire could demonstrate that the Federation had been behind the theft. The Klingons had threatened to side against the aggressor in a conflict between the Empire and the Federation, and the meticulously planned appropriation of the Romulan flagship from this side of the Neutral Zone would certainly qualify as aggression.

"We need to send out a message," Vokar said to Linavil. "To Romulus, to another vessel, even to the crew in the evacuation pods. We must expose the Federation plot." The intruders had obviously sabotaged communications so that the crew would not be able to broadcast a distress call, but probably also as a precaution should not all of the crew evacuate the ship.

"There's long-range communications equipment in the shuttles," Linavil noted.

Vokar nodded. "Go now," he said. Linavil headed for the turbolift, but stopped when Akeev spoke up.

"Admiral," he said, urgency in his tone. "Sensors have detected a comm signal . . . originating in . . ." The science officer tapped at his panel. ". . . lower engineering deck . . ." He looked up, the pale glow of the sciences display reflecting on his face. ". . . port maintenance connector forty-seven."

"Can you get a fix on their life signs?" Linavil asked.

"Trying," Akeev said. "Negative, but . . . they've tapped into internal sensors from the same location."

"Shut them out," Vokar ordered.

"Yes, sir," Akeev said. He worked his controls for a moment, and then said, "I can't isolate their connection for some reason."

"Disable the surrounding links into the network," Linavil said.

Vokar felt the change in *Tomed* before he heard it: the initial vibration of the ship, carried through its structure, through the bulkheads and decking, as the warp drive began operation. He raced to the helm, seeing confirmation there of *Tomed*'s transition to light speeds, even as the bass pulsation of the engines rose around him. He began working the panel, attempting to regain control of the ship.

Linavil dashed up beside him. She observed for a moment, and then said, "They've locked us out." She quickly dropped to the floor, onto her back, and reached up beneath the console. "The helm's still operational, though. I can reroute the panel, manually bypass the lockouts."

"I can do that," Vokar told her. "You get to the shuttle compartment and send out a message."

"Yes, sir," Linavil said, rising back to her feet. Once more, she headed for the turbolift.

"Admiral," Akeev said, "I've shut down their sensor access. I'm also reading a major decrease in the destabilization of the containment field; it's suddenly drawing power through different relays."

Vokar acknowledged Akeev, then stopped Linavil before she left the bridge. "Subcommander," he said. She turned back toward him as the turbolift doors glided open.

"Sir?" she said.

"Make sure your disruptor is set to kill," he told her.

Harriman clambered through the equipment conduit, his muscles no longer aching as badly as they had been. The repeated, awkward movement through the cramped maintenance tunnels during the time on *Tomed* had taxed his body, but the flow of adrenaline eased much of that pain right now. Still, he would have preferred his own discomfort to the reasons for his heightened physical state. The continued presence on the ship of six Romulans endangered not only this mission, but the Federation itself. If word of Starfleet personnel attempting to commandeer *Tomed* reached Romulus and Qo'noS, war would be the consequence, with the two empires uniting against a common foe. The loss of life in the Federation would be unimaginable.

Around a corner in the conduit, the beam of Harriman's beacon picked out a maintenance hatch just a few meters ahead, where he'd expected to find it. He crawled forward, anxious both to be free of these restrictive surroundings and to meet the threat of the Romulans still on board. Since he had first conceived of this plan so many months ago, and through the more detailed plotting that had begun after the Romulans had taken the world of the Koltaari, this had always been the stage most susceptible to failure. Had the entire crew abandoned ship, the flight to the Neutral Zone would likely have been uneventful, but now . . .

Harriman could only hope that the Romulans in the escape pods knew nothing of the special ops team aboard their vessel. The timing of events suggested that to be the case, but if not, then all had already been lost. Providing he, Gravenor, and Vaughn could subdue the remaining Romulans, he could take the ship back to the escape pods and allow the containment field to fail. The result would be the deaths of all of them—*Tomed*'s crew and the special ops team. But even if Harriman could find the justification to take such an action—and he did not know that he could—such an uncommon accident occurring within Romulan territory, after *Tomed*'s close contact with *Enterprise*, would rightly be construed by the Empire as an attack by Starfleet. In that circumstance, Ambassador Kamemor might well come forward to confirm what little she knew of the plan, and how she had been duped by Harriman. Again, the outcome would be war, with the Klingons siding against the Federation.

No. The only course of action he could take right now would be to attempt to complete the mission.

Harriman arrived at the hatch. He set his beacon down and reached for the tricorder hanging at his waist. Using the device to scan for life signs would reveal his position, but better to risk that than to open the hatch and find a disruptor pointed at his head; he would not be staying in this location anyway. He performed a sweep of the surrounding deck. No life signs registered.

He deactivated the tricorder and returned it to his waist, along with the beacon, exchanging them for his phaser. The hatch opened beneath a heavy push, and Harriman scrambled out of the conduit. As he dropped onto the deck, he ducked low, flattening himself against the near bulkhead. Despite what the tricorder had told him, he looked hurriedly from side to side, ensuring the absence of any Romulans here.

Although he saw and heard nobody, the corridor in which he found himself left him feeling vulnerable. It ended at a T-shaped intersection a short distance to his left, but it stretched a long way to his right—the direction he needed to travel. Perhaps seventy meters long, it crossed several other corridors and afforded few places for concealment; he glimpsed what appeared to be a couple of recesses along the way, but hatches, access panels, and equipment—rather than doors—lined the bulkheads. If he had not left here by the time the Romulans arrived to investigate his tricorder signal, he would probably not be able to hide from them.

He pushed the hatch closed and proceeded cautiously down the corridor. He stayed low, hugging tight to the bulkhead, his phaser raised before him. As he approached the first intersection, he paused, choosing not to scan again, but listening intently. He heard nothing but the rhythms of *Tomed*'s warp drive.

Just as he started forward again, though, a sound reached him, like a foot shuffling along a deck, or a shoulder brushing against a bulkhead. Harriman froze, then aimed his phaser toward the intersection, toward the corner nearest him. He waited . . . one second . . . two . . . and then a Romulan emerged from the cross-corridor, a disruptor in his hand.

Harriman's arm tensed, even as the inconsistency struck him. Only a moment ago, his sensor scans of the area had detected no life signs. And as the Romulan glanced in his direction and spotted him, Harriman hesitated.

"Vaughn," he said in a hushed tone resembling a stage whisper, just loud enough to be heard above the background hum of the warp engines. As Harriman lowered his weapon, it occurred to him that the lieutenant no longer looked silly in his Romulan masquerade, but threatening. He had no idea how he'd managed to avoid firing on Vaughn.

"Captain," the lieutenant said, trotting over, his sensor veil obviously still functioning. "I'm on my way to the shuttlebay." Harriman nodded. He knew that had been the plan, of course, but the statement confirmed for him that nothing had happened to prevent Vaughn from undertaking his tasks there. "The access ladder to the next deck is this way," the lieutenant said, hiking a thumb back over his shoulder.

"I know. I'm headed past there," Harriman said, glancing around to make sure that the corridor remained clear. "We have to go now though. I just used my tricorder, so the Romulans will be here soon."

"Yes, sir," Vaughn said.

Harriman began down the corridor again, and Vaughn fell in alongside him. When they reached the first intersection, they peered carefully around the corners. "Take cover here," Harriman told Vaughn. "If we encounter Romulans now—" He motioned down the long corridor that lay in front of them. "—I don't want both of us at risk." No matter what happened, at least one of the special ops team needed to survive and remain free long enough to complete the mission.

"Yes, sir," Vaughn said. He took a position off of the main corridor, where he could look around the corner to follow Harriman's progress.

Phaser in hand, Harriman moved swiftly, staying low to the deck and close to the bulkhead. He stopped twice before intersections, traversing them guardedly, and then a third time at an equipment recess, where he ducked out of sight. Across from him, in a small bay, stood the ladder leading to the next deck, and just a few meters to his right, a corridor reached away in both directions from where this one ended.

Leaning out of the recess and peering around, Harriman waited several seconds, listening for the sounds of anybody approaching. Hearing nothing, he reached his empty hand out and gestured toward Vaughn, waving him forward. The lieutenant rounded the corner immediately and began down the corridor. After he had navigated the first intersection, and then the second, Harriman held up his hand, palm out. Vaughn stopped, allowing them both to look around and listen once more for any Romulans who might be heading this way.

Finally, Harriman signaled to Vaughn by pointing across the corridor. The lieutenant's gaze seemed to take in the ladder, and then he lifted his own hand and pointed toward the end of the corridor, obviously asking about Harriman's own plans. Harriman nodded and stepped out of the recess. He offered the lieutenant a final look, feeling a solidarity of purpose with him. Then he turned and continued on toward his objective, knowing that Vaughn would do the same.

Harriman sped through a half-dozen more corridors, pausing only before intersections. Doors eventually replaced the equipment and hatches and access panels, reminders of the crew who had recently stridden these decks. Still under power, the beat of its engines still permeating the hull, the ship seemed eerie for its emptiness. Despite knowing what had taken place here, Harriman recalled the centuries-old Earth tale of *Mary Celeste*, a sailing vessel found abandoned in midvoyage. This somehow felt like that—mysterious, and even haunting. Except that whatever presence leaped out at him here would be far more dangerous than some imaginary specter.

When he neared his objective, he began reading the rectangular plates set into the bulkheads beside the doors. The rounded-block forms of the Romulan characters identified an auxiliary-computer control site, a life-support monitoring station, a conference room, and finally, his destination.

Clutching his weapon before him, Harriman darted toward the doors. As they parted and he traversed the threshold, he tucked and rolled. Across the small room, he come up onto one knee, his phaser held up in one hand and steadied by the other. His eyes rapidly scanned his surroundings, right to left, from a circular platform, to a freestanding console, to a bulkhead faced with displays, controls, and access panels. Like most of the rest of the ship, the room was empty.

Harriman rose and moved to the console, a long, arcing station supported by a narrow column reaching up to its center. He examined the Romulan markings there, familiarizing himself with a layout slightly different from the one he had seen in intelligence briefings. When he had distinguished all of the controls that he would need, he set his phaser down atop the panel and activated the sensor matrix. He scanned the ship for life signs—doubtless giving up his position once more—and located the six Romulans still aboard *Tomed*. Two roamed near the maintenance junction that Gravenor and Vaughn had left not long ago, while a third moved inside the junction itself. A fourth rode in a descending turbolift, and Harriman guessed that they were headed either for main engineering or for the shuttlebay. The final pair of life signs emanated from the bridge; he targeted those two first, assuming that one of them would be Admiral Vokar, who surely would have been the last to vacate the flagship.

Moving his fingers deliberately across the transporter console, Harriman locked on to the two Romulans. He specified the remainder of the settings, verified them, and then engaged the activation sequencer. A series of lights running laterally across the panel illuminated one after another as a deep buzz rose in the room. After he had beamed the first two Romulans into—

Nothing happened.

The whirr of the transporter faded to silence as the chain of lights, all of them glowing, winked off. Without delay, Harriman ran through the preparations a second time, confirming the operation of the console and the two sensor locks. He reviewed the rest of the settings, then initiated the activation sequencer once more. Again, the row of lights began to brighten one at a time, and the drone of the transporter grew out of the silence. But he already knew what would happen: nothing.

Vokar, Harriman thought, certain that it had been the admiral who had thwarted his plan. A long time ago, Harriman had utilized a transporter to defeat Vokar. Clearly the leader of the Romulan Imperial Fleet would not allow such an occurrence to happen a second time.

Harriman grabbed his tricorder and scanned the sections of the deck surrounding the transporter room. He read one life sign, Romulan, moving away from the maintenance junction and seemingly headed in this direction. They were still far enough away, though, that Harriman would have time enough to escape.

Snatching his phaser from the console, he rushed for the doors. At the last instant, as they failed to open, he rolled his shoulder forward, absorbing the impact with his upper arm. He stepped back and looked to either side of the doors, spying a small control panel in the bulkhead to the right. He hastily pulled it open, searching for a manual override. A lever promised freedom, but failed to work. Obviously, the transporter room had been completely locked down from another location, probably the bridge.

Harriman checked the tricorder again. The Romulan would be here shortly. He peered around the room, but saw no place to conceal himself. He could take a position behind the transporter console, but standing on its slender base, it would provide him little protection.

With no other choices, he retreated across the room. He stood opposite the doors, with his back against the bulkhead. Then, keeping his eyes focused on the tricorder display, Harriman raised his phaser and waited for the impending confrontation.

Sublieutenant Alira T'Sil stood outside maintenance connector forty-seven, uncomfortable with the feel of a disruptor in her hand. Although she served as an officer in the Romulan Imperial Fleet, she considered herself an engineer and not a soldier. In her nearly seven years of duty, she had never fired a weapon outside of compulsory drills. She found herself far more anxious now than when she'd been aiding in the attempted repair of the singularity containment field only moments before it had been expected to collapse.

Ahead of her in the corridor, Lieutenant Elvia operated a scanner, searching for indications of the intruders on the other side of the closed maintenance hatch. T'Sil watched the rangy engineer take sensor readings, the lieutenant's fingers moving across the controls of the scanner with such fleet precision that they almost seemed choreographed. Beside T'Sil, Sublieutenant Valin also watched, a disruptor drawn awkwardly in his hand.

"I'm not picking up any life signs," Lieutenant Elvia said, studying the display on her scanner.

"Admiral Vokar said that the intruders couldn't be directly detected using sensors," T'Sil offered.

"I know what the admiral said," Elvia snapped. T'Sil knew *Tomed*'s lead engineer well enough to understand the target of her discontented tone. The lieutenant aimed her frustrations not at T'Sil for her comment, but at Admiral Vokar for having ordered engineers to take on the mantle of security.

Elvia stepped back from the maintenance hatch, taking hold of the disruptor hanging at her hip. "All right," she said, looking over at T'Sil. "Open it." The lieutenant lowered her scanner and raised her weapon.

T'Sil attached her own disruptor to its place on her hip, then moved over to the hatch. The rectangle of burnished, lightweight metal extended about as broad as her shoulders and half her height. She took hold of the handles on either side of the hatch, facing her reflection in its glossy surface. Her rounded cheekbones, delicate nose—turned slightly upward at its tip—and straight black hair seemed familiar, but the unconcealed look of fear in her eyes did not.

"To the side," Elvia said, as though T'Sil might have been oblivious of the situation, opening up the entrance to the maintenance connector while staying in the line of fire. T'Sil said nothing, though, as she tightened her closed fists about the handles and pulled. The hatch came free with a pair of metallic clicks, and she swung her body around, flattening her back against the bulkhead. In front of her, Elvia glared into the access port, her disruptor a minatory sight at the end of her outstretched arm. T'Sil tensed as she anticipated the shrill scream of the weapon, waited for blue packets of lethal energy to streak past her and into the maintenance connector.

Instead, Lieutenant Elvia paced across the corridor to the open hatch. She peered inside for a few seconds, then dropped her disruptor to her side. "There's no one here," she said. As Elvia moved to hook her scanner and weapon to the waist of her uniform, T'Sil turned and set the hatch down on the decking, leaning it against the bulkhead. "Come with me," Elvia said to T'Sil, then looked back over her shoulder at Valin. "Stand guard, Sublieutenant." Valin nodded.

Elvia leaned against the bottom of the hatchway and swung a leg across it, then stooped and climbed inside. As the lieutenant disappeared from view, T'Sil glanced over at Valin, exchanging a look with the stout engineer—a slight shifting of the eyes, a slight raising of the eyebrows—that told her that he felt as uneasy as she did about this duty. Then she followed Elvia through the hatchway.

Inside the small, circular compartment, T'Sil saw the dozen or so equipment conduits accessible here—some high on the bulkhead, some low—and she realized just how many places for concealment *Tomed* offered. Elvia moved to one of the conduits and peered into it. She had drawn her disruptor again, T'Sil saw, but she held it at her side, unprepared to fire even if she spied one of the intruders.

T'Sil looked around the enclosed space and saw no evidence that anybody—intruders or crew—had been here recently. "I'll check the equipment," she said as Elvia moved from one conduit to another. T'Sil turned to the bulkhead, bent down, and reached for the nearest access plate. Pulling it clear and putting it down on the deck, she studied the layout of circuitry revealed. Nothing seemed amiss, at least not from a visual inspection.

She replaced the panel and moved to the next. She'd examined four equipment configurations when Elvia said, "There's nobody here." A mixture of disappointment and relief seemed to lace her voice. T'Sil peered up at her to see that she had circled the compartment, obviously having checked each of the conduits. "What about there?" Elvia said, nodding toward the exposed circuitry.

"No indications of any tampering so far," T'Sil said. "Not that I can see, anyway."

"Complete a visual assessment," Elvia said, waving one finger in a circular motion, clearly indicating all of the access panels within the connector. "If you don't find anything, we'll use scanners to do a thorough examination. I'll assist after I contact the admiral."

"Yes, Lieutenant," T'Sil said.

She sidled over to the next access plate as Elvia started through the hatchway. Before she'd made it back into the corridor, though, the stern voice of Admiral Vokar suddenly filled the maintenance connector. "*Vokar to Elvia,*" he said. Not long ago, T'Sil had heard him contact the lieutenant to inform her that the deterioration of the containment field had been slowed, a claim borne out when the predicted moment of its complete failure had come and gone without incident. And yet T'Sil now imagined that he would retract that information, letting the engineers know that they were once again just moments from death.

Still inside the compartment, Elvia sat on the threshold of the hatchway. She reached up and, with a touch, activated the communicator wrapped about her wrist. "This is Elvia," she said. "I was about to contact you, Admiral. We've entered maintenance connector forty-seven and found it empty. We've also seen no evidence—"

"*Lieutenant, we've located at least one of the intruders,*" Vokar interrupted. "*They're in transporter room three, and the room has been secured. Proceed there immediately.*"

"Yes, sir," Elvia said, although she seemed less than enthusiastic about the order. "Do you want me to detain the intruders there, or elsewhere?"

"*Detain?*" Vokar asked, irritation plainly coloring his voice. "*I want you to kill them.*"

Elvia looked over at T'Sil, stricken. The lieutenant had paled, the yellowish tint of her flesh completely drained away. But she said, "Yes, Admiral."

"*Vokar* out."

Elvia remained motionless on the edge of the hatchway, her face now expressionless, though her dark eyes betrayed the distress she felt. T'Sil thought the lieutenant might talk to her about the orders she had just been given, but she only said, "Keep looking for sabotage. I'll be back." Elvia then left the maintenance connector, and T'Sil heard her tell Valin to continue to stand watch in the corridor.

With difficulty, T'Sil returned her attention to her task. She pulled open the next access panel and peered inside the bulkhead at the circuitry there. All appeared as it should, and she covered the equipment back up and started for the next panel. It was bad enough that the ship had been sabotaged and the crew endangered, but to learn that the saboteurs remained on board, and that she and the other two engineers would have to function as security, and even have to—

As she removed the next access panel, T'Sil saw a batch of fiber-optic lines jammed haphazardly inside. The lines clearly did not belong here. She traced a finger along them until she reached their ends, many of which had been broken off, and none of which connected to anything. T'Sil leaned into the panel for a closer look, and spotted fiber-optic fragments protruding from several pieces of equipment. The lines might not have been connected to anything right now, but it appeared that they had been—connected, and then ripped out.

T'Sil carefully grasped the fiber-optic bundle and pulled it toward her, searching for the other ends of the lines. She quickly found them, also not connected to anything, but their perfectly intact tips suggested that they might at some point have been linked to an external device. It occurred to her that some sort of system reconfiguration might have been executed from here. She read the identification markings on the equipment and saw that helm and navigation functions routed through this panel.

The significance of that pushed T'Sil immediately to her feet. Not only had singularity containment been damaged, but the intruders might well have taken control of the ship's course and velocity. Needing a scanner and other equipment both to determine the extent of what had been done, and then to attempt to effect repairs, she crossed the maintenance connector and maneuvered through the hatchway. In the corridor, she raced up to Sublieutenant Valin, who stood several strides away.

"Alira," he said, obviously concerned by her agitated manner. "Are you all right?"

"I've got to get some equipment from main engineering," she told him.

"Ah . . . I think Lieutenant Elvia wanted us to remain together," he said.

"Rennis, I've discovered modifications to the helm and navigation systems," she said. "I need to find out exactly what's been done, and then try to undo it."

"All right," he said. "But when you . . ." His voice trailed off, and she saw him look over her shoulder in confusion. She turned and followed his gaze down the corridor. A Romulan officer, small in stature, marched in their direction. T'Sil did not recognize her. That was not unusual in itself—*Tomed* normally carried hundreds of crew—but the woman wore the dark blue sash that denoted engineering, and T'Sil doubted that there was an engineer aboard whom she didn't know—particularly an officer.

T'Sil looked at Valin. She saw him begin to raise his weapon, and she realized that he must have come to the same conclusion as she had. The shriek of a disruptor suddenly filled the corridor, confusing T'Sil for a moment, because Valin had not yet aimed his weapon. But then a flash of electric-blue light surged past her, and Valin flew from his feet, sailing backward several meters. He landed with a dull thud, his arms and legs askew, his disruptor skittering along the deck beyond him.

T'Sil turned to face the unfamiliar officer, who now held a weapon in her hand. The woman came abreast of the open hatchway and peered inside, momentarily pointing her disruptor in that direction. T'Sil took that instant to reach for her own weapon. She had actually raised it up to fire by the time the wail of a disruptor blared once more. T'Sil had just enough time to register the visual sensation of brilliant blue light before she hurtled backward herself.

And then blackness took her.

Vaughn ran toward the large, reinforced doors at an angle, cutting diagonally across the corridor. They opened at his approach, and he sprinted into *Tomed*'s shuttlebay, his disruptor held out before him. He scanned the room with his eyes as he moved, searching for any of the Romulans who had remained aboard after the rest of the crew had abandoned ship. Of those six, none had been near the shuttlebay when Commander Gravenor had executed her sensor sweep in the equipment junction, but Vaughn could not afford to assume that nothing had changed since then. In fact, with *Tomed*'s external communications down, the comm systems in the shuttles seemed an alternative to which the Romulans could reasonably be expected to turn.

When he reached the lateral bulkhead without seeing anybody, Vaughn stopped and surveyed his surroundings. The shuttlebay stood two decks tall, with an observation platform overlooking the landing stage on either side. A control room sat behind a transparent wall on the near platform.

The facility housed four full-sized shuttles, he saw, along with twice as many smaller craft. The two-person pods probably functioned as maintenance vehicles, allowing *Tomed*'s crew to perform inspection and repair of the ship's hull and exterior equipment. Boxy, with viewing ports in their curved fore and aft bulkheads, the simple, basic pods did not interest Vaughn. Although speculative as to whether or not a shuttle could survive the end of the mission, simulations had demonstrated conclusively that the pods could not.

Vaughn started toward the outer bulkhead, heading for the great clamshell doors that separated the shuttlebay from the unforgiving vacuum of space. He studied the vessels as he walked, still alert for the presence of any Romulans. In contrast to the pods, the shuttles had been designed not only to satisfy function, but to complement the distinctive bird-of-prey style of the Romulan fleet. The long, sleek hull, colored the characteristic grayish green of most Romulan vessels, tapered to a point in front of the forward viewing port, an effect evocative of a beak. The small-scale warp nacelles, capable of achieving warp two, sat atop graceful, arcing pylons that swept upward from the main body, like the wings of a bird swooping down from flight.

Satisfied that he was alone in the bay, Vaughn went to the shuttle nearest the outer doors. He read the name of the craft—*Liss Riehn*—printed beside the door in deep-red characters barely visible on the dark hull. The words translated as *Blood Hawk*.

Vaughn jabbed at a small panel beneath the name, and it opened with a click, swinging upward to reveal a control pad beneath. He studied it briefly, then reached up and worked the controls. A mechanical hum emanated from the craft, and a door appeared in the hull, pushing into the cabin and then sliding away to the left. Within, overhead lighting came on automatically.

He stepped up into *Liss Riehn*. The cabin ran the length of the shuttle, with no interior bulkheads providing any separate compartments. Two chairs sat before forward control panels, with two more chairs behind those. Benches had been built into the side bulkheads, accommodating perhaps another ten or twelve passengers. The cabin narrowed aft, with a short corridor reaching to a rear viewing port, set between two equipment columns in the corners there. One item that Vaughn did not see, but that he and the others had hoped to, was an emergency transporter.

Swapping his disruptor for the small case of tools hanging from the waist of his uniform, he moved to the forward stations. He set the case down there and examined the panels, scanning them once quickly, and then more carefully on a second pass. Confirming his observation, he found no transporter controls.

Wonderful, Vaughn thought. *Just when I was starting to think this wouldn't get any harder.*

He strode to the rear of the cabin, to one of the two equipment columns. Vaughn pulled open a door that reached from the deck to the ceiling, exposing a maze of circuitry. He started at the top and followed it down, searching for what he needed. Not finding it, he moved to the second equipment column, looking out through the aft viewing port as he did so. The sight of the shuttlebay doors stopped him.

Eventually, those doors would have to be opened. The shuttle possessed only minimal armaments, he knew, probably insufficient to penetrate any section of the hull. But even with more powerful weapons, the special ops team could not simply blast through the doors; leaving them open would go unnoticed, but shooting a hole in them would produce a readily detectable energy signature, not to mention questions without satisfactory answers.

Vaughn returned to the forward stations and looked for the controls that would open up the shuttlebay, leaving only a forcefield between the landing stage and space. The original plan had called for the doors to be opened later, but it had also counted on the entire crew abandoning *Tomed*. With six Romulans still aboard, Vaughn felt that he could

not risk waiting to open the doors, when he could potentially find his efforts blocked, without even the few minutes
he would require to counteract the Romulan resistance.

The controls extended across the top of the port-side station, but Vaughn realized that he would not be able to lock
the doors open from here. To prevent the Romulans from
overriding his commands, he would have to reroute and re-
program the main panel in the shuttlebay control room. It
would be a relatively simple matter to accomplish, but he
needed to do it now.

Drawing his disruptor again, Vaughn stepped down out of
Liss Riehn and jogged over to one of the two ladders that led
to the nearer observation platform. He climbed at a brisk
pace, heading for the control room once he had alighted. Inside, the landing stage and its dozen craft spread out before
him on the other side of the transparent wall.

Vaughn set his disruptor down and examined the panel
there. Only a few systems could be operated from this location, he saw: shuttlebay environmental control, forcefield,
homing beacon, tractor beam, and the clamshell doors. As
quickly as he could, he reprogrammed the OPEN/CLOSE controls, then pulled the panel up and removed the circuitry
that would allow them to be operated from another location
on the ship. He considered modifying the other controls for
the other systems, but did not want to take the time to do so.
No matter how much he had trained for this mission, he
could not be sure how long it would actually take him to
complete his assigned tasks here in the shuttlebay.

Vaughn worked the modified panel, then peered out
from the control room. In the center of the clamshell doors,
a dark line appeared, reaching from the top of the shuttlebay
down to the decking. As he watched, the line widened. The
two great doors folded into themselves, leaving only the
forcefield in place, its functioning marked by a lighted blue
ring rimming the opening. Stars became visible, seeming to

stretch out into slender segments as *Tomed* passed them, a result of the warp effect.

Not waiting for the doors to open completely, Vaughn retrieved his disruptor and exited the control room. He glanced around at the landing stage below, then started back down the ladder. He had descended two-thirds of the way when he felt as though he'd been struck by something along the entire side of his body, from head to foot. The disruptor flew from his grasp as his hands tightened about the ladder. Air gusted past him. He looked toward the doors, which continued to open, but he saw that the forcefield had been deactivated, the blue ring signaling its operation now inert.

As the atmosphere in the shuttlebay rushed out into space, Vaughn felt his Romulan scanner pull free of his uniform. He dropped a hand from the ladder and reached for the sensor veil at his waist. He grabbed the small device, not wanting to risk losing it, then hooked his arm around a rung of the ladder. Staying focused, he turned away from the doors and inhaled deeply. Seconds passed as he waited out the storm, his hand and arm holding securely to the ladder.

Finally, the atmosphere in the shuttlebay had emptied completely into space. Vaughn glanced down to judge his height above the landing stage, then loosed his grip on the ladder and dropped the rest of the way. He bent at the knees as he landed, absorbing the impact, then raced for *Liss Riehn*. He climbed inside and moved to the forward stations, where he operated the controls for the shuttle door and life-support. He felt the vibrations of the door as it closed, but he could not hear it in the absence of a medium to carry the sound to his ears. An indicator on the starboard panel began to glow, a bar of light rising through different colors as it measured the atmosphere pouring into the cabin. When it peaked, Vaughn exhaled and gasped for air. He took several fast, deep breaths, then worked to slow his respiration to a normal rate.

Obviously, the Romulans knew that he was here in the shuttlebay—or at least that he had been here. They had no doubt monitored the clamshell doors opening, and when they'd been unable to override, they'd chosen to drop the forcefield instead. They probably hoped that he'd been blown out into space, but he guessed that they would not take that hope for granted. Soon, he would have company.

Vaughn identified the controls for the shuttle's passive sensors and activated them. Then he picked up his tools—still sitting atop one of the forward stations—and returned to the equipment columns at the rear of the cabin. He opened the second one and searched again for the system he needed, eventually locating the craft's deflectors.

While he awaited the Romulans, he set to work.

As Harriman waited, preparing himself for battle, his thoughts drifted to Amina. Death did not scare him, but the prospect of never again seeing the woman he loved did. He also knew that thinking of her in this situation would not improve his chances for survival. With an effort, he left his emotions behind and concentrated on the task at hand.

He scrutinized the display of his tricorder, measuring the gait of the approaching Romulan. Strangely, they did not move as swiftly as he would have expected in these circumstances; they didn't run or even trot, but seemed to walk at a normal, unhurried pace. Harriman wondered for a moment if they might actually be heading elsewhere, but then they turned in to the corridor leading here to the transporter room.

They're being cautious, he thought. *No, not cautious; tentative.* Harriman recalled that the six Romulan crewmembers left aboard had been divided between the bridge and engineering, perhaps indicating the absence of any of *Tomed*'s security officers. If so, then his chances of surviving the coming encounter might have improved significantly.

Glancing up from his tricorder, Harriman ensured the high power setting of his phaser. Then, leaning back against the bulkhead, he let himself slide down to the deck, minimizing his profile as a target. He reached out and rested the side of his forearm atop his raised knee, steadying his aim as he pointed the phaser across the room at the doors. The tricorder showed the Romulan only a few strides away now.

Harriman waited tensely, anticipating the precise moment to take action, attempting to time his attack effectively. In the corridor, the tricorder told him, the Romulan neared. Three steps away, two steps—

The Romulan stopped before reaching the doors, moving close against the bulkhead just outside the transporter room. Harriman guessed that they would operate the doors manually, opening them without stepping in front of them and becoming a target.

Harriman fired, his index finger squeezing the pressure-sensitive firing plate of his phaser. A concentrated shaft of red fire leaped from the emitter crystal, slicing through the still air of the transporter room. Accompanied by a high-pitched whine, the beam struck the closed doors halfway up, along the line where they met. They absorbed the powerful phased energy for only an instant before blasting apart.

The sound of the explosion filled the transporter room. Harriman continued to fire for several seconds as smoke and dust emerged from the disrupted matter of the doors. He concentrated on the rolling, gray swirls, searching for the darker colors of a Romulan uniform moving within. But the clouds spread thickly into the room, obscuring his view.

Harriman released the firing plate of his phaser and immediately rolled to his left, into the corner. He came up to a sitting position and raised his weapon again, taking aim in the direction of the doorway. He fired five short blasts, high and low, left, right, and center.

The room quieted with the screech of his phaser at least

momentarily silenced. Tiny specks of debris floated down onto the deck, producing a sound like the gentle tapping of a light rain. The soft, almost peaceful noise provided a vivid contrast to the blare of his weapon and the concussion of the explosion.

Harriman waited, unmoving, his eyes seeking the enemy. Time seemed to slow as the seconds passed. He kept his phaser trained on the doorway, but he neither saw nor heard any indication of his Romulan adversary.

Finally, he risked a look at his tricorder. He raised the device and studied its readouts. In the corridor outside the transporter room, in the surrounding sections of this deck, there were no Romulan life signs.

Harriman attached his tricorder to the belt of his uniform, then rose to his feet. Covering his mouth with his free hand to guard against the smoke and dust, he started forward. He did not take his gaze from the direction of the doorway, and he did not lower his phaser.

At the threshold separating the transporter room from the corridor, Harriman removed his hand from his face and waved at the clouds. As the air shifted, he spotted a narrow, mangled section of one door, its ragged edge reaching up less than a meter from the deck, rising at an angle to where it met the jamb. The rest of the doors had been destroyed.

Out of his long-ingrained training, Harriman dashed into the corridor. He spun around as he moved, bringing his weapon to bear on the last location the tricorder had shown the Romulan to be. Harriman reached the far wall and braced himself against it. Beside him, a fist-sized triangular slice of a door jutted from the bulkhead, evidence of the force of the blast.

Nothing moved in the corridor but the swells of smoke and dust. As the billows waned, the bits of debris settling, a shape became visible on the deck: a boot, recognizable as a component of a Romulan Imperial Fleet uniform. It was empty.

His phaser still held out before him, Harriman pushed away from the bulkhead and walked slowly forward. He stepped past the boot, wading through the thinning clouds. A stockinged foot appeared, and as Harriman squatted down beside it, the rest of the body to which it belonged appeared too. Thrown onto her back, a Romulan woman—an engineer, according to the blue sash adorning her uniform—stared unseeing at the ceiling of the corridor. A chunk of flesh had been torn from the side of her face, a wide trail of green blood reaching down from the wound to where it had pooled on the deck. On her right side, a section of the door had cut through the upper portion of her torso, from front to back. Patches of her sallow skin showed through her shredded uniform. Blood had splattered everywhere.

A hollow feeling twisted through Harriman's gut. *This wasn't supposed to happen,* he thought, echoing his words to Sulu after the unexpected injuries to the crew of *Ad Astra*—and the probably mortal wounds to his father. Harriman had devised this plan, and had then fought—with his father and others—for its particulars. The death of a Romulan officer—or even the deaths of many—would not impact the outcome of the mission at all, but Harriman had contrived to avoid killing. What morality would there be, he had argued, in killing to avoid war? The certain murder of one could not be mitigated by the anticipated deaths of billions.

He reached forward and rested the tips of two fingers against the neck of the woman. He felt no pulse, the vital throbbing of her heart—two hundred forty beats per minute for the average Romulan—now stilled. *I'm sorry,* he thought.

But he had no time to mourn, he knew. He could not reverse what had happened, but he could try to make sure that the price that had been paid actually obtained something of value. He had to complete the mission.

Harriman peered around the corridor, the dust and smoke

now reduced to a haze. A couple of meters beyond the Romulan engineer, he saw what he had been looking for, resting in the right angle formed by the bulkhead and the deck: a disruptor, which the woman had obviously been carrying. He stood up and walked over to it. He retrieved the weapon and verified that it still functioned, then hooked it onto his uniform belt.

Allowing himself a final moment of anguish, Harriman looked back down at the dead woman. Then he let the emotion go, and turned toward a future he still hoped to shape for the better. But with or without his efforts, whether he succeeded or failed, he knew that future would arrive very soon.

Harriman marched away, hurrying through the corridors of the Romulan flagship, heading for *Tomed*'s bridge.

While he awaited word from Subcommander Linavil and Lieutenant Elvia, Vokar continued his attempts to wrest control of his vessel's direction and speed from the intruders. Lying on his back beneath the helm, he disconnected a series of fiber-optic lines and rerouted them to a different network link. He affixed them using a spanner, then rolled clear of the console and rose up onto his feet. Reaching over to the helm panel, he touched a control, but it remained dark and emitted an atonal buzz, signifying its inactive status. He tapped another touchpad, which flashed red and beeped. "Can you read that?" he asked Lieutenant Akeev.

"Yes, sir," Akeev replied, checking the readouts at his station. "You've bypassed one of the downed relays." The science officer looked up and faced Vokar across the bridge. "You're one step closer, Admiral."

One step closer, Vokar thought bitterly. *One step closer to regaining control of* my *vessel.* If the Federation criminals could be captured, he would tear the flesh from their bones himself. And if Harriman was among the group of intruders, Vokar would do worse than that.

"Admiral," Akeev called urgently. "Sensors are detecting

weapons fire on the lower engineering deck . . . outside port maintenance connector forty-seven." He worked his panel, obviously seeking more information. His controls blinked and chirped, and Vokar could see text advancing across his display. "A single disruptor, it appears."

"Yes," Vokar said quietly, though he understood that nothing guaranteed that the weapon had been fired by one of *Tomed*'s crew. He reached across the helm and pressed a control to open a comm channel. "Vokar to—" A few minutes ago, he had ordered Elvia to transporter room three—to deal with the intruder he had managed to confine there—leaving the other two engineers at the maintenance connector. "Vokar to T'Sil," he said.

There was no response. On the bridge, the reverberation of the warp drive underscored the lack of voices. Vokar waited, his confidence in the engineering team dwindling, and his anger with the intruders escalating, with each second that passed. At last, he tried again.

"Vokar to T'Sil," he repeated. "Vokar to Valin." He waited again, and then looked to Akeev. "Are they receiving me?"

The science officer worked his panel once more. "They are receiving you, Admiral," he said. "The comm channels are open. They're just not responding."

Vokar knew the question he had to ask next, though he wasn't sure he wanted to hear the answer. "Are there life signs down there?"

"Scanning," Akeev said haltingly, a sign that he too dreaded what the sensors might reveal. But instead of determining whether or not T'Sil and Valin were still alive, he reported something else. "I'm picking up more weapons fire, this time in transporter room three."

"A disruptor?" Vokar wanted to know.

"No," Akeev said. "A Starfleet phaser . . . and there's been an explosion." Then, not waiting for Vokar's order, he said, "Scanning for life signs."

But Vokar already knew what had happened: *Tomed*'s remaining crew of six had been halved, Elvia, T'Sil, and Valin cut down by Federation operatives—by Federation *savages*. A moment later, Akeev confirmed at least part of that conclusion.

"I read no life signs in or around transporter room three," he said. His voice seemed mixed with both fear and anger.

Vokar stood in the middle of *Tomed*'s bridge and considered his options. He reviewed everything he knew about the situation, analyzed all of the variables, worked through the best- and worst-case scenarios—and found that few differences separated the two. Given the current circumstances, he could reach only one end.

On the navigation console, a light began to blink yellow. Vokar stepped over to the station and examined the indicator. "Where's Linavil?" he asked at once.

It took Akeev only a moment to respond. "The subcommander's almost reached the shuttle compartment."

Vokar brought the meaty side of his fist down on a touchpad to open a comm channel. "Vokar to Linavil," he said, already moving his hands to work other controls.

"*This is Linavil*," came the immediate response.

"Somebody's opening the shuttle-compartment doors," he told her. "I'm closing them now and—" The doors would not respond to the commands he sent to them. "They won't close," he said. "I'm going to try to drop the forcefield." He operated the console. "It worked," he said, actually surprised that something aboard *Tomed* had functioned as it should. "Restore it from your end when you get there, Subcommander. You have to reach a shuttle and get a message out. And if the comm systems have been damaged, then take a shuttle and deliver word of what's happened in person."

"*Yes, Admiral*," Linavil said.

"Vokar out." He closed the channel with a touch, then peered up at the main viewscreen. Stars shot past *Tomed* as it hurtled through space. Somewhere ahead lay the Neutral Zone, and beyond it, Federation space. If Linavil could send a message out, if she could get to one of the shuttles before the intruders had incapacitated all of their comm systems, one of the Romulan vessels patrolling the Zone might be able to intervene. But even if a ship could reach *Tomed* in time, its crew would likely not be able to do more than what Vokar had chosen to do right now.

"Lieutenant Akeev," he said, "is the self-destruct system operational?"

"It's tied to the singularity containment field, sir," Akeev said. "As long as it stays active . . ."

The containment field had been reinforced by the intruders, Vokar knew, with power being supplied to it through alternate relays. "Akeev, I want to find out where power is being routed to containment," he said, "and sever it."

"Yes, sir," Akeev said. Although he sounded less than enthusiastic about the prospect of destroying *Tomed*, Vokar knew that the lieutenant would faithfully discharge the order assigned him.

Vokar sat down at the navigation console and reconfigured its panel, bringing up a control layout that would allow him to launch an examination of the ship's power relays. Either he or Akeev would locate the flow of power to the containment field, and then Vokar would stop it. No matter what else happened, he would not permit the flagship of the Romulan Imperial Fleet to fall into the hands of the Federation—even if he had to destroy *Tomed*.

Main engineering spread out before Gravenor. Dominating the large space, two warp-power conduits reached high up from the deck, slanting diagonally from the center of the room out to the lateral bulkheads. Contrasting with the standard gray-green coloring favored by the Romulan Imperial Fleet, the conduits glowed the same vibrant blue as their counterparts on Starfleet vessels. Past the conduits, a transparent bulkhead stood tall and wide, containing a swirling mass of spectral light, ranging from the longer wavelengths of red to the shorter wavelengths of violet. Inside, Gravenor knew, the kaleidoscope of color marked the containment field that allowed the massive gravitational forces of an artificial quantum singularity to be harnessed as a power source, and that prevented the microscopic black hole from tearing apart both the ship and the space it occupied. Captain Harriman had sabotaged that containment field beyond repair. After the crew had abandoned ship, he had slowed the rate of its decay, but nothing could prevent it from failing completely; within a day, the quantum singularity would be loosed, endangering everything in its proximity.

Gravenor walked toward the warp conduits, before which sat a large master console, more than two meters wide and twice as long. On its surface, cutaway views of *Tomed* detailed the layouts of major systems throughout the ship. She found the system she needed, saw the location of its primary equipment in relation to main engineering—in a separate room connecting to this one on the starboard side—and headed in that direction.

Though she expected no resistance, Gravenor held her disruptor at the ready. She had encountered the three Romulan engineers while on her way here, and she'd cautiously followed them until she'd been able to attack, taking two of them out. As she had headed to main engineering for the second time, Captain Harriman had contacted her to let her know that the third engineer had also been removed as a threat. That left three of *Tomed*'s crew with whom to contend, but a quick sensor scan had shown none of them to be in or near main engineering.

Gravenor walked past an impressive display of state-of-the-art equipment and consoles. She would have expected nothing less of Admiral Vokar's vessel, not only because of its place as the flagship of the Empire, but also because of Vokar's hubris. He draped himself unapologetically in his arrogant belief in the superiority of the Romulan people.

For this mission, the covert capture of any primary vessel of the Imperial Fleet would have sufficed. But Captain Harriman had expected that sending *Enterprise*—the Federation flagship—to Space Station Algeron to deliver the hyperwarp drive specifications would compel the Romulans to send *Tomed* to accompany it. His prediction had been correct, and while any Romulan battle cruiser and its commander would have served the needs of the mission, *Tomed* and Admiral Vokar would do so better than any other vessel and officer could have, specifically because of Vokar's position and his staunch Romulan chauvinism.

Gravenor arrived at a set of doors in the starboard bulkhead, near the aft end of main engineering. She read the Romulan lettering that confirmed the equipment housed beyond, as well as issued warnings about unauthorized personnel being forbidden to enter the secured area. Reaching up and operating a control pad, she attempted to open the doors. She tried several different command paths, without success, the controls buzzing beneath her touch.

Stepping back, Gravenor adjusted the setting on her disruptor, taking care to select a power level that would compromise the doors without causing an explosion. She could not risk damaging the equipment she sought—not if the mission was to succeed *and* the members of the special ops team to survive. Of the two goals, though, the safe return to the Federation of Gravenor, Vaughn, and Harriman was secondary to their accomplishment of the mission.

Gravenor raised her disruptor and fired. The whine of the weapon echoed in the cavernous engineering section. Blue pulses of energy struck the doors midway up, causing an almost immediate glow. Gravenor continued to fire until an irregular hole, about a meter in diameter, had been opened in the doors.

With a quick glance around main engineering—a long-standing habit that had developed as a consequence of her work—Gravenor approached the breach. Carefully avoiding the edges of the newly created aperture—which would be extremely hot from the disruptor fire—she lifted one leg through, then ducked her head down and entered the room beyond the doors, pulling her other leg in after her. The temperature in the enclosed space—already warm due to Romulan environmental preferences—had been raised several degrees by the blasts that had penetrated the doors.

Gravenor moved quickly to the center of the small room, where a circular console rose from the deck. Atop it sat the piece of equipment she needed, a cloudy sphere mounted on a tapering metal base. The entire assemblage measured a meter tall and about half as wide. Knowing the amount of time it would take to cleanly uncouple the equipment connections, Gravenor set to work immediately.

She first examined the console, and saw that it had been laid out differently than what she had seen in her intelligence briefings. But she had studied not just the details of the few such panels Starfleet had gathered, but the theory of the equipment as well. With an urgency fortified by confidence, Gravenor attacked the console, working as quickly as she could to remove *Tomed*'s cloaking device.

The hiss of air flowing into the shuttle compartment slowed, and then stopped. Linavil raised her disruptor in one hand, and used her other to work the control pad beside the outsized doors of the compartment. The metallic sound of locks being released rang in the corridor, and the doors parted and slid open.

Linavil stood motionless, waiting and listening. Hearing nothing, she waved her empty hand out from the side of the doorway, attempting to draw the fire of the intruders, should any of them have survived the dropping of the shuttle compartment's forcefield. She assumed that the intruders had operated the outer doors from one of the shuttles, and therefore had probably been unaffected when the admiral had deactivated the forcefield.

Eliciting no response, Linavil braced herself, then sped into the shuttle compartment. She rushed to the nearest vehicle, one of *Tomed*'s work pods, and took cover beside it. Dropping down low, she leaned out around the curved forward hull and peered about the landing stage. Past the cluster of work pods sat the ship's four shuttles, arrayed in two lines of two against the backdrop of stars visible through the opened outer doors. The thin blue line of the forcefield, reactivated by Linavil before she'd restored the atmosphere to the compartment, bordered the wide opening, framing the starscape.

Nothing moved in or around the shuttles, but through the forward viewing port of one of those nearest the forcefield Linavil saw interior lighting. A *ruse*, she thought immediately, an attempt to draw her into an area upon which Federation weapons must even now be trained. But though Linavil ached to meet the intruders, to deal them punishment for their attempted theft of *Tomed*, she had a different duty to fulfill right now. If the comm systems of all the shuttles had not been damaged, she would send a message to all Imperial Fleet vessels, and to Romulus; otherwise, she would take a shuttle and, as Admiral Vokar had ordered, deliver word of the Federation deception in person. Either way, the effort to steal the Romulan flagship would go neither unrevealed nor unpunished.

Ignoring the interior lights of the one shuttle, Linavil ran to another of the craft, the one farthest away from the first. She reached to the small panel below the name of shuttle— *Liss Ornahj*—and pushed it. It clicked, and then hinged open, allowing access to the door controls—

Movement flashed above Linavil, and she looked up to see a figure crashing down on her. In the last fraction of an instant before she was struck, she jerked her head to the side, and even as she tumbled to the deck, she understood that the small shift had been what had kept her from losing consciousness. And that, she assumed, had also kept her from losing her life at the hands of the enemy.

Vaughn resisted moving until he heard the click of the access plate opening, not wanting to risk divulging his presence too soon.

Just a few minutes ago, as he had worked on the deflector interface aboard *Liss Riehn*, the passive sensors had told him in quick succession of a lone Romulan nearing the shuttle-bay, of the reinstatement of the bay's forcefield, and of the reintroduction of an atmosphere here. He had checked the shuttle for weapons, but he hadn't found any, and he hadn't had enough time to improvise. Without waiting for the air to finish completely filling the bay, Vaughn had exited *Liss Riehn* and sprinted to another of the shuttles, *Liss Ornahj—Fire Hawk*—and had climbed atop it.

The move had been a gamble. If the Romulan had come into the bay and approached one of the other shuttles, then Vaughn would have had to jump down and cross the landing stage in pursuit of them, a risky proposition since his disruptor had been blown out into space when the forcefield had dropped. But Vaughn had relied on the perception and intelligence of the Romulans to lead them to the understanding that, in order to foil the commandeering of their ship, they need only let the Empire know what had happened aboard *Tomed*; he counted on the Romulan entering the bay and *avoiding* contact with him until after they had broadcast a message.

And so Vaughn had lain unmoving, facedown, atop *Liss Ornahj*, listening intently to the footfalls of the Romulan as they had entered the shuttlebay. Vaughn had kept his muscles tensed, prepared to move. He had defied the strong impulse to lift his head and follow the Romulan visually, but with the loss of his disruptor, the only weapon he possessed now was surprise, and he could not chance losing that.

The click of the control panel opening sounded unnaturally loud to Vaughn in the otherwise-silent bay, like the unexpected crack of a whip. He surged forward, pulling himself along and swinging his legs around, aiming his feet toward the door of *Liss Ornahj*. As he cleared the top of the shuttle and came down, he saw the Romulan look up at him at the last moment before the heels of his boots struck her head—a hard but glancing blow, and not the full contact for which Vaughn had hoped. The woman collapsed onto the deck. Vaughn, knocked sideways by the impact and his circular momentum, landed lengthwise, his arms coming up before him to cushion his fall.

He pushed himself up at once and whirled toward the woman, set to rush her. She'd already risen to one knee, he saw, and she peered about, obviously searching for something. Vaughn looked too, and caught sight of a disruptor lying beside the shuttle; the weapon must have been knocked loose from the woman's hand or uniform when she had tumbled to the deck. Vaughn lunged for it, but too late; the woman had spied it as well, and she grabbed it up and started to bring it around toward him. He planted one foot and kicked with the other, the tip of his boot striking the woman on her wrist. Her arm flew backward, and the disruptor sailed from her hand, arcing high and far, the view of its landing among the work pods obstructed by the body of *Liss Ornahj*.

As Vaughn brought his leg back down, attempting to find his balance, the woman charged forward. Her shoulder hit Vaughn just below his solar plexus, and he plunged backward. He struck the deck hard, but he allowed his momentum to carry his legs upward, at the same time grasping the Romulan's shoulders and lifting with all of his strength. The woman flipped over him, and he heard a grunt escape her as she landed on her back.

Vaughn rolled over as quickly as he could and then rose to his feet. The woman stood up too, her chest heaving as she gasped for air, the wind apparently forced from her lungs when she had slammed onto the deck. He noticed a smear of green on the side of her face, and he saw that the upper tip of her ear had been ripped partially through, probably by the heel of one of his boots.

The woman—a tactical officer, according to the pale green coloring of the right side of her uniform shirt—squared off opposite Vaughn, and he wondered how he could defeat the greater strength of a Romulan when he did not have the benefit of a weapon. Surprise no longer seemed the asset he had needed it to be. As though offering proof of that, the woman charged again. Vaughn waited as long as he could to move, then threw himself sideways, hoping to escape the attack. But the woman's arm reached for him, and she grabbed hold of the black-and-silver mesh of his Romulan uniform before he could get away. She continued forward, carrying him backward and heaving him against the side of *Liss Ornahj*. Now Vaughn felt the air rushing from his own lungs, and he heard himself begin to wheeze as he tried to breathe.

Before him, the Romulan's face looked flush, streaks of bright green crawling up her cheeks. With her eyes wide and her teeth gritted, her rage appeared pure and unstoppable. She brought her fist up, and all Vaughn could do was push himself away from the shuttle so that his head would not pound back against the metal surface when the punch landed. The woman hit him hard, her knuckles darkening his vision as they rammed into the center of his face. He felt his knees weaken, and he chose to let them fold. He dropped onto the deck, the Romulan's fingers still clutching the chest of his uniform.

Vaughn tried to fall backward, but the woman would not let him go. Instead, she reached down with her other hand and took hold of his arm, then hauled him upward easily, as though the artificial gravity of *Tomed* had been suspended for her. She let go of him with one hand and raised her fist again, cocking her arm back. Concerned that if she hit him again, he might pass out—dooming Commander Gravenor and Captain Harriman, as well as the mission—Vaughn swung his arm up and frantically reached for the side of the Romulan's head. His fingers found her wounded ear, seized it, and pulled. The flesh and cartilage came away with a sickening, carnal sound, and blood spurted from the coarse wound.

The woman cried out, her voice seeming to carry less pain than anger. She released her grip on him as her hands reached for the side of her head. Vaughn started to sidle away, but the woman stepped forward and dropped her hands, took hold of his upper arms, and heaved him into the air. He soared several meters before crashing onto the deck.

Searching his mind for anything that he could do to overcome his opponent, Vaughn struggled back to his feet. He anticipated another attack by the Romulan, but he saw that she had not yet moved toward him again. Instead, she bent down, slipped her fingers inside one boot, and pulled out a shape perhaps twenty centimeters long. Vaughn recognized it immediately as a knife.

The woman held the weapon before her, as though displaying it for Vaughn. Then she reached up and removed its sheath. The blade, half the length of the entire knife, glistened a deep, reflective black. In that moment, Vaughn knew with certainty that, before this battle ended, the Romulan's dagger would slice into his body.

Forming a desperate plan and wanting to regain the initiative, Vaughn ran toward the woman. As he came at her, he saw her brace herself, bending her knees and pulling the dagger back, clearly readying to thrust it forward. But

Vaughn dived downward, pitching himself at her shins. He knew that she would not have enough time to reverse the haft of the knife in her hand in order to bring it down into his back, but she lowered it enough that he felt it pierce the top of his shoulder as he struck her legs.

The Romulan flew forward, her legs taken out from under her, and she toppled to the deck as Vaughn passed beneath her. He'd hoped that she would let go of the knife, but her hand stayed wrapped tightly around it, and the blade carved through Vaughn's shoulder and emerged from his back. Pain shot through him, but he ignored it; he could do nothing else.

He rolled onto his back, intending to hurry to his feet and continue his attack. But already the Romulan had risen, and as Vaughn began to stand, she pounced on him. He landed on his back again, and she came down on top of him, her legs straddling his midsection, her knees pinning his forearms. She reached down past his face and pulled off the artificial tip of his ear, then repeated the process on the other side. An expression of repulsion decorated her features as she examined the bits of mock flesh. After a few seconds, she cast them aside.

The movement caused a globule of the Romulan's blood to drip from her face onto Vaughn's uniform. She looked down to where it had fallen, and then glared at him with raw hatred. She dropped her empty hand onto his wounded shoulder and pressed down. Pain seared that side of his body, and for the second time, he feared that he would pass out. Whorls of white light spun across his vision, and he opened his mouth and screamed. Above him, the woman's eyes gleamed with the enjoyment of her cruelty.

"*Do it!*" Vaughn yelled at her. "*Kill me!*"

With sudden speed, the Romulan raised the knife above her head. Vaughn moved with equal swiftness, recognizing his opportunity. He yanked one arm free from beneath her knee, then flung his hand upward. As she brought the knife down, it punctured his palm, the blade passing out the other side. He could not ignore the agony, but he refused to give in to it; the stakes were too high. Instead, he wrenched his arm sideways and down, knowing the damage the ebon blade would do to his hand, and not caring.

The knife came free of the Romulan's grasp, and Vaughn tugged his other arm from beneath her knee. As she scrambled to reclaim her weapon, he grabbed its handle with his uninjured hand. The woman reacted, but not quickly enough: Vaughn pulled the blade out of his palm and then drove it forward, into her rib cage. She threw her head back and howled in obvious distress, reaching automatically to where her own weapon had injured her. But Vaughn wasn't done; he slid the knife back out, and then sent it slicing back into her body, up on the right side, where her black heart still beat within her. She tried to take hold of Vaughn's hand, but her strength had gone now. He pushed at her upper body, and she fell backward and to the side with a dull thud, one of her legs coming to rest draped across his knees.

All at once, Vaughn felt numb. The pains in his hand and shoulder had not abated, but had somehow transformed; they had mutated into dull and pulsing sensations, horribly unpleasant, but survivable. He identified it not as anything that he had managed to do, but as simple instinct, the natural reaction of his body and mind to protect themselves.

He lifted his mangled hand up to look at it. Blood flowed freely from the wound, actually hiding the worst of it, but he could move only his thumb and none of his fingers. He knew that he would have to tend to his injury—injuries, he amended, thinking of his shoulder—or he would die from blood loss. Unable to help himself in any other way at the moment, he forced himself up into a sitting position, then placed his damaged hand beneath his opposite arm. He squeezed as gently as he could, but forcefully enough to stem the flow of blood. It hurt him no more than what he had already been through.

Extracting himself from beneath the Romulan woman's leg, Vaughn leaned over and reached awkwardly to her wrist with his healthy hand. He felt for a pulse and found none. *Good,* Vaughn thought, and then felt immediately uncomfortable for his satisfaction at the death of another. He had always believed in the sanctity of life—*all* life. If he could have incapacitated the woman somehow, he would have, but . . .

I killed her, he thought, the foreign notion terribly troubling to him. Worse, though, was his certainty that, given another opportunity, he would have taken the same actions. He did not regret what he had done, but he regretted having had to do it. Until now, his duties with special operations had avoided matters of life and death, at least in such a direct and personal manner. He also realized that, in other times and other places, circumstances such as these would recur, and he would again do what needed to be done. Unquestionably, he had crossed the Rubicon.

Vaughn removed his fingertips from the wrist of the dead woman. As he withdrew his uninjured hand, he saw it stained in blood, both the green of the Romulan and the red of his own. *No,* he thought. *There will be no going back.*

He fought to get to his feet, then staggered back to *Liss Riehn.* When he had earlier searched for weapons aboard the shuttle, he'd come across a medical kit. He would use it now to tend to his wounds and mask his pain. However he would need to deal with what had just happened, with what he had done—with what he had *lost*—it would have to wait.

Right now, he still had a job to do.

Harriman ascended the ladder, climbing into the limited, dimly lighted space between a turbolift and the wall of the vertical shaft. At the top of the ladder, he dismounted onto a narrow walkway, careful to make sure of his footing. He circled around the lift—which sat parked at the starboard entrance to *Tomed*'s bridge—and entered the horizontal shaft that ran in an arc to the port-side doors.

Taking the beacon from his belt and switching it on, he walked to the other side of the ship and began searching along the bulkhead. It did not take long for him to locate a knockout panel that allowed emergency access to and from the bridge. *And this,* he joked to himself, *qualifies as an emergency.*

Lowering himself from the walkway to the floor of the horizontal shaft, Harriman moved back to the starboard turbolift. He found the knockout panel in its shell, once more using the beacon. Then, with great care, he set his shoulder against the bottom of the panel and applied gradual pressure; he did not want the square of metal falling into the lift and either making noise or activating the automatic opening of the doors.

When he had pushed the panel inward a few centimeters, Harriman pried its top edge downward with his fingers, eventually allowing him to pull it completely free. He set it on the walkway, then reached to his belt and traded the beacon for his phaser. Selecting its stealth mode and an appropriate power level, he set the weapon to overload, with a trigger of sixty seconds. He began counting down in his head as he gently deposited the phaser inside the lift.

As Harriman made his way back over to port, he drew the disruptor he had picked up from beside the dead body of the Romulan engineer. He verified its setting, then climbed back up onto the walkway and readied himself in front of the emergency access panel. As he waited to take action, though, his thoughts returned again to Amina, just as they had down in the transporter room. And as he had done then, he pushed those thoughts away, knowing that they would not serve him right now.

He counted down to twenty, and then to ten, and then to

five. He tensed his muscles as he awaited the explosion, not wanting to move before his diversion manifested itself. He counted to three, two, one, and as though he had willed the detonation himself, the phaser overloaded.

Harriman surged forward at the sound of the blast, driving his shoulder against the knockout panel and pushing forward onto the bridge. The explosion seemed to occur in two places at once, both behind him, in the turboshaft, and to his right, in the lift. He hit the deck and rolled, coming up onto one knee with the disruptor held out before him. Ignoring the effects of the phaser blowing up, he assessed the situation as quickly as he could. He saw a figure pulling itself up from beneath a console at the center of the bridge. Harriman immediately put the officer in his sights, but he'd expected to find two Romulans here and—

Something shifted position on the far side of the bridge. Harriman dropped at once to the deck and crawled behind the nearest console, not waiting to find out what had moved. Above him, the air suddenly sizzled as disruptor fire roared past and hammered into a station behind him. He brought his own weapon up and fired it around the corner of the console, aiming not in the direction from which the disruptor shots had come, but toward the Romulan he had seen in the center of the bridge. He heard the body fall to the deck just before more disruptor shots screamed out, this time striking the front of the console providing him cover.

Something flickered off to Harriman's right, and he glanced that way to see a series of small flames dancing in the starboard turbolift. One of the two doors had been blown completely off and now lay on the deck, he saw, while the other still stood, but had been badly bent and scarred. When the disruptor fire stopped a moment later, it left the crackle of the fire as the only sound on the bridge.

Harriman peered around at his immediate environs, looking for anything he could use to his advantage. Cautiously, he rose onto his knees and peeked over the edge of the console. Keeping his head low enough that it would not become visible from the other side, he read the Romulan markings on the panel to see which ship's system it operated: environmental control. He considered several options, then reached up and worked some touchpads.

The lighting went out. The fire in the turbolift sent an eerie, orange glow flickering across the bridge. The numerous consoles threw long, wavering shadows along the deck and against the bulkheads.

Harriman waited, listening fixedly for the slightest sound of movement. He let a full minute pass before he pulled the beacon from his belt. Covering the beam, he activated it, then tossed it spinning away from him with a flick of the wrist. The disruptor fire began almost at once, blasting in the direction of the beacon. Staying low, Harriman emerged from behind the console on the other side. In the semidarkness, the point from which the disruptor was being fired made itself plain. Harriman raised his own weapon and pressed the trigger. Blue light streamed across the bridge, briefly illuminating the face of the Romulan as it struck him.

Both disruptors quieted. Not taking any unnecessary risks, Harriman jumped back behind the console and consulted his tricorder. In seconds, he had confirmed that neither of the two Romulans on the bridge any longer posed a threat.

Harriman stood up and reached to the environmental controls, bringing the light back up. He walked the perimeter of the bridge, over to the Romulan he had just fired upon. The man lay on his side, one arm stretching out above his head, the gray sash of his uniform distinguishing him as a technical specialist. His disruptor sat on the deck a few centimeters from his open hand. Harriman reached down and picked it up.

Walking to the center of the bridge, he regarded the first Romulan he had shot. The man lay prone on the deck, but

Harriman did not need to see his face to recognize him. Small in stature, and with the royal purple of his uniform indicating his high position within the Imperial Fleet, Admiral Aventeer Vokar seemed to exude an aura of authority even now.

Starfleet Command deemed Vokar one of the most dangerous people in the Romulan Star Empire, a prime architect of the present lust for war with the Federation. Harriman did not entirely agree with that assessment: he considered the admiral to be *the* most dangerous Romulan. In addition to Vokar's staunch conviction in the preeminence of his people, he constantly sought the defeat of all those he considered inferior—the Federation, the Klingons, and others—and he had allies in the Senate, the ear of the praetor, and command of all Romulan space forces.

Harriman peered down at Vokar, stunned into unconsciousness. The admiral had a spanner in his hand, and had obviously been working to restore helm control to the bridge. Harriman peered at the flight-control readouts and verified that *Tomed* remained at speed and on course. He saw a disruptor sitting atop the helm panel.

He contemplated his own disruptor, and visualized pressing its energy emitter against Vokar's temple. He recalled his first encounter with the admiral, when Vokar had launched unprovoked attacks on *Dakota* and *Hunley*. He had killed Captain Linneus and dozens of others, and would have captured and tortured the rest of the crews had he not been stopped. Surely those actions alone justified Vokar's death, even all these years later—perhaps *especially* after all these years; the admiral had lived free for three decades after committing multiple murders. There hadn't even been any ongoing hostilities between the Federation and the Empire to qualify him as a war criminal; Vokar was simply a criminal.

Anger grew within Harriman as he remembered that terrible time aboard *Hunley*. Vokar's death right now would not only avenge all of those he had killed and maimed, both back then and in other incidents, but it would also limit the risk of *not* killing him. If Harriman permitted Vokar to live, there would always be the threat that he would reveal the mission. Starfleet special ops would take measures against that, of course, but the threat would exist as long as Vokar remained alive.

He adjusted the setting on his disruptor, then squatted beside the admiral and pushed the weapon against the back of his head. Beads of sweat formed on Harriman's skin. The weight of the disruptor felt right in his hand.

He did not press the trigger.

For all of the evil Vokar had perpetrated, Harriman could not kill him in cold blood. He had not done so all those years ago aboard *Daami*, and he would not do so now. But he would do everything he could to see the admiral imprisoned for the rest of his life.

Harriman stood up and found the tactical console, intending to scan the interior of the ship. On the readout, though, he saw that an attempt had been made to engage *Tomed*'s self-destruct. Vokar had evidently made some progress with it, as some of the power couplings Harriman had himself rerouted to the containment field had now been isolated and cut off. As a result, containment would now fail sooner, but fortunately not before the mission had been completed.

He operated the ship's internal sensors, and read four life signs, all Romulan: two here on the bridge, and the two Commander Gravenor had stunned down near the maintenance junction. Including the engineer Harriman had killed, that left one unaccounted for. He pulled out his communicator and flipped it open. "Harriman to Gravenor," he said, choosing not to use the Romulan names they'd assigned themselves.

"*Gravenor*," the commander responded.

"I've taken the bridge and captured two Romulans," Harriman said. "That means there's one more aboard, but I haven't been able to locate them with the ship's sensors."

"*Understood,*" Gravenor said.

"What's your status?" Harriman asked.

"*I'm preparing for our departure,*" Gravenor said.

"Very good," Harriman said, understanding that the commander meant that she was working on the cloaking device. She also had not utilized the prearranged word that would have functioned as a distress signal, something she would have done if, for example, the sixth Romulan had been holding her prisoner. "Harriman out." He reached up and reset the channel on his communicator, then said, "Harriman to Vaughn."

Several seconds passed, and he grew concerned. He envisioned a scenario where the sixth Romulan had incapacitated—or killed—Vaughn and now utilized the lieutenant's sensor veil to mask their own position. But then Vaughn's voice came across the comm channel. "*Vaughn here,*" he said.

"Are you all right?" Harriman asked, hearing something—weariness? pain?—in the lieutenant's tone.

"*I've been injured,*" Vaughn explained. "*One of the Romulans came to the shuttlebay.*" He seemed about to say more, but then paused. As the silence drew out, Harriman worried that Vaughn might have passed out, but then the lieutenant continued. "*She's dead.*"

Like Gravenor, Vaughn did not employ the word that would have indicated that he spoke under duress, which meant that all six Romulans had now been neutralized, two dead and four captured. He explained that to Vaughn.

"*Understood,*" the lieutenant said.

"What's your status?"

"*I'm preparing a shuttle,*" Vaughn said, "*but I'm having some difficulty. I've lost the use of one hand.*"

"All right, Lieutenant," Harriman said. "I'm on my way to help. I've got to deal with the four remaining Romulans, and then I'll be down to the shuttlebay."

"*Yes, sir,*" Vaughn said. "*Thank you, sir.*"

"Harriman out." He closed the communicator and returned it to the back of his waist. He exhaled loudly, as though he'd been holding his breath. *Haven't I been?* he thought. For months, for years even, figuratively holding his breath as he waited for the start of the interstellar war everybody considered inevitable.

But now, at last, that wait would end. Whether he, Gravenor, and Vaughn would survive the end of the mission was problematic, but it had become clear now that the mission would succeed. After all this time, after all the planning and effort, they were almost home.

Vokar awoke by degrees, becoming aware of himself first, lying on his side, and then of the hard surface beneath him, and finally of the muted sounds of voices, speaking as though from a distance. He remembered the explosion on the bridge, and the events that had led up to it. Assuming now that he had been captured, he kept his eyes closed, giving no indication to anybody who might be watching that he had regained consciousness.

With little movement, Vokar tested his muscles, flexing them lightly and feeling for any limitations. He found himself encumbered only at the wrists, held together before his thighs. Finally, needing more information to act, he slit one eye, the one closest to the deck.

Ahead of him, he saw the back of another Romulan, stretched out parallel to him. The gray sash of the uniform told Vokar that it was Akeev. Beyond the science officer sat a couple of shuttles and several maintenance pods.

The shuttle compartment, Vokar thought. *But why the shuttle compartment?*

Vokar heard a hiss behind him, like that produced by a hypospray, and a few seconds later, he heard another. "Captain," a man called from nearby, "they're awake."

Realizing the futility of continuing his subterfuge, since

he'd apparently been brought back to consciousness by the intruders, Vokar raised his head from the deck. He looked first at his wrists, which he saw had been placed in electromagnetic restraints, evidently appropriated from *Tomed*'s own armory. Then he peered past his feet, toward the source of the voice. He saw a quartet of antigrav stretchers, and a man walking past them toward the bow of a shuttle. The man had both a disruptor and a hypospray clasped in one hand, and a bandage wrapped around the other, with that arm in a silver mesh sling. He wore a Romulan engineering uniform, though he was clearly not Romulan: his round ears and feathery brown hair provided ample evidence to that effect. "Akeev," Vokar whispered, looking forward again.

"Sir," the science officer said. "Are you all right?"

"How long have we been unconscious?" Vokar asked, ignoring the question.

"A long time, I think," Akeev said. "Ten hours, fifteen . . . maybe more."

"Then we must be close to the Neutral Zone," Vokar concluded.

"Yes," Akeev agreed, "if we haven't already crossed it into the Federation."

But Vokar knew that they hadn't. If they had, then why would they still be aboard the ship, and in any case, why would the intruders be in the shuttle compartment? He saw now that he had erred in assuming that they'd wanted to commandeer *Tomed* for their own uses—he had erred not in that deduction, but in *stopping* at that deduction. He thought that he now saw their purpose in appropriating his vessel.

Footsteps approached from the direction of the shuttle. Vokar looked up to see a Starfleet officer, a disruptor in his hand. He stopped a couple of meters short of Vokar's feet.

"Admiral Vokar," Harriman said.

"My serpent," Vokar intoned, "returned to me." He chose not to hide his hostility.

"You can think that," Harriman told him, "but I'd suggest that the serpent lives in your own house, sits in your own chair."

"Perhaps," Vokar said, "but I'm not about to kill hundreds—or is it thousands—of my own people." Harriman's eyebrows went up, and Vokar knew that he had unmasked the human's plan. "All to coerce the Klingons to ally with the Federation against the Empire. And what do you imagine the Klingons would do if they learned of your cowardly act?"

Harriman lifted a hand to his face and wiped it across his mouth. "Two of your officers have been killed," Harriman said then, apparently unwilling to respond to Vokar's accusation. "There are four of you left—"

"Also to be killed shortly," Vokar interrupted, a comment intended only to bait Harriman. If the Starfleet captain had truly wanted to take the lives of Vokar and his other three officers, he would have done so already.

"Actually, you have a choice, Admiral," Harriman said. "I'm aware of the prerogative of Romulan commanders to destroy their own vessels, and to kill themselves and their crews, when faced with capture, and I remember your own personal desire to go down with your ship." Vokar used his hands to push himself up to a sitting position, and he saw T'Sil and Valin also beside him, their faces turned up to listen to the conversation. Linavil and Elvia, then, had been killed. "But in this instance, you can stay here," Harriman finished, "or you can come with us."

"And where would 'we' be going?" Vokar asked, already having a good idea of the answer, and knowing that he would *never* consent to being a prisoner of the Federation.

"You and your crew will be taken to a planet far from Romulan space," Harriman said.

"Where we'll be kept as prisoners," Vokar said.

"Yes," Harriman said. "But you won't know it. We've developed an experimental technique to erase memory."

"You're going to *experiment* on us?" Akeev asked, obviously fearful of such a prospect.

"Your memories will be erased," Harriman said, "but otherwise, you'll be unaffected. You'll be permitted to live out your lives in a comfortable setting."

Even if Vokar believed Harriman—which he didn't—the notion of Federation doctors performing experimental techniques on his brain repulsed him, as did the idea of living the rest of his life in captivity. As he had been trained to do, Vokar would die with his vessel. But he also knew Starfleet, and he understood that Harriman offered this choice to Vokar not for all four of them, but only for himself; Harriman would allow the others to make their own choices.

"Captain," the man with the bandaged hand called. "Thirty minutes."

"That's it," Harriman said, looking at each of the four Romulans. "You need to make your decisions now, all of you. Are you coming with us, or are you staying here?"

Vokar waited. Valin spoke up first. "I . . . I'll go with you," he said quietly.

"I will too," T'Sil said. Vokar felt nothing but disgust for the young officers.

"I'm staying," Akeev declared, defiance apparently overcoming his fear. Vokar nodded his head in approval.

"Admiral?" Harriman asked.

"We'll all go," Vokar said. "Including Akeev."

"Sir?" Akeev asked, his voice rising in obvious surprise.

"We'll all go," Vokar repeated.

"All right," Harriman said, then called back over his shoulder, "Lieutenant." The man in the ersatz Romulan uniform appeared again from around the bow of the shuttle and approached the group. Vokar saw that he now held only a disruptor in his unbandaged band. "We're going to have four more passengers," Harriman told him.

"Yes, sir," the lieutenant said. He circled the group at a wide remove until he'd gotten behind them.

"Everybody up," Harriman said, gesturing with his own disruptor. "Slowly." Vokar and the others all rose to their feet. "Now, one at a time, I want you to walk toward the shuttle."

Vokar peered over at Valin, ordering him without a word to go first. The sublieutenant stepped forward and started toward Harriman. Vokar waited for only a moment, and then he moved. He brought his hands up in their restraints as he rushed over to T'Sil, bringing them down around her head. "Akeev," he yelled, hoping the science officer would understand his duty. Vokar twisted with all of his might, and heard with satisfaction the fracturing of T'Sil's neck. He turned then, toward Valin, and saw the sublieutenant falling to the deck from Akeev's grasp. A flash of intense blue light streaked across the shuttle compartment, and Akeev crumpled where he stood. Beyond him, Harriman stood with his disruptor aimed. Vokar took a step toward him, and Harriman fired.

His last thought consisted of a single word directed at the Starfleet captain: *Die!*

In the aft portion of the shuttle cabin, Gravenor executed the test sequence for the third time. Before her, the cloaking device she had removed from *Tomed* sat on the deck between the two equipment columns. Fiber-optic lines ran in jumbles from numerous junction nodes on the device over to the exposed circuitry of the shuttle. She confirmed the operation of the cloak, its connections to the deflector interface, and the rate of the power drain.

Finished with her testing, Gravenor turned toward the front of the cabin, to where Lieutenant Vaughn sat at one of the forward stations. She saw the sling he wore and wondered again just what he had been through here. He had reported killing a Romulan officer whom he'd believed had come to the shuttlebay to transmit a message about the commandeering of *Tomed*. But the spatters and smears of red and green blood on the deck, the lifeless body of a subcommander, and Vaughn's own injuries had all testified to the ferocity of the battle that had taken place, something the lieutenant had not mentioned. That omission, as well as his reluctance to provide details of the encounter, troubled Gravenor. Of more concern to her, though, was Vaughn's manner in the hours since the incident. He continued to behave and act professionally, but where he had always been open and communicative, he now seemed reserved, almost closed off. Gravenor had initially suspected the lieutenant to be suffering a post-traumatic reaction to his experience, but she now suspected that there might be larger matters at issue.

With a few minutes before they needed to launch, Gravenor stood up and walked to the front of the shuttle. "How are you doing, Elias?" she asked as she took a seat beside him. She rarely used his first name, and she did so now as an indication of her concern for him.

"I'm fine, Commander," Vaughn said, looking up from the console for just a moment. "Thank you." Although polite, the response promised no elucidation.

"Are you in much pain?" she persisted. Vaughn had initially treated himself with a Romulan medkit he'd found in the shuttle, but Harriman had later tended more carefully to his injuries. The captain had also provided him with medication for his pain, but the analgesic hadn't been able to mask it completely.

"There's some pain," Vaughn admitted, now keeping his focus on the panel, "but I'm getting through it."

"Good," Gravenor replied. She wanted to say more, wanted to help her colleague deal with the issues affecting him right now, but she also knew that there would be a better time than this to do so. Instead, she glanced down at the chronometer on the console. In just thirteen minutes, she saw, the shuttle would have to launch. "What's Captain Harriman's location?" she asked Vaughn.

The lieutenant worked his controls, and then said, "He just arrived at the brig."

After Harriman had stunned Admiral Vokar and the other Romulan—Akeev?—he'd wanted to load them back onto the antigrav stretchers so that he could take them to the brig. Gravenor had considered the decision an overly cautious one, since the two Romulans would not regain consciousness prior to *Tomed*'s destruction. But the captain had insisted, and Gravenor had realized that he'd had a reason other than caution: justice. The two Romulan officers had murdered their own crewmates, and Harriman had wanted to see them spend the last moments of their lives paying for those crimes—and in Vokar's case, she was sure, for other crimes as well. It might have been only a gesture, but she believed it to be an important one, and she respected Captain Harriman for making it.

She thought about trying to discuss the matter with Lieutenant Vaughn, but decided instead to allow him the solitude he seemed to need right now. "I'm going to run one more test sequence," she said as she stood from her chair.

"Understood, Commander," Vaughn said simply.

Gravenor returned to the rear of the cabin and attempted to pinpoint once more just what the chances were of the special ops team ever seeing the Federation again.

Harriman watched as the stimulant he'd administered took effect. Vokar's eyes blinked open, and he lifted his head from the antigrav stretcher and peered around the small cell. When he spotted Harriman standing outside the doorway, he froze, and then said, "So, are we to die together?"

Harriman said nothing. On his way here with his two prisoners, he'd thought of many things to say, but he realized now the pointlessness of whatever words he might utter. Vokar had lived a life devoted to beliefs and actions impossible for Harriman to justify rationally, and nothing he or Vokar might say now could change that.

Vokar rose from the stretcher and paced toward the doorway. "No, I guess we're not going to die together," he said, "because you're going to run away before that, aren't you?" Harriman maintained his silence. "You've set your plan in motion, and you're going to slink away before it's done. And no doubt you'll cast the blame my way for all the deaths you'll cause, all in the name of the survival of the glorious Federation." Vokar stopped about a half-meter from the forcefield that sealed the cell.

"Actually," Harriman said, "you *are* the cause of these events."

"I am?" Vokar asked. "By spying on Starfleet's testing of a first-strike weapon? By conquering a weak, inferior race like the Koltaari? Or perhaps you mean that I drove you to do this by my attempt to protect my people from a Federation starship and freighter trespassing in our space thirty years ago?"

Harriman smiled without humor. "You don't even believe any of that yourself," he said. "You caused this by trying to find any excuse to go to war with the Federation—by trying to *provide* any excuse."

"The superior will survive," Vokar said, as though quoting personal doctrine. "Tell me," he said, turning away and pacing back across the cell, "where is Lieutenant Akeev? Or have you left him in the middle of the shuttle compartment?"

"He's in another section," Harriman said, "in another cell, paying for his crime while he's still alive."

"Crime?" Vokar said, whirling around to face Harriman again. "Is that why you've brought me here, to exact some form of retribution for crimes you imagine me to have committed?"

"I just watched you murder one of your own crew," Harriman said.

Vokar walked back to the doorway, until he stood only centimeters from the forcefield, his cold gray eyes glaring at Harriman. "What you call *murder,* I call discipline. Unlike Starfleet, members of the Romulan Imperial Fleet are trained to give up their lives when duty requires that they do so." Vokar reached up and tapped at the forcefield. Harriman did not move as a flash of blue-green buzzed through the doorway. "Is that why *you're* here now?" Vokar asked. "To see me pay for my so-called crimes?"

"No," Harriman said simply.

Vokar said nothing, apparently waiting for an explanation. When he received none, he said, "Then why are you here?"

"Just to tell you that I've relieved you of your command." Harriman held up his hand before Vokar's face. In his fingers, he clutched the long patch of stylized starbursts that identified the Romulan Imperial Fleet rank of commanding admiral. Harriman had removed it from the neck of Vokar's uniform.

Vokar stepped back, reeling as though he'd been struck across the face. He reached for the collar of his uniform, and found his rank missing. He said nothing for a moment, and then seemed to force an expression of nonchalance onto his face. "You have no authority to relieve me."

Harriman shrugged. "Nevertheless," he said, and he dropped the rank patch onto the deck. Then he turned and walked away.

It required all of Sulu's concentration not to display the anxiety mounting within her as *Enterprise* approached Foxtrot XIII. She resisted the urge to tap the arm of the command chair, or to stand up and pace the bridge. Still in shock at the audacity of Captain Harriman's plan, she wanted to take action as quickly as possible, see it completed, and put it in her past.

"Captain," Linojj said from the helm, "sensors just detected a vessel in the Neutral Zone."

"Heading in which direction?" Sulu said, careful to ask the questions she should be asking, as though she knew nothing beyond what had just been reported to her.

"Toward Federation space," Linojj said.

"Lieutenant Tenger," Sulu said, "can you identify the ship? Is it one of ours?"

"Scanning," Tenger said from the tactical station. "It is a Romulan vessel, *Ivarix* class . . . it is *Tomed*."

Sulu rose and stepped forward, both playing her role and finding an outlet for her restlessness. "Open a channel," she said.

She heard the tones of the communications station being worked behind her, and then Lieutenant Kanchumurthi said, "Channel open."

"Romulan vessel *Tomed*," she said, "this is Commander Sulu of the Starfleet vessel *Enterprise*." She peered at the main viewscreen, where the stars shot by as the ship sped through Foxtrot Sector.

"There's no response," Kanchumurthi said.

"*Enterprise* to *Tomed*," Sulu tried again. "You are in violation of the Neutral Zone and heading for the Federation. You must alter your course immediately and return to Romulan space."

"Still nothing," Kanchumurthi said.

"Lieutenant Tenger, course and speed of the *Tomed*?" Sulu said.

"The ship is traveling at warp nine," Tenger said, "on a direct heading for Foxtrot XIII."

Linojj looked up at Sulu. "They're going to attack," she said in a low voice, obviously horrified. The declaration actually underscored the need for Sulu's next order.

"Ensign Tolek," she said, "plot an intercept course."

"At maximum warp," Tolek said, "we will intercept *Tomed* just as it reaches the outpost."

"Set course, maximum warp," Sulu said. Tolek and Linojj acknowledged the order and worked their consoles. "Are there any Starfleet vessels in the vicinity?"

"*Agamemnon* is on patrol there," Tenger said.

"Captain, Foxtrot Thirteen and the *Agamemnon* are both transmitting warning messages to the *Tomed*," Kanchumurthi said. Sulu glanced over and saw the communications officer reaching up to his silver earpiece, obviously listening to the transmissions.

"Let them both know we're on our way," Sulu said.

"Captain," Tenger said, "there are indications of a singularity containment failure in progress aboard *Tomed*."

"If containment fails at warp . . ." Linojj said, but she did not need to finish her statement. Almost everybody on the bridge would know that the introduction of a quantum singularity into a warp field would have devastating results.

"A few months ago, they installed those new defenses," Lieutenant Kanchumurthi said hopefully. "Perhaps that will be enough to protect the outpost."

"No defense known to Starfleet could withstand such an event," Tenger said soberly.

"What can we do?" Sulu asked, already knowing the action she would take. "Can we evacuate the outpost? Can *Agamemnon*?"

"We're not close enough, "Linojj said. "And even if we were, there isn't enough time to beam up three hundred people."

"We can attempt to destroy *Tomed*," Tenger said.

"Too risky," Linojj said.

"What if—" Sulu started, speaking to the entire bridge crew. "Can we get close enough to transport the microsingularity off of the *Tomed*, out of its warp field?"

"It seems unlikely," Tenger said. "In addition to the highly condensed matter overloading the transporter circuits, we would be attempting transport from a vessel moving at warp speed."

"Unlikely," Sulu said, "but not impossible."

"It may be impossible," Tenger said, "but a thorough analysis would be required to determine that."

"I'm going to try," Sulu declared. "Xintal, I'll be in transporter room one. You have the bridge."

"Aye, aye," Linojj responded.

Sulu walked over to the helm and made eye contact with Linojj. "If I'm not successful," she said, "if there *is* an explosion, get the *Enterprise* out of here immediately."

"Understood," Linojj said.

Sulu headed for the turbolift. She felt extremely uncomfortable at having to deceive her crew, but she could not think about that right now. Instead, she needed to concentrate on trying to save Captain Harriman.

"Thirty seconds until launch," Vaughn announced, reading the chronometer in a panel set into the side bulkhead. He had moved to the second row of seats in the cabin so that Commander Gravenor and Captain Harriman could take the two forward positions. The captain would pilot the shuttle, while the commander would operate the cloaking device. Vaughn's duty would be to monitor the time and the sensors, and then to transmit a disguised signal to the retreval vessel sent by Admiral Harriman—or by Admiral Sinclair-Alexander, he supposed, if the elder Harriman was still incapacitated.

"I'm bringing the warp engines to full power," Harriman said, working his console.

"Initiating power to the cloak," Gravenor said.

Around them, the shuttle hummed to life. Vaughn glanced quickly to the aft of the cabin and saw the sphere of the cloaking device begin to glow. "Twenty seconds," he said, looking back to the chronometer.

"Commencing antigrav liftoff sequence," Harriman said, his fingers roaming expertly across his panel.

Through the forward viewing port, Vaughn saw another shuttle and several work pods seem to descend as *Liss Riehn* lifted from the landing stage. A moment later, the shuttle stopped rising, and then it yawed to port. The bay slipped away in the opposite direction as the stars came into view, the warp effect stretching them into thin lines as *Tomed* raced through space. "Ten seconds," Vaughn said.

"Activating cloak," Gravenor said. The lighting in the cabin immediately dimmed, a signal both of the cloak's operation and of the enormous amount of power it drew.

"Aft thrusters at the ready," Harriman said.

"Three seconds," Vaughn said. "Two . . . one . . ." As he reached "zero," the shuttle surged forward into the starscape, the bay slipping past the viewing port until it was no longer visible. "Subspace threshold in three seconds," Vaughn said. He knew that navigating the border between a ship's warp field and normal space could be accomplished safely and easily at speeds slower than warp five, but at *Tomed*'s current velocity—

A jolt thundered through the shuttle, and it skewed laterally from its course. Vaughn flew from his chair across the cabin. He raised his uninjured arm in time to absorb the impact as he struck the bulkhead, but the wounds in his shoulder and hand screamed in pain. A loud drone rose in the enclosed space, and Vaughn recognized the sound of the structural-integrity field straining to protect the shuttle.

The vibrations in the cabin increased as he pushed himself away from the bulkhead and staggered back to his chair. He saw Commander Gravenor also pulling herself back up to her console, but Captain Harriman had somehow braced himself and had maintained his position. Past the two officers, a faint translucent glow, golden and the consistency of vapor, shined outside the viewing port.

"The cloak is holding," Gravenor yelled above the din.

"We're almost clear," Harriman said, also raising his voice to be heard.

Vaughn checked the time, grabbing hold of the panel to steady his gaze. "Five minutes, forty-five seconds until containment failure," he called, indicating the time left before the destruction of *Tomed*. "Forty-five seconds until we need to go to warp." In order to escape the ensuing shock wave, the shuttle would need to put some distance between it and the Romulan flagship.

All at once, the shuttle stopped shaking. "We've cleared the subspace threshold," Harriman said.

Vaughn peered over at the viewing port. The stars moved in counterclockwise spirals out in space, he saw, the shuttle obviously in an uncontrolled roll. Then he checked the chronometer. "Thirty seconds until we need to go to warp," he said.

Captain Harriman operated his controls. "Starboard thrusters," he said beneath his breath, his words almost inaudible. The spinning of the stars slowed, and Vaughn imagined that he could feel the decelerating effects of the thrusters as they braked the shuttle's roll, although with no external gravitational reference, he surely could not.

"Fifteen seconds to warp," he said.

"We'll make it," Harriman said calmly. Through the viewing port, the stars coasted to a stop. "Laying in our course away from *Tomed* and Foxtrot XIII," he said, working his panel once more. "Going to warp."

The hum of the warp engines filled the cabin, accompanied by a controlled vibration. Through the viewing port, Vaughn watched the stars streak past the shuttle as it rocketed to lightspeed. Then he turned to his own panel. "Transmitting our signal," he said. Using his uninjured hand, he activated the control sequence that would cause a random dispersion in *Liss Riehn*'s navigational deflector. "Signal away," he confirmed when he had completed his task.

Five minutes later, Captain Harriman brought the shuttle out of warp. The stars returned to pinpoints as the cabin quieted and stilled. "Maneuvering thrusters," the captain said. "We are at station-keeping." Then he turned in his chair and faced both Commander Gravenor and Vaughn. "Drysi, Elias, well done," he said. "You've completed an incredibly difficult mission. And an *important* one. Your actions may have saved billions on both sides of the Neutral Zone." He paused, and then added, "If I could, I'd put each of you in for the highest commendation."

"Thank you, John," Gravenor said.

"Thank you, sir," Vaughn said.

"John," the captain told Vaughn. "Right now, you can call me *John*."

"Thank you, John," Vaughn said.

Harriman and Gravenor both turned back to their consoles, and Vaughn looked at his own panel. Their duties completed, they sat in silence, waiting to learn whether or not they would survive their mission.

Linojj stared from the command chair at the tactical readout displayed on the main viewer, having trouble accepting what she saw. An icon representing the Foxtrot XIII asteroid sat in the center of the screen, with concentric circles drawn around it to indicate distance from the outpost. A representation of *Tomed*, a small, green starship symbol, sped toward the center of the display on an unwavering course.

"It's headed directly for it," Ensign Fenn said from the sciences station, her voice low, her tone one of disbelief.

"*Tomed* is nine billion kilometers from the outpost," Tenger reported. "The containment field will fail completely in eighteen seconds."

Linojj didn't need to work through the mathematics to know that the explosion would occur extremely close to Foxtrot XIII. Even at a greater distance, though, the unleashing of a quantum singularity within a warp field would send such a powerful shock wave through subspace that the outpost would still be destroyed. And with *Tomed* traveling at warp nine, the entire sector might be at risk.

"We're within visual range," Kanchumurthi said.

"On screen, maximum magnification," Linojj ordered.

The viewer changed, the tactical display replaced by a starscape, with the brown, irregularly shaped oval of Foxtrot XIII visible at its center.

"Four-point-five billion kilometers," Tenger said. "Eight seconds to containment failure."

Linojj felt helpless, unable to bring *Enterprise* close enough in the final seconds to help in any way. She could only hope that that *Agamemnon* would be able in the last moments to force *Tomed* out of warp. If containment failed outside a warp field, the microsingularity would cause localized destruction, but there would be no threat to the outposts.

"*Agamemnon* has opened fire on *Tomed*," Ensign Fenn said excitedly.

"Two-point-two billion kilometers," Tenger said. "Three seconds . . . two . . . one . . ."

Linojj peered around the bridge and saw all eyes focused on the main viewer. She looked there herself, in time to see a brilliant flash of white fill the screen, the protective filters unable to compensate for the intensity of the light. Linojj squinted and looked away for a moment to protect her eyes.

When she looked back, Foxtrot XIII was gone.

ZERO: TOMED

In Tomed's *main engineering section, containment failed. With the complex fields that tamed its effects gone, the microscopic black hole that powered the starship reached out into the universe. Matter tore apart under the relentless draw of the singularity, and then disappeared into the pure darkness. Space and time, bound together seamlessly to form the structure of reality, rent beneath the force, twisting and wrinkling as portions of the continuum sank into the ultimate gravitational vortex. The black hole pulled at everything, devouring all it captured, its appetite insatiable.*

Around Tomed, the warp field generated by its faster-than-light drive carried the ship through subspace. The alternate realm existed within and without the starship, allowing it to travel at speeds not possible in normal space-time. Loosed in this domain, the singularity continued to feast, consuming the fabric of this other existence.

But as subspace folded in on itself at warp factor nine, it filled the black hole. The actuality of velocity overwhelmed the potentiality of force. The singularity, infinite in its dimension, could not contain the greater infinity of subspace collapsing into it.

Gravity turned. Matter transmuted into energy, and the

energy shifted, reversed, pushing from the negative, through the zero, and into the positive. Subspace grew into the superior power, transcending the might of the singularity.

The black hole became the black entrance, the black portal. Subspace pushed backward, flowed from the point of its virtual demise and rushed, born again, back into the universe, carrying with it matter and energy previously consumed.

In the space occupied by the disintegrating form of Tomed, subspace asserted itself with its new force, destroying the rest of the starship in a fraction of second. And the wave of energy continued on, expanding in every direction, coursing through and beneath space and time with little resistance.

The shock wave caught Agamemnon, and an instant later, Agamemnon was no more. The inconspicuous asteroid dubbed Foxtrot XIII provided more opposition, withstanding the onslaught of subspace energy for an entire second before crumbling into nothingness. And still the great sphere of the wave expanded.

The shuttle Liss Riehn lasted as long as each of the two starships had, its distance from the source of the shock wave keeping its smaller form intact longer than it would have had it been closer. And still the subspace wave spread.

It chased another starship, Enterprise, which escaped only by virtue of the greater speed allowed by the separate subspace field projected around it.

Foxtrot XII vanished next, its matter blown apart in seconds. Outposts XI and IX followed, gone as though they had never been, so complete was their destruction. Two unnamed asteroids and a comet in the Neutral Zone were pulverized.

Finally, the vastness of space and time over which the shock wave had traveled took its toll. The subspace wave, its energy diminishing at each point as it expanded, began to fade. It demolished Foxtrot X, but took a half-minute to do so. Outposts VIII and VII each disappeared in a minute, and Foxtrot VI in two.

As the wave weakened and slowed, it lost its ability to devour. Four of the remaining five Foxtrot asteroids shattered, but left progressively larger chunks of themselves floating through the void. Foxtrot I withstood the initial assault relatively intact, its hollow center caving in, but the asteroid itself not breaking up for more than an hour.

And then at last, the wave died, its energies spent on trillions of trillions of cubic kilometers of space.

In its wake, Foxtrot Sector was gone.

PLUS ONE: RUINS

Sulu stood alone in the transporter room, peering down at the hooded sensor display in the center of the control console. She tapped a series of touchpads, trying to cast a wide net, but not *too* wide. The dispersion in the Romulan shuttle's navigational deflector would not be differentiable from the background noise of the universe at too high a level of granularity.

As *Enterprise* raced toward Foxtrot XIII, Sulu had to continually adjust the targeting scanners. As she did so, she could not help thinking about Linojj and the others attempting to reach the outpost in time to protect or rescue its crew. Their efforts would ultimately prove fruitless, and there seemed to her an inherent cruelty in that. While they would mourn the loss of the almost three hundred personnel stationed at the outpost, they would also have the burden of watching the event unfold. And they would witness, via sensors, the deaths of not just those on Foxtrot XIII, but also those on each of the other dozen outposts, and those aboard *Agamemnon*. After initially suffering herself the grief caused by the loss of *Universe* and its fifty-one personnel, Sulu could only imagine what the *Enterprise* crew—along with the rest of Starfleet and the Federation—would feel at the murder of more than four thousand men and women.

Sulu understood the value of the plan Captain Harriman had devised and then carried out. If the consequences of what he had done played out as he'd intended—and she saw no reason now to believe that they wouldn't—then war would be averted, and countless lives would be saved. Was that worth the sadness that would be inflicted on the people of both the Federation and the Romulan Empire? She had to agree that it was, and yet she wanted to go to the bridge and tell her crew—tell *everybody*—that nobody had died, that nobody would die—not aboard *Universe*, not aboard *Agamemnon*, and not in Foxtrot Sector. She wanted to remind them of all the equipment *Enterprise* had recently ferried to the outposts, and to reveal to them that the ship hadn't been delivering new defenses or weapons, as all had believed, but equipment to simulate the life signs of a crew of three hundred. *Enterprise* had rotated personnel off of the outposts, but no replacements had been delivered by *Agamemnon*; instead, a skeleton staff from that ship had installed the new equipment, and then had left their empty ship orbiting Foxtrot XIII, its functions automated—including a final run at *Tomed*, phasers firing. Captain Harriman's plan had been so meticulously plotted—

Accompanied by a short tone, a tiny point of light flashed on the sensor display. It pulsed once and vanished. Sulu initiated the transporter's targeting lock, but the sensor contact had already faded. It could have been anything—a burst of radiation from a distant star, the ionization of interstellar gas—but Sulu believed otherwise, having seen firsthand the readings of a dispersion of a navigational deflector. Trent's duplicity had paid yet another dividend, in addition to having lured *Tomed* into the area of the Bonneville Flats, where its crew had witnessed the destruction of *Universe* and thus set these events in motion.

She worked the controls, narrowing the search area considerably, centering it on the brief reading she had just seen. With a smaller volume of space to scan, she would increase the effectiveness of the sensors, and thereby increase the chances of locating the dispersion.

The point of flight flared again on the display, another tone signaling the sensor acquisition. As the light began to fade, Sulu quickly focused her scans even more. The point pulsed twice and then steadied. She followed the signal to its source and executed a scan for life signs. She found three, all human.

Once more, Sulu activated the targeting sensors. In only seconds, the transporter had locked on to the three life signs. She reached forward on the console and pulled a trio of slide buttons toward her. The whine of the transporter filled the room, and white motes of light formed above the platform. When the sound and lights faded, Captain Harriman, Commander Gravenor, and Lieutenant Vaughn had materialized. Both Gravenor and Vaughn wore Romulan uniforms, and Vaughn had one arm in a sling and bandages wrapped around one hand.

Despite whatever misgivings she might feel about Harriman's plan, Sulu could not prevent herself from smiling widely. "Welcome back, Captain," she said.

"It's good to be back," he said, stepping down onto the deck. "I wasn't sure they'd send you and *Enterprise*, but I thought they might." Sulu understood the veiled reference; Harriman's expectation of her involvement in the mission had come from his mentioning Iron Mike Paris to her twice. The captain hadn't been able to reveal the highly classified details of the mission—or even its existence—to her, but he'd obviously hoped that she would come to discover it on her own. "What's the situation?"

"*The Tomed* is heading for the outpost, its containment field failing," Sulu said. "It should happen any time now."

Harriman gestured toward the transporter console, toward the center section that housed the sensor controls. "Let's take a look," he said.

Sulu operated the panel at once, bringing up the sensor

readings of Foxtrot XIII. Harriman walked around the console to stand beside her, and Gravenor and Vaughn descended from the platform and joined them. They had to wait less than a minute before the readings changed dramatically, numbers and measurements spelling out the unleashing of the singularity at warp, and the subsequent destruction of the outpost. Even knowing that nobody had died in the maelstrom, the vastness and speed of the destruction chilled Sulu.

She looked from Harriman to Gravenor to Vaughn. Whatever satisfaction each of them felt must have been muted by their obvious exhaustion. Noticing again Vaughn's sling and bandages, she asked him, "Do you need a doctor?"

"I'm fine," Vaughn said, although he did not sound particularly convinced of his own answer.

"The lieutenant probably does need a doctor," Harriman said, "but we'll have to treat him ourselves right now. Have you got quarters ready for us?"

"Yes," Sulu told him. "There are three adjoining guest cabins on deck seven, all secured. I can beam the three of you there, unless you'd like me to beam you to your own quarters, Captain."

Harriman offered a wan smile. "Much as I'd like you to, the three of us need to talk." He walked out from behind the console and mounted the transporter platform again, followed by Gravenor and Vaughn. Sulu reset the transporter with the new coordinates. "Once we've beamed into guest quarters," Harriman said, tapping at a small device attached to his belt, "we'll reactivate our sensor veils." As far as the *Enterprise* crew were concerned, Captain Harriman was still aboard the Romulan space station, and that would have to continue to be the case. "I'm sure you know what comes next," Harriman said.

"Yes, sir," Sulu replied. Admiral Mentir had provided all the details of the actions she would need to take at this point.

"Then I'll see you at Algeron, Demora," Harriman said. "Energize."

Sulu nodded, then reached across the console and pushed the slide buttons forward. In seconds, she stood alone in the transporter room once more. She inhaled deeply, not sure how she would get through the next few hours, the next few days. She had trained for many situations during her years in Starfleet, but not for something like this. She had trained for the reality, and not for the artifice. Still, even if only she and Captain Harriman and a handful of others knew the truth, at least nobody had actually died in the destruction of the Foxtrot Sector.

She erased the logs of two transports she had just performed. Then, knowing that she now had to finish this, Sulu steeled herself and headed back to the bridge.

Stillness filled the *Enterprise* bridge. Seated in the command chair, Linojj could not seem to tear her gaze from the image on the main viewscreen. In front of the ship, which now held station outside the Foxtrot Sector, space had been transformed. *No, not transformed*, she thought. *Devastated. Ruined.*

Space looked like a rumpled black cloth, tattered and frayed. It seemed somehow to have *holes* in it, with a strange blue-gray tone visible in clumps through them. Sensors provided evidence that the space-time continuum had been both misshapen and torn. Pockets of subspace emerged through the tears, rendering warp travel impossible in the region. Linojj doubted that any type of space travel would be feasible.

Her emotions swung like a pendulum, from profound sorrow to unspeakable rage. The unprovoked attack on Foxtrot XIII—on *all* the outposts—recalled for her the initial invasion of her homeworld thirty-five years ago. And while she had lived a childhood in which the death of the innocent had been commonplace, the mass murder of four thousand people still seemed unthinkable.

"Ramesh," Linojj said, "open a channel."

"Commander," Kanchumurthi responded quietly, the terrible destruction they'd just witnessed clearly affecting him. "To whom?"

Linojj heard the turbolift doors open, but she did not look over, instead keeping her eyes on the viewer, on the twisted remains of space-time. "To Starfleet Command and all Starfleet vessels in the vicinity of the Neutral Zone," she told Kanchumurthi. "Transmit the following message. For reasons surpassing rational comprehension, the Romulan flagship *Tomed* has launched a wanton attack on all Federation outposts in the Foxtrot Sector. All outposts—repeat, *all* outposts—have been destroyed with all hands." She hesitated, wondering if her level of authority would permit her to say what she had thought to say. *Right now,* she told herself, *you command the* Enterprise. By leaving her in charge of the ship, Sulu had given her the authority to take action. "The Romulan Empire has committed a heinous and cowardly act of war. All available Starfleet vessels, proceed to the Neutral Zone." Linojj knew that a segment of the fleet traveled with battle plans specifically designed for the outbreak of war with the Romulans, including in circumstances such as an unexpected attack. "Lieutenant Commander Xintal Linojj, in command of the *U.S.S. Enterprise.*"

"Belay that," a voice said. Now Linojj peered over to the turbolift doors and saw that Commander Sulu had entered the bridge, returned from her obviously unsuccessful attempt to transport *Tomed*'s singularity off of the ship. "Lieutenant," Sulu said to Kanchumurthi, "broadcast the message not only to Starfleet vessels, but on all Klingon and Romulan frequencies as well."

"Romulan?" Kanchumurthi asked.

"Yes," Linojj said, standing from the command chair. "Unlike the Romulans, the Federation does not launch sneak attacks."

Sulu walked over to the command chair, looking aft toward the tactical-and-communications console. "The message is from Commander Demora Sulu, in command of the U.S.S. *Enterprise.*"

"Yes, Captain," Kanchumurthi said, working his panel.

Sulu turned to Linojj. "Take us to the edge of the Neutral Zone," she said. "Maximum warp."

"Aye," Linojj said, and she relieved Ensign Verant at the helm. She waited for Tolek to plot their course, then took the ship to warp. On the main viewscreen, she saw the mutilated space of Foxtrot Sector sweep away to port as *Enterprise* headed for the Romulan Neutral Zone. After all of the political tensions of the past years, and amid all the desperate hopes for peace, war had finally arrived.

Beneath the red glare of alert lighting, Sulu stood beside Tenger and peered over his shoulder at the tactical display on his panel. Icons representing a sizable assemblage of Starfleet vessels extended along a red ribbon denoting the Neutral Zone. As she watched, another icon—the thirty-seventh—appeared and maneuvered to the flank of the battle group. *Enterprise,* the first ship to arrive, had taken point.

On the other side of the Neutral Zone, an even greater number of Romulan ships—forty-eight at last count—had taken position.

"We are being hailed again," Kanchumurthi said from his console. "It's the *Aspire.*"

"On screen," Sulu said. She had been communicating with the fleet for most of the day, ever since she had transmitted word of *Tomed*'s attack. She made her way down to the lower section of the bridge and stood beside the navigation station. On the main viewscreen, the starscape disappeared, replaced by the image of a long, wide bridge, at least half again as large as that of *Enterprise.* Alert lighting flashed red there as well.

In the center of the scene, in a command chair with a high, tapered back, sat an officer Sulu did not recognize. He had thick brown hair, and his heavy eyebrows, mustache, and beard covered a great deal of his face. Sulu could not see his mouth, but his flat, circular nose, wide and upturned, along with his deep-set eyes, identified him as a Tellarite.

"Commander Sulu," the man said. *"I am Captain Renk of the* U.S.S. Aspire. *We received your message regarding the attack on Foxtrot Sector."* He hesitated and glanced around his bridge. Many of the officers there, Sulu now noticed, had their eyes cast downward. *"My crew,"* Renk said. *"We are . . ."* He could not seem to find the proper word to describe what he wanted to say, but his meaning was clear.

"I understand, Captain," Sulu said. "The crew of the *Enterprise* feels the same way."

Renk nodded, accepting the sentiment. *"Have you heard yet from Starfleet Command?"* he asked.

"Not yet," she said, "but we anticipate a response soon." Any orders from Starfleet would come from the officer responsible for operations in this and the neighboring sectors: Admiral Mentir. Sulu actually hoped not to hear from him. If the Starfleet vessels amassed along the Neutral Zone received either the command to advance or to retreat, then it would mean that Captain Harriman's plan had failed to provide the outcome he had expected—the outcome for which he had risked so much.

"I'm sure you'll keep us informed," Renk said.

"I will, Captain," she said. "In the meantime, maintain battle stations." As the commander of the Starfleet flagship, Sulu also functioned now as the de facto leader of the battle group. Renk nodded once to Sulu, and then to an officer on the *Aspire* bridge. The transmission ended, the starscape appearing once more on the viewscreen.

"Captain," Tenger said, "sensors are picking up movement along the Klingon-Romulan border, not far from Federation space." Sulu moved back up to the raised outer section of the bridge and over to where Tenger worked his panel. She studied the display he had configured, and now saw not only Federation and Romulan space, but Klingon territory as well; the lines of confluence of all three powers hung in space not far from Foxtrot Sector. Several more Klingon vessels had moved into the area, bringing the total to twenty-one. As she'd expected, her transmission to the fleet and the subsequent gathering of Starfleet forces along the Federation side of the Neutral Zone had not gone unnoticed by either the Romulans or the Klingons.

Shortly after *Enterprise*'s arrival here, an *Ivarix*-class vessel had appeared in nearby Romulan space. They had made no attempt to contact *Enterprise,* and Sulu had not tried to contact them. In the intervening hours between then and now, more and more ships on both sides had moved into position along the Neutral Zone, and in the last few hours, Klingon vessels had also begun arriving in the region abutting both Federation and Romulan space.

Sulu looked up from the tactical display and over at the main viewscreen. She considered the massive amounts of weaponry now aimed in each direction, and wondered how long she would have to wait. Captain Harriman's entire plan had been predicated on how this military buildup would end. As long as Chancellor Azetbur remained in power—and Starfleet Intelligence did not believe she faced any imminent threat of removal—Harriman believed strongly that he knew precisely what would happen. He had, in fact, believed so strongly that he had been willing to endanger his own life and the lives of others, and to cause anguish throughout the Federation and the Romulan Empire—anguish that would not soon be forgotten by either side.

Sulu stepped away from Lieutenant Tenger and began walking the perimeter of the bridge. She paced past the engineering stations and the starboard turbolift, and then past the main viewscreen. As she neared the sciences station, Ensign Fenn peered up at her, a stony expression on her face. Sulu noticed the bandage still on her finger. "How are you feeling?" she asked, motioning toward Fenn's hand. In the next couple of months, she knew that the young woman would have to take a leave of absence from Starfleet, so that she could return home to undergo the Shift.

Fenn lifted her arm from her console and looked at her finger. "My pain seems inconsequential right now," she said.

"I know, Borona," Sulu said, putting a reassuring hand on Fenn's shoulder. "I know." And she thought: *This* has *to work*. The sense of loss engendered by the supposed attack on the Foxtrot outposts would be far too high a price to pay for this not to work. She understood Captain Harriman's belief that the reality of peace, and of the saving of billions of lives, would be worth that pain, and she even agreed. But she didn't know if she agreed that merely the *possibility* of peace was worth it. For if war could not now be averted—

"Captain, we are being hailed," Kanchumurthi said again. "By a Klingon vessel."

Sulu felt her eyebrows rise on her forehead, not in surprise, but in hope. It took an effort for her to remain calm. "Put them on screen," she said.

As she headed back toward the command chair, the image of a multitiered Klingon bridge appeared on the viewer, the dark atmosphere almost brooding. Atop a raised, thronelike chair sat a large, thickset man, the silver metal torso of his uniform appearing to strain along its seams. Pulled back against his head, his hair might have been long or short, she could not tell which. His dark beard and mustache were well defined, even against his swarthy complexion. "*I am General Kaarg,*" he said, "*of the* I.K.S. NuH Bey'."

"Commander Sulu, of the *Enterprise*," she said, standing before her command chair.

"We have monitored your transmissions," Kaarg said. "As I'm sure you intended us to do."

"Yes, General, we did," Sulu admitted freely. "We wanted everybody to know what happened, and to know that *we* know what happened."

"Indeed, everybody does," Kaarg said. "Four Klingon warships, on patrols near our borders, registered the Romulan vessel on long-range sensors. They witnessed the attack."

"The *cowardly* attack," Sulu said pointedly, and then thought that she shouldn't have. She did not need to overplay her hand.

"I must admit that I do not always share the opinions of Federation citizens when it comes to matters of cowardice or honor," Kaarg said. "But in this case, I have no choice but to agree."

"I'm pleased to hear that, General," Sulu said.

"I would imagine that you are. And as I'm sure you know, Chancellor Azetbur has been quite clear in stating the Klingon position regarding hostilities between the Federation and the Romulans."

"I do know that," she said.

"Good," Kaarg told her. "Then I will not now have to explain myself." He looked to his side and barked an order, and the image of the Klingon bridge vanished from the screen, replaced by the starscape.

"Captain," Tenger said at once, "I'm reading movement along the Klingon border."

"Give me a tactical display, Lieutenant," Sulu said. "On screen."

The readout Sulu had viewed at Tenger's station now appeared on the main viewer. The red sweep of the Neutral Zone still flowed through the center of the display, Federation territory marked on one side and Romulan territory on the other. At one end of the Neutral Zone, the expanse of Klingon space began, and there, the phalanx of ships had begun to move, advancing toward the area where the three territories intersected.

And then they turned, traveling directly toward the Starfleet battle group.

"We're being hailed by several—make that *many*— Starfleet ships," Kanchumurthi reported.

"Open a general channel," she ordered.

"Channel open."

"This is Commander Sulu of the *Enterprise*," she said. "All Starfleet vessels, maintain position and hold your fire." Then, wanting to be sure, she said, "Tenger, sensors. Are the Klingons arming weapons?"

"Scanning," Tenger said. She waited, staring at the viewscreen as though she could see all that was transpiring across the vast distances of space. Finally, Tenger said, "Negative."

After a few minutes, Kanchumurthi said, "Several of the Klingon vessels are entering visual range . . . including *NuH Bey'*."

"Let's see it," Sulu said, expecting that the general's actions would provide the lead to the other ships.

On the viewer, the tactical graphic winked off, and a Klingon warship appeared in space, heading toward *Enterprise*. *NuH Bey'* swooped in, then arced away in a tight turn. It slowed, then came to stop directly ahead of *Enterprise*, its bow pointed in the direction of Romulan space.

"The Klingons are now powering their weapons," Tenger said. "All of their vessels are falling into formation with ours."

As relief flooded over Sulu, she turned toward Kanchumurthi. "Lieutenant, send to General Kaarg: the Klingons are people of their word, and you are a man of honor."

"Yes, Captain," Kanchumurthi said, a smile on his face. Sulu realized that she was not the only one who felt relief.

She sat down in the command chair, knowing that it only

remained to be seen what action the Romulans would now take. But Sulu knew: it was over. The praetor and the people surrounding him might believe in the natural superiority of the Romulan genome, but they also understood *numerical* superiority; if not for the uncertainty about what the Klingon Empire would do, the Romulans would have attacked the Federation long ago. Now, faced with a combined Federation-Klingon force, the Romulans would move away from their ambitions for war.

An hour later, they proved Sulu right. "Captain," Tenger said, "the Romulans are disarming weapons and pulling back."

All eyes on the bridge turned to Sulu. "We've won?" Linojj said.

Sulu smiled, but she said, "No. We haven't won. But with our new allies, we just guaranteed that we won't lose either." Linojj nodded, apparently satisfied, and turned back to the helm. "Lieutenant Kanchumurthi, open a channel to all Starfleet and Klingon vessels."

As Sulu prepared what she would say, she thought about Linojj's question. And she thought that maybe the Federation had won after all. And so had the Klingons and the Romulans. There would be no war now, thanks to Captain Harriman.

Ambassador Kamemor fixed her gaze on the standing figure of the Starfleet officer, but only so that her eyes would not be drawn to the far wall, to the multihued patterns of the Algeron Effect glowing there. She sat at the conference table, listening to the statements of Commander Sulu with only half an ear. Already, Kamemor had heard all that she had needed to hear. That the Federation and the Klingons offered ample proof of their claims mattered little at this point. The crews of several Romulan starships had witnessed *Tomed* streaking through the Neutral Zone, heading directly for the Federation outpost, and wiping out an entire sector. *Tomed*'s own crew, rescued after a power-source problem had forced them to flee into space, had disclosed that they had expected their ship to be destroyed only minutes after they had evacuated it. But the ship had survived enough hours beyond that to take it into Federation space, and the fact that six of the crew—including Admiral Vokar and three engineers—remained unaccounted for pointed to their obvious complicity in the plot. There seemed insufficient cause for anybody to declare that the act had not been deliberate.

At the end of the table, Federation Ambassador Endara and his staff listened in rapt silence to Commander Sulu's descriptions of what had taken place. All of them seemed affected by the words, appearing alternately disbelieving, sad, and angry. Even the normally reserved Endara had paled.

Ambassador Kage and his two aides also concentrated on the commander. In Kage's case, he looked less engaged emotionally than interested in the diplomacy that would necessarily follow from here. His belligerent young aide, though, seemed more confused than anything else, as though he did not know how to react to the situation without direction.

As she spoke, Commander Sulu raised the padd she carried in her hand, drawing Kamemor's attention back to her. "There was no price paid higher than that in lives," the Starfleet officer said. "But there were other costs." She reached forward and set the padd on the table, its display faceup.

Kamemor glanced down and saw the strange, grayish masses she had seen in another image, one captured from a Romulan vessel at the Neutral Zone. The picture disturbed her. Like the shimmering fragments of planet that marked the tragic end for the inhabitants of Algeron III, the splintered ruins of space would be a constant reminder of catastrophe.

"Thank you, Commander," Kamemor said, looking up. "We appreciate your time in sharing your experience with us. We also empathize with you for your loss."

"Thank you, Ambassador," Sulu said. She turned and retreated across the room, taking a seat against the far wall between a Klingon general and Captain Harriman. "General Kaarg," Kamemor said, "we would like to hear from you now."

The Klingon officer stood and lumbered across the room, hauling his hefty frame to the spot where Commander Sulu had delivered her statements. Kamemor raised her eyes to meet his. "During the time of which we speak," he began, "four Klingon warships were on patrols near the borders—"

As the general continued, Kamemor noted that her aides, Subconsuls N'Mest and Vreenak, grew restive. Seated to either side of her, the two shifted several times in their chairs. Vreenak in particular moved excessively—not that he moved very much, but the somber circumstances called for quietude. Kamemor wondered which caused his unrest, the calculated murder of four thousand people, or that the crime had been perpetrated by a man she knew he had admired.

Or perhaps he is not entirely comfortable feigning sorrow for the deaths of beings he considers inferior to Romulans, she thought cynically. In the brief time she had known Vreenak, Kamemor had come to appreciate his quick mind and his willingness to commit to an opinion—something many young diplomats failed to do—but too often his opinions seemed motivated by an unflagging belief in the preeminence of the Romulan people. While she disagreed with such biases, and vigorously opposed employing them as the basis for Romulan policy, she had not dismissed Vreenak from her employ, because she hoped to guide the young man from his narrow views. Her experience had demonstrated to her that the world of diplomacy required expansive perspectives. When all factions in a negotiation considered issues from all sides, and not simply from the standpoint of their own needs and desires, much could be accomplished. Although the months of negotiations prior to the *Tomed* incident had failed to produce a treaty, she felt that progress had been made, in large part owing to the consideration of the larger picture by the Klingon and Federation ambassadors.

Captain Harriman possessed a wider view as well, she thought, not taking her eyes from General Kaarg, but keenly aware of the captain's presence across the room. After what had happened at the Foxtrot outposts, the concerns that she had harbored about helping him—transporting him and his two colleagues onto Vokar's ship—had vanished. Harriman's claim that the admiral had intended to commit an act of violence against the Federation had been borne out. She did not know how the captain had survived the ordeal, but he obviously had, though he had just as obviously failed to prevent Vokar's attack. She had not yet had a chance to speak with him privately, but when she had first seen him upon his return to Algeron, he had looked at her with an expression that she had interpreted as acknowledging both his gratitude for her assistance, and his torment for his failure.

When General Kaarg had finished delivering his statements, Kamemor thanked him. After he had withdrawn, returning to his seat beside Commander Sulu, Kamemor stood up to address all those assembled. "I appreciate everybody's time and tolerance in dealing with this matter so soon after the tragedy. I will bring these reports back to my government, and we will, I am certain, take action." What actions the praetor and the Romulan Senate might take, Kamemor did not know, but she also understood that it would likely not make any difference in the current flow of politics among the three powers. The Klingons had made their choice of allegiance, and they would not forsake it— at least not in the foreseeable future—no matter what the Romulans had to say; even the unlikely exoneration of Vokar would be met with enough skepticism to prevent Qo'noS from changing sides. "I again offer, on behalf of the praetor, the Senate, and my people, our most solemn condolences on the disaster the Federation has experienced. I also want to assure all parties that if Admiral Vokar and others did commit this heinous crime, then they did so on their own, and not under the aegis of Romulus. We unequivocally condemn these actions." She peered slowly around the room, being sure to make eye contact with each person present. "Thank you," she said at last, ending the meeting and dismissing the participants.

The Klingon and Federation delegations exited the room in silence, leaving Kamemor with her two aides. She stood up, preparing to leave herself, but first she wanted to know the thoughts of the people with whom she worked. "What are your impressions of the situation?" she asked.

"It's a tragedy," N'Mest said at once. "Commander Sulu was correct in her assessment that this was a cowardly and immoral act."

Vreenak conspicuously said nothing. Kamemor moved out from her chair and circled out from behind the table. Stopping opposite her aides, she said, "Subconsul Vreenak, have you no opinion on the attack on the Federation?"

"It's a lie," Vreenak said simply.

"A lie?" N'Mest said, incredulous. "Do you believe that the Federation outposts were not actually destroyed, that the region of space around them was not decimated, that four thousand people did not lose their lives?"

"Admiral Vokar," Vreenak avowed, "is not a terrorist."

"If your characterization is not inaccurate," Kamemor said sternly, "it is at least irrelevant. What has been done cannot be undone, and that includes not only the act of destroying the Federation outposts, but the alliance of the Klingon Empire to the Federation. What we must do now is not dwell on the past, but focus on the future."

"And if it is a future based on a lie?" Vreenak asked.

Kamemor moved forward, placed her hands flat on the conference table, and leaned toward Vreenak. "The future we now face, young Merken," she said, admonishing him for his impertinent attitude, "is one of peace. The praetor and the Senate will not seek to go to war against a force combined of Starfleet and the Klingon Defense Force. And the Federation, despite being viciously attacked, despite being provided superior numbers by the Klingons, has not responded with violence. So at least for now, there will be peace. We should all be thankful for that."

This time, Vreenak did not respond, apparently chastened enough to hold his tongue. Kamemor turned and headed for the door. Before she left, she looked back toward the conference table. "The lie, Subconsul Vreenak, is believing in something contrary to all evidence." Then she turned and left, not waiting to see if he would brave a reply.

Captain Harriman walked beside Demora Sulu through the brightly lighted corridors of Space Station KR-3. He had not yet had an opportunity to discuss with her everything that had happened; he hadn't even found time to contact Amina. While *Enterprise* had traveled to Algeron, he had remained in seclusion, and during the return to KR-3, he'd spent most of his off-duty hours in conference with Gravenor and Vaughn, putting together the verbal report that they would deliver to Admiral Sinclair-Alexander. Within the next few days, though, he felt sure that he and Sulu would talk.

When *Enterprise* had arrived at the space station just a few minutes ago, Admiral Mentir had asked to see Harriman at once. But while Mentir's desire for an immediate debriefing about the mission seemed reasonable, and while Harriman had agreed to it, he had decided when disembarking the ship to first visit his father. This time, he would not allow Blackjack to keep him away. Demora, always a supportive friend, had asked if she could come along.

Now they entered the station's infirmary. Only two of

the biobeds in the main section were occupied, he saw, one by a sleeping man, and another by a woman whose ankle was being tended to by a nurse. The scene put Harriman in mind of all the dancing he and Amina had done over the years, since he had twisted his own ankle from time.

As he and Demora approached the wide door of the intensive-care section, it glided open before them. They started inside, but stopped at the threshold when a voice called from behind. "Captain Harriman," a man said. Harriman turned to see the tall, lean figure of the station's chief medical officer coming through a doorway on the other side of the room.

"Dr. Van Riper," Harriman greeted him.

"Captain," the doctor said after he had crossed the room, "I'm terribly sorry."

Harriman nodded knowingly. "We all are," he said, unsure that he would ever feel completely comfortable speaking about the apparent loss of the four thousand people in the Foxtrot Sector—and the fifty-one aboard *Universe*—when he knew the truth. "The attack on the outposts was a terrible thing."

"Oh," Van Riper said, and then he motioned with an open hand into the intensive-care section. "Let's go in here," he said, moving past Harriman and Sulu.

And Harriman suddenly realized that the doctor had not been referring to the events that had unfolded in Foxtrot Sector; he had been offering compassion for the death of Blackjack. "My father," Harriman said, still standing in the doorway. "My father is dead?" The words, and his speaking them, seemed surreal.

"I'm afraid so," Van Riper confirmed. "He died just a few hours ago. The injuries to his brain were just too severe."

Harriman peered past the doctor, toward the far bay, where they had been treating Blackjack. An urge rose in him to race over and peer inside, to confirm that his father no longer lay in the biobed there. But there was no point; the doctor was not lying.

Harriman felt a touch on his forearm, and he glanced down to see that Demora had reached out a hand to him. He looked up at her face, and saw an expression of sympathy and sadness, as well as complete understanding. In her childhood, he knew, she had lost her mother, and as an adult—

"Captain," the doctor said. "I'll give you a moment to yourself. Please don't hesitate to call on me if you'd like any questions answered." He walked back out into the main area of the infirmary. Harriman turned in the other direction, moving farther inside the intensive-care section. Demora followed, the door sliding closed behind her.

"I'm so sorry, John," she said, and she reached out to hug him. He put his arms around her back and held her close for a few moments. Even though he felt as though he'd taken a phaser on heavy stun, the kindness and caring of his friend was not lost on him.

When he stepped back from her, she said, "Are you all right?" Then she shook her head quickly, as though she had asked the most ludicrous question possible.

"It's all right," he told her. "I'm . . . I'm . . ." *I'm an orphan*, he thought. The idea—however foolish for a man of fifty-two—produced an awful, hollow feeling inside him. Not wanting to say that, though, he told Sulu, "I'm in shock, I guess. I think I believed that Blackjack would live forever."

"He certainly was . . ." Demora shrugged. ". . . larger than life."

Harriman surprised himself by smiling. "Yeah," he said, "he was that." Sulu smiled too, and the moment helped him. But still, the reality of his father's death remained— would *always* remain. It seemed incomprehensible that Blackjack no longer existed. It seemed *wrong*.

He reached both hands up to his face and wiped with the

tips of his fingers at his closed eyes. Fatigue washed over him like a wave, trying to carry him away. *I need sleep,* he thought, and knew right away that running from this would be no answer.

"Do you want to go back to the ship?" Demora asked.

He did, but he said, "No, we have to meet with the admiral." It occurred to him that this was why Mentir had wanted to see him right away. "I'm all right," he said.

"You're not all right, John," Demora said gently. "But you will be."

Harriman looked at his friend and saw her deep concern for him written across her face. He tried to reach inside himself, into his emotions, to define all that he felt—or at least *understand* all that he felt. There were so many different emotions: anger at his father for having driven a wedge between them, and for having treated him not as a son, but as a subordinate; guilt for not having worked harder—or worked at all, really—to mend their relationship; frustration for not having insisted on seeing his father after the accident.

Ironically, for all of the Starfleet officers who had supposedly died during the mission, it had been Blackjack who really had. Although the mission had been successful, there had been things that had gone wrong: Vokar and five others staying aboard *Tomed*; the Romulans interpreting the *Universe* trial as the testing of a new weapon and not a new drive; and the explosion, more powerful than expected, slamming into *Ad Astra*. In another sardonic twist of fate, it had been Blackjack who had first proposed the *Universe* ruse. He'd foreseen being able to use the event to maneuver Azetbur, to cause her to proclaim that the Klingons would side against the aggressor in any hostilities between the Federation and the Romulans. Harriman had then found a way to use the test as a means of delivering him and the special ops team into Romulan space, proximate to an Imperial Fleet vessel.

None of that really mattered now, though. What really mattered was that his father was gone. And of all the complex emotions churning within him, Harriman found that what he felt more than anything else was simple sadness.

"John," Demora said, and Harriman looked up at her, not realizing that he had dropped his head as he'd lost himself in thought. "I spoke with your father before I took the *Enterprise* to Foxtrot XIII." Harriman blinked, startled. Demora had said nothing to him about ever having visited Blackjack. "We didn't have much time," she said. "He was very tired. But he told me . . . he told me that he loved you, John, and that he was sorry."

Harriman's jaw set, and the muscles in his face tensed. A tightness formed behind his eyes. He inhaled deeply, feeling his nostrils flare. He could not believe how quickly Demora's words—his father's words—had affected him.

"I loved him too," he said, his voice now a whisper. He moved forward, back into his friend's embrace. He hugged her for a long time, holding tightly to what he had not lost.

EPILOGUE: DESIGNS

Elias Vaughn gazed through the viewing port in the conference room, his eyes drawn to the line of shimmering objects that had once been Algeron III. Though strikingly beautiful, the polychromatic fragments, born of a devastated world, reminded him of Foxtrot Sector, its thirteen asteroids smashed into oblivion. And like one domino toppling another, the memory of Foxtrot Sector forced him to recall that last moment with Renka Linavil. Two months afterward, Vaughn could still feel her flesh yield as he thrust the knife into her body.

Behind him, he heard the murmur of excited conversation as people arrived in the conference room. In his mind, though, he heard the flat thud that the subcommander's body had made when it had fallen, lifeless, to the deck. He automatically tried to bury the memory, but then fought the instinct, knowing that he had to deal with this in order to overcome it.

Vaughn turned and scanned the room. Commander Gravenor and Captain Harriman talked with each other over in a corner, he saw; Vaughn and the commander had assumed their roles as envoys again, and the captain had been invited to the treaty signing by Federation Ambassador

Paulo Endara. In addition to Endara, Vaughn recognized several of the dignitaries present—including Ambassador Kage, General Kaarg, and Senator Vorex Ontken—as well as a couple of the functionaries who'd recently begun to appear in intelligence briefs—Merken Vreenak and Ditagh.

It had been in such a brief, one from six years ago, that Vaughn had learned the name of the woman he had killed aboard *Tomed*. After returning from the mission, he had found numerous reasons to review old intel, refusing to admit to himself his true motivation. The tagged photograph he had located had originally arrived at special ops from an Yridian operative, from images captured at a military summit. Younger, and with her face not contorted by rage, Linavil cut an attractive figure.

From there, Vaughn had sought other information about her. More recent intelligence had revealed that she had been instrumental in promoting and then carrying out the occupation of the Koltaari, and that, like Vokar, she had favored war with the Federation. But he had also learned that Linavil had graduated at the top of her class from the prestigious R'Mala Military Academy, that she had competed and placed in *voraant* competitions on Romulus, and that she had a sister and niece living on Terix II. When he had discovered that her parents had died a decade ago, he'd been pleased to know that they would not experience the misery of dealing with their eldest daughter's death, or at least with her disappearance.

It had been at that point, when Vaughn had practically rejoiced that Linavil's parents were no longer alive, that he'd realized his emotional state had veered significantly off course. He had gone to Commander Gravenor, asking to be relieved of his field duties, but she'd encouraged him instead to see one of the counselors assigned to special ops. Vaughn had agreed, and in the month since then, he had grown more able to cope with having taken a life, and even with the likelihood of having to do so again. He no longer obsessed over finding out the details of Renka Linavil's life, but tried to bear in mind the wrongs that she had wrought in the universe. Vaughn would have preferred to have brought her to justice—rather than having killed her—for whatever crimes she had committed, but naïve as it might be, he still believed in doing battle against evil.

What remained most troublesome now were the visceral memories of the confrontation: the sound Linavil's flesh had made when he'd torn off the tip of her ear, the resistance to the knife entering her body, the heat of her blood on his hands. Vaughn knew that he could overcome his fixation on these terrible recollections, and the distress they caused him. But he also knew that it would take time for that to happen—far longer than it had taken for his physical injuries to be treated and to mend.

"Elias," somebody said, and Vaughn looked to his left to see Captain Harriman approaching.

"Captain," Vaughn said, and he clasped Harriman's outstretched hand.

"John, please," Harriman said.

"John."

"It's good to see you again," Harriman said. They had not seen each other since their return to Space Station KR-3 from Algeron almost two months ago—and since the captain's father had died, the result of the injuries the admiral had sustained aboard *Ad Astra*. Vaughn considered the unexpected death of the elder Harriman a tragedy, particularly for the captain.

"It's good to see you," Vaughn said. They could say nothing more right now, and they didn't have to. The captain turned and headed toward the Federation ambassador.

On the other side of the room, the door slid open and Romulan Ambassador Gell Kamemor entered. Vaughn took note of her purposeful stride, several black, hardbound folios clutched to her breast. She made her way around the conference table, to the empty chair at its center. Her aides seated on either side of her, Kamemor stood there rigidly, waiting, her demeanor not what Vaughn would have expected for such a momentous occasion as a treaty signing.

By degrees, conversation stopped. Silence settled in the room, and all eyes turned toward the Romulan ambassador. Vaughn watched as several smiles faded, clearly indicating that he had not been the only one to notice Kamemor's bleak mien.

"May we begin?" she said flatly. Her words might have formed a question, but there seemed little choice in the answer. As though previously choreographed, people gravitated toward their places. The Romulan aides seated at the table, along with one of Endara's staff, rose and moved to chairs ringing the room; the other aides and staff members and minor officials—including Gravenor and Vaughn himself—retreated to the perimeter as well. At the table sat Ambassador Endara and Captain Harriman, Ambassador Kage and General Kaarg, and Senator Ontken. Ambassador Kamemor continued to stand.

When everybody had stilled, Kamemor reached forward and set the top folio in the center of the table. Even from his vantage at the side of the room, the volume seemed to Vaughn to have some weight to it, measuring at least a couple of centimeters thick. "This," Kamemor said without inflection, "is the trilateral treaty document negotiated for many months, and finalized in the past two." Vaughn saw stealthy smiles blossom around the room. An accord to which the Federation, the Klingon Empire, and the Romulan Empire were all signatories would be historic.

If, Vaughn thought. *If*. He perceived some quality, some . . . *restraint?* . . . in the Romulan ambassador that made him think that this conference would not proceed as originally intended by all involved—including Gell Kamemor. The ambassador confirmed Vaughn's suspicions with her next sentence.

"The Romulan Star Empire will not sign it," she said.

Where there had first been conversations, and then smiles, there now came the mutter of confusion. Even Ontken, a member of the Romulan Senate, peered up at Kamemor bewilderedly. "Ambassador, I don't understand," he said. "The Senate voted to authorize the praetor to—"

"The praetor contacted me early this morning," she said. Vaughn found it surprising that a woman so skilled in the means of diplomacy would interrupt a Senator, especially in front of others. It reinforced his observations that things were not right. "The praetor expressed to me his absolute condemnation of the attack on the United Federation of Planets perpetrated by Aventeer Vokar. An order for the arrest and trial of the admiral, should he still be alive, has been issued throughout the Empire, and the praetor is considering trying him in absentia."

"And for that reason," Ambassador Endara asked, confused, "you won't sign the treaty?"

"Yes," Kamemor said. "The praetor feels that, because of the odious acts driven by one man and committed by him and his associates, the Empire has been asked to concede too much, and has also been willing to concede too much."

Slowly, as though trying to contain his emotions, Ambassador Endara rose from his chair, his hands on the edge of the table. "After the tremendous efforts that we've all put in—that *you've* put in, Gell—the praetor is going to undermine the peace process because the Federation and the Klingon Empire think that what Vokar did was wrong?" His words climbed in volume as he spoke, his agitation plain. Seated beside him, Vaughn saw, Captain Harriman maintained a stoic expression.

"No," Kamemor said, "the praetor is not going to undermine peace." She set down on the table the other folios she carried, all three of them the same size, and with not nearly as many pages as the first volume she'd set down. She lifted the top folio from the pile and handed it across the table to

Ambassador Kage, then picked up the second and walked it down to the end of the table and gave it to Endara. As she returned to stand in front of her chair, she said, "This is a revised version of the treaty, greatly simplified."

Endara opened the folio and began paging through it, his gaze moving swiftly over its few pages. The Klingon ambassador placed his copy on the table in front of him without opening it. "Pardon me," Kage said, "but it is not reasonable to expect us to begin negotiating a new agreement after we have already finalized a previous one."

"By order of the praetor," Kamemor said, "Romulus will no longer negotiate. What is contained in these documents are the only terms to which we will agree. They can be amended in no way. They must be signed and ratified within ten days."

"Or?" Endara asked, looking up from his copy of the treaty.

"Or there will be no accord," Kamemor said. Vaughn did not think that she necessarily agreed with what she had been ordered to do and say.

"Allowing ten days for full consideration by the Federation Council is unrealistic," Endara said, now seeming resigned that there would be no treaty signed today.

"Even the Klingon High Council requires some time to battle their way to concurrence," Kage added.

"The terms of the treaty are simple enough to warrant agreement within the prescribed time frame," Kamemor said, apparently not willing—or not permitted—to cooperate in any way. "The Neutral Zone currently established between the Romulan Star Empire and the Klingon Empire will be reaffirmed, and any violation whatsoever of the Zone will be deemed an act of war. The identical reaffirmation of our borders will occur with the Federation. Finally, the Federation will agree to ban the research and development of cloaking technology in exchange for the Empire leaving the world of the Koltaari."

And there it is, Vaughn thought: the final result of Captain Harriman's plan. The failed trial of *Universe*'s so-called hyperwarp drive had been intended to draw the Romulans' disapprobation, and a concomitant accusation that the Federation was seeking a first-strike capability through the development of a vastly improved engine system. That, in turn, would force the Klingon chancellor to move toward choosing an allegiance.

Although the Romulans had believed the destruction of *Universe* to be due to the testing of a metaweapon and not a drive system, the outcome had been the same. Starfleet had handed over the hyperwarp specifications to both the Romulans and the Klingons in order to demonstrate that the Federation did not possess a first-strike capability, if for no other reason than that hyperwarp did not work. The "development" of the "new" drive had merely been the introduction of cloaking technology into the field configuration of a transwarp engine.

And transwarp was simply a failed technology of the past.

Hyperwarp would *never* work. But the Romulans would note the Federation use of cloaking technology, and they would want to stop it in order to maintain that particular military advantage. It would not matter that Starfleet had always declared its aversion to the use of cloaking devices, because the Romulans had never believed that. And so when it came time to negotiate a treaty, the Federation would be able to give up what it never had and never wanted, placating the Romulans and getting something from them in return—in this case, the freedom of the Koltaari.

"If the treaty is signed and ratified within ten days by both the Klingons and the Federation," Kamemor continued, and then she paused, and it seemed obvious to Vaughn that she did not like the orders she had been given. "If the treaty is signed and ratified, then we will withdraw."

Nobody responded for several seconds, and then Ambassador Endara said, " 'Withdraw'?"

"We will close our borders," Kamemor declared.

Endara paged through the treaty again. "That does not seem to be in here," he said.

"It is not," Kamemor said, "because we of course wish to control our own space. But the praetor has chosen this direction, and he has the support of a majority of the Senate." From Senator Ontken's raised eyebrow, it seemed to Vaughn that he was likely not among that majority.

"Ambassador," Endara said, "we do not seek to isolate Romulus. We would choose peace. We would choose friendship."

"You will have one of those," Kamemor said. "It is for you to decide if it is enough." She leaned forward and reached for her copy of the treaty. She paged to its end, then pulled a writing implement from her sleeve and signed the document. "I have already signed your copies," she told Kage and Endara. Then she hurried around the table, headed for the door. "N'Mest, Vreenak," she said along the way, and her two aides followed her out.

In her wake, Kamemor left shock and uncertainty. But as much as what Ambassador Endara had said was true—that the Federation did seek friendship with the Romulans—Vaughn knew that the treaty would be signed, and that there would be peace.

And that, he knew, was something that he could definitely live with.

Chancellor Azetbur emerged from her private study into the large main room of her office. She skirted the dais situated just outside the door, and upon which sat the great chair that she occasionally used to receive official guests. Overlooking the conference table in the center of the room, the old throne had been passed down through a long line of chancellors, who had draped its wide back with various trinkets: a gold ceremonial sash, a scabbard, an ornamental chain, and other personal items. No matter where she stood in her office, her eyes always seemed drawn to a silver medallion her father had for years worn.

As she came out from behind the dais, Azetbur noted the chill in the room. A cold snap, unexpected at this time of year, had enveloped the city as the sun had set. The wintery air invigorated her, though it had grown too frosty now even for her tastes, her breath puffing out in front of her in a pale cloud. Rinla, her assistant, had already closed the dozen tall, peaked windows in the outer wall, she saw.

A hammering sound, three loud knocks, filled the room, the noise echoing off of the stone blocks of the walls. Azetbur looked to the timepiece standing beside the great chair and saw that her visitor had arrived late. She presumed the disrespect to be deliberate. How could she have believed otherwise of this man who wanted her dead, who might even have requested this meeting to in some way further that end?

With calm and deliberate movements, Azetbur stepped up onto the dais, turned, and assumed her place on the great chair, various of the mementos there rattling as she sat. She waited until the knocks came again. "Enter," she called.

The doors to her office opened, each of the pair of floor-to-ceiling panels pushed inward by a guard. *Kaarg's officers*, she thought. She had taken his point about the uncertain trustworthiness of the members of Klingon Internal Security who normally protected the Great Hall and the chancellor. For now, Azetbur had reassigned those officers elsewhere.

General Gorak walked forward into the room, his strapping form impressive in his military uniform. As he advanced toward Azetbur, she saw a sheathed ritual sword lashed to his side, as well as a horde of medals adorning his chest plate. Her right hand found and gripped the top of her walking stick, which leaned against the side of the

throne; it galled her to be in the presence of a man considered a hero of the Empire, but who she knew wanted to betray her. She did not fear him, especially not at this
moment, with Kaarg's officers just outside; Gorak had kept
his designs in the shadows, demonstrating his cowardice, no
matter his military record. He would not act against her
right now with reprisal just beyond the doors—although
Azetbur had not been averse to the other precaution that
Kaarg had suggested.

But while she did not fear Gorak, she had tired of his
continual, concealed threat. When Kaarg had informed her
of the traitor's request for a meeting, she had concurred with
his counsel to grant that request, in the hope that she could
learn more of Gorak's intentions. With the Romulan menace sufficiently defused, and relations with the Federation
stabilized, she wanted to focus now on securing her position
and addressing domestic issues.

Azetbur waited for the general to stop in front of her before she spoke. "Gorak," she said, choosing to deliver the
minor dishonor of omitting his rank.

"Chancellor," the general said, his breath blowing out in
front of his face in gray wisps. Then he actually bowed his
head. His fraudulence turned her stomach. She had to defy
the urge to heft her walking stick and pound his head with it.

"You appear . . . rested, General," she said, an oblique reference to the month of peace they'd experienced since the
Romulans had pulled back into their space and closed their
borders. She did not know how long that would last, of
course, but she had begun lobbying the High Council to
begin applying Klingon resources elsewhere than at the edge
of Romulan space. Gorak had publicly supported such a
shift in policy, but Kaarg had informed her that such was not
the case in private.

"I am rested," he said readily, not appearing to perceive
her veiled insult.

No one can be insulted less, her father used to tell her, *than those who deserve insult most.*

"Your wing departs Qo'noS tomorrow," Azetbur said, her voice rising at the end, not as a question, but to invite comment. She typically did not track the movements of the Klingon Defense Force closely enough to know where individual officers would be—not in peacetime, anyway. Gorak would know that, and so her awareness of his coming assignment would send him a message that she was watching him carefully.

"Yes, we leave at dawn," the general confirmed. "We are planning a defensive sweep along the Gorn border."

"Are you expecting trouble from the Gorn?" Azetbur asked.

"I am not 'expecting' trouble," Gorak said, "but it is always a good idea to watch your enemies and potential enemies, and to let them know that you're watching."

Azetbur smiled, despite her impression that the general had begun to bait her. "I agree," she said. She understood and appreciated this type of exchange. Gorak might not have been speaking plainly, but at least he was speaking *to her,* in the light and not from the shadows. She suddenly held out hope for this meeting. "And what of enemies here on Qo'noS?" she asked. "How will you manage to monitor them while you are gone?"

"Chancellor?" Gorak asked. "I don't believe I have enemies on Qo'noS." He seemed to reconsider his words, and then added, "I suppose I must, but none worth watching so closely."

Azetbur rose quickly to her feet, bridling at the general's arrogance. Bad enough that he plotted to overthrow her, to take her life, and now he stood here and slighted her? "Why are you here, Gorak?" she said, lifting the saber-tooth walking stick and thumping it once on the dais.

"I am here at your behest, of course," he said.

Azetbur grew tired of the game. She descended onto the floor and closed to within an arm's length of the general.

"What is your purpose in requesting this meeting?" she said angrily. "State either your true reason or the false one you intended to give, but tell me one of them now."

"Chancellor, I did not reque—"

A glint of light flashed to the left of Azetbur's head, and in the next instant, Gorak staggered backward. His hands came up quickly, and the sudden movement caused Azetbur to reach for the *d'k tahg* at her side.

Her hand closed on empty air.

Did I neglect to arm myself? she thought. *Or did Gorak somehow disarm me?*

Before her, the general dropped to his knees, and now she saw the blade—not her *d'k tahg*, another sort of knife—sticking from his neck. As she watched, his hands clutched at the handle and tried to pull it out. Blood coursed through his fingers and down the front of his uniform. A gurgling sound escaped him, and a glistening purplish bubble of saliva formed on his lips. After a few seconds, he dropped backward and fell still.

Behind her, Azetbur heard footsteps. She did not have to turn around to see who it was. General Kaarg had suggested that she not be alone when she met with Gorak, and now one of his staff—a tall, heavily muscled man named Morahg—walked out around the dais, from where she had left him in her study. He squatted beside Gorak's head and reached toward him. Azetbur thought that Morahg would remove the blade, but instead he pulled a black, studded glove from his own hand and placed two fingers by Gorak's nose and mouth. She did not see any breath above Gorak's face in the still-cold room.

"This is more than taking a 'precaution,'" Azetbur said. She understood Morahg's loyalty to Kaarg and therefore to her, and she would have killed Gorak herself if it had come to that, but she did not like this action being taken without her sanction. She told Morahg as much.

"Gorak was an enemy," he said, sliding his massive hand back into his glove.

"I know that," Azetbur said, "And General Kaarg and you know that, but many people don't." As she spoke, Morahg took hold of Gorak's sword, moved it to the right, then drew a *d'k tahg* from the dead general's side. "We are alone in my office," she went on. "This is going to require an explanation."

Morahg put his hands on his knees and pushed himself upward, rising to his considerable height. "The explanation is simple," he said. "I killed Gorak after he attacked the chancellor of the Klingon Empire." He held up the *d'k tahg*. "After he attacked you with this."

"Of course," Azetbur said, but she thought about all of the other details that they would have to provide about exactly what had happened here. She peered down at the lifeless form of Gorak, and she had to admit that she felt relieved at his death. "I think—" she began, but then fire sliced through her chest. Her hand fell from the walking stick and it slammed to the floor. Looking down, she saw the hilt of a knife protruding from her chest. "What—?" She looked up at Morahg.

"Gorak was an enemy," he repeated. "If you were to have died, Chancellor, then he would likely have succeeded you. And with his reputation, and his popularity among the Klingon Defense Force, he would have been difficult to unseat. Now, in death, he will be a coward and a traitor."

Azetbur looked back down at the knife that had buried itself in her body. Attempting to ignore the pain, she grasped the haft and pulled. As the blade came free, she cried out, the pain excruciating. She collapsed to the floor, barely able to bring one hand up in time to prevent herself from striking her head.

Above her, she saw the vaulted ceiling of her office. Her vision narrowed, black areas seeping in around the edges. Small tufts of white curled above her and vanished, the vapors of her breathing, now coming in short wheezes.

She wondered if Morahg had turned on General Kaarg, but then realized that she had made a terrible mistake in accepting Kaarg as an ally, in trusting in his loyalty. She recalled all the subtle and overt signs of that loyalty, now so obviously meant to deceive. A *backroom planner*, some called him, mocking his choice to win battles through careful strategy, rather than through force. He had convinced her that Gorak had been plotting against her, had—

Kage, she thought, and the realization caused more agony than the knife had. Had her friend also betrayed her? Kage had told her that Ditagh had revealed the name of Gorak as the traitor they had suspected. Had he been lying, or had Ditagh?

"Di . . . Ditagh," she managed to say.

Morahg's face appeared above her. "I am Ditagh," he said, a smile contorting his features. "And I play the role of the fool well. I serve General Kaarg . . . who will be, with you and Gorak gone, the obvious next chancellor of the Klingon Empire."

As Azetbur lay dying, she thought of her people, of the recent progress made through the isolationism of the Romulans and the alliance with the Federation. That Kaarg had maneuvered Gorak, had maneuvered her, seemed immaterial compared to the question of what would befall the Empire now. Would Kaarg dissolve the pact with the Federation? Would he resume the push to war just recently abandoned by the Romulans? Would he undo all the progress she had made over all these years?

Ditahg continued talking—she could see his lips moving—but she barely heard his voice, as though he spoke from far away. Her breath, which had been visible in the cold room, had gone now. She resisted death, not because she feared it, but because she did not want to leave her people. She had led them for so long now, protected them, guided them, the responsibility for their safekeeping left to her by her father—

Father.

Her heart flew as she realized that soon, in *Sto-Vo-Kor*, she would finally see him again.

I'm going to see Father, she thought.

I'm going to—

I'm—

And then nothing.

As Commander Demora Sulu gazed at the stars gliding by on the main viewscreen of the *Enterprise* bridge, she had to stifle a yawn. She did not feel tired, though. After her shift ended, she still planned on joining the primary command staff—Linojj, Buonarroti, Morell, Tenger, Kanchumurthi, and Tolek—for a gathering to bid farewell to Ensign Fenn; Sulu also hoped that Captain Harriman would join them, although he had been somewhat reclusive of late. Borona would be leaving the ship tomorrow, beginning a leave of absence that would last at least two months, as she returned to her homeworld to undergo the Shift.

During the last few weeks, as Dr. Morell had been able to determine an accurate timeline for Borona's condition, Sulu had attempted to learn more about it, beyond what little she had already learned from the doctor, the captain, and Borona herself. She hadn't found much literature about the Shift, but the few pieces she had read all indicated that the process could be extremely painful—and not just physically, but mentally and emotionally as well. That didn't surprise her. When she thought about herself, she could say that she had been substantially the same person for all of her adult life. She had certainly changed as she'd learned new things, and as she'd grown older and more experienced, but such changes had been gradual, and largely a matter of her own choosing. But Borona had no choice in what she would go through. Sulu hoped that the young woman would be able to get through the experience as well as possible, and that once she had undergone the Shift, that she would still be the same person. For apparently not every Shift went well, and not every Frunalian who went through the process emerged recognizable as who they'd previously been. And in a few cases, some Frunalians did not retain their sanity.

Borona would be disembarking the ship tomorrow, once *Enterprise* had arrived at Starbase 77. From there, she would take a transport bound for home. The *Enterprise* crew, on the other hand, would remain at the base for three days while special scientific equipment was installed on board.

Other than having to say goodbye to Borona, Sulu actually looked forward to reaching Starbase 77, because the ship's next mission would launch from there. *Enterprise* would head out into uncharted space, toward the Röntgen Wall, an unexplained cosmological anomaly. Unlike so many of the ship's assignments for so long now, this would be a mission purely of exploration. The anticipation among the crew in the past few days had become palpable; the notion of doing something other than patrolling the Neutral Zone or conducting defense drills or delivering weapons to military outposts had everybody excited.

I just hope it hasn't been canceled, she thought suddenly, recalling the eyes-only transmission that Captain Harriman had earlier received from Starfleet Command. Politically and militarily, though, the last three months—since the destruction of Foxtrot Sector—had been relatively calm. The last month in particular—since the treaty had been signed and ratified—had been extremely peaceful. Although the accord contained little goodwill within it, it had already begun to serve its purpose. The Koltaari had been freed and were now receiving aid from the Federation, and the Romulans had retreated into their empire and closed their borders. Nobody knew how long the latter development would last, but with the strong relationship between the Federation and the

Klingons, the consensus was that the Romulans would stay away, at least for some time. Sulu certainly hoped that would be the case.

To her right, the starboard turbolift doors opened, and Ensigns DeYoung and Verant entered the bridge. Sulu glanced down at the display in the arm of the command chair and saw just three minutes left before the end of the shift. She stood up and greeted both officers, then quickly reviewed ship and crew status with DeYoung, who relieved her.

"Ship's lounge," she said as she entered the turbolift. She would miss Borona, but she had been looking forward to this gathering tonight. She wanted very much to spend some downtime with these people whom she considered her second family.

"*Harriman to Sulu,*" came the captain's voice over the comm system.

"This is Sulu," she said. "Go ahead, Captain."

"*Commander,*" he said, "*would you please meet me in my quarters?*"

She considered asking if whatever issue the captain wanted to discuss could wait until tomorrow, but then decided against it. "I'll be right there," she said, and after the captain had signed off, she restated her destination for the turbolift. She wondered why the captain wanted to see her so late in the day.

As the lift descended, Sulu thought about the captain. She had been concerned about him since he'd returned to *Enterprise.* She had hoped that after the success of his mission aboard *Tomed,* and after he had mourned his father, that he would rebound from the incredible pressures he had obviously been feeling in the months leading up to recent events. Instead, he had continued to be less talkative, less social, than usual, and more reticent, more solitary. She had thought that perhaps he needed to talk about all that he had been through,

and he had talked a little bit about it with her, but not much —
not enough. And there were very few people with whom he
could discuss all that had happened; as far as she knew, only six
people had knowledge of every step of the mission: Harriman
and Sulu, Starfleet Commander in Chief Admiral Sinclair-
Alexander, Admiral Mentir, Commander Gravenor, and Lieutenant Vaughn. The small team that had "created" hyperwarp
drive and mounted it in an existing prototype starship, and the
skeleton crew aboard *Agamemnon* who'd installed the life-signs
generators at the abandoned outposts, had been aware only of
their own roles, but nothing beyond that.

As the turbolift slowed its descent, and then accelerated
horizontally, Sulu wondered if the captain felt guilty. He
had likely saved billions by his actions, averting a war that
virtually everybody had considered inevitable. But he had
also done some things in the furtherance of that goal that
might be disturbing him. For one thing, he had helped hide
the deaths of Starfleet officers during the year or so prior to
the mission, so that real people with real histories could be
included among the rolls of those who'd supposedly per-
ished aboard *Universe*, the Foxtrot outposts, and *Agamemnon*. And for another thing, Harriman and his team had
been responsible for the deaths of six Romulans aboard
Tomed. Had Vokar and the others not remained aboard, then
none of them would have died, and only Vokar would have
paid a price; for if he had evacuated *Tomed* before the ship
had decimated the outposts, then he still would have been
believed responsible for the attacks, and the Klingons would
still have sided with the Federation against the Romulans.

And on top of all that, the captain had lost his father. Sulu
knew that the two had been estranged for almost twenty years,
but she also believed that the captain had nevertheless loved
his father. It probably hurt him a great deal to know that any
hope of ever reconciling had now been taken away for good.

The turbolift eased to a stop, and Sulu exited into the corridor, heading for the captain's cabin. She thought about what she had told him his father's last words to her had been. She wondered now if that had been the right thing to do—perhaps it had simply made the situation harder for the captain, causing him to miss his father more, or to take himself to task for not having attempted to reconcile with the elder Harriman. But she had made that choice, and she could do nothing now to change that. Given the opportunity to do things differently, though, she felt that she would do just what she had done.

She arrived at the captain's cabin and touched the door chime. A moment later, the door withdrew into the bulkhead. Captain Harriman stood in the middle of the room, and he invited her inside.

"How are you tonight, Captain?" she asked as she entered.

"I'm doing very well," he said, motioning her toward a chair. "How are you?"

Sulu smiled, pleased to see him in such good spirits. "I'm doing very well too," she said, taking a seat on the sofa. Harriman sat down in a chair across from her. "I was just on my way to a small farewell gathering for Ensign Fenn." She paused, and then added, "I'd hoped that you might join us."

"Actually," he said, "I already stopped by the lounge, but I had to come back here to speak with Starfleet Command."

"I hope that our mission to investigate the Röntgen Wall hasn't been canceled," she said.

"No, it hasn't," the captain said, "but there has been a slight change of plan."

"Oh," Sulu said, feeling immediately disappointed.

"A change made at my request," Harriman added. He stood back up and paced across the room, as though with nervous energy. He seemed to be in a strange frame of mind. "Demora," he said, "I miss my father."

"Oh," she said again, surprised at the apparent non sequitor. "That's understandable."

"Maybe," he said. "You know that we weren't close . . .

that we didn't even talk beyond professional communications. But he was my father, and even if we were apart, I always knew that he was out there somewhere. Now . . . well, it's hard."

"I'm sorry," Sulu said, feeling bad for her friend.

Harriman walked back across the room. "I've really enjoyed my time aboard *Enterprise*," he said, seeming to change the direction of the conversation again. "As a boy, growing up on Starfleet vessels, that was the only world I knew. And it's obviously still the one I know best."

"I think that shows in your command," Sulu told him. "You're an exceptional captain, John."

"Thank you," he said. "A lot of credit has to go to the crew. And to the best first officer in the fleet." Sulu inclined her head and closed her eyes, acknowledging the compliment. "As you know, I missed my father by hours," Harriman said, appearing to change the subject once more. "He died just a few hours before we returned to KR-3. I missed him."

"I know, John," Sulu said. "I'm sorry."

He sat back down in the chair. "I don't want to miss the most important things in my life," he said. "So I've decided to resign my position as captain of *Enterprise*."

"What?" Sulu said, shocked.

"That was what the communication from Starfleet Command was about," he said.

"Starfleet's accepted your resignation?" she asked.

"Actually, I'm not resigning my commission," Harriman said. "I'm giving up my position, not my rank. I haven't decided what I'll do next exactly, but for now, I'm still a Starfleet captain."

Sulu shook her head. She felt numb. "So Starfleet approved your request to change positions?" she asked.

"Oh, they accepted that request a month ago. Tonight—" He reached out his closed fist toward Sulu, then opened his hand to reveal a Starfleet insignia pin designating the rank of captain. "—they approved my replacement."

Sulu looked up at Harriman. He reached up, removed the rank pin from her right shoulder, and replaced it with the new one. "Congratulations, Captain Sulu."

She felt her mouth drop open, but she said nothing.

"And *Enterprise* will still be going to the Röntgen Wall," Harriman said. "That will be your first mission as captain."

"I don't know what to say," Sulu finally managed. "Thank you."

"You've earned this, Demora. You're a fine officer, and you'll make an excellent starship captain." He smiled widely. "You're also a damned good friend." He stood up and moved toward her, and she rose as well. They embraced, and when they parted, he said, "Since you're a captain now, I no longer outrank you. But I do have seniority, so I hope you'll accept one final suggestion."

"What's that?" she asked.

Again, Harriman held out his hand. Now it held the rank pin he'd just removed from her uniform. "Xintal has been promoted to commander. It's your choice, of course, but I think she might make a fine first officer."

Sulu beamed. "Shall we go tell her?" she said.

Harriman shrugged. "Why don't we let this night belong to Borona? I'll be leaving *Enterprise* before it departs Starbase 77, but I've scheduled appointments tomorrow with each of the senior staff. I'll have time to say goodbye, and you'll have time to make your announcements."

"All right," Sulu said. She took the commander's insignia from Harriman's hand and exchanged it with her captain's pin. Then she looked up at her old friend. "I'll miss you," she said.

"I'll miss you too," he said. "But I'm a good letter-writer, and I know you are too." It was a skill she'd learned from her father. "And I hope we'll get to see each other from time to time." He paused, and then said, "Now go see Borona on her last night. I'll see you tomorrow."

She nodded and thanked the captain again, then crossed the room to the door, which opened before her. She stopped just outside Harriman's cabin, feeling overwhelmed by what had just happened. She felt both sad, knowing that she would miss her friend, and exhilarated, marveling at what her own future would hold.

Gathering herself, Captain Demora Sulu headed for the turbolift, striding through the corridors of her first command, *U.S.S. Enterprise*.

Harriman walked past the unmarked door, but then came to the end of the long corridor. *That has to be it,* he thought. He turned around and headed back the way he'd come.

He had to smile. It had taken him two starships, two transports, and a shuttlecraft to get to this remote outpost, and now he couldn't find the right room. *I was a helm officer,* he joked to himself, *not a navigator.*

Harriman reached the unmarked door again and stopped before it. He looked both ways down the corridor, attempting to get his bearings and decide whether he really had arrived at the right place. But before he'd come to a conclusion, the door slid open.

"John!" Amina said. "What are you doing here?"

He smiled. "I love you."

"I love you," she said, and they stepped forward into each other's arms, their bodies fitting together as though they'd never been apart.

Into Amina's ear, he whispered, "Will you marry me?"

"Yes," she whispered back.

"When?" he said.

"Every day."

Harriman pulled back so that he could see Amina's face. "How about today?" he asked.

ACKNOWLEDGMENTS

I would like to thank several people for their assistance, generosity, and support during the writing of this novel. I first wish to express my gratitude to Marco Palmieri, both for offering me the opportunity to play in the *Lost Era* sandbox, and for all of his unstinting efforts along the way. Marco's professionalism is unmatched, and his editorial skills and sensibilities always improve my writing. His patience and understanding are fortifying, and his vision and enthusiasm for the work galvanizing. Marco is a good man, and I feel fortunate whenever I have the chance to work with him.

I would also like to thank several of the *Star Trek* novelists. Peter David magnanimously allowed me the full use of Admiral John "Blackjack" Harriman, and Michael Jan Friedman, with equal magnanimity, the full use of "Iron Mike" Paris. Keith R.A. DeCandido provided me with Ditagh, and I gave him Kaarg, so that we might generate a bit of fun continuity for those who read both this book and Keith's own *Lost Era* entry, *The Art of the Impossible*. I am grateful to Dayton Ward, who graciously answered several questions about the *Trek* universe that I posed him. Lastly, I want to thank Peter David and Armin Shimerman for generously giving of their time by stepping in for me at a writer's workshop when I was unexpectedly unable to attend.

On a very personal note, thank you for everything to Paul "Stick" Roman, #40, now gone. Paul and I shared so many wonderful moments together, both on and off the baseball diamond. His sense of humor and his loyalty were just two of the many things I could always count on (unlike his fastball, which wasn't always fast, and his curveball, which didn't always curve). One of my closest friends and a best man at my wedding, Paul lived a quiet life of greatness. His legacy of kindness cuts a broad path through many lives, and I am a better man for having known and loved him. I will miss him always, and Jackie, Becky, and Ryan Roman continue to have important places in my life and in my heart.

I am thankful, too, that my life intersected with that of Terry Weinstein, now also gone. Terry's love of the game and his wit—not to mention his hitting, fielding, and running abilities—always made it enjoyable to step onto a baseball field with him. It's not the same without him, and never will be. I miss him, and I keep Ellen Gordon and Terry's family in my heart and thoughts.

I want to thank Colleen Ragan for her love, friendship, and support. One of the funniest people I've ever known, Colleen also manages to impress and encourage me, by bravely and boldly taking her life in new directions. And of course, she is truly the queen of all she surveys.

Thanks to Marty Nedboy, another person whose incredible sense of humor never fails to brighten my days. Marty is a dear and fabulous man, and absolutely one of a kind. I still can't wait for him to take his comeback show to Vegas.

I want to thank Anita Smith for her unflagging love and support. She's a terrific woman, and I appreciate the happiness she brings to life.

I want to thank Patricia Walenista, a woman to whom I always look for love, support, and guidance. There is no question that she has, in so many ways, contributed wonderful things to my life. I respect, admire, and love her.

And finally, thank you to Karen Ragan-George, who in addition to fulfilling my life in countless ways, also managed to save it this past year. After all this time, she still makes me laugh harder than anybody else ever has, and my heart still beats faster when I'm with her. She provides continuous inspiration to me on so many levels, a Renaissance woman whose beautiful smile makes everything worthwhile. Karen is the love of my life, for now and ever.

About the Author

Serpents Among the Ruins marks David R. George III's fourth writing foray into the *Star Trek* universe. David's previous contributions include a first-season *Voyager* episode, "Prime Factors," and two *Deep Space Nine* novels, *The 34th Rule* and *Twilight*; the first of the four-book *Mission: Gamma* series, *Twilight* also composes a part of the DS9 novel "relaunch." In addition, David will be penning one of the entries in the upcoming *Worlds of Deep Space Nine* series of *Trek* novels. He also continues to write mainstream fiction, and hopes to complete a film screenplay shortly.

Born and raised in the magnificent metropolis of New York, New York (the city so nice . . .), David has subsequently lived all over the country. He called upstate home when he attended the State University of New York at Plattsburgh, where he earned a Bachelor of Science degree in mathematics and scientific computing, with minors in writing and philosophy. He resided in South Carolina when he attended graduate school at Clemson University, where he earned a Master of Science degree in mathematical sciences, with concentrations in operations research and scientific computing. Since then, he has lived in Kansas, Washington, and northern and southern California.

David loves to travel, and has done so all over the United States, from Key West, Florida, to Anchorage, Alaska; from Kalae, Hawaii, to Burlington, Vermont. Outside the U.S., he has visited Russia, Switzerland, Tunisia, Spain, Italy, France, Monaco, England, the Bahamas, Mexico, and Canada. He hasn't been to the moon or Mars yet, but both places are on his agenda.

David loves the game of baseball, and he plays both in regular tournaments and in a league. While he used to want to watch a game in every Major League ballpark, he now hopes to *play* in every one; he has already done so twice at Candlestick Park, once at Oakland–Alameda County Coliseum, and three times at Dodger Stadium. He's also played in numerous Major League spring training stadia in Arizona and Florida, and in several minor league parks in California and Nevada.

In addition to baseball, David plays racquetball regularly, and he and his fabulous wife, Karen, love to dance and play softball together. They are passionate film aficionados, voracious readers, and devoted—if often unrewarded—New York Mets fans. They currently live in southern California, still one step ahead of the law.

STAR TREK
— COMMUNICATOR —

3 ISSUES FREE!

FOR A LIMITED TIME you can get 9 issues of *STAR TREK COMMUNICATOR* magazine for $19.95 – that's 3 FREE ISSUES!

STAR TREK COMMUNICATOR is your source for the inside scoop on all incarnations of *Star Trek!*

HURRY AND TAKE ADVANTAGE of this offer – simply call **1-888-303-1813** to subscribe!

Or send your name, address, phone number and payment to
STAR TREK COMMUNICATOR
P.O. Box 111000,
Aurora, CO 80042

We accept checks, money orders, Visa, Mastercard, AMEX and Discover Cards.

Please reference code **TBOOK** when ordering.

Canadian 1 year subscription $22.95, Foreign 1 year subscription $34.95. (U.S. funds only)

Offer expires 7/31/03

Asimov's
SCIENCE FICTION

Science fiction at its best
CAN BE YOURS!

Now the leading science fiction and fantasy magazine
in this world (and who knows how many others?)
__IS YOURS FOR THE ASKING__!

Each issue of *Asimov's Science Fiction* features
novellas and short stories from today's leading
science fiction and fantasy writers.

**Kristine Kathryn Rusch • Janet Kagan
Esther M. Friesner • Susan Shwartz
Karen Haber • Pamela Sargent • Joe Haldeman**

ORDER YOUR SUBSCRIPTION TO ASIMOV'S TODAY!
CALL: 1-800-220-7443
Visit us on the web - www.Asimovs.com

- -

Mail to: Asimov's • 6 Prowitt Street • Norwalk, CT 06855

☑**YES!** Send me *ASIMOV'S SCIENCE FICTION* and bill
me. If I'm not completely delighted, I'll write "Cancel" on the
invoice and return it with no further obligation. Either way, the
first issue is mine to keep. **(6 issues, just $14.98)**

Name _____

Address _____

City _____ State _____ ZIP _____

❏ Payment enclosed   ❏ Bill me

We publish a double issue in October/November, which counts as two issues towards
your subscription. Please allow 6-8 weeks for delivery of first issue. For delivery
outside U.S.A., pay $19.98 (U.S. funds) for 6 issues. Includes GST. Foreign orders must be
prepaid or charged to VISA/MasterCard. Please include account number, card type,
expiration date and signature. Billing option not available outside U.S.A.   5T92.01

STAR TREK DEEP SPACE NINE®

MISSION: GAMMA

•TWILIGHT•
David R. George III

•THIS GRAY SPIRIT•
Heather Jarman

•CATHEDRAL•
Michael Martin and
Andy Mangels

•LESSER EVIL•
Robert Simpson

On sale now!!!

MIGA.01